EAR
TIDE'S END

MW01222578

In *Tide's End*, Meredith Egan lovingly invites us to wade through the gray matter of life that we would frequently prefer to approach in black and white. In the peeling of the layers, she reveals the beauty of human vulnerability. But perhaps the most unique thing for me with this story is that, as I mop my heart back off the floor, days later I find myself thinking about Taylor and other characters in the novel and wonder how they are doing? Rarely have I felt compelled in that way at the conclusion of a novel.

Heidi Epp, Artistic Director and Choral Conductor, #MeToo

Tide's End is a deeply engaging novel which explores the multiple impacts of violence and sexual assault on victims and how the path to recovery is fraught with conflicted, uneven and sometimes self-destructive attempts to get to the other side.

Tide's End is artfully told through multiple narratives however Egan has created a surprising and endearing protagonist in Taylor Smythe through whom she surfaces the complex experiences of child victims of sexual abuse. We follow Taylor as he copes with the rippling effects of sexual abuse in multiple situations in his adult life.

It is a powerful statement on the capacity of humans to forgive. And the generosity and caring of spirits made kindred through their shared experiences. In exploring the emphasis placed on the rehabilitation of offenders, Egan deftly exposes how victims can be forgotten or worse - asked to contribute to the redemption of their abusers.

This novel carries you deeper into the complexities of these relationships. I found myself caring for each of these characters, empathizing with their struggles and rooting for them to overcome. It is a novel about the power of love, forgiveness and hope. A wonderful read, right to the end.

Janice Robinson, Executive Director, Halton Children's Aid Society

Tide's End captured my attention from the first page and kept me engaged for the next day and a half as I went back to it at every opportunity wanting to know what everyone was up to and how it would all sort itself out. As with her first novel, *Just Living*, it didn't disappoint, and I look forward to Meredith Egan's next offering as well. The book is reminiscent of work by Jodi Picoult, Wally Lamb and Anna Quindlen - works of fiction which draw the reader into social and family issues. A social commentary which keeps asking us to think well and hard about right and wrong, and all of the nuances which factor into our decisions.

Renata Karrys, Former Street Outreach Worker (Youth),
and Former Family Support Worker (Youth in Care/Foster Families)

Tide's End is a story about resiliency, and most of all, it's about hope. It delves into the world of being a sexual assault survivor and the many facets that entails — including the realm of conflicting emotions. Learn about the role which a support circle can play in a survivor's arduous journey of healing.

And no journey is complete without its challenges. What happens when you're told to perform a series of tasks, you actually complete them, and the rules suddenly change? The rug gets pulled out from underneath you. What do you do then? Can you summon the strength to keep going?

Tide's End makes you want to root for the underdog who struggles to do the right thing. Life's decisions seem like they should be so simple — especially when looking in from the outside.

Meredith's book illustrates just how complicated life's journey can be—when the bond of family or community support is ever-changing. Even a small amount of love, guidance and acceptance can make all the difference. And that can move you forward in unexpected ways.

Cathy – a lifelong learner

Building on the vivid journey Meredith Egan took us on in *Just Living*, exploring the experiences of federally incarcerated men and those who support them, she now turns the volume up on the silenced voices of victims of sexual abuse. Egan perfectly captures the emotions, struggles and strengths of victims in their journey towards becoming survivors. She also helps readers understand the current risks and realities of sex trafficking within our communities.

Avery Hulbert, MA, Criminology Instructor,
College of the Rockies, #MeToo

IN PRAISE OF
JUST LIVING – A NOVEL

There is so much more to this fine novel than meets the eye, and its rich exploration of the human experience touches the soul deeply on many levels. With Meredith Egan's keen and compassionate understanding of correctional services and community, her respect for Aboriginal and other spiritual teachings, and led by her finely drawn and authentic characters, we are helped to stand in many places, and come to yearn for justice in new ways. Absorbing! Compelling! Genuine! Heartwarming!

Jane Miller-Ashton, Criminology Instructor, Kwantlen Polytechnic University Senior Manager, Correctional Service of Canada (retired)

Just Living grabs your interest from the start...the pace is maintained by flashbacks and forward reflecting the complexity of life for people who have had horrific experiences in their lives, and have caused serious harm to others. This is a good read for those who hope for a better future in justice with its wide rippling consequences. It's also a good read for those that seek a love story in exceptional settings.

Tim Newell, past Prison Governor (UK) and founder of Escaping Victimhood

Meredith Egan deftly walks us carefully full circle around the complexities of trauma and its aftermath; letting us feel the hurt, the fear, the shame and the wretched losses that ripple from the broken-heart center of it all.

Along the way she weaves a container to hold the pain, its threads made from life's simple, joyous pleasures; the breaking of bread, the turning of soil, and the caring of animals. *Just Living* teaches us by example what it means to live restoratively and offers hope for the way we can do justice.

Katy Hutchison, Author of "Walking After Midnight: One Woman's Journey Through Murder, Justice & Forgiveness"

Just Living is a good tale well told. It's filled with mystery, intrigue, life, spirit, and, best of all, healing.

Brent Bill, Author of
"Life Lessons from a Bad Quaker" and other books

Just Living is emotional honesty. Meredith Egan's compelling characters catapult readers into the world of brutal injustice whereby intergenerational trauma wreaks havoc. In the terrain of both the literal and the figurative of 'doing time' we come to better understand the power of compassion, of healing, of reconciliation, of resilience.

Margot Van Sluytman, Victim/Survivor,
Founder of The Sawbonna Project for Living Justice.

Just Living is a wonderful book, filled with characters that moved me. Each of their stories was so unique, and yet they were all connected to one another. I felt I knew all of them.

Beth is an awesome character, all of her doubts and faults, and emotions and goodness, she is a model for those of us who want to change the world.

At one point she shares, "What is the point of blame when there's so much healing to be done?" This sums up all of our lives, whether we are victims, prisoners or people who work and volunteer in Corrections. We all have things that need to be healed and need places like *Just Living* to be able to do so.

Thank you for bringing this story alive.

Marlyn Ferguson,
Valley View Funeral Home Homicide Support Group

A compassionate and challenging read. Meredith Egan has taken up the complex challenges of addressing the many issues experienced by marginalized peoples in our Canadian society, and has succeeded in creating believable, sympathetic characters whose human strengths and foibles carry us along in this fascinating narrative. *Just Living* will affect readers in a real and memorable way.

Alison Lohans, Award-winning author of 26 books for young people

Just Living is an adventure, an open-hearted search for ways to recover from harm. What happens when people respond to harm by listening to the deep reasons for it, and focusing on bringing healing out of the consequences? It's life, it's exciting, and it takes courage.

Gianne Broughton, Author of "Four Elements of Peacebuilding"

TIDE'S END:
a just living novel

MEREDITH EGAN

Copyright © 2019 by Meredith Egan
Amity Publishers edition published 2019

National Library of Canada Cataloguing in Publication
Egan, Meredith
Tide's End / Meredith Egan
ISBN 978-1-7770080-0-0

This book is dedicated to everyone who helps –
the healers,
the lovers,
the sisters, and brothers, and complicated families,
that we are born to or create,
the first responders,
the soup-makers, and neighbours,
all companions to those who suffer,
who walk alongside, listen so carefully, and gently wipe tears,
sometimes without knowing the stories,
even while carrying their own.

Without your Light, the world would be so bleak.

Thank you.

CONTENTS

CHAPTER 1
WARMING UP

If this is what I have to do to rescue Jenny, I'll figure it out, I thought as I drove along the dark, narrow roadway. *My little sister is worth it, even if I feel like throwing up.* Occasionally the overhanging trees dropped massive dumps of water onto my car. Or rather, into my car through rust holes and windows that didn't seal. Every time there was the thunder of falling water, I ducked.

What the hell have you gotten me into, Marta? I thought, wishing daggers at the social worker who'd sent me here. Crawling further up the driveway, I turned a corner and gasped.

Holy crap, I thought, staring at the building in front of me. I'd stayed in dodgy motels. Run down apartments. *But I'd never been in a place like this before.* Ever. In my life. This place was huge, and gorgeous, and knew I wouldn't fit in. I'd registered for the Survivors of Sexual Assault Retreat, but *would it be okay?* What would it take to blend?

The money I'd need to pay for the rest of the damned retreat was in my torn duffle. But this looked decidedly upper class, and, well…here I was hoping my junker would make it up the driveway. It'd been my home for the last three months…so not upper class.

Is this really what I need to do to get Jenny back? I'd just turned 19, and getting custody of Jenny Benny, being an epically amazing big brother for a change…that was the most important thing to me. Marta thought I'd better deal with my sexual…history first.

My mind bounced all over. Then it landed on *maybe tonight I'll get warm*. Like, to my bones, warm. I smiled.

Smoke was drifting out of the rock chimney above me. *Tide's End*, the huge retreat centre, was built of logs – the biggest I'd ever seen. Two or three stories, with whole wings that stuck out from the main building. I'd never understood what was meant by "wings" on a building before. Of course, I also couldn't get my head around *Tide's End*. I thought tides never ended…something I could rely on. Not?

Wow. Looking up, my brain registered only wow.

I swallowed my fear and remembered the promise I'd made to myself and Jenny. I would get everything I could from this. It would cost me every penny I had (and some I didn't, but I'd borrowed those), and I wasn't going to let a lack of courage hold me back. Besides, warm, right?

I parked as far away as I could from the building. A warm light shone through the stained-glass windows on either side of the huge wooden door, and I felt a bit of hope.

Then it started to pour, of course. I reached around behind me, pulled my sleeping bag and pillow away from the door in case the window leaked again, and wrapped my arms around my old duffle. I made a dash for it. As I slammed my car door, the "thunk" sounded different, and not good, but I kept going.

Running through the front door, I stopped as it swung closed behind me. The room was incredible – a huge stone fireplace, two stories, with a roaring fire. I tried to look nonchalant, but my mouth kept falling open. There was a balcony that wrapped around the main space. Beautiful blankets – maybe quilts? – hung from the banisters, and more than one was made of a First Nations design. I wondered who had enough blankets to hang them as decorations in winter. And yes, matching light fixtures.

Chairs were spread out in front of the fire, and I wanted to sink into one and put my feet up. There were two women in front of the fireplace, one with a clipboard. *That's who I have to talk to*, I thought just as the door behind me flew open, and I jumped. My duffle hit the floor like a rock, and everything spilled out. I stumbled and barely caught myself, but not before my wet sneakers smacked the floor. Twice. Shit.

My face was burning, and I could feel every eye in the place on me. Women peered at me from everywhere, and the ones who'd bumped me were now fussing. I scrambled to pick up my stuff, and knew they were trying to help, but really? Did I need you to see my dirty, second-hand clothes? Old journal? Russet, Jenny's old stuffed toy? I jammed the cat back into the bag and headed for a corner under the balcony. I knew how to hide.

The woman with the clipboard quickly found me. She stuck out her hand, and I think I shook it.

"Hello, I'm Kate. How can I help you?" she said, and I remembered a story I'd heard from a black friend who'd visited the South.

I saw the lady at the door to the church say, "Welcome," over and over again to all the white people who were granted entry. And then when I walked up, she said, "How can I help you?" and I knew I wasn't welcome. For a second, I wondered if I was in the right place.

"Hi, I'm Taylor Smythe. I'm here for the Survivors Retreat." Kate started flipping through papers on her clipboard.

"Welcome, Taylor. Let me check you in," she said, leaning against the wall under the balcony. So much for the warmth of the fire, I thought. She waved an older woman in a big apron over.

"Sally, can you get Elder Rosie for me? We need to talk," she added, and my hackles raised. I *needed* this retreat.

"What the heck? Didn't you get my deposit? I have the rest of the money in my bag," I told her, reaching for my battered duffle. She smiled at me.

"No, Taylor, that's not the problem. Really. Just give us a few minutes, okay? I'll be back," and she steered me towards a couple of armchairs. I flopped into a deep one, slid down to get comfortable.

An old woman in a long, patched skirt and cardigan came over.

"Rosie! Thanks for coming. Taylor's registered for the retreat. Do you know…should I talk to Beth?"

What the literal fuck? I thought. I'd wanted to leave five minutes ago, but now I was determined to stay. I listened in.

"Beth's with Hugh. They're busy," she said. "I promised not to bug him," Rosie said, reaching into her pocket for a kerchief, wiping her face. "Do we really need her?" the old woman asked. Kate steered Rosie a few feet away, and I heard her say something about, "Well, he can't stay here," and my stomach dropped. I closed my eyes.

Kate put her phone to her ear, making a call.

"Beth? Where are you?" she asked, waited a minute. Whoever Beth was, she had something to say. "Can you drop by on your way home? Sure, bring Ben," I overheard her say. I sighed, and opened my eyes, trying not to look at them.

Behind the fireplace was another room set up with big tables and chairs, maybe a dining room. The back wall was made of glass, and I think I saw a small lake out there. The deck was lit up, so the darkness wasn't too…well, dark.

I did a mental count of the people I'd seen. Ten, I think. Ten women. Hmmm. Soon, they forgot I could hear them. I've never had trouble listening…it's kept me safe.

"What the fuck? I thought this was for survivors," one tough chick whispered to still another middle-aged woman.

"Well, that's interesting. Didn't expect a guy," someone upstairs said, and my gut clenched.

Taylor. Every year in school I'd had to remind some of my teachers that some Taylors were boys. Thank you, Taylor Swift. I didn't remember seeing a tick box for Male or Female on the application form.

"Maybe he's f2m trans," a younger woman piped in, leaning over the balcony. She was stunning — long, black hair, wearing torn jeans and a baggy T-shirt. Broken as I am, I still notice cuteness. Even though I'm *not* a tranny, I liked her, and not just because she dressed like me. Or because she was brown, like my best friend in school.

Shit. I might have to get out of here, I thought, but then realized that even over here in the corner, I was actually getting warm. *I'll just stay until they kick me out. Maybe I'll get dry. And I'll make them give me my deposit back,* I thought, as drowsiness kicked in. I closed my eyes, thinking back to last month, in Marta's office.

"Really Taylor. I can't tell you where she is. You can't just come in here and demand stuff. You know that." She was pissed at me, but I didn't back down. I'd never been lippy because she'd been in charge of me, but now I'd show her pissed.

"You promised, Marta. You said if I could stay clean until I was an adult, you'd help me find her. I ain't used once, not even a joint. It's not fair!" My hands clenched by my side, and I didn't care that I was being loud. Jenny needed me, and the last time I'd seen her I'd promised I'd come for her.

Three whole years.

And no doubt, wherever she was, Jenny was living in a hellhole. I'd heard from a friend that Mom was back on the streets, turning tricks and using, so maybe Jenny was free of her. But no matter if she was in foster care, temporary care, or even at a relative's…it all sucked, and my heart hurt when I thought about it. I had to get her out. She'd be safer with me.

That's what big brothers are for, right?

That's what I'm for. I'm certain of it.

That day, I was escorted out of the office, dismissed. Marta told me to come back the next day for more information. That day I was escorted out again.

I kept showing up and kept being escorted away. Except when they didn't even let me in. But I kept at it.

A week later I reacted all over her. Mistake.

"You can't just be the age of an adult, Taylor. If you're really going to help your sister, you have to *be* an adult. The assaults…they just have to stop affecting you so much." I'd been stunned. *WTF? I thought I'd hidden it pretty well.*

"Do your work to heal from all that's happened to you. Get on your feet. Learn not to blow up." *Why couldn't I have just listened patiently,* I thought.

She told me what I had to do to get Jenny safe and look after her.

I just hadn't expected it to be so damned hard.

And now, looking around that enormous room, I saw it was filled with the fire's glow and a sense of good spirit, and I felt myself drifting in and out. *Just a few minutes,* I promised myself. I pulled my wet feet from my shoes and nodded off as the warmth blanketed me.

CHAPTER 2
THE POUNDING OF TIDES

"Lift it, please!"

Kate's voice, along with furniture being dragged on the floor, jolted me awake. I checked my shirt for drool.

"We want to protect these gorgeous floors as much as possible." I cringed a little. Why so loud? She grabbed a couple more chairs then started stacking the footstools against a wall. "Let's get these comfy ones into a circle, so we can start," she said to the others. Then she walked over to me.

"Taylor, can you come with me? Bring your stuff and we'll put it in the office." At least she wasn't yelling now. Kate headed down a hallway and I stuffed my feet back into my cold, wet shoes and followed her. She ducked into a back office and told me to stash my bag on a table in the corner. Turning, she put her hand on my arm. I tried not to flinch. Awkward.

"So. You may have guessed. We weren't ready for a guy to be a part of this workshop." She looked away. "We know men are sexually abused, so we should have been more prepared. I'm really sorry. We're still figuring things out," she said. More awkward.

"I've spoken to my supervisor and our Elder, and we'll let the group have a say in what to do. I hope you'll be a part of that." I stifled a yawn that was threatening to escape. "They're on their way. We think you're here for a reason, so we want you to stay." She brushed her pants. "Ready?"

"Can I take a minute?" I asked, and Kate nodded.

"Sure, but we're going to start in about five."

"I'd really like to use a washroom, if I could?" As we headed back towards the big room, there were two washrooms. I waited while she knocked on one that had a paper sign on the door that said WOMEN.

"Anyone in here?" she called out. No answer, so she went in to make sure it was empty. Coming out, she reached up and tore off the paper, revealing the permanent Men's Washroom sign. Which felt oddly welcoming.

"There you go. See you soon," she said as she walked away. I went in and locked the door. Don't ever say no to a clean washroom or a dry place to sleep.

A few minutes later, I walked out. I'd splashed water on my face and tried to tame my curls. No luck. As I glanced down at my T-shirt, I noticed drops of water all over it and brushing them off with my wet hands didn't help. Ah well. Nothing in my duffle would look better.

Back in the big room people were sitting in the comfy chairs in the circle. I felt like I was late to class but I really hadn't taken that long.

There was one open seat, and as I made my way towards it, an old lady wearing braids and a long patchwork skirt stood and lifted her arms. I tried to sneak a look at the cougar beside me. She was gorgeous. Blond hair, tight jeans…sigh. Why's *she* here?

"Welcome, everyone. I'm Rosie, and I'm honoured to be here today," she said, and she waved the long stick she was holding, getting us to stand. It had a carving of a big, black bird on the top and was painted bright colours. There was a large crystal in it, and some feathers fluttered from a ribbon. I liked it, I decided.

"Let's start this evening in a good way, with a prayer," she said. A prayer? Weird.

"Thank you, Creator, for bringing us together tonight. Thank you for the journeys that brought us here, especially the good bits." She asked for kindness on our "healing journey," and open hearts and minds and other stuff. Then she said something I won't forget.

"Creator, we ask you to remind us to believe each other as much as we want to be believed. And to show us new ways to make sense of what happened to us. Help us find a way to go back into the world with less hurting." Less hurting. An idea I could get behind.

"Let's be open to new things, and not be too judgemental." She just stood there for a bit, and when she finally sat, so did everybody else. People were smiling, even me.

"*Tide's End.* I don't know if you know why this place is named that, so I'll try to explain.

"Mission – the train bridge, actually – is the place where the folks who regulate fishing have decided the tides end. The water is brackish until here, up the river delta, but First Nations People have been fishing here since time…forever. At least 10,000 years. We fished the salmon, and the sturgeon, and other fish. And we know about tides, and how they pound and beat on a place. Without ending.

"So, we called this place *Tide's End* because we hope to help with the relentless pounding." She adjusted her skirt and looked at us again.

"We'll talk about Taylor's participating later, but for now, know that sometimes we are going to push you. Ask you to work hard. But you can always say no, if you need to. We just don't want you to be disruptive… stopping someone else from getting what they need in the circle." She smiled and handed the talking stick to Kate.

"Welcome to *Tide's End.* Thank you, Rosie, for your prayers. To start us off, please tell us who you are and why you're here," Kate continued. "I'll start. My name is Kate, and I'm going to help Rosie lead things. I've worked here at *Tide's End* since it opened this past year, so I can help you with any questions. Before this space opened, I worked at the half-way house, *Just Living,* down the road.

"My partner and I have a young son Brock who is almost two, and the only thing that will take me away from you this week is a family emergency. You are my priority!" She took a deep breath and kept going. "Ten years ago, I was working as a nurse in the Downtown East Side, helping out at an injection site. The DTES, you all know it. I was working with people who struggle with addictions, homelessness, mental health issues. While there, I was a victim of a horrible assault and robbery that left me with a brain injury and ongoing PTSD symptoms. I'm managing them, but some days are better than others. It wasn't a sexual assault, as far as I know, but I was unconscious when I was found." I tried to imagine what that was like. Not knowing if you've been diddled. Then the stick went back to Rosie.

She told us her ancestry – her band is from the Interior of B.C. —⊠ and then she told us about residential school. The stories wove together.

"So my mother and father and aunties and uncles were all made to go to residential school and they were all abused – physically, emotionally, culturally, sexually, you name it. And it messed them up. Then my parents had to send me too." She looked at her hands. "It broke them." I winced.

At school, she said, the staff told her she was the "special one," and she thought at first that what they did to her was "special love." Boy, could I relate. I squirmed in my chair. Glancing around the circle, others were squirming, too.

"Now I understand it was sexual abuse," Rosie continued, "but back then it was all confused in my head with learning English, and school lessons, and eating weird food. And not being allowed to talk to my cousins who were there with me, or my parents, or our Elders."

I wasn't taken away from my home like Rosie, but I'd been just as confused. The blood started to rush in my ears, and it was hard to stay focused.

"I was a child, and it was wrong. It took me a long time to admit they'd been abusing me, both the people at the school, and then later folks in the village where I lived. I was tough. I knew *I was different*." Just a little too familiar, I thought. Then, she decided what they did was love because she didn't want to be a victim. Man, I related hard.

I don't know if what happened to me was always abuse either, I thought. *Sometimes it felt good, but at some point I figured out it was wrong. It was, right?*

Rosie ran her fingers over the feathers on the stick a couple of times. Then she looked up, and sighed, and kept going. The room was silent. Still. Everyone focused on Rosie, even the folks who looked away.

"It was easier for me to be angry about the cultural and physical abuse at school, because that happened the same for everyone. But the sexual stuff was more personal. Intimate, I guess.

"And then, because we were so messed up, we kids took all kinds of sexual advantage of each other in the dorms at night. I did that, too, and I still feel dirty when I think about it. I feel ashamed." She looked at the cloth in the middle of the circle, with a bowl and a feather, and some stones on it. "Sometimes I still can't tell the difference between healthy relationships, abuse and sexual assault." My mind wandered a bit, wondering what it would be like to just *know* what's right. Then her next words brought me back in the circle.

"What I know now is there's a path that can take you towards a better life, towards healing." Whoa. Really?

That was *my* secret hope. The one buried so deep I hardly ever let myself think about it. But when Rosie said it, I could almost believe in the possibility. Maybe that was what could connect us. Possibility. Healing. Even for the women who didn't really want me in their circle. *Could the pounding of the tides really end?*

"Survivors," the retreat flyer called us. But one of us was not like the others. I bet everyone but me had survived men.

I'd mostly survived my mom. A woman who was supposed to love me, but not like that. Rosie kept going.

"I don't know what your path is. But I'll help you find it and even have a few tricks that might help." Her eyes sparkled when she looked at me, then the others, one by one, and this time no one looked away except one angry woman across from me. The one who'd been stabbing me with angry looks for a while.

Rosie passed the stick on to the next woman, and the next, and one by one the women introduced themselves. They talked about what had happened to them. And I listened. And squirmed.

Men beat and raped these women. Husbands. Strangers. College boys – men really — who gang raped the young woman with the long, dark hair. Some of them cried when they talked about ruined childhoods, horrible relationships, or the night they were attacked. Some of them didn't because, well, not feeling is easier? And some of them were still raging.

They were attacked everywhere. Some in their own homes, some in the streets. It was terrifying. And I felt like a shit just because…well, I'm one of "them." A potential rapist.

I heard what they said. And what they didn't. Slowly I put some names to faces to stories. The angry dyke made it clear we were to call her Terry – definitely not Theresa. Like I would dare call her that. Her ex-husband had assaulted her "again and again," and she'd hurt him so bad she'd gotten something like ten years and was out. She just wanted to find some peace, she said. She scared me a bit, the chains hanging from her belt loop, her mean eye.

A middle-aged woman, Dianne, reminded me of the secretary at one of my elementary schools. She dressed like I imagined a mom *should* dress, matching top and sweater with a modest skirt, and I felt safe around her. She spoke in sudden bursts about the sexual abuse her husband had rained on her for years. On top of physical abuse. I felt sad again. She'd escaped to a transition house with her two kids and was still staying there. "Luckily, the kids went to their aunt's this week."

The young woman about my age who'd been gang raped was Padma. ("Short for Padmasundara. You can call me Pam if it's easier.") After they raped her at a university social, they had put the video on Snapchat. Of course, someone else recorded it, and then it was everywhere. Forever, I guessed.

She'd had to leave both school and her family. "It's complicated," was all she'd say. *No kidding. Families can be quite fucked up. Something in common with her, too,* I thought. I knew that family honour was big in South Asian families. Complicated wouldn't begin to describe it.

Ophelia, in her late twenties, was a First Nations woman who barely whispered about her experience of incest, a habit that had plagued her family. She was tough, but I liked her vibe. And I wondered what she was hiding. Ayesha, who was about 30, was the one who didn't hide her hate for me. She was still pissed at the guy who raped her, who she said "got away with it." She scared me.

There were others, all kinds of abuse, and I felt ashamed. *Jesus, isn't there something we men should be doing about this? Why don't we care?*

Then I realized I'd have to talk soon, the last person. And the only guy. What could I say, really?

I'd promised myself I'd try to do my work. I owed it to Jenny and my wallet to make this count. I wanted to look Marta in the eye and tell her I'd rocked it.

But what to share? Does too much show weakness? Fuck. I hadn't thought this through. I felt like a chicken at a fox convention. Hiding in the corner…nothing to see here….

Jean, the stunning older woman sitting beside me, caught me by surprise. She said it was too hard to talk about what had happened to her, and just passed the talking stick to me. My mouth dried right up, and I looked down at the holes in my running shoes. Shit. I really was worthless. I couldn't even get it together to have decent shoes. No wonder Marta didn't trust me with Jenny.

"Hi, I'm Taylor. I'm 19 years old, and I was abused by my mom for about ten years until I left when I was 16. It's kind of messed me up, and I'm here to try and figure things out. A counsellor suggested this group a while ago, but I had to save my money. So here I am. Sorry you weren't expecting me to be a guy," I said, looking down. "For this week, I'm gonna try hard to be really honest with myself and everyone here. If you let me stay." Not exactly blending in. After a moment I gave the talking stick back to Kate.

Everyone looked somewhere else, waiting for Kate to talk.

She outlined the retreat plans. Mornings in workshops. Afternoons doing our own stuff – with retreat partners, counsellors, alone, or sometimes even just taking the afternoon off to nap. Most days we'd come together again just before dinner. Then evenings were unprogrammed. Five more days. *I can do this*, I thought.

Then she talked about creating safety, but I zoned, waiting for the question about whether I'd be allowed to stay. I just wanted them to talk about me, the elephant in the room.

Kate suggested we take a short break. She had to talk to her boss at the Retreat Centre.

"Enjoy some treats. We'll reconvene in a bit and talk about everything. Stay close!" she said.

I kept looking at my shoes, pathetic as they were. I could tell my feet were like cold prunes inside, and I wondered if they'd ever be warm and dry. I'd gotten so close earlier, but my soaked shoes had chilled me to the bone all over again.

The front door opened, and a young woman wearing a black shirt with that funny white minister's collar came in. As the door started swinging shut, a big hand grabbed her, and I jumped a little. She turned back, and leaned through the opening, kissed whoever'd reached up and tugged her collar off. Coming into the room, she stashed it in her pants pocket and opened her top buttons. She smiled at Kate across the circle and headed into the kitchen. Kate followed her, and the woman's friend came in a few minutes later and joined them. *Was that the supervisor?* I wondered.

Man, I wished I could be a fly on that wall. Would I ever find a place where I fit in? Felt… relaxed?

I escaped back to the washroom to wait. My stomach hurt.

CHAPTER 3
CRACKS AND CHASMS - MARTA

"I know what the policy says, I just don't agree with it!" Marta felt her voice rise and didn't fail to sense the irony. At least they wouldn't throw her out of her own office like she'd thrown Taylor out last month. She juggled the files on her hip, wanting to settle this with her boss before she headed home with her paperwork.

"Really, Paul, we have to find a different way to support him. It's not working, what we're doing now," she finished.

"But he hasn't applied for assistance. In fact, now that he's an adult, we can't do *anything* for him until he asks. We have no right sticking our nose in his business. Especially since he left our care and we didn't even seem to notice," Paul said, closing the file and putting it on the stack on the credenza behind his desk. "Don't you have enough cases without sticking your neck out for this kid? I heard he was trouble at the group home," Paul finished, dismissing Marta. But she wasn't done.

"His welfare does matter to one of my cases. His twelve-year-old sister, Jennifer, is being cared for by his aunt, but I don't trust the old lady. In fact, I've been trying to schedule a visit, and she's being evasive. I'm worried her aunt would sell her for a pack of smokes. And Jenny isn't exactly thriving there, so I'd be glad to have Taylor be able to take care of her. Look out for her.

"I just want the go-ahead to help Taylor access some counselling. Maybe some funds to get him training, so he can get a job. I *don't* want him working the streets like his mom. Really. That young man has seen enough in his childhood to last a lifetime. He deserves a break, and I want you to authorize his first 20 sessions."

Like where the hell will I find the money for that? Paul thought.

Marta wasn't backing down. She'd felt horrible for Taylor when he'd come in last month, remembering her promise of three years ago. Back then she'd given her word that she'd reconnect him with his little sister once he was an adult, and frankly she never thought he'd remember. Or stay clean. He'd done both, and she believed they deserved to be together, even if he wouldn't qualify for custody.

She'd found him that Survivors Retreat, and even given him some of her own money so he could afford to attend. She had a soft spot for the boy who'd survived so much, but wanted things to be better for his little sister.

She knew this was the kind of work she was trained to do, dreamed of doing her whole life. Damn it, she was going to do it, and do it well. Even if sometimes she messed up.

It was hard not to think about that other young teenager in care, abused by her foster parents, involved in internet porn. That teen wasn't in Marta's caseload, but she'd been involved in her care. Or rather, not involved enough. She'd missed a visit while covering for her colleague, who was off on stress leave. In fact, thinking about that young girl, Marta started worrying again about Jenny. She'd do an unscheduled visit this afternoon to see Jenny in person. Her gut radar was telling her not to allow anything to postpone this time.

"Marta!" Paul summoned as she stopped outside his door. "This isn't that little girl from Maple Ridge. And you didn't do anything wrong," he said, his voice softening but with a really hard edge.

"You just keep telling yourself that, Paul. We'll be lucky if the police find the little girl and get charges against that predator. I was supposed to visit her, cover for Laurence. I couldn't find her.

"Bottom line is, I know I failed her. And her little brother. Yes, I had a ton of cases. Yes, I was overwhelmed. But I reported checking on her when in fact I didn't because I couldn't find the address, and I never went back and corrected the reports in the computer. It gave her foster parents a chance to move. Now I just hope they put in a change of address, to get their cheques. I put a pause on the money until they check in.

"I still get sick when I think about it. Every night I pray for those kids. This is what people mean when they complain about kids falling through the cracks." Paul reached out and put his hand on Marta's arm. It was important to him that this mistake be left behind; he'd chosen to cover for the workers, not report it. And he couldn't afford to lose Marta *or* Laurence. It hadn't been intentional; he was sure of it.

Yes, the department was always short on resources. Yes, he needed to push for more, so this didn't happen again. But Marta had been overtaxed and had just forgotten to amend the report, a simple oversight. Then Laurence hadn't chased down a visit when he returned because the report said a visit had happened. Paul called her back into the office.

"I forgot to tell you. I got a call from the RCMP in Mission; they've got a crew on it. They think they're close to reeling the guy into a sting operation -- they're using officers to pose as a young girl in Mission. Feeding right into his frigging addiction. I'll keep you up to date." Marta started to move down the hall towards her office, feeling a little better.

"I'm going to help Taylor, you know. I don't have to chart it, but I'm not going to keep it a secret.

"He loves Jenny. And she deserves to be with him. He certainly deserves to be in touch with her." Paul needed to know nothing would stop her. She wasn't letting another little girl slip from the case files.

That afternoon, Marta slung her bag over her shoulder and slammed her car door. Chances were, even in this neighbourhood, no one would give it a second glance. There wasn't anything about it, or in it, that said "worth stealing." She glanced at the first-floor apartment in the tenement building and saw the curtain move. Good. Jennifer Smythe's aunt was in.

As she knocked on the door, a neighbour stuck his head into the hallway.

"She's not home. She hasn't been for over an hour. Maybe picking up the little girl," he said, just a little too rehearsed.

"Oh. Then I better call the police, because I saw someone in there!" Marta's authority showed up when she needed it. The guy ducked back into his house quickly. No one wanted to be responsible for a police call.

Marta banged again.

"Mrs. Edgars. It's Marta from Social Services. If you don't open the door, I'll have to put a hold on your cheque." She waited a minute, wondering if she'd have to threaten again to call the police. After a few seconds, the door opened a crack, chain barely holding on to the door frame.

"She's at school. No sense in coming in," Mrs. Edgars whispered. Her voice was raspy, and the smell coming from the apartment was stale and tasted bitter on Marta's tongue.

"No worries. This is about seeing you, too." First rule. Gain entry. Voluntary entry. A couple of moments later, Mrs. Edgars lifted the chain and granted access by shuffling away.

Marta followed her into the single room. It was chaos, and Marta again wondered if Jenny was better off with this aunt, something mandated by the government policy of trying to keep families together.

"I'm here to see Jennifer, and to inspect her space." Marta looked at the clipboard, and noted, "I see you received some funds for bedding, and clothing when she moved in. Where does Jennifer sleep?" There was a dirty mattress on the floor in the corner, and a single bed against one wall, a dirty child's blanket tangled in the corner. Marta guessed the mattress was Jenny's, but wondered about the blanket. She checked the file in her hands again. *She's twelve. Why does she still have a baby blanket?* she wondered.

"Over there," Mrs. Edgar confirmed, waving a hand, a cigarette dangling from her fingers. Marta cringed.

"You know you promised to make your space smoke-free for Jenny." Marta regretted the words as soon as they were out of her mouth. Being the social worker police wasn't going to help her get information about Jenny.

"Anyway, where is she, again? Did she go away for a bit or something?" Marta saw no evidence that Jenny had been here lately. No milk glass in the sink, no small plates on the table. No skinny jeans on the floor, or kids' books lying about.

"Yes, that's right." Marta could see Mrs. Edgars trying to make up the story as she went. "Her uncle came and took her for a few days in Mission. Fresh air, and all that. She'll be home after the weekend." The elderly woman was looking down, picking at her soiled T-shirt. The glass in front of her, smoky with grime, was moved to the counter. Marta doubted that was apple juice in it.

"When did she go? Do you have an address for him?" Marta knew Jenny would be a prime candidate for exploitation. She was young and had been surrounded by so much sexual abuse Marta wondered if she'd even fight.

A half hour later, Marta had an address. She didn't know if it would help the police, but she barely made it to her car before she called the detachment in Mission.

"Inspector Derksen please. I'll wait." And the staff seemed surprised when he took her call right away.

"Mark, I might have a lead. And another young girl in danger. Jennifer Smythe is the girl's name. She's twelve." Marta flipped through the file on her passenger seat.

"No, twelve. Just turned twelve And especially vulnerable because of her history of sexual abuse. Anyhow, her aunt told me she's gone to visit her 'uncle' in Mission. She doesn't have an uncle in Mission. Or anywhere else.

"This suspect's last name is Mason. First name either Sam or Tom. Or a combination of those. Here's his supposed address," Marta shared the address.

"Thanks Marta. Sounds like a solid lead. Some of this matches up with some information we're piecing together. Let us know if you learn anything else," he finished, and they said goodbye.

The next thing Marta did was put a stop order on Mrs. Edgars' cheques. And she smiled while doing it.

She called Paul to report that they really did need to fund Taylor's counselling, and get him as prepared for Jenny as possible.

And she promised herself, Paul and (with a silent prayer) Jenny that she'd work her ass off to find the little girl before she had to face Taylor again.

* * *

BETH AND BEN

"Are we good?" Ben asked Beth as they headed into the office with Kate and Rosie. She turned towards him and noticed how scared he looked.

"We're fine!" She smiled at him. "I met with Hugh, we talked about Martin, which is hard. You know." She took a sip of water. "I tried to explain to you why it bugged me." She laughed a little. "Clearly I didn't do a good job. I must have more thinking to do," she said, turning towards him. "We can talk about it later, love. Something more important is going on here if Kate called us in."

When Ben asked, it was enough to get Beth thinking again about her talk with Elder Hugh that afternoon. He'd been visiting Martin in prison, and even that was hard to think about. Hard to not feel jealous about. She and Martin had been close when Martin had been a resident at the half-way house next door. She'd been a practicum student and, in the end, he'd wreaked havoc on her life, and got himself thrown back in a maximum-security prison where he'd likely spend the rest of his life.

And the fact that Hugh visited him, thought it was important to "keep her updated on his progress" always knocked her off centre. And it bugged her that Ben didn't get it.

Oh, she understood that Ben related to prisoners and institutions and chaplains and Elders better than she did since that was actually his job. And that when they talked, she had to remind him that the systems they worked in forgot about crime victims, didn't even think about the impact their institutional work had on the lives of those most affected. And that frustrated the fuck out of her and pushed her buttons.

But she'd agreed to meet with Hugh later in the week, because she loved the old guy, and always felt a little like she owed him.

"Anglican guilt," he called it. "And I'm not above taking advantage of it. Even if you didn't run them residential schools," he'd said, hugging her. "We'll all feel better if we talk about stuff."

Now she had to break it to Ben that she'd added an evening meeting with Hugh this week, when their lives were already overcommitted.

And she'd promised she wouldn't do that.

CHAPTER 4
BREADCRUMBS

I struggled to stay awake waiting for the circle to start again. Yes, in the bathroom, sitting on the floor. I was tired, and warming up, and my brain was hurting. Usually I just leave when the waiting gets too hard but not tonight.

God, there was a lot of talking. And a ton of listening to those wounded women. What they say and what they don't. And there's lots they don't say. Like how pissed they are. Raging, fucking pissed. Except for Ayesha. She showed the world her anger.

Finally, I got up and joined the larger group. And then Kate called us together. She introduced Beth, and her husband, Ben. Beth actually runs the place, even though she looks maybe 20 years old and wears a minister's collar. Ben (who I thought was in charge) is older than Beth, I think, but quieter. He was wearing a grey cardigan and really clean jeans, and he kinda reminded me of Mr. Rogers. Thinking about watching the reruns of that on TV with Jenny made me smile.

I saw some of the women in the room bristle, though. Terry's eyebrows raised, and her shoulders braced. *How can someone that tough look even scarier?* She leaned over to Ophelia and whispered, "Two guys now?" Ophelia snorted, tugged on the single braid hanging over her shoulder.

But that was nothing compared to Ayesha and Michelle. They were livid and didn't hide it. Arms crossed, Ayesha's eyes darted back and forth spewing daggers at Kate and Beth and Ben. I thought I'd heard Kate tell some of the women during break that Ben was a monk, but I guess not, because monks don't get married, right? After introductions, he headed to the kitchen and Beth stayed. Kate started.

"So let's talk about things. I've asked Beth to join us in case there are any questions. What's going to help you move forward on your journey? What's going to get in the way?" Kate passed the talking piece to Rosie, who reminded everyone that sometimes the Creator asks us to do things that are hard.

The women in the circle talked about feeling scared and that they hoped there wouldn't be gossip. Padma leaned back, not really engaged. Terry grumbled about "allowing men in here," and rattled her chains. Michelle was shooting dagger looks at Rosie and Kate. Ayesha spoke out of turn.

"Yeah. Like what the hell? I didn't come here to be hassled." Before she got the talking stick, she was spewing at me. Literally. I felt the spit across the circle.

Someone else mentioned we weren't being forced to do anything... and then the talking piece came to Dianne, in her lavender sweater set. I smiled.

"So, I agree with everything that's been said so far. We should be brave, and nice to each other. Keep confidentiality. And I hear you about the men being scary.

"But I want to talk about Taylor. I've been living in a transition house with my kids because, well, my husband abused me for years, and I finally snapped when my son Tommy asked me why I put up with it. You see, he's 16 and he's trying to decide if he can leave home for college. If I'd be safe." I was cringing, trying to disappear into the cushions of my chair. Does God strike you down for envying someone? College – imagine.

"A part of living at the transition house is that the women there tensed up around Tommy until they find out he's only 16 'cause he looks older than he is. Men aren't allowed in the house, or even around it.

"I started to wonder what would've happened if I hadn't had the courage to leave this year. What if I'd waited until Tommy was 18? Would I have had to choose between going to the transition house and leaving my son with my abusive husband, or staying and being abused? Bringing only Paula, my daughter? Choosing between my kids?

"There isn't a cell in Tommy's body that would hurt a woman. He's a good boy." God, she was fierce for her son. I believed her. She sat just looking at the talking piece in her hands. Then she looked up, and my heart stopped. *What would it be like to have a mom like that?* I wondered.

"If Tommy had been abused and was brave enough to come to a retreat like this, I'd be pissed right off if a bunch of bigoted women ran him off. Yes, some men are pricks. Assholes. Mean fuckers." Some smiled, others gasped. My inside-my-head voice was cheering her on, and when I looked at Padma she was sitting up straight, and she smiled at me.

"But most aren't and the ones who've been abused need help before they get angry. If Taylor is voted off this island, I'm out of here," she finished, crossing her arms across her chest. Lots of the women were looking at their hands, the floor, anywhere but Dianne. She passed the talking piece to Jean, the woman with gorgeous blonde hair. Jean held the stick with hands that were lined with age, but beautifully looked after. Her red nails were dotted with designs. I'd never seen nails that pretty before.

"I agree with Dianne. We women talk about equality and being better than men because we care more. Here's a chance to show 'em what we mean. Besides, I don't think Taylor's threatening. And I bet you gals don't either. I get your comment, Terry, but I don't really think you're scared of Taylor, right?" The woman across the circle shrugged, looked down. "Let's look after him. Things might be more interesting," Jean finished, smiling.

Rosie took the talking piece.

"Thanks for your perspective, Dianne, and Jean. It's valuable. I'd like to hear from everyone, though, especially if they don't agree." And then *everyone* spoke again, except me. But almost no one spoke about me –

only Terry and Ayesha were still pissed. I was getting tired. Frustrated. Almost ready to leave.

Except I was warm, which kept me in my chair. In the end, Rosie took the piece "to close the circle," as she put it.

"One thing I've heard here that is important to me, too, is that everyone have a chance to participate, and that we help each other make it safe. I'm going to assume that includes Taylor, and that those of you who will find that hard will get support from us. No one said this work would be easy." She was staring straight at Terry, Michelle and Ayesha.

"We haven't talked to Taylor about this yet. We've got a couple of places nearby that Taylor can stay in during the retreat. Of course, he needs a chance to think about all of this, too. Beth has some stuff to check out, and Ben will be around as a male counsellor. Shall we meet again in ten minutes sharp and see how everyone is doing with this before promises are made? And I'll write up the guidelines that we've agreed to moving forward." No one disagreed. Thank God. This wouldn't go on all night, which was good. Sleeping in my car was gonna be some cold if things didn't work out. I guess I was only being voted off the island for sleeping at *Tide's End*.

And then she exploded. Ayesha stood up, knocking her chair over. "You said we couldn't stay if we bugged someone else. Well, Taylor is fuckin' bugging me. Gettin' in my way. You guys are fuckin' liars!" she shouted and stomped out of the circle and upstairs. A couple of minutes later, she was thumping her suitcase down the stairs and out the door. She tried to slam it, but it was too heavy. Rosie sighed, and headed into the night after her.

"Taylor, I get that this is a lot to take in." Kate had called me back into the office. "I want to say again how sorry we are. This should have been arranged before you arrived." She tucked her arms into the pockets of her bulky hoodie, making herself small. I knew that trick.

"So, this is what we've got to offer you. There's a fellow who works here, his name is Kenny, and he stays on-site in a trailer. He's offered his spare room if you want it."

"Really? Why would he do that? That's pretty generous." My stomach clenched.

"Well, that's the other bit. Kenny works here now but he used to be a client at the half-way house. He told me I had to tell you two things before you decide.

"He's finished his sentence, which wasn't for sex crimes. In fact, he wants you to know he's never sexually offended against anyone." I swear, she thought I was going to be scared. Like I wouldn't know how to handle the guy. Any guy.

"And secondly, he's gay, and he thinks he might be in a relationship." *Let me tell you, if you wonder, you aren't,* I thought, but I smiled. "I think if you give him a chance, you might really get along." She put her hand on my shoulder and pulled it back when I flinched. Again, awkward.

"And I have another option. There's a woman, Veronica, who lives nearby. She's offered a room in her house. She's a volunteer here and could drive you back and forth if you want."

And then Rosie stuck her head in the office door and called us back to the circle.

"Just give us a second. Taylor's deciding if he's staying, and where."

"Oh. He'll be best at Kenny's," Rosie said, and I laughed. I looked over at her.

"What does Beth think? Is she mad about me being here?" I asked Rosie and Kate.

"Oh, don't worry so much about what other people think. She'll be fine. And Ayesha has decided to sign up for a different retreat later on," Rosie said.

"Okay, then, Kenny's it is," I answered. I trusted Rosie. But I worried about what Beth thought of it all.

Even when Rosie told me not to.

Luckily it didn't take too long to review the "Circle Expectations" Rosie had written up, and there wasn't any discussion. Padma and I were eye rolling across the circle, and I started to bounce a little. My head was spinning, but mostly I was happy. I think. And I really needed sleep. There was an interesting conversation about Ayesha.

"She decided this wasn't the right time to do the retreat, for a bunch of reasons. Things might get hard. We are going to push you. And we will support you staying, do what it takes," Rosie said.

"But you're also free to leave at any time. We'll follow up with you, but you're adults here to do work, and no one is forcing you. Even those of you who are here because an agency or individual sent you. We aren't locking you in here. You'll have to choose to stay," Kate added.

After circle we headed to the dining room for snacks. Cookies and scones were grabbed up, and the women quickly headed upstairs. I hoped they felt safe, and I was a little envious, both that they were so close to their rooms, and that they'd get to hang out with each other. I dashed into the office to get my stuff, and saw Kate grab the last scones. I only felt a little guilt because I'd already stashed some in my pockets. They were really yummy.

A couple of minutes later, Kate finished answering questions and we headed out into the rain to go meet Kenny. It was a long walk, and we had to cross two main paths to get there. It was dark, and I was surprised how LOUD things are in the forest at night. I tried to be cool with it, because clearly Kate wasn't afraid, but it was kinda terrifying. Now I was awake! And I was trying to keep track of where we were, so I'd find my way back in the morning.

Because I wasn't willing to use the stashed scones as breadcrumbs.

CHAPTER 5
CREATING HOME - KENNY

"Yup. I'm off parole now. Of course, he can stay here. And yes, I know I'm allowed to say no." Kenny nodded into the phone. "Yes, I get it. I don't have to do what you ask any more." He listened to his boss, Beth, for a bit longer, reassured her he really did want to do this, insisted she let the poor young man know he was both an ex-offender and gay, and smiled into the phone. Finally, he hung up after a quick, "See you both later." He put his hands on either side of his face, and grinned. Imagine, a real, honest-to-goodness guest in his trailer! Kenny, a helper!

Heading into the bathroom, his energy bubbled as he rubbed the clean faucet until it sparkled, and he grinned when he caught sight of himself in his mirror. His curly hair was shot through with silver, but he wasn't old. Not really. He brushed a piece of fluff off his white T-shirt, captured it in his fingers and put it in the toilet.

Considering where he was, and where he'd been, life was good. He had a job doing what he loved. Couldn't have imagined being a gardener and landscape designer ten years ago but now considered it a passion. He got to work with amazing people – people who'd made a difference in his life, and for the past few months, he'd been able to pay the rent on this trailer. It had changed hands a few times, but when Beth and Ben moved into the modular home on-site, it was decided to turn it over to him. He loved having his own space, for the first time ever, and this old trailer had never looked better. He was born to take care of things. Including his guest, he decided.

It was easy to see his life had been steadily improving. He thought about driving up the driveway to *Just Living* that first time, so many years ago, no cuffs or shackles, being allowed to move into the Lodge, taking care of the gardens. He'd been young and brash when he'd arrived in prison and hadn't been able to settle down and keep quiet. Which had made life there complicated. And risky. He'd served more years than he'd been sentenced to because he'd picked up new charges along the way.

That life was behind him now. He still cringed and turned red when he thought about what he'd done.

So he intended to stay out of prison. His mom needed him. His sister still loved him, and let him hang out with his nephews, even look after them alone. He wasn't going to let his family down ever again. Or himself.

Then Beth had called him and asked him about Taylor, who needed a place to bunk away from the female participants at the Survivors Retreat. Kenny wanted to make sure Taylor felt as welcomed as he'd felt that first night in the Lodge across the fields.

Kenny smiled, and headed for the spare room to make sure it was still clean. He jumped when his phone rang. It was Carson. Shit. He'd forgotten again.

"Hey, Carson. Forgot to let you know...I'm not coming to town tonight. Sorry," Kenny answered.

"Um...second night this week, Ken. I'd almost think you were avoiding me." *Why does he sound like he's snarling at me?* Kenny thought. And just like that, Kenny's nerves were as tight as piano wire. *If he doesn't get me, he's not the right guy.*

"Something came up at work and I'm needed here tonight. I'm hosting a young man from the retreat." As soon as the words were out of Kenny's mouth, he wanted to stuff them back in. Carson had made it clear he didn't understand why Kenny didn't run fast and far from this place now that he didn't have to stay. He'd even suggested Kenny move back to North Van, where he came from, where he'd run with a tough crew. As if he'd let himself go backwards.

"I was looking forward to seeing you and seeing the movie. Sorry." Kenny's voice tapered off. "Maybe I can cook for you next week," he offered. Carson laughed.

"It's okay. Really. Let me know if you're free, and I'll see if I am, 'kay? That is, if the young man hasn't moved in permanently. Man, I do not get why you hang around that place," he said again, and this time Kenny heard the disdain.

Do I really want to date this guy? Kenny asked himself. In fact, since his partner had died in the prison nine years ago, his heart hadn't been into dating.

Hanging up, Kenny smiled, thinking about hosting Taylor. Imagine, him, making a difference. A few of the guys from his old crew wouldn't believe — Kenny, a Goody Two-shoes. Then he thought about the aquaponics program he wanted to start with Cook – growing restaurant greens and fresh herbs, and eventually tomatoes, year-round in a cold frame with some yummy seafood being raised below – maybe some perch or prawns. He felt his heart race just thinking about the funding proposal he was working on with Beth. If only he could feel that excited about dating. Somehow posh guys from North Van didn't turn his crank any more.

Seems everyone "hooked up" online, and Kenny couldn't get used to it. It was all "apps on phones" now. What had happened to the bar scene? Now bars were filled with either old men (was *he* that old?) or married couples…the young men all met online, and Kenny hadn't learned how. No computers inside, no computers at *Just Living*, and so he couldn't see the point in upgrading his "operating system," so to speak. Oh, he had an old laptop Beth'd given him, but he really only used it to write reports or look up plant and seed prices online. Ben and the other guys bugged him about staying single now that they were both partnered, but Nora seemed to understand.

"Not too many guys jump into relationships right after prison," she'd told him. "Don't worry about it. Everyone inside talks about wanting a special someone when they're out, but experience tells me mostly they want freedom to do things when they want, how they want. Without creating new obligations. Take your time."

He'd learned that listening to Nora made things easier, so he hadn't rushed things. Maybe someday he'd find someone, but for now changing the bed in his spare room (taking off clean sheets and replacing them with really clean sheets), making tea for his neighbours and taking field trips to learn about aquaponics was just about enough excitement for him. God knew, his last few years inside were stressful enough; enough. He was done with that. He smiled at himself.

You're turning into an old softy, he thought. *But why do I feel so much stronger, then?* he wondered.

He moved a few plants into the living room from Taylor's room, so that the kid wouldn't have nightmares about jungles, dusted some clean shelves, made sure there were hangers in the closet and went to put on the kettle just as there was a knock on the door.

Before he knew it, Kate bounced in his front door with a shivering young man, his arms wrapped around a torn duffle. Kenny tried not to look too pitying as he welcomed them into his space.

* * *

BEN AND BETH

Ben cuddled Topaz, their orange furball cat, and glanced over at Beth pouring their tea.

"Honey, you okay?" he asked, aware that he might be heading into dangerous territory. At least for a guy who'd never had any opportunity to get to know women before Beth.

"What do you mean?" she asked, and then sighed. "It's that clear, is it?" She picked up two mugs and brought them over to the table where a plate with two scones and a butter dish already sat. She sat down and took a moment. *Blessedly,* she thought, *that man won't rush me.* When she was ready, she looked across the table at her beloved.

"I don't know. I'm kinda pissed at Hugh, and I don't really get why." Ben's eyebrows raised.

"Hugh?" It was all he needed to say. They both knew Beth adored the Elder who worked at the half-way house, and in the prisons with Ben and the men inside. But something else was going on, and Ben had no idea what it might be. "Hugh?" he said again, taking a bite of scone. He'd married the best scone baker in the world. It'd been the first thing he'd noticed about her…her baking.

"I know. He asked me to come and talk to him this week. Something about Martin wanting something from me. And it got my back up." Her scone was quickly becoming crumbs on her plate, her fingers worked at breaking it into ever-smaller pieces. "I think I'm jealous that Hugh visits Martin. Cares so much about him."

Suddenly, tears crested her lower lashes, and two or three fell down her cheeks. Her husband reached over and brushed them away with his thumbs, cradling her face. She pushed him gently away.

"I'm just having a moment. No one comes and visits me, asks me how I'm doing. And I get that's not rational. That a bunch of people would be here in a New York minute if I asked. But Martin isn't asking Hugh to visit, that's for darned sure.

"I guess sometimes it just sucks when I remember how unfair it is," she said, looking up at him.

Ben was smart enough to wait a minute or two, to let his wife speak again. But she stayed silent, so he didn't.

"It *is* unfair. Bad things aren't supposed to happen to good people, and what Martin did to you, to Glenn's family, was horrible. I've had a few tense conversations with God about it, believe me," he said. "If you're done with beating up that scone, can I have a piece of it? They're the best you've ever made," he said, trying to flatter his wife.

"What the hell, Ben? Really? You think I'm worried about what happened that day? I get there are no easy answers about why that happened. That I might have even had opportunities to intervene." She slid her plate towards him.

"I'm pissed at how much time and energy and funding the fucking criminals get after their convictions...and how hard it is to raise even a penny to help victims. Fucking parole officers, counsellors, Elders, re-integration plans. Half-way houses. Employment counselling. Meanwhile, we have to charge big money from sexual assault victims to attend a few days here. And Hugh is off 'visiting Martin.'" She slammed her mug into the sink and headed into the bathroom.

"Whoa," Ben said to only himself. "Sure got that wrong." He slowly shook his head, stood up and cleared the dishes, loaded the dishwasher. He even wiped the table and counters. Turning off the lights he thanked God and his lucky stars that this amazing woman, whom he barely understood, had married him. And that she was a so amazing that he didn't even think twice about being in trouble when they headed for bed.

As he passed the bathroom door, he heard quiet sobs, and knocked.

The door flew open, and Beth was in his arms, hugging him as if she'd never let go.

"When will I get over this?" she asked, and her partner stayed quiet, comforting her with caresses and murmurs. A few minutes later they headed for their bedroom, where he knew they'd fall asleep in each other's arms.

At least he'd learned enough to not ask her if she was on her woman time.

But he did wonder.

CHAPTER 6
PRAYERS AND NIGHTMARES

I jumped when I saw the bear beside the path, but luckily, I didn't scream out loud. Because, really, a bear-shaped bush shouldn't be scary. Kate hadn't even flinched. I coughed to cover up, so Kate wouldn't think I was a total 'fraidy cat. And then we turned a corner, and there was the trailer, lights blazing through the windows into the night. Kate bounced up the steps, knocked on the screen door, and turned back to me.

"I think you're going to like him. He's great." She opened the door and walked right into the arms of a buff guy wearing jeans and a very white T-shirt. When she turned to introduce me, I saw him pulling fur from his shirt, rolling it into a ball between his fingers. He headed for the kitchen and put it in the compost bucket on the counter even before he said, "Hi!" to me. A clean freak. Oh joy.

"Lighten up, Kenny. I haven't even been over to the kennels today. And honestly, a little fur won't kill you," she teased him.

"I know. I'm just teasing you," he countered, and I couldn't tell who was out-foxing who. But they were both smiling.

"Kenny, Taylor. Taylor, Kenny. I'll just stay long enough to make sure this'll work for you guys. And to share the amazing Beth scones," Kate said, reaching into her pockets.

Kenny smiled at her, shook my hand, and put the kettle on.

"Beth scones?" I asked. The Beth from circle tonight?

"One of Beth's superpowers is keeping the peace. And she does that by baking. Amazing scones are a favourite and Cook talked her into sharing some with us tonight." This just kept getting better, I thought, as I stashed my duffle by the front door. The scones in my bag were apparently epic.

Kenny poured us tea, and soon we were sitting around the wooden kitchen table, chatting and devouring the biscuits with butter and blueberry jam.

"Wow, you have lots of plants," I said, scanning the room. Brilliant me, making conversation. Kate burst out laughing, which seemed to make Kenny smile.

"Yeah. I've only had my own space for a bit, and I like plants. Maybe I overdo it. I spent the last half hour moving a bunch out of your room. It got really bad in there." *My* room?

"You didn't have to do that. I don't want to be a bother."

"Oh, get over it." Kenny barely smacked my shoulder. "You aren't a bother. You might just be a God-send. I'm going to skip going to Mom's this weekend. Sis is coming with the kids, and much as I love them, it's pretty intense."

"Kids are dirty, hey?" Kate smiled indulgently at him, and I tried to figure them out. Friends? Is she his counsellor? Clearly this Kenny guy had a thing for clean.

"I get it," I defended. "I like things clean, too. It just makes me feel better." And I made a mental note to clean up after myself while staying here.

"Don't worry about cleaning up." Christ, is this guy psychic? "I'm used to living with other guys, and some of them were slobs. I just kind of clean wherever I am. Don't know if Kate told you, but I spent time in prison." I nodded, looked down. With my past, I don't judge. At least I'd never been caught lawbreaking, which would help me get Jenny back. He kept talking.

"I'm looking forward to a weekend here to trim the labyrinth, maybe go fishing. I'll drop by Mom's sometime on Saturday to see my nieces and nephews." Kenny looked over at Kate. "It's not the chaos, as much as the noise. I've gotten used to a whole lot of quiet, so it's better if I can come and go. You, Taylor, are what I call 'a perfect excuse.'"

He stood up and invited me to come see "my room." I'd never had a room to myself, like with a door, so it felt weird. I didn't want to take advantage. Or set myself up to be taken advantage of.

"You must be tired. Or at least ready for some space. Let's get you settled," Kenny finished.

He opened the door to the room and stepped to the side.

"There's everything you need there on your bed. Just ask if there's something I missed." I saw a pile of shampoo and toothbrushes and stuff. "I actually won't even come in while you're staying, if that's okay. It's really important to me that you feel like this is 'your space.'" I looked up, surprised.

"Really, man, that's okay. I have friends who are gay. You can come in," I said, blushing as the words came out. "I trust you," and I realized I meant it. I trusted Kenny. And Kate. And Rosie. *WTF?* As my armour started to fall, I yawned. I *was* getting ready to sleep.

"Actually, if you just show me where the bathroom is, I am kinda tired after the drive out and the session tonight and everything," I said, stashing my dirty duffle under the bed.

"Sure. The bathroom's right across the hall. We share it, but don't worry about keeping it clean. Really. I just cleaned up while I was waiting for you." Kate snorted and looked at the old taps that were gleaming.

"Sure. 'Cause usually it's really skanky in there," she teased. "Just one sec, though, Taylor. If you're okay staying here at Kenny's, there's a little paperwork that needs doing.

"Technically, here you're on the grounds of the half-way house, so we need clearance forms filled out. I'll leave them on the counter and get them from you in the morning, okay? You've got the welcome package with the schedule, I hope? I'll come by to get you at eight and you can have breakfast in the dining hall with us." She turned and looked at Kenny. "Fill him in on what he needs to know about staying at a half-way house." Fuck. I bet there *are* lots of rules. And then she was gone, and I was alone in *my* room.

I found myself unpacking, which was unusual. Ordinarily I liked to be ready for a quick get-away, but not here. I put my one pair of clean underwear, three T-shirts and an extra pair of torn jeans in a drawer. My journal went on the table beside the bed. I tucked Jenny's stuffed cat near my pillow. She'd given it to me for safekeeping the last time I saw her, and when I get to see her again, I want to show her I'd done that. Russet, she'd called him, even though the damned thing was black and white.

Tonight, I was happy to give the toy a place of honour in this palace. A quick hot shower later, and I was heading for a warm, clean bed. Such a luxury. I started to relax, "dial it down," as I called it, and then remembered one thing.

The forms Kate had left. Filling them out, they asked for an address. Which I kinda sorta didn't have right now. I decided to use the one from my last group home and hoped they wouldn't notice. Do government departments talk to each other? I'd have to risk it. Kenny was headed for the washroom, and I called out to him.

"Hey, Kenny, what about the half-way house rules?" We got chatting for a bit, and then I must have been tired because I just flat out asked him. "Wasn't it weird over there, being gay?" He chuckled.

"Not really. I'm not flaming, and I don't flirt with the other guys, so they don't really care. Live and let live," he said as he turned back towards his room, "as long as you aren't a rat, or a pedophile."

*Phew...*I thought. *No risk of that.*

Later in the bedroom, I turned off the light and felt my breath even out. I took stock of my day, sent a prayer to Grandma, who'd died when I was six. Drifting off, I wondered if I dared to hope for restful sleep.

I hoped I didn't wake Kenny in the night with my screams.

Please Grandma, not that.

CHAPTER 7
GOOD NIGHT, ALYSSA – PATTY AND THE INSPECTOR

Patty was used to men of a certain rank expecting something from her crew, and it wasn't always good. She hoped Inspector Mark Derksen was one of the good guys.

He'd put her team in the basement, so the air conditioners were working overtime to keep the computers cool. It didn't bother her to be in the basement. The fewer distractions while they were doing their jobs, the better. She got busy helping Arun set up the computers, which might have looked like she was ignoring the Inspector. But truth be told, she was more focused on setting up the webcams, and linking the small computer she used to Arun's machine that recorded and did some high-level search and real-life location stuff. She had mad props for Arun, who worked with her full time now, infiltrating the dark web and luring pedophiles and traffickers into law enforcement's net.

"Hey Neil, Arun, Patty. How are things going?" Inspector Derksen said as he came down the stairs. She waited for Neil, a local cop, to answer, but the inspector kept going. "Anything I can get you? And don't say 'coffee.'" The Inspector smiled at them.

"No, we're good, I think. Patty, he's still taking the bait, right?" Neil checked with her. She liked that. She tossed her asymmetric pink hair over her shoulder, revealing a wicked blue undercut.

"He still thinks I'm an elementary school student at Forest Elementary. We're just doing text chats so far. Thanks for taking us by there yesterday. You were right. It's easier knowing the terrain."

She'd wanted to stay downtown in her usual offices to work this case, but the Inspector had convinced her boss that there was value in borrowing team members for the area where the "child bait" was supposed to be from. He'd told them he thought his people would learn from them, that understanding the nuances of cyberwork, including engaging with suspects without "entrapping" them — would help the detachment once they left.

The team, but especially Patty, were determined to nail this asshole who had a history of luring young girls into webcamming. Currently, the scumbag was working on convincing "Alyssa" (a.k.a. Patty) to allow him to take naked screen shots of her. In good time, she knew she'd reel him in. In fact, she was determined to get his whole distribution list, so that her friends at the FBI could take down the "even bigger" players down south. Her skin crawled just thinking about the networks of creeps who were connected online, all of them into "kiddie porn." It was huge. To think this guy had used foster kids in his care, taken their pictures to make money. Word was there were still a couple of kids living with him, and maybe one more Social Services had lost track of. Her nausea rose just thinking about it.

Really? What the hell? How do you lose track of kids in care? Patty thought unfairly, and then hunkered down, more determined than ever to arrest this creep. *Had they ever lost track of me?* she wondered. She knew how fucked up foster care was.

"Great. Let me know if you need anything, okay?" Mark said. "I'm going to introduce you guys to the next watch, if some of you can join us upstairs soon," he finished. "Then you can talk to our detective about the other cases — the college sexual assault on social media — for example."

"No problem. Alyssa is heading to violin lessons soon, so we'll be able to take a break," Neil answered. Mark turned to head upstairs.

"Don't forget, we're meeting Padma tomorrow at dinnertime. She's got questions about our investigation into her case, and Victims Services will be talking to her about testifying, plea bargains and stuff." *Sheesh, it never ends,* Patty thought, glad to be of help but wishing she could see an end to the depravity.

Patty ducked her head around the corner of the briefing room as Mark was telling his staff about them.

"Heads up, folks. Members of Integrated Child Exploitation moved in downstairs, working with Neil and a couple of other investigators for the next few weeks. Seems we have some locals who are making money selling photos of kids. And those kids are not eating ice cream. We don't want these creeps to move, we want to catch them, and seize their computers. And hopefully get the kids out sooner rather than later."

He glanced at the doorway. "Neil, Arun, Patty, come on in." He kept going, which Patty appreciated. No fanfare, please.

"And, we've got the other case, the college student who was videoed at the bar. In that case, we should be able to get the accused on sexual assault, as well as cybercrimes for sharing the video. With the first case I mentioned, if the Crown thinks we can't prove sexual assault, we will prosecute for sharing the images. Welcome to the world of social media. I hope you know what your teenagers are doing," Mark said. They waved at the other officers, and as soon as they could escape, they headed back downstairs.

Later that day, they sat with a couple of detectives, sharing sushi in the back room. A rumpled detective named Wallace started the conversation.

"Okay, what do we need to know for Padma tomorrow night? Her case is complicated because her family doesn't want her to testify. I'm worried about her safety. Her brothers are pretty angry. I don't want to have an honour killing on our backs." Patty smiled and knew what was coming. Arun didn't disappoint.

"Why is it called an 'honour killing' when it's in my community?" Arun asked. "When husbands kill wives in your community, they call it 'domestic violence.' How is this different?" Arun had been working for months to help the RCMP understand his culture. "Most Indian men love their wives and sisters. Really. The guys who do this are crazy, like your white guys who hurt their partners." Wallace had the good sense to look sheepish. He knew better.

"Sorry, man. I was up all night. You're right. Anyways, whatever we call it, I think she's at risk. We've got her holed up at a retreat centre up north of here right now, and we've got some ex-cons on alert. They'll keep her safe," he finished. That raised Patty and Arun's eyebrows.

"Ex-cons doing our work? I don't even think I want to know," Patty said, tossing her hair over her shoulder.

"Nah. It's okay. It's a different place. We've been working with these guys for a few years. Really." Wallace finished, not wanting to try to explain *Just Living* to cops who were used to half-way houses where ex-cons spent their time planning their next crime. Especially when he was so tired.

"So, anyways, let me know what you need me to say to Padma to make sure we get what we need tomorrow," he said.

"Do you want us to come?" Patty asked. "I could join you, and we could make sure she is comfortable with being a witness, if that's what's needed. Hopefully the guys from the college will plead. I know the Crown is working on it. We just need to know what she's up against and figure out how to make this as easy as possible for her. Of course, if it goes public in court, that's a whole different thing.

"If that happens, her family will freak out. We've got to make sure she's safe. And keep the journalists from sparking another media storm about the case. I don't want another suicide. Or any domestic violence," Patty said, looking at Arun, who snorted.

"Yeah. I can ask my connections in the neighbourhood what we're really looking at. There usually isn't so much fundamentalism in the

Valley, but we should be ready," he said, and Wallace nodded, glad they were working together after his earlier gaffe.

"I heard about another youngster. A Social Services kid who's gone missing. We've got an address, and it matches up with the area we're working on. Feels like we're getting close," Patty said. "We'd better get back downstairs. We've got work to do for tomorrow."

A few minutes later, Patty messaged the suspect, pretending she was a little girl who went to Brownies, and music lessons.

"I'm going to bed now. Maybe I'll be on tomorrow," she messaged. And a chill went up her spine when the reply showed on her screen.

"Looking forward to it. Maybe tomorrow we can take some web shots for that photographer I was telling you about. He's really interested in you. Says he can make you famous.

"Goodnight, Alyssa."

CHAPTER 8
LOST IN THE WOODS

I didn't think anyone could hear my stomach growling as the morning circle closed, but the way Padma smiled at me from under her bangs I figured I was busted. The morning had gone quickly. We'd played with scissors and glue…but it was way deeper than kindergarten. And scarier.

In the dining room an older woman in kitchen whites greeted us. Her dirty-blond hair was falling out of her bun. When I looked over at Jean, I knew she'd never look sloppy like that.

"Welcome, everyone. I'm Sally, the kitchen liaison, and I hope you're hungry!" Padma and I smiled at each other. "Cook has made comfort food for lunch – macaroni and cheese three ways – decadent with bacon, vegetarian with tomato sauce, and vegan deliciousness for those with even more discerning palates. You can pick any of them. There's lots of each. Also, there's salad from our gardens, as well as veggies and dip. I'll bring out an assortment of desserts in a bit. If any of you want something different, let me know. Cook is magic with short order as well."

I'd seen the guy everyone called Cook, big as a tank, usually in the background. He was a quiet, heads-down kinda guy, which I related to. His ink and bald head told me he'd probably done time. I was surprised he'd got caught. Seemed smarter than that.

The name on his kitchen whites, barely covering his chest and belly, and never done up around his enormous neck, told me that he'd graduated to Chief Cook. Hey, who was I to judge? Apparently, he was responsible for all the great food around here. And I remembered the scones he'd scored for us that first night. I liked him already.

I grabbed a bunch of food and headed for the back-corner table and joined Dianne and Padma because we wanted to talk about the morning sessions. I glanced over at Padma, and she was pushing food around on her plate, her hair falling around her face. She was beauty and innocence wrapped up together.

"What did you think of that exercise?" she asked us. We'd cut out pics in magazines and stuck them on a sheet of paper. Collages, they called them. The first one was about our assaults, and what we show the world about our hurt. That was kinda easy because I always pretend nothing happened. The second one was harder. Rosie wanted us to think about *our* relationship with the assault. Today. I'm still pretty pissed so my pictures looked spiky.

When I didn't say anything, Dianne started to talk.

"My first collage was all about being a Stepford Wife. I covered for the bastard Reg for years. I think I was scared at first to admit I'd made a mistake marrying him. Then it just got harder and harder to leave, so it was easier to cover it up. Pretend.

"Now all I want to do is shout from the rooftops about how awful it was, but my family doesn't want to listen. I don't know if they don't believe me, or if they are ashamed of me or what. Anyways, I need new friends because Reg made sure I don't have any anymore. I guess that's something I'll have to figure out." I was happy when Padma reached across the table and squeezed Dianne's hand. Dianne's tears nearly broke my heart.

"Mine was different. I was frustrated at first because the college didn't seem to want to do anything, but the video was proof that it'd happened, so they didn't really have a choice. I'm working with the police now to try to figure out who will be charged for circulating it because it's child pornography. I was only 17, and not consenting, so sharing the video is illegal. They're trying to figure out if someone is making money off it. Off of my assault. Off me.

"So, my first collage was all trumpets and angry, shouting and lashing back at the boys who did it, and the system that screwed me again and again. It was awful." Padma stopped, wiped her eyes. "Sometimes it still is.

"The second was about how tired of it I am. I just want it to be over. The legal stuff. The publicity. Being known on campus. It was so bad I had to leave. I just want to get on with my classes. Get back to who I was, learning about music, and art, and geology." Padma smiled, her eyes moist. "I know. I was still figuring out my major." She sighed and moved some food around on her plate. "You know, I never really knew about the world where this stuff existed before now. Happens all the time. I felt like such a freak at first, but now I just feel sad. People are crazy." She shrugged her shoulders and took a bite of the macaroni and cheese with bacon. I shoveled mine in and looked anywhere but at her.

"And then the nightmares start again. I wonder when it will really be over?" She was strung tighter than a violin string ready to explode. *This sucks*, I thought.

"I'm really sorry men are such shits," I mumbled into my plate. I glanced up at Padma, and she smiled, tears pooling in her eyes too.

"Thank you," she whispered. "I wish my brothers were like you," she said.

"Give them time. A chance," I muttered. "I didn't mean them when I said men are such shits," I backtracked.

"Oh, don't paint half the population as evil," Dianne said. "Most men aren't like that. I bet you aren't. In fact, I even know some young men who are feminists," she said, smiling.

"Most men aren't like what?" Jean said, sliding up to the table. "Mind if I join you?" she asked, and I didn't. She was a beautiful distraction, refined. Together.

"I hope I'm not interrupting. I just wanted to talk about the morning, and everyone else is already in a group," she said. Padma raised her eyebrow at me, as if to say, *We weren't?*

"We were talking about our collages. How was yours?" Padma's voice was sharp. I don't think she liked Jean.

"That was a tough exercise, no doubt." Jean didn't elaborate. "How about for you?" she asked, looking at me.

"Hard. I don't really know when stuff started, and I'm not sure of everything that went on for me. Or if my sister was involved. I don't think it started until my grandma died, but I'm not sure. Anyhow, I realized it'd be good if I tried to find my mom. Just to know if she's okay." It was getting easier to talk about our stuff with each other. "Surprised myself, to realize that."

"And I also figured out that I don't like dealing with it over and over, and that's one reason I want to be done with it. Really. Like who'd want a boyfriend who lost his virginity to his mom when he was ten after four years of foreplay? Or a guy who doesn't really do feelings any more?" Jean put her hand over mine, and I smiled at her. No flinching this time. I couldn't help but notice again how gorgeous her nails were, complete with artwork.

"You heard what Kate said at the end, right? That it's all normal. You'll figure it out, with so much to offer the world. Really," Jean said. I think I snorted.

After an awkward minute or two, Padma coughed.

"Hey, Taylor, let's go get some dessert! You promised!" she said, grabbing my other hand and pulling me away. At the long buffet table, we debated the assets of each dessert. In the end we decided to take the homemade banana custard and break a fresh chocolate cookie on top. Before we could head back, she pulled me into a corner.

"I'm meeting with the police this week so they can talk to me about my case. I'm a bit crazy thinking about it, so if you see me acting strange, you know why." I wondered what it took for her to admit that, and it felt good that she was talking to me.

"That sounds scary. Do you have anyone to go with you?" I asked, really hoping she did.

"Not yet. You offering? I don't trust guys, but you remind me of my brothers before they got all weird about honour. I'm not sure you'd be allowed. But I'll ask 'cause I'd like that."

I swallowed hard. I didn't mean me!

"And I wanted to say you don't have to be friends with everyone here, you know." Our backs were towards the corner table, but I knew she was talking about Jean.

"It's okay. I feel kinda sorry for her – no one wants to talk to her. And she's nice. Really." Was I convincing? When I got back to the table, Jean grabbed my spoon and started to eat my dessert.

"You don't mind, do you?" she asked, smiling. I smiled back.

Padma jumped up and offered to get her some. Jean nodded no.

"This is delicious!" she said, putting down her spoon. "But don't worry, I won't eat it all." Padma's eyes bored into her, but Jean didn't flinch, just stared the younger woman down. Zing!

"No worries! There's lots here. Help yourself," I said, pushing the dish between us. I think everyone noticed our spoons touched as we shared the dessert. Padma only snorted once in disgust. Soon, we were all grabbing coffee and heading back to the group to find out our plans for our "afternoon off." Jean somehow inserted herself between me and Dianne. Padma's linked elbow had the other side of me all locked up. I was getting a little uncomfortable with the tension, I admit, and was glad to get back to circle.

"So, this afternoon, during your down time, I want you to hang out with the art pieces you created -- the face you show the world, and the real face of the trauma you experienced. And what's happened since, because everyone of you is a story still unfolding." Kate took a breath and welcomed us as we settled back into the reason for being together. "You can do it on your own, with your partner from before, or with someone else. Rosie and I will be in our offices if you want to talk. See you for dinner!" And we were off.

Dianne and I decided to work together again, Padma with Ophelia. Jean ended up with Terry, the angry lesbian, and I was glad it wasn't me. Terry is…well…big energy. Big, angry energy.

Jean seemed a little sad that I was with Dianne, so I nodded at her as she went by.

"Hey, Jean, I'll see you later, okay? Hope you have a great afternoon," I said, feeling awkward. Dianne called me to the door and I hurried over.

"How about we go to a bench up ahead? I pass it on the way here from where I'm staying," I said, glad to be outside, and away from all the other eyes that probably weren't looking at me. Dianne suggested we spend a little time in silence, and I was surprised by all the noises coming from the forest.

"Wow. I've never thought of the woods as loud before," I said after a few minutes.

"Have you spent much time in the outdoors?" she asked me. I admitted I hadn't.

"Actually, we've always lived in the east end of Vancouver. Over the years, we moved closer and closer to the dodgy areas," I confessed. "That's a part of why this is so hard for me."

"You're doing really well, Taylor. Really. You came into a difficult situation. You've made friends. You care about us. You're strong," she said, and I blushed.

"So, enough about me. Tell me about your artwork," I deflected. Dianne wrung her hands together and started.

"I knew I was ashamed of marrying Reg," she said. "But I never realized how ashamed I was of being too weak to leave. Ashamed of staying and believing him that it was my fault. And I'm not just ashamed for me, but for Tommy and my family, too. I don't even know how to get over that. Except I want to be stronger." I kept asking her questions from the sheet Kate had given us.

What would strong look like? What advice would she give a daughter in the same situation? A friend? What might be a first step? We talked, and hugged, and we even wept a bit. I learned a lot about her. She's an amazing woman. Her kids are lucky. Then, Kate appeared with some lemonade and cookies.

"How're you doing?" she asked. "There's snacks out. Didn't want you to miss them."

"We're good. Just getting to Taylor's artwork," Dianne started. "He's a really good partner, Kate. He listens better than any young person I've met. I'm kinda freaked about the plan I'm developing. I never imagined I'd get this far in the whole retreat, never mind after the first day." I blushed and said something about her making it easy, but Kate put her hand on my shoulder.

"Okay, Taylor. Well done. Now it's your turn, and no ducking, okay? You came here to do some work too, and you deserve the attention from Dianne.

"Let's gather back in the Great Room at about 5:30 to debrief before dinner. Take a break before then if you want. Just bring the dishes back inside later," she said, heading down the pathway.

We settled back into quiet when a big, black bird started talking to us from up in the trees. It was kind of freaky, and I started looking around, trying to keep track of it when it flew from branch to branch above us. Dianne laughed.

"I think it's a crow or something. Maybe a jay. But someone's been feeding it. It wants our snack," she said, throwing a piece of cookie. Sure enough, the big bird landed in front of us, and ate the cookie pieces Dianne and I threw. I was entranced, until finally it was done and flew away yelling, "Skreeka!" at us. I wondered what it was like to be that free to come and go.

After a few minutes, Dianne started at me.

"So, I heard a little last night, about your frustration with unclear memories, and maybe some guilt about your sister. But I'm still not clear…what is it you're afraid of?" I wiped at my cheeks, surprised they were wet. I played with the string on my old hoodie.

"I think I'm broken. That I can't really be fixed, and because I'm damaged…that I'll never be normal." She let me breathe for a moment.

"Never be normal like have a job, and pay your bills? Go to a game with friends? Or normal like enjoy a relationship with a woman your age?" She got me thinking about things.

"I think I'm afraid I'll never fall in love. And then I'm relieved because I'm terrified of falling in love and then not being able to be a good boyfriend. Or maybe I'll mess up being a father. Really fuck up a family.

"I'm worried that I'm so fucked up that I'll be afraid to tell someone how fucked up I am. And all the ways I'll let them down. People deserve better than me," I finished, and when I looked up, I saw Dianne was wiping her eyes.

"Oh, Taylor. Really. What does 'not fucked up' look like? And when you fall in love, won't you want to know about your partner's struggles?"

Somehow that woman got me to admit over the next hour that hope might be possible. And to consider that as a kid I wasn't responsible for what happened to Jenny (although a small part of me still wished I could have been our superhero, even at eight years old. Because, after all, we could have *really* used a superhero.)

And although I want it, I'm not sure I'll ever be open to love. Family love. Mother love. Sexy love. Brotherly love. And that's why I still think I'm seriously broken. Dianne hugged me and begged me to be patient. She offered to take the dishes back to the Lodge, and I headed to Kenny's for a nap.

And I found my way without getting lost in the woods.

CHAPTER 9
CUPCAKES AND CONVERSATIONS

We got together for the pre-dinner check-in circle and it took me a minute to figure out what the heck was going on. Terry could barely sit down. In fact, I thought she'd explode. But then I saw him. Ben was sitting in an extra chair in the circle, decked out in khakis and polar fleece. Kate summoned us, and we got going.

"So, I told you Ben will be around this week. Rosie and I are also available to counsel any of you. Rosie welcomes you – even if you don't identify as First Nations." I looked around and caught Padma smiling at Rosie. What would it take for me to be brave enough to talk to her? She's terrifying. I have no idea if I'm First Nations, or what it would mean if I am, but Rosie is badass.

"Ben's available too. He's a chaplain at *Just Living* and the prison, and we wanted Taylor to know that we're comfortable with working with men. Taylor, Ben wants to talk to you after supper, if that's okay. And all of you have appointments to book one-on-one with one of us for counselling. Okay? You get two sessions, maybe three, over the course of the remaining workshop. Use us. There's also a psychologist on call if you want to talk to him." Then she asked us to share about our afternoons.

"Feel free to share as much, or as little, as you want. It's all voluntary, and remember we agreed to keep confidences," she said, and passed the talking piece to Ophelia, who spoke so quietly we could hardly hear her.

"First off, you can call me Phee if you want." She smiled. "I guess one of the things I'm starting to get is how complicated it is. It was always pretty messed up that I loved my uncle but hated what he did. And what my brother did, too. I really loved my auntie, who tried to keep me safe, but was mad that she yelled so much at her brother." Ophelia crossed her arms over her chest, looking like she wanted to disappear inside her belly. "It's hard to figure out what parts of my family I love, and what parts I hate." God, I felt for her. And I got it. She took a breath. "Mostly, it's hard to figure out what parts of me I hate," she finished, holding her arms open. "Or maybe the parts I don't hate. Are there any?" She presented her body as if it was something to be ashamed of, and although she was chunky, or even large, she was also pretty. And I could only look at my shoes. Which were only marginally dryer than last night.

I knew the names of everybody in the circle now, but I didn't try to keep them straight. I listened to everyone, but it was easier with Dianne, and Padma. And Jean. A few minutes later she got the talking piece.

"So, I'm ready to share now. I've been abused by men, big men, and scary men, for most of my life. When I dropped out of high school, I got involved with some guys who rode motorbikes, who wanted to be gang members, and my life has kinda been fucked up since then."

I felt my heart squeeze listening to her.

"First, I was proud to be their bitch. Then, once they knew they had me, they treated me bad. Shared me around. I cooked and cleaned and everything else for them. And I started to hate me.

"Eventually, I became an old hag, and they ditched me. I'm glad I got out, but now I'm trying to figure it all out, because I just want a quiet, easy life. No drama. And I have enough saved up to look after myself." She passed the piece. Rosie closed the circle.

"A great start to the week, everyone. I'm remembering the idea of tide's end, and wondering what other forces, other than the tides, have been pulling on us, or maybe pushing us along. Think about what you need from each other, from your friends, so that we can start to talk about which waves are still swamping you, and which ones you're surfing on top of."

I smiled, and before I knew it, we were finished circle for the day. Kate warned us that tomorrow morning Kate would talk about trauma and normal, but I kept thinking about getting ready for the meeting with Ben. I ate by myself, quickly, and kept hoping Kenny hadn't shared about any screaming from last night.

Later, full of spaghetti and garlic toast, I grabbed two cupcakes for sharing with Kenny later, and headed into a "quiet room" to talk to Ben. I was still nervous, but I'd remembered my promise, so I decided to pour my guts out if it would help.

After all, I still owed it to Jenny.

"Hey Taylor, good to see you again." We shook hands, and I sat in the comfy chair across from him. "I know Kate billed me as a counsellor, and technically I do some counselling, but you get to be in charge, okay?" He promised he wouldn't breach confidentiality unless he was afraid I was going to hurt myself or someone else. I wiped my sweaty palms on my jeans and was surprised at how calm I felt. Even with sweaty palms.

"So, why don't you tell me about it?" he said.

And I did. About my mom abusing me, and how confusing it was when I realized it was wrong. And when it felt good. It was easy, but really hard, too. An hour later when Ben said our time was almost up, I was stunned. I hadn't stopped talking the whole time. But I felt better. I thought talking about it would just churn shit up, but this time it helped.

"Really? Wow. I'm sorry. I guess I don't get to talk about it much," I said. I thought about the only other "counselling" I'd had, at high school, where the glass walls and bells every half hour meant I'd never opened up.

"We have a few more minutes. I'm wondering if you have any questions for me," he asked.

"I do. I've been wondering if there's any chance I'll get better," I asked, picking at my holey running shoes. "Any chance I'll grow up. 'Cause I kinda feel like a child…."

"What do you think?" he asked. We waited.

"God, I hope so, because otherwise…what's the point? And how do I help Jenny?"

"And when you say, 'get better,' what do you mean? What would 'better' look like?" I sat thinking about it for a bit. It was weird. I didn't feel rushed, even though I knew our time was short. I didn't want to duck the question. For Jenny.

"I guess be good enough that I can think about the future. What I want to do. What job I want, and if I want to learn something else, or decide to get an apartment or something," I said. "Just normal stuff everyone does, maybe have a girlfriend," I said. We sat for a few minutes in quiet calm. I hadn't known quiet calm for a long time.

"Tell me, Taylor, how are you feeling today compared to yesterday on the drive up?"

"Well, less scared of the retreat. More calm, I guess." I swallowed. "Surprised so many people are in the circle. They all seem so normal." Ben looked over at me, steepled his fingers under his chin.

"What if I told you that you'd hardly believe how many people have been seriously hurt in all kinds of awful ways? And lots of them go on to be happy. Have jobs. Families. Even go on to help others," he finished, smiling at me.

"Really? Like I could maybe be in a relationship?"

"I don't know. You just told me you made four or five friends in the last day. People who are rooting for you. I think anything is possible if people keep moving towards it," he finished. "How about we talk again tomorrow night?"

"Sure. If it's early enough could we walk around outside? I've never really been outside the city. I like it here," I asked.

"I think we could," Ben said to me while we grabbed our stuff and headed out into the night. "And I live on-site, so if you want me during the day just let Kate know. I work at the prisons down the road part time, but not this week."

Jean was just outside on a bench and stood up as we walked by her.

"Hey Taylor, mind if I walk with you?" she asked. We headed off towards Kenny's, and weirdly our steps matched up. The sun had set and I noticed Jean was shivering. She wrapped her posh gold sweater tighter around herself, and I felt compelled to add my beat-up jacket to help keep her warm. After all, I still had my hoodie.

"Sorry. It's not great, but it's all I've got," I said, shrugging. We walked, sometimes talking, just hanging out. It felt good, but I got weirded out as we got closer to the turn-off where I'd be on half-way house property. I didn't know how to not invite her up the path, but I didn't want to break any rules I didn't know about. Pretty sure she hadn't filled out a security form.

"Well, this is where I head off," I said. "I hope you have a good night, Jean. Thanks for walking with me." I admit, I was hoping she'd leave. "I'll get my jacket tomorrow. Stay warm while you walk back." And miraculously, she took the hint.

"You're welcome, Taylor. Thanks for walking with an old lady, and for keeping me warm." She smiled back at me. "It's good to just walk with someone sometimes. And thank you. You treated me well today, Taylor, and I noticed. I think you're doing a great job of figuring out who you want to be. You should be proud," she finished, turning and raising a hand in a quick goodbye. I smiled and turned towards the path to Kenny's trailer.

Kenny was in the corner of the living room talking on the phone when I came inside. I took off my shoes and picked them up to take to my room.

"Fuck off, asshole. I'm not coming back. Get over it." He was pacing a little, staring out the window, and I realized he didn't know I was there. I crept to my bedroom, but that didn't prevent every word from reaching me.

"What the hell? You threatening my sister?" he asked whoever he was talking to. "Really. You're going to ask her what's going on with me? I'll tell you what's going on. You go anywhere near her or her family and I will…." Whoa. Sisters. We had that in common. What the hell *was* going on?

"No. You wait. You cannot come back after all these years and expect me…. Fuck off. I don't care what you heard. I will not fuck with you and you'll leave me alone. Got it?" Several seconds went by and I realized I was in trouble.

"Fuck you. You think I don't know people who will fuck with you? Where the hell have I been for the last few years? DOING YOUR TIME. Fuck off." There was no way I couldn't hear that. Kenny had no idea I was here, and I'd have to come clean. I opened my door and peeked out the crack. He hadn't moved from looking out the window, so I picked my shoes back up and crept back towards the entrance.

"Whatever. I don't get it. Why you need to see me. Fuck off. Nothing more to say about it. And don't you dare call my sister." His hands were tugging at his hair, and he was starting to pace again.

I slammed the front door after putting my shoes on the floor. He saw me and waved. I waved back and headed for my room.

"Look, I'm done. Don't call again. Leave me alone. Got it?" Kenny hung up his phone and tossed it on the couch. "Hey! Good to see you. Tea?"

"Sure. You okay?" I asked. "That sounded intense." His eyes narrowed briefly.

"Yeah…. I'm fine. Why?" Ah. Okay. I can pretend.

"Always yes to tea. Out in a second!" I called back. I was trying to forget what I'd heard.

We sat with our tea, and shared a huge cupcake.

"These are great, but about 10,000 calories each, I think," Kenny said, putting down his plate. "I just can't get away with a whole one any more." I wondered how to make small talk. This being with people all day was exhausting. Trying to remember that I didn't hear him threaten someone a few minutes ago wasn't easy. Ask questions, I remembered a teacher telling me.

"What did you get up to today?" I asked him.

"Oh, cleaned some kennels. Started staking out ground for the aquaponics bed. Did a little weeding. How was your day?"

"It was good. I met Ben. I like him. The group did some collages, and stuff." Kenny nodded. I wanted to change the topic, so I looked over at his book shelves.

"Borrow any books you want while you're here," he said, and I snorted.

"You are so effin' generous," I said. He just chuckled when I took a cookbook off the shelf.

"You like cooking?" he asked me.

"Not sure. I've never really had a place to cook," I admitted. "I'd love to try, though. Who doesn't like great food?"

"Are you still in school? What're you taking?" I didn't know how to answer, so I just shut up.

"Oh Christ. I didn't mean to pry. Really." Once again, awkward. I seem to bring that into any situation. I decided to tell him what I could.

"Nah. I'm done high school. Not sure what I'm going to do next," I said. "I've never really thought about getting a job before now. My life was a little chaotic," I confessed. We drank our tea, and I finished one of the cupcakes.

"Ben suggested I build a 'to-do' list. Next steps and stuff. While I'm here I'd like to clean my car out. That might be tough 'cause I don't know if it'll still drive." I snuck a peak at Kenny to see if he was judging me. Not yet, I don't think.

"Then, once I've done that, I can get my papers together. I think lots of them are in the car. And I promised him I'd go to Social Services to ask if I'm eligible for assistance." I asked for half his cupcake.

"Wish I could get away with that," he teased me. "Looks like you could use some flesh on you, though. Help yourself to anything in the cupboards," he said, as we headed to bed. "And I'm happy to help with the car, even just getting it running," he offered as we put our dishes in the sink. "There are other folks here who would help too, you know," he said.

"I know," I answered. "It's kinda weird. I had no one three days ago, and now there's a whole team. But I also get that I'm only here a few more days. I gotta stand on my own two feet, be an adult."

At the doorway to my room I stopped.

"I wouldn't mind meeting some of the other guys, though. It's weird hanging out with women all day." I looked down at the floor, stumbling as my throat got thick with gratitude. "I hope I wasn't too loud last night," I mumbled.

"Hey, no problems. Really. I've heard lots worse where I come from, so I use ear plugs. And really, I had nightmares, too, until I worked with a counsellor. Hopefully Ben helps you," Kenny offered. I smiled.

I realized I'd already started to think of it as "my room" as I started to get ready for bed, pulling back the blanket. Clean sheets two nights in a row. I picked up Russet and kissed the kitten, saying a prayer for Jenny. Maybe she wanted to be called Jennifer now. My eyes teared up.

I admit, as I showered before bed, I wondered, *Kenny, who seemed to have his life together (but took threatening phone calls), had used a counsellor. Maybe I'm not such a big freak after all?*

CHAPTER 10
ANGRY WOMEN –
TERRY AND JEAN

Terry unlocked her dorm room and invited Jean in. She offered her the comfy chair, then made sure the door was shut behind them. They'd decided to come up to her room with their coffee and cupcakes after dinner because, frankly, Terry was up to her eyeballs with those women and their shit. They didn't even have the guts to fight back when they were attacked, and she just didn't get them. No pride. But Terry thought maybe Jean was different.

She sat down cross-legged on her bed, and leaned back against the wall, taking it all in. Only her course materials were on the table, which was good. No need to show anyone, not even Jean, her stuff. Nothing to see here.

Terry undid her thick, leather belt, with the chains attached to her wallet and keys, and put it on the bed. She pulled the sheathed knife from her jacket pocket and tossed it beside her wallet — still within reach. It wasn't that she meant to put Jean on notice; she just didn't remember how not to. She flexed her shoulders, drawing circles to try to loosen them. She snuck a sniff of her armpit and was relieved that she didn't smell of BO. Or fear.

"What the fuck? Can you believe those chicks?" Terry's voice was gravelly, deep, and she ended with a quiet snort. "They couldn't fight their way out of a Care Bear rumble. When will they learn to stand up for themselves? How do they expect to get respect?" She glanced sideways at Jean to see her reaction. Meeting new people was always risky.

Jean's lips softly turned up a little at the corners, and she worked to keep a gentleness in her eyes as she looked at her coffee and cupcake. She understood Terry; it was easy to understand an angry dyke. Terry was more like a pissed-off biker right now than anyone else at the retreat, which made her familiar. And Jean knew how to go with what you know.

"Yeah, they're pretty weak. But I could tell you were different. That, and the rumours," Jean said, smiling up at Terry. "Something about parole, and being required to attend," she finished, putting Terry on notice that she had access to all kinds of information.

"Like that's a secret," Terry said with a snort. "The assholes running this place aren't exactly careful about sharing," she said. "I know, for example, that that Paki chick is working with the cops."

Jean sat quietly for a moment, thinking hard. Was Terry friend or foe? She decided not to point out that Padma had told the circle she was struggling to decide whether to work with the cops or not. Hardly a state secret.

"Yeah, I know," Jean said, deciding. "But you're different. That's all I meant. We've got grit those other women can only dream of having."

Terry smiled, and Jean noticed.

"Yeah, well, I took shit for years, and when I'd had enough, I lost it. I didn't kill him, but I'm glad only because then I'd be doing life. 'Course, another part of me is still pissed that he didn't get anything for all those years of forcing himself on me, beating *me* up. If I had a few more minutes with him alone now…." Terry's voice trailed off. Jean resisted pointing out that for years Terry'd taken his abuse – just like the women she ridiculed.

"Well, at least he can't come near you if you aren't allowed near him. You're done with the bastard," Jean sympathized. "And in the end, you *did* put up a fight. He won't mess with you again."

They chatted for a while about work, and life, and lovers.

"I'm good with knives," Terry said, grinning. "I line prep for a great chef who runs the kitchen in a pub downtown." Jean could see her, cussing and throwing things, hidden back of house. She didn't doubt that Terry worked hard and didn't disappoint. But she'd never work in front of a customer. And she'd never get rich chopping veggies either.

So either Terry was in a dead end, or she had other sources of income on the side. Jean wondered if Terry was an opportunity for her.

"And I have a great gal, who tolerates my shit," Terry said, not missing a beat. It took Jean a moment or two to figure out what her new friend was talking about. Of course. Terry wasn't single. "I don't know what I did to deserve Bobbie, but she treats me real fine."

"And I bet you take care of her, too," Jean said. "In all kinds of ways. There's lots about you that I'd find attractive if I was into women." Jean knew flattery could bend anyone, really.

"Yeah, I can't believe she's with me sometimes. I'll always have a record. I really did want to kill that fucker. There were *years* of pissed off that showed up in that steel bar that night.

"Pissed off at him. At my sisters who hadn't warned me about my dad. At my dad and uncle, who thought they were God's gift to teaching 'their girls' about sex. At the whole God-damned world who didn't listen to us when we complained."

"That's awful," Jean said. "I just wish I was surprised. But really, scumbags who love sex with youngsters are so fucked up. And the cops just ignore them." Jean hoped she'd hit the right balance of shock and sympathy.

Terry, she thought, was like everyone else. She wanted to survive. Win. Be on top.

Because she thought she was special.

Just like everybody else.

Then, Jean shared a little about her life.

"I work with young guys on the streets, helping them get their lives together," she said. "And right now, I'm on the market, dating. I'm a bit gun-shy I admit. Not ready to trust someone after…." Jean paused.

"He was older, and I'd been his girl for a while. Sometimes that meant he was rough on me. Really rough, if you know what I mean. Then, one time, I was at his place with a lot of his guys and got a little drunk. I complained. And he went ballistic. Beat me up, stripped me down, and shared me around.

"Later that night they all passed out, and I grabbed my clothes and some of their cash and ran. Didn't stop running until I hit the West Coast, and then I took control of my life. Ain't no one gonna overpower me like that again," she said. And Terry believed her.

That night, Jean had been ready to leave those assholes. And didn't want to be vulnerable ever again. Over time, she'd learned the rules of their business, and was irked that those stupid guys thought only men could run their products on the streets.

When she'd landed across the country, she'd set up shop. Started small, and stayed small, taking only enough to keep herself comfortable. Well, maybe a little better than comfortable, but she didn't get too greedy. Jean knew better than to piss off any big players but made sure they knew she was out there in the corner of their turf, doing a little commerce. And they tolerated her because she fed them information and extra product or people when they needed it.

Of course, when she told Terry her story, Jean changed a few details — made it seem like the assault had happened locally. Recently.

That she was still tender in all the places that she'd been hurt.

That a colleague had suggested she come and take the course, that it would help her heal.

She didn't mention she was forced to come, just like Terry. That the police had tried to bust her for trafficking the boys, and she'd claimed innocence, that she was being abused. They'd called her bluff and forced her here or promised charges if she didn't agree.

Then, this afternoon, the monkey on her back, the one she'd been carrying since childhood had started to whisper to her. When she yelled enough in her mind about the police stuff it covered the whisper in her heart that said, "What if?" What if she could heal from all the abuse, and the multiple rapes from those men 20 years ago?

Jean shook her head, wondering why she was still here with Terry, what the woman could offer her. Her intuition told her there might be a good reason to keep Terry in her life, so she stayed a bit longer. She let Terry trash talk the other women. Fed the anger, and let Terry believe she was on side. Then, Terry went after Taylor.

"Can you believe that little shit? What a puss, afraid of his own shadow. I kinda hope his sister finds someone stronger than him to look after her," Terry said, and Jean's eyes flashed anger, but just for a second.

"You think? I think he's kinda cute. And mature for a young kid, showing up and staying after some of the others tried to run him off. Besides, maybe he'll be a little fun on the way," she teased as she headed out the door for her own room.

It'd been a long time since a fresh young man had turned Jean's head, and Taylor made her positively glow.

This could prove to be very interesting. Hot, even.

Juicy hot.

* * *

BETH AND THUD

Beth walked over to her husband, brushing her fingers through his curly hair to comb out some of the hay. She'd known Ben would be in the barn, feeding his horse and helping Tom with the chores. Thud nickered at her as she hung her arm over the stall door.

"Hey, big guy, how you doing?" she asked, and he offered his head for scratches. "How is he?" she asked. She knew he'd had a sore leg, but Ben had told her earlier in the week that he was pleased with the progress.

"He's doing great. Put him out alone for an hour today and he didn't try anything foolish." Beth smiled. When Thud and Tex were happy, her husband was, too.

She wondered if Ben knew how much she adored him, especially when he didn't freak out at her for being a hot mess like last night.

"I brought you some coffee," she said, holding up a thermos. "Do you have time?" Ben put on a drawl that always made her laugh.

"Always have time for you, Mugwump."

"I wanted to explain about last night," she said. "I've been thinking about things." A few minutes later their mugs were empty, and Ben was trying to make sense of what she'd said.

"So, you're worried about these strong feelings that you're having about this talk with Hugh. But you don't even know what he wants to talk about, and you get that it's...premature to be kept up at night about this. And you wanted to warn me because you feel really unsettled, but you don't know why. But you think it'll be big. Both the feelings, and however this affects you. And our situation here." He looked down at his hands. "Does that about cover it?" Beth almost got angry...pissed, really....at how trite he was being except...well, he was sincere.

And that really did sum it all up.

"Yup. Guess so," was all she said, kicking the dirt floor.

"That sounds awful," he said, drawing her into his arms. "I hate wrestling with demons I don't really understand. But it's okay – I'm here. And I'll still be here next week. Next year." They stood, rocking in each other's arms for a bit, Ben kissing his wife's hair, the horses munching their dinner in the background. "Any ideas of someone you could talk to about it, other than Hugh? Someone who could maybe sympathize?"

"Fuck, Ben, I don't know. I just feel so weird. Maybe Veronica could help. She'd get it," she said. "Maybe I'm not the first crime victim to feel weird about this stuff."

They agreed to keep checking in with each other, and Beth gathered up the mugs to take home.

"Maybe we can connect again before dinner tomorrow. I'm seeing Hugh in the evening," Beth told him.

"I don't know if that'll work. I promised Kenny and Taylor I'd go hiking with them. I'm sorry." He heard his wife sigh. "I won't stay out much after dark," he reassured her, and as she closed the barn door, he heard her disappointment.

"It's okay. Really. Taylor's important," she said.

But not as important as you, he thought.

CHAPTER 11
HIKING WITH FRIENDS

Walking up the hill, I did a quick pat-down of my pockets. Tap. Wallet. Tap. Keys. Tap. Where my phone should be. It was a habit I'd gotten into on the street and had become a ritual. Soothing, even. Kenny was hiking in front and Ben was behind me, and I felt Ben's hand on my shoulder. I turned, and Kenny kept going.

"Hey, Taylor. It's okay to relax. You know your stuff is safe, right?" Ben said to me, quietly. I must have looked confused.

"Just saw you checking your pockets and stuff," he reassured me.

"Oh God!" I said and then started to blush. He's a monk. Awkward. "I'm not worried you'll take my stuff! I don't even realize when I'm doing it," he said. Kenny had turned on the path and called back.

"Everything okay?"

"Sure," I answered. I thought about the ending to the circle earlier in the day. It'd been a busy day, but different than the first.

I hurried to catch up to my roommate.

Ten minutes later, Kenny suggested we stop for a rest. The trail had opened up beside a large rock, and there was a break in the tall, green trees. Around us, on the ground, were ferns, and some other small plants. It was lush, and damp. It sure smelled good in the forest.

From where we stood, we could look out over the property, and see the fences, gardens and all the buildings. The fire pits and tipi made it look like one of those models other kids made in school. We leaned ourselves against the rock, and took long drinks from our water bottles. I rummaged around in my backpack and pulled out some banana bread I'd baked that afternoon with Cook's help.

"Oh God, Ben, just wait. You're gonna love this. Thick and not too sweet…another reason I'm glad Taylor moved in!" Kenny said. My first banana bread was getting rave reviews. I'd figured out this recipe with yogurt and granola, and it was more like a breakfast feast than a dessert.

"Least I could do after all you guys have done for me." I looked down at the boots on my feet. "Ben, thanks again for letting me use your hiking boots."

"Those're yours now. Beth'll be glad they aren't taking up space in our closet any more," he said, and I squirmed. "Really." He put his hand on my arm. "I have the ones on my feet. No need for two pairs," he said.

"I know. But you all keep giving me stuff I don't deserve. What have I done to help you? Or Beth? Nothing." I knew I was the charity case. Again, my face turned red.

"Whoa. Everyone deserves good shoes, and clothes that fit, Taylor. A warm bed. Food." Kenny said. "Besides, you give lots. Like banana bread. And we like to support people. It's kinda what we do." Kenny sounded like he was defending their generosity, which made me smile.

"I know. I know. You've told me before. But I'm not used to it, okay?"

"How was today?" Ben asked. I knew he was just making conversation.

"It was good. Different. Kate talked about trauma, and what normal is. It was kinda weird." Kenny snorted.

"I remember when I learned that stuff inside. Every time I heard, 'It's normal to feel your face flush and your heart race when you're triggered,' I'd look around and we were all, like, red-faced, flushed. My heart was pounding. It was so strange to know those reactions I'd been having for…well, years…were normal after you've been through something like we had. Prison."

"Man, you are psychic. That's just what it was like. All those things – panicking and then crashing, heart pounding, not remembering…we'd all felt them. Anyways, I've got lots to think about. It's weird to know my body was just…trying to protect me?" It felt strange to talk to these guys about it. But enough already.

We were finishing our snack, and I started to pack up. Kenny picked up a stone and threw it down the hill. Ben followed, trying to knock Kenny's out of the air. Later, Kenny knocked Ben's. He turned to me.

"No rush, Tay," he said. "We've got nothing to run off to. I want to stay for a bit if you don't mind, just hang out…." I immediately tensed up. *What? Was I being sent away or something? What had I done?* Kenny chuckled, a gentle sound coming from deep inside his chest.

"It's okay, Tay. Honest. Ben loves Beth, but sometimes he misses being alone. He just likes us to come up here and sit for a while." They kept throwing their stones, and a few minutes later, I joined in, rarely hitting the pebbles down, but enjoying trying. I smiled. Who knew a few rocks on a mountainside could be fun? A few minutes more, and Kenny picked up his pack.

"Let's go, Taylor, give Ben some space. We'll wait for you down at the next bend," he said to Ben. "No throwing stones," he called back as we hiked maybe 25 metres down the path. And as we sat on a log, Kenny started telling me about his arrival at the half-way house.

"Maybe it's weird that we help each other out all the time. When I first got here, Sally arrived in my room with muffins, and towels, and sheets. She had her arms filled with stuff for me, and I was…suspicious. No one had given me stuff without strings attached since my partner had died. Really.

"The first week, I just watched and tried to keep my jaw from hitting my chest. Couldn't believe it. I kept waiting for someone to take advantage, get called out." He laughed again.

"And it happens. People can be jerks. Some were. But amazingly, that didn't stop other people from helping. Really. That's why I want to live here. It's different," he said.

"Sure is," Ben said. He'd snuck up on us, and I jumped. "Oh man, sorry. But you're right, Kenny. It is different, and people can still be jerks. Or maybe just misunderstood. But it's worth it.

"I'd only known living in the order where we didn't exactly always agree, but we were never…outright disobedient…well, that's not quite true. But mostly we weren't — except for the brothers who abused the students. Sexually. Fuck." Ben looked down, stomped his foot. He had a small rock in his hands, and he was running it between his fingers, never letting it be still. I hadn't expected him to swear and was almost afraid to breathe. Kenny reached out and squeezed Ben's shoulder.

"I'm sorry, Ben. Evil exists everywhere. It's only when we're so arrogant that we think it can't happen in our community that it really grows." They were both looking pretty intensely at the ground. Clearly these guys had known some shit. I took a breath.

"Wait," I said. "You left the monkhood, or whatever you call it, because there were monks diddling kids? And then you married Beth? I'm confused," I admitted. Kenny laughed.

"Just about sums it up. Luckily it happened in that order," Kenny said. "No pun intended." Ben brushed his jeans off, got that dreamy look in his eyes I'd seen when he thought no one was watching him watching Beth.

"I thought I'd always be a monk, until I found out some of my brothers were hurting the kids. And when I said something, they told me it was being handled. Only I knew it wasn't. No investigation. The kids were still…hurting. So I walked out and found work as a prison chaplain.

"The day I met Beth, the day she climbed into my old car for a ride out here…well, that might have been the best day of my life. Really. Except I didn't know it at the time because I was so daft. I'd never dated. Never even really looked at women that way. Or at all, really. Because…" and he ran his hands up and down, pointing to himself, "well…monk." He smiled.

"I appreciated her humour, and voice, and…baking…but it took me months before I knew what I felt was love. Romantic love. She had to show me." I couldn't believe it. Ben hadn't been with Beth for decades? They were so comfortable together!

"How did you know once you figured it out?" I asked. I'd never been in love and was trying to imagine what it felt like. I knew lust, but love was different, right? Ben looked down at his hands, and there was that silly grin again. We started towards *Just Living*.

"It feels like sunshine, and happiness. Warm custard with fresh berries. A perfectly pitched canon sung in the dark with my brothers." He looked around. "Where's Julie Andrews when you need her?" He smiled, then looked back at me, maybe thinking I wouldn't know the reference. But Mom'd loved that movie. Fuck! When would I ever be able to just do me?

"You know," Ben continued, "at first it felt all sparkly and new. But then after a bit, it just felt…right. Comfortable. Safe. And good. Like even when we fight, and we do…it's still gonna be okay. And when I don't understand her, I just want to. I don't need to be right, or control her, or give in to her…I know that if I want us to be together, and she wants to be together…and we know we are meant to be…then…it's just more important to work on love than get short-tempered or angry. I guess that's what it feels like."

We smiled at each other, and I hoped I would get to feel that sometime. But he wasn't done. I was glad the trail had widened into a path, that we could walk side by side.

"One of my favourite poems is by a guy named Hafiz, from a long time ago. Thirteen hundreds. It goes:

Even after
All this time
the sun never says,
'You owe me.'
Look what happens

with a love like that.
It lights the whole sky.

We stopped at the fence by the Sacred Grounds, I sat thinking about that for a while. Wow. Had I known an adult who didn't think I owed them something? Not sure. But I knew Jenny didn't owe me anything. Maybe I did have a feeling close to love.

"But don't think I'm a saint, Taylor. I don't deserve Beth's love. I abandoned those boys. I didn't stay and protect them. Which is why I struggle every day to face myself.

"Luckily God forgives. And so does Beth. Because I don't know how to forgive myself most days. I hope the boys who were hurt get all the help they need." He took a sip from his water bottle.

"And I've been working hard to try and help other folks who've been hurt ever since," Ben said. "Sometimes in prison, because lots of those guys were abused, but lots of other places, too. We have to help each other, and not just let hate take over. Because it so easily could," he said, standing up. "Thanks for that. I don't usually get to talk about myself to somebody who really listens.

"And if we don't get home, that lovely wife of mine will give me heck. It's not good to poke a bear." I couldn't believe it! Beth! A bear! I picked up my bag. Couldn't help but rise to her defense.

"Like she'd get angry at you for being late!" I said. Is this what having men friends feels like? I wasn't sure I'd ever had any. Teasing, eating, hiking. I liked all of it. Kenny laughed.

"Who says 'heck' any more?" He pushed Ben's arm, all in fun.

"Ah. She won't care if I'm home late," Ben clarified. "She's on duty tonight at the Lodge. She told me to get *you* home before dark, and with enough time for you to enjoy some evening without being bugged by the likes of me," he said. It was my turn to laugh.

Heading down the path, Kenny asked Ben how he stayed focused.

"You always seem to be doing something else good. How do you do it?" he said.

"The next right thing," he said. "I always look for the next right thing. Like right now, she's…struggling. And I'm just supporting her, without trying to fix it." We walked a little more.

"What about you guys? What's your next right thing?" he asked.

"I'm cleaning my car. Going to Social Services. Then I've got to find a place to live, get myself a job so I can help my sister," I confessed. How much did they know about Jenny? It was weird not worrying so much who knew what any more.

"I'm trying to get out more, live a little beyond this property," Kenny said. "And learn more about hydroponics. For growing vegetables, not weed," he confessed.

We headed down the path towards the Lodge just as the lights went on in the kitchen. Maybe there were some snacks on hand, I thought. Or something I could do for Cook.

"I think I might go see if I can help," I said. "I'm feeling good." Now we were all smiling.

A few minutes later, we parted at the door. Kenny headed to the trailer, and Ben joined me. I walked into the kitchen and could hear Cook's low rumble singing off-key through the door.

Yes, life was very, very good indeed.

I liked hiking with friends.

And felt brave enough to go thank Cook for his help with the banana bread. And show him by washing his dishes.

CHAPTER 12
TORN - SALLY

Sally smiled over at Cook, puttering in his already-cleaned kitchen. She'd slipped Taylor a few dollars after he'd helped her man clean up from baking, even though Cook told her not to. She knew a young man needed a little jingle to feel…well, confident. And he deserved to feel confident, after all she'd heard about his life. She put her head down and got back to writing her poetry.

Torn

Pleasure we have known
And Pain that haunts
Hurt doesn't live forever (does it?)

Torn
Between the space and places
That haunt our todays
From yesterdays of trembling
Denying
Defying

And being and feeling and knowing and
Laughter

Always laughter
Compelling us forward towards wholeness encircling
Touching
Being together
Imperfectly glorious
Scarred and scared

Torn
Between hurt-in-the-past
Or always alive, yet really?
Living (sort of) a life
Of cotton-wool wrapping and
Rainbows and unicorns
And always a smile
A warm bed

Waiting in fear for life to be

Torn

There. She put down her pen and reread it. Felt suitably disgusted. First drafts always left her feeling that way, but at least she was writing. She looked over at her beloved Cook and smiled again.

Her publisher had been on her. Last chance, they'd said. She hadn't published, or even read her poetry publicly for more than a decade, and they were starting to talk about her "lifespan" as if her poetry was only a commodity, a product to support them. She'd collected a few poems over the last few years, but she hadn't shown them to anyone because they were crap.

Sitting at the table, she grudgingly admitted that it felt good to be writing. *Just Living,* and now *Tide's End,* had been good for her soul but hard on her poetry. Of course, being super busy helping others didn't leave much time for the angst required for poetry to form, to craft, to become, but she really didn't mind. And being in love after so many years was a delicious distraction.

It hadn't come easy, letting Cook into her life. One day, a few years ago, she sat with him over tea at the little table beside the kitchen window and told him about her life, her heartache, and the poems. Until then, no one had known they had a poet laureate serving breakfast.

She started by telling him about her failure as a mother when her children were babes and she was alone. She'd been overwhelmed and made mistakes.

Teddy, her oldest, was ferocious about protecting his sisters. At four, he'd stood up to that huge street dog and got between it and baby Carmen. He took a bite on his face for his baby sister. Sally knew in that moment that she was a failure, not watching, not careful, not attentive. So she'd dropped him off, with his little face swollen and stitched, and the sisters he adored, at a doctor's office with a note, and wandered for days on the street. Finally, she decided to head up north. She'd been feeling the tug to use again, so she'd headed for the oil rigs to cook and clean. She knew it'd be easier up there to avoid getting wired.

Telling Cook about it, she wondered if Teddy was still putting himself between those he loved and danger. Cook had reached out and squeezed her hand, ever solid, always there for her.

She'd sent money to the social worker every month to make sure the kids were kept together in foster care. He'd told her it would help, but had pocketed the money and split them up, eventually asking her to relinquish custody so they could be adopted. She was doing the best she could, she told herself at the time. Being a mom was just so damned hard when you were poor and sad and yearning for the warmth of smack.

Being up north had been good for her. The work was hard, and no one expected her to want a fix, so she hadn't. It was that simple.

And at night on the platform, while missing her babes and the warm embrace of the smack, trading one rig for another, she'd started to write poetry, to write the yearning, to write the pain. And someone read it, and encouraged her, and apparently, she was good at it. Good enough to make money, not a given for a Canadian poet. But she stayed in the oilfield, too, because that was what worked for her. And she had money to send to her kids.

When the yearning got strong, she'd reached out to her babes. She remembered how they smelled so delicious in the night when they cuddled her, and how Sarah always woke her afraid of the darkness and the shadows that seemed to shake her soul.

Was her little girl writing poetry too? Were they all adults now? Hard to believe.

She got an address from the social worker and wrote to them. She'd even said, "I love you." They hadn't believed her. In fact, they spewed venomous anger, which she knew she deserved. Yes, they were fine, thank you very much, but not because of her. And then the truth that still burned.

Teddy told her about the babies. She'd hoped that she could redeem herself, could love again, could feel the warmth of a little one's breath on her neck…she knew she'd be an amazing grandmother. Six! Six little ones, all healthy, all loved, all knowing love, and not pain or yearning, or the teeth of a mad dog.

But her children had said she was not worthy. Not wanted. Her time had passed. They had found one another again (she knew it was Teddy who did that) and didn't need her. Didn't want her. So please go away. And she wondered if it was so hard to know your mother only through her poems and the fame she enjoyed (small as it was, and like she enjoyed anything without them). And she knew why they were angry. But that didn't take away the pain. Cook had wiped her tears. What if she'd never found him?

She remembered moving to *Just Living*, to heal, and explore the pain differently, perhaps with colour instead of living in muted grey tones. She worked hard and, one by one, she'd let people in, and they understood without even hearing her story. The colour started to trickle back into her life, just at the edges at first, and then showing up with a smile for a moment, then a day.

She'd started to care and, even in her gruffest voice, to love the men who were broken and the people they had hurt. And she started to heal herself. She wove all of it together into something quite strong, quite useful and surprisingly beautiful. She loved her life and her job. These people. And then she'd realized she loved Cook. And now Taylor.

At *Just Living*, there had been another young man like Taylor. Ricky had struggled to belong, and when he couldn't deal with the pain any more, he'd decided to leave them forever. It had torn at Sally's heart and she hadn't leaked hurt like that since losing her kids. She'd cried, alone and then with Cook, and the sobbing took over, and became a torrent of decades of sadness, of disconnect. Cook had held her after Ricky died, and stroked her hair, and washed her face, and brought her soup. And never once told her to stop crying. So she'd cried some more.

And in that moment, her heart opened again, but this time light shone through the cracks, and (miracle of miracles) she wanted to write poetry again. And she was okay if it was horrible, because either it would become better, or she would. Or maybe (miracle of miracles) they both would.

Now, as she looked out at her strong man straightening his storeroom, she thought about Taylor. She remembered the night Cook lamented that he'd had no children, had only a nephew he'd never known.

"I wish…." he'd said, "I just wish there was someone I could hang out with, show the ropes to. Do guy stuff."

"Like baking?" she'd teased, and then they'd both laughed out loud.

"Yeah. Like baking. And not drinking." It was the only night she'd really felt his sadness. It was a part of why she smiled now, when he worked beside Taylor, the caring between them after only a day or two. Who knew what this boy would mean to Cook in a year or two?

Sally knew she had to take care of Taylor. She'd seen the way that older woman checked him out, and she couldn't help but be protective. She'd heard he'd had a hard time being welcomed, and she'd felt so small. Unable to help. To heal.

A few dollars here and there would only help, right?

Could she risk losing another young man if she started to love? Risk having him torn from her heart like the others? Did she have a choice if Cook ended up loving him?

Would she ever feel mended?

CHAPTER 13
CAMPFIRES AND CONVERSATIONS
– BETH AND HUGH

Beth pulled a colourful blanket off her shoulders and laid it over the log beside her bag. She was on duty tonight, but the men knew where to find her if she was needed. She smiled when she thought about sitting with Elder Hugh to talk about life, and other complicated things. But her lips pulled tight, and she knew the smile didn't quite reach her eyes.

She grabbed her headlamp and headed into the nearby forest to find some kindling; she still liked to go get some "wild wood" to start her fires, even though the men split logs into small pieces for her. She knew it was important to thank the Mother Earth for giving her the warmth from her fire; she had learned these lessons, and many more, from the Native Brotherhood here at *Just Living*. She was glad for the space to talk around the fire, glad for Elder Hugh, glad for the Teachings. Well, most of them.

Over the years this fire pit had become an important part of the Grounds, where folks met to talk about life, and being. Beth never forgot that the place she'd built while trying to belong was still important years later.

Being responsible for the day-to-day operations at the half-way house meant her brain was usually a jumble of details, which kept the memories away. But tonight was different. Tonight, Hugh had asked to meet her by the fire to talk about Martin, who lived apart from them in prison now.

As she bent to put a match to the dry tinder, her head exploded with memories of her early days at *Just Living*.

"At least you didn't build a white-man's fire," Martin, as he was now known, had said to her when she'd built her first one in this little ring of rocks off in the far corner of the Sacred Grounds. She remembered him back then, long braids, blue jeans and plaid shirts, often accompanied by a scowl.

Beth blew gently on the fire, and the small flames caught some larger logs.

"Well, Princess, it's been a while. Not feeling sorry for yourself, are you?" Beth turned and saw the orange tabby, Timex, limp towards her. Beth wasn't the only one who heard the cat's voice in her head, but it still bugged her. She reached out and stroked the cat's head as it wound itself around her calves.

"You old crank. I'm fine," she said to the beast. "I can't believe you're still alive. Who've you fought off this week?" Beth asked, aware that the limp was a combination of an open sore, and hard living.

"I'm just fine. Look at us, bein' all fine. Hugh's coming, just so you know," the cat seemed to say.

"Thank you, Spook," Beth replied, and the cat lay down on a corner of her blanket and started making a noise like a broken chain saw. "You purring? I don't believe it," Beth laughed, and kept petting her friend. A few moments later, she saw Hugh step through the three-rail fence, which pulled her to the present, and another item for her current "To-Do list." Get fence painted. This time, though, she wouldn't be doing the painting.

"Here Beth. Cook sent this out," Hugh said as he handed Beth a plate with a bagel and cheddar cheese. "He said to take care of yourself, and he has some scones to grill with you when we're done here. He gave me one for now," Hugh said, holding up a bundle in a piece of paper towel. They sat quietly for a while, wrapped in blankets, nibbling their food. Beth reached down and unpacked a thermos of herbal tea from her bag, offering some to Hugh. Soon there was only what was unsaid between them.

"I saw our friend last week," Hugh began. "He asked about you." Beth let that land. Her stomach clenched knowing that she had been a topic of their conversation.

"He didn't send a letter this time. He asked if I would to talk to you about something. He was uncomfortable asking, but I told him I would." Hugh took a sip of tea. "I know it's hard, Beth, but he's trying to be careful. And generous. That's good for him." He looked at the flames, got up and added a log. The conversation wasn't over yet.

"He's carved some boxes for Adam and Bruce. Toy boxes, big ones. Wanted to know if it was okay to send them to the boys through me. Or if you'd like to take them, maybe save them until the right time."

Beth noticed her stomach clenching. Bruce and Adam were brothers, sons of a friend. Beth was like an auntie, so it wasn't strange to ask her. But she didn't want to ask their mother, Donna, about this stuff.

"Really. Let me get this straight. Martin wants to give the boys a gift." Beth nudged her boot up to a stone by the flames. "I have to think about this. He promised not to bug me again until I was ready, but here we are," Beth reminded Hugh. "I wanted to give myself a break," she said, poking the fire with a stick. Seconds crept by.

"Did he take up less space in your head during your break?" Hugh asked. Beth knew he was actually curious, so she thought about it. It was her turn to sip her tea.

"Yes and no," she answered. "I probably think about him as much, and I'm wrestling with stuff for sure, but truthfully, it's easier.

"It's at my pace, in my way. I know it's been years, Hugh, but I have a lot to figure out. Like, I'm still asking myself about all the Teachings he taught me, and whether or not they cease to be true when he rips my heart out. You know, simple stuff." Beth finished her tea, and looked over at her friend, and mentor.

"What do I do with that, Hugh? I don't even know if that's a human question or a God question. And I really don't think I'm any closer to figuring it out. He almost destroyed me, Hugh. And I don't know what I'd do if he did it again.

"I've talked to wise people about it. Maybe I'll wrestle with it forever," Beth said. She started to pack up her bag, putting the plate from the kitchen beside the thermos and mugs from the tea. Hugh didn't make a move to leave, so she settled in. She knew it'd be disrespectful to leave before the Elder was ready.

The silence hung in the air, until finally she settled, and felt her heart open just a little bit.

"That's a tough one, Beth. I know. Lots of Teachings are shared and lost over the years, lots of pain and hurting gets in the way of being fully alive." Hugh started to poke the fire again but didn't get up to feed it. "You know I've said before that, for me, Truth *is*. You recognize it when you see, or hear, or feel it. It's not about the messenger for me. But like everything, you'll know Truth when you get there."

Hugh smiled over the flames at the young woman who'd hurt so much, but still came back to help others. And did an amazing job.

"Teachings, on the other hand, Teachings are a Truth that you discover again. One you've forgotten. Or haven't recognized meeting before. But one you know is Truth." Beth sighed, looking at her old friend watching the fire.

"Let me think about it. I'll get back to you. Can you hold onto the boxes for Martin and the boys until I figure this one out?" she asked. She didn't want to be contrary, but inside she was *screaming*.

How could they think those precious boys should even be asked to think about this? Shouldn't they be free to live their lives, figure out why their Daddy never came home? But that visceral gut punch was too final, too hard. She wasn't willing to rush this. She had to figure it out slowly, and maybe she'd get why she was so mad at Hugh. Maybe Veronica *could* help her. She leaned in to her stomach, curling her fists together and pushing on her gut.

"It gets me right here, Hugh. And I can't help but want to scream. Give me some time…." She wrapped her arms around herself.

"Of course," Hugh answered. "You'll get there, Beth. You always do. Never doubt yourself, or the Creator," he said, rising and inviting Beth into his huge heart with a hug. Which she lost herself in.

On the way back to the Lodge, Beth reminded Hugh that they had a new resident at *Just Living*, and she'd really appreciate it if he'd talk to Taylor, welcome him. Ground him in the place, the men, and his journey. She knew Taylor was talking to Ben, but she wasn't sure if he identified as First Nations, and she wanted to offer the young man every possible support. Hugh snickered.

"You always think about everyone. You know I'll look in on the boy. You said he's carrying a lot. Here you are again, taking in those who need it. It's why I love this place."

In the kitchen, Beth put her dishes in the sink and gave Cook a hug.

"Thank you, friend, for looking after me." She was always amazed that Cook knew exactly what to feed her in any moment. His meals brought comfort, nurture. And yes, fuel for her work.

Ben was sitting at the table by the window, and she looked over at him with such love in her eyes.

"Hey, handsome. You waitin' on someone?" she asked, smiling.

"I was told if I was patient an amazingly beautiful woman would pass by. Look at that. God's right again." He smiled back at his wife, astonished at how great his life was, even when it was hard.

"That wasn't God. That was me," Cook teased.

"Well, some say your cookin' is heavenly," Sally teased back. They chuckled, and Beth lost herself in Ben's arms.

"Ready to head home?" he asked, holding up a warm package. "Cook snuck me some treats. I came back here looking for you, and I found grilled scones instead."

"You know it," was her quick answer. They waved as they headed out the back door.

Hugh grabbed his own bundle of warm baking to take to his wife. He hugged Cook and Sally, and headed home. On the drive, he thought about Beth, the amazing young woman who ruled this space in such a gentle, caring way.

He couldn't force her to live in her heart more. In fact, he thought, it might mess up the amazing gifts she had if she started to think less. And goodness knew this place needed every gift she brought to the work.

And so did the men who followed after Martin.

Oh, Creator, Hugh prayed in his own tongue, *please show Beth a clear path. And make it no more difficult than it needs to be for her greatest good… and the world's. Especially my boy, and those he hurt….*

CHAPTER 14
FAMILY FIGHTS

I understood why Rosie did it, but it didn't make my story easy. The next day, after we settled back into opening circle, we were moved into groups, and I guessed they were based on the *kind* of sexual assault we'd experienced. There was a small group of women who'd been hurt by their partners. Some who'd been hurt once by strangers. Some who'd been assaulted by a group of men. And Ophelia and me.

I couldn't tell if our group was "child sexual assault" or "incest," so just decided it was both. A weird club to belong to, I know.

I think we were supposed to talk with survivors who really understood what we'd experienced. Well, that kinda blew up, which hurt because I was starting to trust this group. Feel the hope, the possibilities, in the circle. I don't know what I expected, but it wasn't "being slayed by a new friend."

We shared stories about our childhoods, and it was nice talking to someone who "got it," without having to share details. She knew what it was like to realize at some point that you'd been doing shit that wasn't good for a long time. And to feel responsible for your part in it, even if you hadn't asked for it. Or wanted it.

Or what it was like to realize you did want it, at least some part of it. Hard to bring that up over coffee at work…I know.

We were sharing about our experiences and giving each other support when she pushed me to explain.

"I know you were messed up by your mom…abusing you. But what changed so you left?" she asked.

"Some shit went down with my mom's boyfriend I didn't like. I bugged out. Been living on the street for a couple of years. It's not easy." I wanted to make sure I didn't romanticize how hard living in a car, turning tricks for food and avoiding drugs had been for me. She felt bad that she hadn't gotten out earlier, and I didn't want her second-guessing herself.

"Yeah, I hear you. It was always hard, but then when I heard my uncles and brothers bragging about being my baby-daddy, I snapped. No one got it. I didn't ask to get pregnant. I didn't want to be a mom. I wanted to go to school. So I finally got the nerve to talk to this counsellor.

"When I told her, she was so tired, like I was the 500th student wanting help that day. Anyways, I finally got what I needed. To see a doctor. To go to a clinic to take care of that baby. To connect with foster care to take care of me. So far, I've been pretty lucky – the foster family isn't perfect, but no one's abusing me.

"And I only have to see my brothers at school. Mostly they leave me alone. They tried to start rumours about me being pregnant, but then when I didn't get bigger, people just ignored them.

"I think they figured out what I'd done. I don't feel bad, even though those people at church think I should. Really. Like they didn't stop the child abuse, but they want me to bring a kid into the world who'll probably be retarded because of in-breeding." We sat for a bit, and then she poked the bear.

"At least we didn't have to worry about leaving sisters behind to be used. My brothers were assholes, but they were abused as kids." Ophelia shrugged. And I could only be quiet.

"Right?" she said, looking at me across the table. I sputtered.

"Well, I had to get out," I said. I already felt so fucking bad about Jenny that I didn't want to talk about it.

"What the actual fuck, Taylor? Did you leave somebody there?" she demanded. Like, in my face, getting kinda loud. Other people started looking at us in the corner of the dining room.

"I was fucking 16, running with no idea where. I couldn't take her, okay?" My voice was quiet, flat. Like a robot. "I wasn't the one abusing anyone. I tried to keep in touch with her. I wanted her to be safe. I just had to look out for myself for once." I looked down into my mug, and I knew my Adam's apple was bobbing, and I was trying not to cry. "At least I reported Mom to Social Services. I didn't know if Jenny'd be hurt," I finished, barely heard. Every cell was feeling defensive.

But Ophelia didn't let me duck. And she wasn't gentle.

"What the fuck Taylor? You KNEW she'd be hurt by those bastards. You KNEW it. And you didn't *do* anything?" She stood up and walked about five paces away. No, stormed. Then she turned around and stormed right back.

"What the fuck did you THINK would happen? And why haven't you gone back to get her?" she demanded. "TWO YEARS you said!"

I put my head down and thought I would cry, but then the rage started. First, it was really small, a spark really. But soon it was bubbling up in me, on fire, and I couldn't keep it in. I stood up, chair flying behind me, and headed for the big glass doors at the back of the dining room. I hit them full on and burst out back onto the deck. Soon I was stomping down the path, then I was running. Away – away from this place, these people. And about five minutes later, I realized I was trying to outrun my past.

Which surprised me. I'd talked to Marta, thought I'd worked out all my stuff, but saying it out loud to Ophelia stirred a dragon in me. One small corner of my brain reminded me I was still too fucked up to get custody of Jenny if I was out of control.

Why *had* I left Jenny? What *had* broken in me that I never went back? At least Ophelia said it like it really was. I was tired of these adults all treating me like I was some kind of a hero for running away from home. *I* knew I was an asshole. The worst brother ever. And then just when I was working to make it okay by asking for custody, it got worse. She was gone. Fucking Social Services.

I kept running. I was following paths I'd never been on but didn't care. I wasn't afraid of the bears and cougars any more. In fact, I might have welcomed a good mauling. And then I cracked. Started to cry, just a trickle at first, and then a sob. I stopped by a big rock and leaned against the thick moss. Leaning over on my knees, I felt the rage bubble up again, and I turned and punched. First the rock, and that hurt like hell, so then a big old rotten log beside it. And I kept punching until the ants were running everywhere. I didn't care, and kept punching, until finally they were running up my arms, into my shirt.

I had no idea if these ants would bite, but I got that they were mad. So I tore off my shirt and started whipping them. Myself. The tree. It didn't make sense, but by then the feelings were so consuming I wasn't trying to make sense. I just kept on hitting my back, brushing my arms, sobbing, screaming out loud, a low angry bellow. I don't know how long I kept on, but the feeling of disgrace was drowning me.

Eventually, I looked up, and there was Rosie. Behind her, hiding, was Ophelia. Glancing at the two of them, I turned my head towards the stone, hiding my shame. Ophelia looked afraid of me when, really, I was the weak one. We stayed that way for a while, and I listened to the sound of water running, the animals in the trees. Even that big, black bird was around, and I swear I saw Rosie pull something from her skirt pocket and throw it for the damned thing.

After a few minutes Rosie tucked my hoodie, that I'd left behind in the dining room, around my shoulders. I pulled it tight, trying to disappear into it. She left her hand on my back.

"It's okay, Taylor. You did the best you could. That's all the Creator asks," she said. "Jenny has her own path to figure out, and you're going to be a huge help to her, but you couldn't do it back then. You didn't know how." Rosie was trying to let me off the hook, and I wasn't ready. But I didn't have any energy to fight left in me. I slid down the rock, and sat on the forest floor, beside the path. Rosie spread her skirt and plunked down behind me. And started to pray in her own language. The not-words-to-me were soothing, embraced me. My head bowed, I wiped my face and my bleeding knuckles with my T-shirt.

And then she started to sing, and Ophelia joined in. And then, I heard Cook and Kenny behind them, big voices holding the Honour Song from below, a song I had heard every day in Circle. And now it was being sung for me, not because I was honourable but maybe because I wasn't. Soon I was slumped onto the rock, and Rosie still held her hand on my back as the song ended. I'd never seen her sing sitting on the ground before. And I missed the drums, but I heard my blood pounding in my brain.

And the silence was deafening.

"So, my little scrappy otter, are you ready to talk? You don't have to be, but when you are, I'll be over on that log," Rosie said, and I could hear her smile. "If Cook and Kenny can lift me up," she finished. I felt her body leave, and felt a smaller, tentative hand on my back.

"I'm sorry, Tay. I just really wanted someone to rescue me and that got all mixed up in your story," Ophelia said, sounding as sheepish as I felt.

I wiped my face again and struggled to put my hoodie on. She helped untangle it from around me. As my head popped out, I looked up and saw Rosie sitting quietly, eyes closed, with Cook on the log. Kenny was standing behind them, his hands on their shoulders. He was looking right at me, not with sympathy, but maybe understanding.

"No rush, Taylor. Take your time. Feeling horrible because of something you've done isn't unfamiliar around here. It takes the time it takes," Kenny said. "And Taylor? For what it's worth, I don't think you did anything wrong. Sometimes saving yourself is the first step." I thought about that. Still didn't feel it completely, but maybe a small piece shifted in me. And Rosie kept praying. But that bird was back, talking to Cook, who, I swear, was talking back.

"Yes, Little One. You are beautiful. And you've eaten the last bit of everything I brought." I looked over at them, and Rosie and Ophelia each had their hands out, some crumbs for Cook to offer the bird.

"Oh, you knew, didn't you! They were holding out. Here's some scone, you spoiled girl," he said, holding the crumbs on his palm and scratching the bird's head as it ate the sweet baking. Soon, she flew off, watching from nearby, and I couldn't believe what I'd just seen. Had Cook tamed a wild bird? I turned and sat with my back to the rock, arms on my knees.

"I didn't just leave Jenny, Phee. I got her kidnapped. She's being held by some internet child porn freaks. And it's my fault. I'm doing what I can to help, but it's not…I just don't know what else to do," I said, my voice trailing off as my head hung between my knees. Rosie started to speak, and her voice was hard. Like steel. Or the voice of the principal after she catches you running in the halls. For the second time. In five minutes.

"Listen up, little scrappy one. I know you're feeling bad about Jenny. It's awful that such things go on.

"And I would have some very hard questions for that social worker if she was here. Because it was *her* job to keep Jenny safe. *Her* job. You reported your Mom. That was your job and you did it." She let that sink in for a bit.

"But Jenny – you couldn't keep her safe and you safe, too. And I know if anyone is responsible for what's happening to her, it's the creeps who are doing it. We *have to* hold *them* accountable. And maybe the police who didn't catch them sooner, or the people who hurt them when they were children.

"But really, Taylor, I will not let you do this. *You did nothing wrong in getting yourself out."* We sat for a bit longer, my breath slowing down, the cold air seeping into my body. Finally Cook spoke up.

"Hey, Taylor, this Rosie? She's a strong woman. And she *never* lets a guy blink who needs to take responsibility, 'kay? You can listen t' her, 'kay? But she's gettin' cold, and so are Ophelia and that flake Kenny. An' it's gettin' dark, and stuff, when the cougars are comin' out so we're gonna think about headin' back soon.

"You can stay out tonight if you want, though, 'kay? But th' ants are still kinda angry you punched them," he finished, grinning.

A few minutes later, we walked out, quietly, heading for dinner. Ophelia and I hung back, and she apologized again, but I didn't let her.

After all, she was right. Right?

CHAPTER 15
SWEETGRASS AND UNDERSTANDING – KATE AND OPHELIA

After dinner, Kate invited the lovely First Nations woman into the smaller office.

"Ophelia, come in, make yourself comfortable." Ophelia snuck by the woman and pulled some braided grass from her pocket. *Why did I ask for this meeting?* she wondered. But after that stuff with Taylor, she knew she needed Kate.

"Here Kate. Thanks for meeting with me." Ophelia had been taught well that she shouldn't visit an Elder without something to offer, so she'd dug into her bag and found the sweetgrass now in her hand. Kate wasn't her auntie, like Rosie, but she'd grown to respect her over the past few days, and so hoped the gift was appropriate. She held the long braid up to her nose, then offered it to Kate.

"Oh, Ophelia, thank you!" Kate held the sweetgrass up to her face, just like Ophelia had, and breathed in its sweetness. "Did you want to go smudge with it now?" Ophelia had rarely met white people – colonizers, her Elders called them, or settlers – who understood the importance of medicine, of her People's ways. But these people at *Tide's End*…well… they got it.

"No, it's okay. I smudged earlier with Rosie. But thank you. Thank you for making time for me."

"Shall we start with a little silence? Ben taught me that. Slows stuff down and it helps me to catch up to my body," Kate said. And so they sat, and Ophelia was grateful that Kate didn't rush her like lots of other people had tried to do. After a bit, Kate looked up and asked her a simple question.

"So, Ophelia, what did you want to talk about?"

And Phee burst into tears. Kate let her cry, gave her tissues and time. A few minutes on, and Ophelia had steeled herself again, and was ready to show Kate the face that she usually brought to the sessions. She sniffled a bit and tossed her braid over her shoulder.

"So, I think I was a complete jerk to Taylor." She tugged at her braid. "No, I was a complete jerk. How do I hold my shit in?" she asked, looking at Kate with tears in her eyes. "I freaked out when I found out he abandoned his sister. Who I didn't know existed before our…." Her voice trailed off. "Abandoned is maybe a bit strong…." she sniffed. "But it's the word I used."

Kate patted Ophelia's knee. And had no idea what to say, so stayed quiet. Offered another tissue.

"Will he ever forgive me?" she asked. "I like him. But maybe I couldn't believe he was a good guy, so I had to make him a bad guy?" Kate realized these young, resilient survivors might never stop surprising her.

"Oh Phee…I am so sorry. I say shit all the time that gets me into trouble with people I care about. That sucks." And waited a bit longer. *Silence is my friend*, she thought.

"I think I want to figure out what to say to him. How to show him I understand." Ophelia wiped her nose as concentration took over her face. "I know I can show him."

"So…what's worked for you? When someone has said sorry, what's helped you believe them?"

Twenty minutes later, after more tears and a little laughter, there was a knock on the door. Sally came in with a tray with tea and cookies.

"We're closing up the kitchen. Thought this might belong here. Just leave the tray on the table – we'll get it in the morning," she said. She smiled at Ophelia. "Sleep well, both of you." Both Kate and Ophelia got up and hugged Sally goodnight.

Kate took a sip of the tea.

"Let me see if I heard you, Ophelia. Your life has been…hard. I think your family was like many others. They had a horrible habit no one talked about. Until they did and then they didn't talk about anything else." Ophelia snorted in agreement.

"But you've been working hard this week. And then today, you and Tay were paired up and you said some stuff you wish you hadn't. So where to now, after our talk tonight?"

"I know even more now that incest sucks. And it's…well, it'll fuck you up. I want to pretend to be carefree. No. I do pretend. I can pretend." She pulled at some threads on her sweater, looked at Kate from under her bangs.

"But under it all, it's always there. Always. Reminding me I'm ugly. Dirty. Alone. And I say shit, clearly. Mean shit." She sniffed, grabbed a tissue. "I think I'm ashamed of who I am. My family." She shrugged, and her long, shining hair tumbled from her shoulders. She'd pulled out her braid and finger combed her hair over and over. "And I wanted Taylor to be ashamed, too."

Kate took a breath, tears leaking from her eyes.

"And it's everywhere," Phee continued.

"What do you mean?" Kate asked. "That every reserve has it?"

"Every neighbourhood. But on reserve we talk about it. Admit it. That's the first thing you have to do." She took a cookie, dunking it in her tea. A piece dropped into the cup.

"Oops. Anyhow, it's messy. And it happened in my family. And his. But it happens in lots of families who don't talk about it. And if we don't talk about it, we can't stop it."

"How did you get to come to the retreat, Phee? Who helped you get help?" Ophelia started swinging her legs, looked up.

"I don't know. Suddenly everyone started talking about it. In the last couple of years, maybe because of the TRC? Blaming residential schools. Each other. But they also accepted it. Like it wasn't the worst thing. I met an amazing young woman at my school who came and told her story. And she was like...famous. An author. But it happened to her, so...basically...I guess I can be anything I want?" She looked up, smiling a gentle smile that didn't leave her lips, didn't touch her eyes. She took a bite of cookie. "It's better than before. When we didn't talk," Ophelia concluded. "I guess." They sat for a bit.

"And Taylor? Who does he have?" Kate asked.

"Taylor...he doesn't have anyone to talk to about it. No one to admit it to. It's like white people think it couldn't happen to them. Child abuse, yes. Pedophilia. Maybe. By priests or Scout leaders. But incest? Nope. They think it's just ours, an Indian problem," Ophelia said. She kept swinging her legs. "They *really* don't like to talk about it. And he was trying, and I freaked on him. I've gotta tell him how sorry I am. Fuck! This stuff is hard," she said.

"And your generation, you courageous young people, you're going to help everyone. You're not going to sweep it under the rug any more. I feel more hopeful now than I've felt in years," Kate admitted. "It seems the #MeToo movement could actually make a difference."

"Oh my Creator!" Ophelia smacked her jeans, stood up and started pacing. "And he's a guy! They don't admit they've been molested. I remember now from the guys on my reserve. Not wanting to admit it until an ex-con came back to town and talked about it. About how it happened to him. About how we have to talk about it. Fuck! And Taylor was talking about it and I shut him down! Fuck." Ophelia started to run out of the room, dashed back and hugged Kate.

"I gotta talk to Taylor." She turned as she headed to the door.

"And Kate? I'm worried about Jean. I think she's…I don't know. I'm just worried about Tay when she's around." Phee flipped her hair in her hand as she turned again and rolled her eyes at Kate. She bounced back and forth on her toes and gave Kate a quick hug.

Kate laughed as the young woman burst out of the room. She gathered the cups and headed for the table by the kitchen door. Maybe tonight she and Nora could debrief some of this.

They were doing good work. The energy in the circle, the strength of these survivors…folks were getting better, right?

CHAPTER 16
AN EVENING WELL SPENT

After dinner I couldn't just hang around. I needed to do something. My afternoon had made me restless. I was getting together with my new friends later to hear about their afternoons. Because of my freak-out, I'd promised a late-night meeting in their dorms. Sneaky, I know.

I'd decided to get to that list I'd made with Ben and headed out to my car with garbage bags. Sally'd offered to take on any laundry I found moulding in the back seat (brave woman that she is) and I wanted to look for the papers I needed. Kenny'd convinced me over tea yesterday that facing my stuff meant I might get to go to post-secondary school for free — something about a new program for ex-foster kids. I'd never drunk so much tea in my life. I could get used to it.

About a half hour in, I'd found an old wallet in a garbage bag of stuff that I'd stashed when I'd run from the last group home. (Who knew that old canvas wallets can mould?) It had my license in it. ID! Score!

I'd excavated some shoes that might work (or might leak), and gross stuff that went into the "garbage" garbage bag. I located my set of free weights a cool foster mom had given me one Christmas. And lots of dirty laundry for Sally to try to transform. Even a jacket that might come in handy if some stains could be cleaned.

I tossed a couple of games that I'd grown out of. They were so wrecked that my idea of saving them for Jenny was trashed along with them. And some old photos were ruined.

Sally wandered out of *Tide's End* with a hand vacuum after I'd taken her my laundry and tossed the trash. I was putting stuff back in the hatch-back and she offered to help vacuum the back seat. It felt awkward accepting her help, but she kinda insisted.

A couple of minutes later I was actually humming while we puttered together on my car (that wouldn't start, btw).

"You been looking for this? It was under the front seat," she said, and held up an old flip phone I'd been using last year. I'd accused a guy in the last group home of stealing it.

I banged my head extracting myself from the car and hurried around to her side. The thought that this was the phone number I'd given Jenny exploded in my head. Would it log calls if it was dead as a doornail? I couldn't even remember if I still had service. Who was paying for it? It might have been pay as you go, but I didn't know if I still had money on it.

"Oh my God. That's my old phone. I thought it was stolen," I said. "I wonder if Kenny'll have a charger." Sally looked on the bottom of the phone.

"Not many guys at *Just Living* have phones, but this is pretty common. I bet Kenny has one for his music player," she assured me. "If not, let me know. I have a couple. In fact, let me get you one you can keep," she said, and she headed toward the kitchen.

I quickly packed up the rest of my stuff to get ready to go over to *Tide's End*.

A few minutes later, I'd plugged in the phone and it was charging in my room. I'd put the bag of stuff to be cleaned and sorted in my room under my bed, so it wouldn't bug Kenny. And I headed back to *Tide's End*. Jean met me at my car, peering in the window.

"This looks way better, Taylor. Looks like you were busy this evening." She turned and looked me up and down. I don't think I blushed.

"Yeah, found some stuff I need. Threw out some other stuff. The car didn't start though, which sucks. I'll have to get it towed, looked at. Hopefully I can leave it here until I can afford that," I said, maybe revealing too much.

"We're meeting in Padma's room. There's back stairs to get you in," she told me. I felt like I was being inducted into a secret club. Nobody said I couldn't go into the centre after dinner, but…this felt badass.

Heading up the stairs, Jean put her hand on my back. It dipped onto my butt once, and I turned and smiled at her. It felt good to be noticed, and Jean was noticing in all kinds of ways I liked. I reached out for her hand and we wove our fingers together. At the top of the outside stairs, I brushed my fingers over her wrist, squeezed her hand and smiled at her when I let it go. Her eyes sparkled when her smile flashed her pearly whites at me.

And just as I got into the door, Ophelia grabbed my free hand and pulled me back out, away from Jean.

"Oh, Taylor. I talked to Kate. And realized what a bitch I've been. I'm so sorry. You did not deserve my crap this afternoon." She kept on firing words at me about reserves, and white people, and incest and our stories and men not admitting it…I couldn't follow any of it. So I gave up. Gave in.

"Whoa…whoa…Phee. It's okay. Really. Slow down. I'm good. We're good." I laughed, and she threw herself into my arms. Kinda crying, but laughing too?

"Is everyone waiting for us? 'Cause we can talk later," I said. She laughed.

"I realized so much today. I have to tell you. But maybe not now. Are we good though?" she asked, and her eyes reminded me of puppy eyes.

"Yes. We're good. Really. I cleaned my car. Got lots done. You said some stuff that was harsh, but some of it got me off my ass, which was good. I'm not feeling so sorry for myself. I've got work to do." I told her about the phone charging at Kenny's and we headed inside.

When we got into Padma and Phee's room, Jean patted the bed beside her, and I sat down. She snuck her manicured hand under my leg, and I smiled.

I was welcomed into the room with snacks, smuggled for me by Dianne and Sally, apparently. Sally was becoming my champion in all kinds of ways. Scones, ginger cookies, and a thermos of tea were all put out on a tray. I dug in while my pack filled me in on what I'd missed.

"Terry freaked out at dinner, where we missed you by the way. I'm getting tired of her," Padma said. I noticed she looked a little pale. Her hair wasn't in a smooth ponytail, and I don't think she was wearing any makeup. Not that she needed to, but it was different. Ophelia, on the other hand, was glowing.

"She sure was. You should have heard her, Taylor. She was nearly frothing at the mouth. That is one angry woman. *I* wouldn't want to piss her off. And a couple of the other women just kept feeding her. You should have seen her going after Rosie and Barb.

"Poor Barb said that maybe she could have been nicer to her family, and they would have believed her. I guess nice is off the table with Terry. Maybe a sign of weakness." Jean gave me a glance that made my blood stir.

"She's got some stuff to work out. But I see her point. Her family should have believed her, even if she was grumpy. People who are assaulted are allowed to be grumpy." I loved that Jean used older words like "grumpy." It made me feel warm inside, like she was from a time when mothers stayed home and baked cookies. But she wasn't done.

"And if Terry's angry, she could use that anger for something good, if she could just find something," she finished. She smiled at me. "Anyhow, Terry gets to decide how much she participates. She did meet with her group today. She's still here."

"So what's gonna happen now?" I asked, wanting to seem like I was curious about the whole workshop, but really just wanting to know if it'd impact me.

"Well, Rosie and Kate talked to Barb and Terry. Barb kind of dug in her heels — she's not going to let Terry bully her," Dianne said. "I was proud of her. And once Terry left the circle for a bit and cooled down, things got calmer. They felt a little sheepish, I think. So tomorrow we're all going to have circle together. I think it kinda freaked them out when you and Ophelia had your…meltdown?" Dianne patted my knee, and I realized I thought of her as a friend. I hadn't expected that from this retreat — a middle-aged woman as a friend.

"We were given some homework we haven't talked about yet. It's for tomorrow. We're supposed to think about the stories we tell ourselves about the people in our lives who we struggle with. Kate talked about this psychologist, Brené Brown, and how we tell ourselves stories with a…perspective. Dr. Brown calls it a 'shitty first draft.' I know I've been thinking about it, and there's lots of stuff I tell myself about my ex that's convenient more than truthful."

"Like what?" Padma asked. I could tell she was struggling with this.

"Well, I told myself that after we got married, he changed, and became harder. But I knew he was dangerous when we were dating. I just thought I could change him. That I was different, and that at least I'd have someone. I was scared of being alone." That seemed to bring a downer into the room.

We talked a little about our evening plans, and what time we were starting in the morning. Jean didn't look happy when I mentioned I had to get home to help Kenny. I wouldn't have minded hanging out with her instead, but had to go.

As I headed for the path, Padma called me from under the overhang outside the big room.

"Hey, Taylor, can I talk to you?" Her voice was thin, tired. Turning, I felt weirdly big-brotherish towards her. I put my arm around her and steered her to my car. We got in the front seats.

"Sorry it's cold and damp. I can't get it to start, or I'd warm it up. What's up?"

"So, remember I said I'd be meeting with the police, and they told me that it'd help them if I cooperated? Well, I decided I really want to. But last night my Dad told my Mom that if I do, I'm out of the family. My brothers were yelling at me over the phone when I was talking to her. I don't know what to do," she told me. God, I wondered, does she know if her family is crazy enough that they might try to hurt her?

I took off my jacket and wrapped it around her legs when I saw her shivering.

"God, Padma, I'm so sorry. That's so shitty. When do you have to decide?" I was rubbing her arms, trying to help her warm up. I noticed tears were leaking from her eyes, but she was weirdly quiet. When Jenny, or even my Mom cried, the whole world knew.

"I don't know. The police want to meet with me tomorrow evening. They're taking me for dinner. I wondered if you'd come. I just feel so shitty about myself I thought maybe you'd drive me. But your car isn't working," she said, beginning to sob.

"I'll go with you. For sure. And I'll ask Kenny about getting a vehicle," I said. "Maybe I can borrow one, or he can drive us," I promised, wondering why anyone would lend a car to someone who can't even keep his own cleaned and running.

"I'm so worried about my Mom. I know she loves me and is sorry about what happened to me. But that's making things hard for her at home. I feel like I'm to blame for telling people about what happened."

I wiped her face with my sleeve.

"You aren't to blame Padma. Those horrible guys drugged you and took pictures of you. You didn't ask to be assaulted and you *really* didn't ask for those pics to be taken. They did all of that. They're to blame," I tried for forceful enough to convince her I was on her side. She sniffled a bit.

"Yeah. If only my Dad and brothers saw it that way. They're just so ashamed of me right now." I tried to hug her over the console.

A few minutes later I was hurrying down the path — I wanted to get home. Kenny and I were "doing tea," and I wanted to see if the phone worked.

Over tea and cookies Kenny talked about a plan he had to grow food for restaurants with some of the guys from jail working with him. Cook wanted to open a restaurant in Mission to train guys in "culinary arts" or something. A partnership with a college nearby maybe? I just knew when they talked about cooking school, my stomach went a bit funny.

"They teach people to cook?" I asked. "I'd really like to learn about that, I think," I said. It felt kind of wild to be thinking about going to school, like I was rushing plans. Let's face it, a week ago I was living in a broken-down car, trying to figure out how to get Social Services to let me see my sister. Living off food I stole from the grocery dumpster and hanging out in soup kitchens trying not to get lured into drugs.

Kenny thought it'd be easy for me to go, learn about cooking.

"Really, Taylor. My life changed totally once I started learning about plants. Might be the same way for you with food. Worst case? You can cook a wicked meal at the end to impress women," he said. It was nice to dream. I begged off for the night because I wanted to check the phone, see if it was working, by some miracle.

"No problem, roommate. I'll do the dishes tonight."

It felt so good to just hang out with Kenny, doing guy stuff. I told him I'd help with the horses again tomorrow morning. As I headed to my room, my heart started pounding thinking about my phone.

I don't know what I was hoping for, but it wasn't what happened.

CHAPTER 17
HEARING THE CALL

I was whimpering when Kenny opened the door to my room ten minutes later. I wanted to think I was hiding it well, but he pointed out that the jiggling of my leg up and down was creating quite a lot of pounding on his wall.

"You okay?" he asked, poking his head around the corner.

"Yeah. Sort of," I lied. And I started to leak out of the corner of my eyes. "I think I have to go for a walk," I said, jumping to my feet. And immediately realized that it was late, and really dark out. Kenny hadn't even made it back to the trailer from barn chores before he'd put his head lamp on (something everyone who lived here seemed to have.) I'd be lost out there tonight.

"Really? Any place in particular?" he asked, and I had to admit I had nowhere to go. I shrugged.

"What's up? Something's changed," he said, and the way he said it, I trusted him. I went from leaking eyes to dripping nose with occasional sobs, and it wasn't pretty. He sat on the bed and put his arm around me and handed me his cloth hankie, neatly pressed into a square.

"It's Jenny," I sobbed. "She needs me, and I don't know where she is. I don't even know when she called. I'm such a failure. I told her I'd be there, and fuck. I don't know what to do." It didn't get better, so I got up and started pacing.

"Tell me about Jenny," Kenny said. And I told him about my little sister, who I adored and hadn't seen or been able to take care of for six years, ever since I ran away from home.

"Listen to this," I said, and handed him the phone to hear her voicemail.

"Taylor…are you there? I need you Tay," she whispered. There was a bang, and she whimpered. "Tay, he hurts me. Can you come get me? Please? I'll be good." Then a quiet scream and she hung up. It unraveled me a little more every time I heard that little scream.

"I don't even know when she called. I lost my phone a couple of weeks ago. I just found it today, and Sally helped me charge it.

"This was in my voicemail when I turned it on just now, but I don't know when she called," I finished.

"Oh shit, Taylor. That's awful. We have to do something. You don't know where she is?"

"No…I guess she's not with Mom. A foster home, I think. I could call my social worker, I guess, but it's late." I couldn't even figure out what would help. Not winning at adulting, that's for sure.

"What about Beth? We might talk to the cops, if you're okay with that. Jenny seemed really scared," he said. "But I don't want to be the one to place that call, for obvious reasons. Let me call Beth." He whipped out his cell phone and left the room.

I wouldn't have thought of the cops in a million years, so I couldn't believe that was the first place Kenny went. It felt good that he was taking this seriously, at least. I blew my nose and grabbed my wallet and stuff in case we had to drive somewhere. It felt good to be doing something, even if I kept hearing Jenny's voice in my head. Shit, I was a crappy brother. Why the fuck couldn't I even figure out what to do when she needed me?

Ten minutes later, boots were tromping up the stairs, then three people came flying in. Kate started.

"Okay, Kenny. Nora's coming. We've got some ideas." Her voice burst out, barely contained. I felt like I'd awakened the troops.

"Can we listen to the call? We believe you and Kenny, but I'll know more if I hear it myself," Ben said. Made sense, so I played the call again, this time on speakerphone. A moment later, Kate had a plan, and we were out the door jogging down the path to *Tide's End*.

"Okay, Beth called Inspector Derksen. He's going to wait for us at the detachment. He says he can find out when the call was placed," she said. "Some of us can take the truck. Can you drive Kenny and Ben down?" she asked, and I realized I'd have to admit that my car wasn't working.

Except as I rounded the corner to the parking lot I didn't have to 'fess up because the car wasn't there.

"What the fuck? It's gone!" In my imagination I was screaming. "Not that that would have helped. It wasn't running. I don't know where it is, though. It was here this afternoon when I cleaned it out," I told them.

Kate grabbed her phone again. "No problem, I'll get Nora to bring ours. Just waiting for Sally to look after Brock."

It seemed like no time before we were being buzzed into the detachment in Mission. Even though it was after hours, they were waiting for us. I hadn't voluntarily shaken hands with cops before, but here I was, meeting and greeting the Inspector of the detachment – middle-aged, in a white shirt with lots of bling and black pants with a stripe, but looking decidedly like he'd been wearing it for a very long day. He was with some other people dressed like civilians. I wasn't sure who they were except one of them had pink hair. Her name was Patty. Another one was Neil and the fourth guy's name I didn't catch.

"These folks are from the Integrated Child Exploitation Team. ICE we call it. They're working a case here. Let's play that message and if you can give Arun the phone, he'll plug it into his computer and see if there are any background noises we can identify." Arun. Must be the fourth guy.

I admit it wasn't easy handing my one connection to Jenny over, but Arun (clearly the geek) treated me, and the cell phone, like he knew it mattered. Soon, we were listening to the call over the bigger speakers hooked up to Arun's computer, and he was taking down information so he could call the phone company and get the data from the call.

"I hope she was calling from a cell phone, but I doubt it. Kids in care don't get phones," he said, and Inspector Derksen left the room with Arun's notes to get someone to deal with the phone company. Something about figuring out when and where the call had been placed.

I just tried not to shake.

Patty took me into a coffee room and started to interrogate me. Kenny sat on my side of the table, and it felt good having someone there for me.

And maybe Patty was just getting information about my social worker and stuff, but I couldn't forget that these were the cops, and they were a part of a club that hadn't always treated me and my friends well. Of course, the social worker club hadn't proven to be exactly supportive either.

I gave her Marta's details, and Jenny's and my history, including my suspicion that my Mom was dead. And the last phone number I had for Mom in case she wasn't. Neil fed me awful cookies that made me miss Cook, and some coffee that tasted like dirt. Kenny pulled a face when Patty and Neil weren't looking. We were used to better than this.

Of course, Kenny heard my whole story. Patty tried to reassure me that they were taking everything seriously and were going to work to find Jenny, but I really didn't see how they were going to do that with what I'd given them. She also said she'd look into my Mom, and I made her promise not to hassle her. She may have been a bad parent, but she had her own demons to deal with. As Patty left the room, I asked for my phone back to be sure I could call Marta myself, hassle her until I knew where Jenny was.

A few minutes later, Inspector Derksen came in and handed me my phone.

"Taylor, call me Mark. Thank you for bringing us all this information," he began. "I can't tell you too much because what we're working on is sensitive, but I can tell you this. What you've just told us is not only going to help Jenny, and we're going to find her, but it's also going to make a big difference in another investigation we've got going on. Really." He put his hand on my arm, but it didn't work. I didn't trust him. In fact, I sensed we were being dismissed.

Nora and Kate and Ben had left to get back to *Just Living* because supervising parole dudes apparently takes a few people at a time. Once we were escorted to the sidewalk outside the detachment Beth, Kenny and I piled into the truck and headed up the Valley. I may have gotten my phone back, but I'd had to promise "Mark" that I wouldn't bug the social worker until the morning, because Marta was "busy helping Patty."

Interesting that even though my head was full of horrible pictures of what was happening to Jenny, and my car might have been stolen, I felt the forest wrap around me as we left town and drove into the tall, shadowy trees. It was weird that I felt more at home here after less than a week than I did in the city, even after 19 years. And I felt safer, too, even living with an ex-offender, a bear-shaped bush, and being scared of some of my fellow participants. Like Terry. Her door slamming and chair tossing made me jump.

Driving home, Kenny and Beth tried to keep me distracted with small talk.

"So, Taylor, what are you going to do when the retreat ends?" Kenny asked.

"Find Jenny, and get her away from that creep," I said with attitude.

"Where are you guys going to live?" Beth asked, and it may have been chatting, but it felt condescending. I barked at her a bit.

"Why should that concern you? We'll figure it out," I snarked. We drove on a bit further. An uneasy quiet settled in the car. I looked over, and Beth was whispering to herself, biting her bottom lip from time to time. I was such a prick – as if she needed my attitude, especially when her and Ben weren't getting along. Or so I imagined after what he'd said the other night.

"What's the prayer?" Kenny whispered to her. WTF? The prayer?

"I'm praying for Jenny. That's all." A couple of seconds later, she whispered, "And Taylor." I may have snorted. Like praying would make a difference. I'd prayed to many gods over the years, and it hadn't changed a thing.

"Don't waste your time on us," I said, looking out the window.

"Hey, Tay, Beth's just trying to help, 'kay?" Kenny said, looking over at me. I banged my head on the window.

"I know. I'm just such a shitty brother. I shouldn't make you guys pay, though," I admitted. "All you've done is help me."

"No…it's okay. Really, I get it," Beth said, and I might have heard some tears. "I've had lots of days of feeling shitty about myself." Her voice broke, and with it I felt a small crack my shell. Tears leaked onto the window when I put my cheek on the cool glass. Beth offered me a Kleenex, and I smiled a weak smile at her as I took it and wiped the window. She handed me another.

"I intended it for you, Taylor. Sally or I can clean the glass later if it needs it. Honest." And I believed her just a little more. Poor Kenny, the two of us sputtering.

"Sorry I'm such a wreck," Beth said as we headed into Kenny's trailer. "I don't know what's wrong with me lately. Try to get some sleep, Taylor. I'll check in with Mark tomorrow and let you know what I hear," she promised. I waved and turned and headed inside. I knew what I needed to do, but I'd be up all night figuring out how I was going to do it.

Help Padma.

Finish the retreat.

Convince Kate and Ben and Rosie and Marta that I was fixed.

Find my car. Get it working.

Find a job, and a place to live.

Find Jenny. Talk Marta into letting me look after her.

Just a short list.

I was even more determined to throw myself back into the circle and do what I had to do to get custody of Jenny.

No matter what it took.

CHAPTER 18
DOUBLE DATE

I was still swearing at myself as I blundered up the path towards *Tide's End*. I had been so stupid to leave Jenny. Lose my phone. I was counting my faults, and then rounded the corner and remembered I had also lost my car. That's me. Taylor Smythe, taking failure to new heights.

Damn! I kicked a stone big enough that I felt it in my big toe. And didn't care.

In fact, I deserved it.

So much to set right.

I hardly slept, and that left me grumpy, to paraphrase Jean. But at least I'd gotten up early and the horses were fed.

I looked up, and there was Dianne, walking towards me, taking me from pissed to smiling in ten paces.

"Hey you. Good to see you. Kate told me you might need a friend this morning, so I thought I'd come get you," she said, greeting me with a hug. Would that ever get old?

"Yeah. Rough night. Didn't get much sleep, but I'm ready. Even if I do smell like horse. What's on for this morning?" I asked, aware that we were closing in on the end of the retreat. And I didn't feel one bit like I was fixed. Dianne smiled.

"Well, this morning we're talking about what we've learned about ourselves so far, and resilience. Light stuff." She smiled at me. "Then this afternoon I think the plan is to think about ongoing support once we're done here tomorrow."

"And hey, do you know what happened to my car?" I asked.

"Oh! I think I heard your car was towed. Jean was there," she said, and I must have looked surprised. She had a conspiratorial grin on her face. "I *told* Padma you didn't know," she said.

"What the heck?" I could feel my blood heating up, and I was getting all prissy in front of Dianne. I tried to cover my attitude. I still wanted her to like me.

"Heck? I think I'd be using stronger language than that if someone towed my car." Her crooked smile made me grin as she took my arm.

As we rounded the corner of the path into the parking lot, Jean came out the front door of *Tide's End*. She was wearing tight beige jeans, and a western top with lots of bling…and a jacket that might have made Dolly Parton blush, it was so…tight? Jean's cleavage was too tempting, so I didn't bother to avert my eyes.

"Hey Taylor. I was just looking for you," she said, rushing towards me. "I wanted you to know what happened with your car, but I couldn't find you last night. I have some friends who own a shop, and they came to look at it. They couldn't fix it here, so I told them to take it in." My stomach churned.

"Really? You just took my car without asking?" I bristled.

"Don't worry, I'll pay for it." She dismissed me with an airy toss or two of her hand. Then she took my other arm and patted it. I felt so mixed up inside, between Dianne, who made me feel capable, and Jean, who, well, gave me different feelings.

Under it all, though, I was churning inside. I couldn't forget about Jenny, so I tried to shake Jean off, reclaim some space for myself. She took a step back and stopped on the path.

"I'm sorry, Taylor. I didn't mean to piss you off. I thought I was helping. Maybe I shouldn't have bothered." She turned towards the front door. "I just wanted to give you a good surprise," she said, crossing her arms over the view. She was miffed. Dianne patted me on the back.

"I'll see you inside, 'kay? There's breakfast for a few more minutes," she said, and I tried not to believe she was using my stomach to get me inside quickly. When it growled, she grinned, and headed for the door.

"It's okay, Jean. Really. I just wish you'd asked me first. I needed my car last night, bad, and didn't know what had happened. And I have some stuff in it. I could have needed that."

"Oh, you couldn't have used the car. It was tanked, my mechanic said. And it's not much of a surprise if I ask first, is it?" She smiled coyly, now that we were alone.

"Yeah, but I didn't know it was tanked, did I?" Even I could hear how strident I was being. "It freaked me out when I thought it was stolen," I said, feeling a bit guilty. Here she was, doing nice things for me, and I was bitching. Besides, if I was honest, there was a part of me that was kinda hoping it *had* been stolen so I wouldn't have to worry about it any more. And then I was agreeing to go for a walk with her in the woods after the afternoon session finished.

How do I go from hot to cold to hot so fast?

I heaped some scrambled eggs on my plate and grabbed a big glass of orange juice when Sally waved me into the kitchen. She was juggling a hot, grilled scone between her fingers, and quickly tossed it on my plate. I almost kissed her. I'd never had a scone grilled in butter before *Tide's End*, but I would never stop loving them, I was sure. Sally smiled as she gave it to me.

"Pardon my fingers, this is the last one and I was keeping it warm for you," she said, and I smiled back at her. "I heard you had a rough night last night."

"I'm okay," I lied. "And thanks, Sally. It smells delicious."

"Cook made them with blackberries for you this morning. I'm glad you got one." I ducked my head in gratitude and slipped over to the corner to eat. Quickly. I had about four minutes, I figured. Cook came out of the back room as I was shoveling in my eggs.

"You okay?" he asked me, concern etched on his forehead. I knew I couldn't lie to the man.

"It's complicated. I'll tell you later," I promised him. "Besides, isn't it your day off?" I asked.

"He doesn't ever really leave," Sally teased.

"No one to leave for," he said, and I felt a little sad as I brushed him on the shoulder on my way out of the kitchen.

Moments later, Padma slipped beside me and helped herself to a small corner of my scone. I smiled.

"Tay, can you do that favour?" she said. I nodded with my mouth full. "I got permission yesterday afternoon to bring you to meet those police people after dinner. Will you come with me? Please? They're going to drive us." Padma was shredding a paper napkin into tiny pieces onto my tray. I could hear the tremble in her voice. Damn! That girl was *so* alone in this.

"Of course, I can," I said, wondering how I'd juggle the walk with Jean and the meeting with Padma. But I'd make it work. Cops twice in two days. Strange world.

Moments later Kate was calling us to circle, so I pulled a new napkin from the dispenser, wrapped what was left of my scone in it and put it in my pocket, and headed to the kitchen with my tray. "Let's talk about it later, 'kay? I'm happy to come, but I'd like to understand why you want me there, so I don't embarrass you," I said. I'd had to tell Kenny my whole story last night, and Padma might not want me to hear hers.

And then we were in circle, talking about how far we'd come in just a few days. What no one seemed to want to talk about was how far we still had to go.

Was I the only one who still felt broken?

Jean came and found me after group. She was wearing colourful cowboy boots I hadn't seen before. I think that's how I'd describe her — colourful. Her furry jacket and tight jeans, fluffy green scarf -- well, it was different from me with my clothes barely held together with patches. She slipped her gloved hand into my elbow, and off we went, looking like a lady with her gardener.

I took her behind the retreat centre, near where Dianne and I had gone on that first day. I walked with her around the small lake. Kenny had told me the path was an easy one, with lots of privacy. We stopped to look at one of the waterfalls spilling into the lake. It was beautiful even as the sun was setting.

"Hey, let's sit here. There's sort of a bench," she said, and I tried not to flinch at how cold my butt was when I lowered it onto the log. I do not get the attraction to going commando, even when it's necessitated by a lack of underwear. Less insulation isn't fun.

"What're you going to do when the course ends?" Jean asked. God, I was glad I had an answer.

"Actually, Beth and I are meeting tomorrow. I think they're going to let me stay on at Kenny's for a bit. We're looking into some stuff, maybe going to school to learn to cook," I said. Kenny and I had chatted about it again over "first breakfast," as I'd come to call our coffee and muffins.

"Well, if you need help, or a place to stay, just let me know," she said, putting her hand on my thigh. Quite close to my…commando. And yes, many parts of me noticed. I turned towards her, in part to move her hand lower on my leg so I would…well…notice a little less and found myself looking into her eyes.

"So, you think we could see each other after tomorrow?" I asked, trying to sound more naive than I felt.

"If you want to," she answered. I took a breath and smiled. Yes, I would like to. I may not be ready for a romp on a bench in the forest, but I was ready to see her after the retreat.

"Maybe when my car's done we could get together for coffee. I'll figure out how to pay you for the work," I said, and then sounded like a fool. When I lived on the street, I'd been paid for sexual favours. My face turned red, thinking about it.

"Oh, Tay, I'd like that," she said, and next thing I know we were kissing. Like full-on, make no mistake about intentions, making out. And I was having trouble stopping, she tasted so good. My hands were behind her head, and she was getting her hands closer to my...excited bits, and both of us were panting.

And then I heard a stick crack.

"Shoot," Padma said, when she turned to run back down the path. I called out to her.

"Padma. Come back! Jean and I were just heading back to the centre. I know we've got plans." Jean smiled at Padma while she dug her nails into my inner thigh. Hard. I tried not to flinch.

"Of course, you do," she said. And then whispered in my ear, "But you better be back early." I laughed a little, feeling uncomfortable for all kinds of reasons. Including that I really couldn't stand up.

"The ride's here," she said, looking me in the eye. Jean squeezed harder when I tried to stand up, which took care of any swelling that may or may not have been going on. I grabbed her wrist gently and moved her hand.

"I'll let you know when I'm back," I said, extricating myself. "But I also have to meet with Beth sometime," I reminded her.

Soon, Padma and I were in the back of an undercover cop car, driving towards town. I was only a little embarrassed that I couldn't offer to drive us, but hey, what's a guy gonna do, right? At least my car will be fixed. I hoped it wouldn't be too expensive. And that it was worth it.

The cop dropped us at a sushi restaurant in town. It looked expensive, and I'd forgotten my wallet. But I like miso soup, right?

CHAPTER 19
A TRIBE CALLED FED

I squinted in the dim light and then spotted them. Shit! Neil and Patty were sitting in a corner booth. WTF? Could it get worse? I grabbed Padma and dragged her back outside before she saw the cops.

"Padma, I know them. I can't really explain right now, but I know these cops. I'm not sure you want me here." I hadn't told Jean, or Padma, or even Dianne about Jenny's situation yet, and dumping that on Padma now seemed like not really supporting her at all.

Of course, abandoning her at the door wasn't exactly textbook support either.

"What the hell, Tay? You said you'd come. Are you in trouble?" she asked. I knew for her to be swearing, this mattered. So perceptive, I am.

"No, not in trouble, but I just found out my little sister is in trouble, and these are the cops Beth brought me to. Are you sure you want me in there?"

"Are you kidding? Who would get it better than you? I asked you to come, Tay. It's okay," she said, and she took my elbow and we went back in the restaurant. Patty was on her way down the aisle, no doubt looking for us after our quick exit.

"Hi Padma. Taylor! Good to see you again. I didn't know you knew each other," she said, and I was glad I'd come clean with Padma. Padma just smiled. No secrets with these cops around. "Let's sit down, and order. Dinner's on us," she said, and my stomach was glad. I love sushi, and free sushi is my favourite kind. Imagine me, accepting dinner from cops. Life is interesting.

After a while, we got to talking about Padma's case. Neil and Patty kept reassuring us that it was going to be okay. To the point that I…well, trust isn't high. Could they say it would be better? They talked about *it* without ever "saying" anything, which made it a little easier to talk about it in the restaurant.

"Well, Padma, I don't know that we can prove those guys meant to release it to the guys selling over the net, because Snapchat deletes stuff so quickly. But they did put it up and tag some friends, and even videoing you was illegal, so we'll get them. I'm sorry you have to deal with this, after all you've been through," Patty said.

Wait. What? Padma's video was being marketed? Fuck. That's evil. It'll haunt her forever. She'd never be able to work things out with her family. Even her mom will freak out. Her brothers and uncles and dad will never be able to hold their heads up. If there's a market for brown-girl rape porn, almost certainly some of the consumers are people in their community. Shit.

"We'd like to use any information we can get from the guys we've charged to track down the internet merchants. But we'd like your permission before we do that, because we're taking info from your case that we'd only get with your cooperation and building a bigger case. Your call, because it's your plea. I mean, yours and the prosecutor's call.

"If the guys cooperate, it'll reduce their charges to whatever is negotiated. If they give us the contact info for the guys who sold it, maybe even help us with a sting for the buyers, we could locate bigger players. Right now, they're just ghosts who keep moving their product around on servers internationally. We're convinced they are locals, because of the background in some of the photos they're using. Local places," Patty finished. She and Neil got quiet. Padma started to squirm. "If you agree, it could help us catch them."

"Hey, Pad, you don't have to decide now," I reminded her.

"He's right," Neil said. "It's a lot to take in. In fact, we won't ask you again. You come to us if you're ready. Talk to your Victim's Assistant Worker about it. I'm glad you can talk to Tay about it, too." He asked the waitress for more green tea, and she refilled our waters, too. It reminded me we weren't the only diners in the restaurant. The paper screens around our table made it easy to forget, but I'm sure some people could hear us.

Fuck, I thought. *This could be directly tied to Jenny. Talk about a conflict. How do I make it okay for her to say no?*

"So, Tay, this is kinda awkward, but hey, can we talk about your case?" Patty asked. "We don't want you to pressure Padma, not that we think you will," she said. I nodded at her, my throat closing a little. Finding Jenny was the most important thing. What was I doing having dinner with them and Padma, especially if my supporting Padma would jeopardize their investigation and leave Jenny hanging? I wanted Padma to agree so badly, but knew I was biased. *Of course, she was free to say "no," right?*

I inhaled my tea too quickly and choked. I used that as an excuse to duck out to the washroom.

"I'll be back," I said, coughing.

Out of habit, I headed into a stall. Sitting at the table had made me aware that my thigh, where Jean had used her nails, was sore. I was so stiff that I was glad there was a grab bar. I coughed once more to convince myself I wasn't going to choke to death.

Then I looked at my leg. Black and blue. Shit. Had Jean known she was hurting me? I had to believe she didn't, that she'd just wanted to keep on holding me. A couple of minutes later I was drying my hands as I returned to the table. I worked hard to walk without a limp. At least there wasn't blood on my jeans — no broken skin. I headed back to the table.

"So, Neil, you can talk about Jenny. I trust Padma," I said. And five minutes later, without letting the other diners know we were talking about a kidnapping, and a sex ring, Padma heard the story.

"Oh Tay. I can't believe it. You weren't even distracted today," she said to me.

"Yeah, I was. I knew Neil and Patty were working on getting Jenny back, so I needed to do my bit. I want to get custody of her, look after her once she's safe, and I need to show the social worker that I'm 'fixed,'" I said, using air quotes. "I tried to focus on being fixed today, but let me tell you, I was distracted," I confessed.

"Well, we're doing our part," Patty assured me. "Arun has started to work the file with the cell phone info. We're working to confirm where your sister is. We aren't sure where she's located yet, but we're working on it. It would help us if we had a photo of her, and Social Services can't give us one. Can you help Arun with that?" I reached into my wallet.

"I have this photo. I don't want to give it up, though. It's the only one I've got," I told them. "And it's old. Like four years old. I kept asking her to send me new ones, but she didn't have any," I confessed. "I should have worked harder to see her. To get a more current picture," I said, and the tears started to swell. I just hadn't wanted to let her know how I was living, what I was doing to survive.

"Taylor, it's okay. This will help. Arun will send it to Vancouver, and they can work with it."

"Except I'm not giving it to you," I reminded her. Neil put a hand on mine. Gently, like.

"No worries, Tay. I can take a picture of it?" he asked, holding his hand out. He put it on the table, held his phone over it and took the photo. Two seconds later, Arun had it.

"We do think she's close by," Patty continued. "The server transfer patterns are similar to the guys in the other case. We're within a few days of getting the ISP to give us an address, I think. I'm working on it. We won't even need your help with that part, and hopefully it will lead us to Jenny," Patty said.

"But you keep in touch about what you want us to do with the guys who had your video, Padma. If we have a two-pronged approach — our sting, and information from your guys, our chance of success rises greatly. As does our chance of making a charge stick."

Neil and Patty offered to drive us back to *Tide's End*. On the way up, Padma and I were whispering in the back seat.

"Tay, I can't say no. *Of course* they should try to get those guys to cooperate," she started. "And it'll keep it out of the courts...."

"Too easy, Padma. You have to think about this. Maybe talk to Kate or something. If you say yes right now, I'm gonna feel awful, like I pressured you."

"I think it's a really good idea to talk to somebody up there," Patty chimed in from up front. So much for covert conversation with cops around. "Inspector Derksen suggested Beth, or someone like her. They really understand this stuff and will have a totally different perspective. How about we call you tomorrow?" Patty said as they pulled in front of *Tide's End*. WTF? They knew Beth?

Who didn't they know?

It was weird caring about people again. First Dianne, and Ophelia. Today it was Padma. And I knew thoughts of Jean would keep me awake tonight.

In a good way. Except for the bruises.

CHAPTER 20
TEA WITH FRIENDS

I had my arm draped over Padma's shoulder when I walked through the wooden front door and bumped into Nora and Beth.

"Hey, you two, warning. The space is occupied," Beth said. I jerked away from Padma, who laughed out loud.

"It's okay. I was just trying to convince Taylor that I can get myself inside," Padma said.

"But I'd promised tea," I said. "Is that okay?"

"Sure. Join us. Beth and I are just talking about woman stuff," Nora said, smiling. That got me moving to the kitchen fast. I put on the kettle for a fresh pot.

Ten minutes later, we were sitting around a table in the dining room, eating some cookies and drinking tea, just as I told Padma we'd be. I introduced Nora when she joined us, and Padma knew Beth's husband Ben, Cook and Sally.

I got up to check out my leg in the washroom again, and when I got back to the table Padma was telling everyone about our meeting with the cops. And then they were asking about stuff I hadn't thought about.

What did she really want to happen to the guys who'd hurt her? Padma didn't think before answering.

"I want them to be punished." The steel in her voice told me that was clear.

"Why?" Nora asked. Padma picked at her fingernails for a bit, then looked up.

"So they don't even think about doing something like this again." Sally brought more tea, and hugged Padma. Padma put her head on Sally's shoulder.

"Oh honey, I get it. But in order to be sentenced, they'll go to court and usually claim to be innocent. Will fighting their guilt in public, minimizing their involvement, help them remember not to do this again?" Nora said. Everyone let that sit for a bit.

"What about if you asked for a couple of things in return for a plea deal? It's not only the lawyers and cops that can ask, you know," Beth suggested. "It's just an idea but think about it."

"Like what? Admission of guilt?" Padma asked.

"How about they have to talk to you, or apologize on video, or do community service somewhere that matters to you? They usually have to admit guilt to get a plea deal," Nora said. "Really, there are lots of possibilities. People just don't realize it." We sipped some tea, ate some ginger cookies. I was glad the focus was off me, but not for long. Cook came into the room.

"Hey, Taylor, I hear you're interested in learning to cook?" I blushed.

"Yeah. Not sure I'd be any good at it," I said, feeling stupid in front of a guy who clearly knew how to make amazing food.

"Well, how about you stick around here this week after the retreat and help me over at *Just Living*? There's a big party going on over there, a public tour and stuff on Wednesday. I could use some help," he said, and I almost believed him.

"No, I'm not makin' this up. I need someone in the dish pit," he said, ruffling my curly hair with his big fist. "Unless you got somewhere to be when the retreat ends," he added. "Beth said you could stay on for a bit, and Kenny likes you, so…just an idea. Let me know."

"There's nothin' in my budget to pay you, but room and board isn't bad. Maybe we can talk about pay down the line," he said.

"Besides," Kate needled me, "you need to get your stuff together to apply to Social Services. Find those papers in your car." I smiled.

"I'm starting to get it together. Found my papers," I laughed. "But I don't have an address. I can't even get a bank account." I knew I'd need one to get any government help because they don't do cheques any more.

"We'll figure that out, Taylor. Let me talk to Kenny," she'd replied.

I turned around and Kenny strode into the room. I wondered how much he'd heard.

"Thought I might find you here. You moving out? Really, Taylor, I'm good with you stayin' on a bit. You can use my address for the government," and I felt like the luckiest guy. How did I end up here? Really, I didn't deserve this break.

My face went flush, and Cook steered me into the kitchen. I swear the man could read a room even better than me and was protecting me from losing it. Soon, I was drying dishes, and putting them away.

Cook and I listened to the conversation in the front room. Kate, Beth and Nora were still talking to Padma, and soon I was shaking my head. Cook chuckled.

"These people think of stuff I never even consider. What'll teach those university boys to respect women? When did that become a thing you could ask police to do?" I wondered out loud. Cook grabbed some ingredients and started to make something with butter and flour and stuff.

"Well, might as well think about it, 'cause the jailhouse never made no one think about that shit," he said, and I realized he'd just confirmed he'd done time. I decided to ask him about Kenny's call.

"So, Cook, what if I think Kenny might be in trouble? I heard him on the phone the other night…and it sounded like someone is threatening him. What do I do with that?" I asked.

"Hmmm. Remember those rules? We don't hear other people's conversations. Ever." He added a few more ingredients to the dough he was making.

"And if we do hear, we never, ever, talk to somebody else about it. No good comes from that," he said. "You can trust Kenny, though."

"Okay…." I answered. "What phone call?"

Soon he had me "kneading dough," something I had zero ability for. We were making scones, he said. For Kenny and me. He pulled some soggy berries in a plastic bag out of his jacket pocket.

"These were blackberries, from the back of the Sacred Grounds," he said. "We picked them ourselves last July." He poured the juice into a small glass and gave it to me to drink. It tasted like summer. We stuck the mushy berries onto the scones, rolled them out and put them in the oven.

Then, before I knew it, Cook and Sally were putting on their jackets to leave, and Cook was giving me instructions about when to pull the scones from the oven, and what to do with them. Kenny was chuckling.

"I'll remind him, Cook. Ten minutes, check that they're lightly browned, cool them on a rack. It's all good. Thank you for the baking," he said. Cook peered at me.

"I had to check that he'd be any help in the kitchen. He'll do," he said. "And be sure to take those scones home with you. You've got the day off, remember. But you can always come by the kitchen and help." I was embarrassed until Kenny told me that "he'll do" was high praise.

Once the kitchen was cleaned, we joined everyone around the table. Padma looked happy.

"I'm gonna call Patty tomorrow. I know what I want to ask for," she said. "I want the boys to work at the rape crisis line — not taking calls but serving the women who do. I want them to know what it's like. And understand what they did."

"I wouldn't hold my breath," I said. "Guys don't really 'get it.' They just breed it." God, I sounded jaded.

"You get it," she said, whispering. "I have to believe they might."

"Well said, Padma," Kate added.

"And you can take a half-day or so to really think about it," Beth said. "Making them wait a bit for an answer might help them...learn the lesson." They promised to check in with her the next day, and then I ducked out to text Jean that it was too late to get together. She didn't answer. Padma found me, and I snuck a warm scone into her pocket, which made her laugh.

And it only started raining a little as I ran down the path with Kenny. A few days ago, I didn't know these people, this place. And already, I could run down the path in the dark, and didn't feel afraid.

Much. Not why I was running. Honest.

That night Kenny and I talked more about my plans. He asked me about Padma, and I admitted that I wasn't interested in her as a girlfriend.

"She's kinda vulnerable right now. And I guess I am, too. We talked about it, but we just aren't...interested?" I told him. "I think she's smart. She said she needs a friend right now more than a boyfriend."

"Are you still dating that guy? Gonna see him again?" I asked.

"Nah, we're not lookin' for the same things. Anyhow, I'll see you tomorrow, right?" And he was gone.

As I drifted off to sleep, thinking about my whole day off, a 'rest day" Kate called it. And about the changes in my life and feeling grateful. I thought about everybody deserving better. Me, Padma, Dianne. Phee. My Grandma would be proud.

And then I remembered Jenny. I felt like a shitty brother.

I knew I needed to do better.
Starting tomorrow. No excuses.

CHAPTER 21
FAMILY COMPLICATIONS - PADMA

Padma smiled as she entered the restaurant looking for her mother's sister, Masi Rampreet. She was excited. Rampreet was her favourite aunt and their families had been close forever. They'd even lived together sometimes. Padma hoped that the invitation for lunch meant her family was ready to let her come home. It had been so long since she'd felt at home, and it hurt. She sat at a table for two and ordered tea.

She looked around the restaurant. There were two guys her age sitting in a corner at a table, and she felt her heart start pounding. She talked herself down, remembering some breathing exercises Kate had suggested. Then she thought about Kenny, waiting for her next door, and wondered why it was she felt so safe with him but not those guys in the corner.

Ten minutes later, she had drunk her tea, and was still waiting. Her stomach had begun to hurt. She was glad Kenny had insisted she take a few dollars in case she had to pay for her tea.

Finally, her aunt came flying into the restaurant, apologizing for being late.

"I couldn't get away. I'm so sorry! I hope you weren't worried...." Padma's smile was weak, and she knew in that moment that her parents, or her uncle or brothers had tried to prevent her aunt from coming. Damn.

"It's okay, Masi! I'm so glad to see you," Padma said, standing to hug her aunt, while trying to cover her disappointment. Soon they were feasting on dishes she'd been missing since having to leave home: dahl, aloo gobi, pakoras, and tandoori chicken. Her aunt had ordered enough for four, maybe to compensate for the bad news to come. After some small talk, Padma couldn't wait any more. Her stomach hadn't stopped hurting.

"How are my brothers?" she asked, too afraid to ask after her parents.

"They are fine. Bad. Up to no good, and your parents won't believe me. But going to school, doing alright there for a change. They are boys." Masi Rampreet was waving her hands, perhaps being just a little too enthusiastic.

"Really Auntie. It's okay. How are they? And Maa and Pita?" Padma was close to tears; she missed her parents madly. She had thought they were a pain in the neck when she'd lived with them, but now that going home wasn't possible, she felt lost, unanchored when she thought about them. She *had* to figure out her life going forward. Her aunt took a deep breath.

"They are sad, Padma. So sad. They miss you," she began, and Padma's heart hurt, squeezed between losing her family and maybe having a chance to have them back in her life.

"Can I visit yet?" she asked.

"No, Patheeji. Not yet." It had been years since Padma had heard the Punjabi endearment from her aunt. She fought the tears pooling in her eyes.

"They are still sad. Sad that their little girl didn't follow their guidance, and now the world knows you don't honour them," she said, her voice trailed off.

Honour. It was always about honour. Screw honour. Did they honour her? But deep down, she knew she'd done wrong. As a daughter. A sister. A niece.

"It's not my fault!" Padma said, working hard to keep her voice down in the quiet restaurant. She didn't want those guys at the back noticing her. "I didn't ask for this! My life is wrecked! It was those boys! I was only drinking fruit juice, but they drugged it!" she said, the tears spilling over. Her aunt put her hand over Padma's and squeezed it, trying to support her niece who had fallen from grace.

"I know, sweetie. You didn't ask to be assaulted, but you *did* go to the party. Alone. No brothers, no cousins to look out for you. And now the world knows. Your Pita's world." And in that moment, Padma realized her family blamed her, even though she hadn't gone looking for sex, or even drunkenness. No matter what she did, she knew she'd be a disappointment to them forever. The video online assured that. She finished her tea, and started moving her food around on her plate, her appetite gone.

"I guess that's it, then. I won't ever be able to come home, see my family," she said, wiping her nose on her sleeve. Tears dripped from her chin, and she kept wiping them away. At least she wasn't sobbing. Her aunt offered a handkerchief, which she gladly accepted. She wrung it between her fingers, determined not to let it go. What she really wanted was for Masi Rampreet to give her hope, but the handkerchief would have to do.

"Padma, I *want* to help you. I do. But it's hard." She poured some more tea.

"Why did you want to meet me? If I am the bad one." Padma's heart cracked open. She could have sworn it was leaking in her chest, making it hard to breathe. Would she have to say goodbye to everything? Her mind went blank, couldn't imagine the shift in her world. She couldn't even think about what was next. Her aunt started to gather her things, reached out for her hand, but Padma knew she would burst into tears if she looked at her favourite auntie.

"Well, I have some of your things in the car, and I'll keep them for you until you get settled. I think I'll be able to help you a little with some money, but not much. Not enough to go back to school. I can't let the others know I'm keeping in touch after this week.

"Your Pita agreed that your cousins and I can come get the rest of your things this weekend. I wish it was because he wants to help you, but I think it's because he wants your stuff out." She sighed. "I had to warn you. You are not the first woman this has happened to in our family," she said.

"Wait — you're going to get my stuff? Maybe I could come, too?" She *knew* if she could just talk with him, take her Dad's hand and smile up at him like she always did on the walks to the park after dinner, she could make him understand. He still loved her, right? Surely her Maa didn't want her living outside the house. Who would she talk with while cooking dinner? Maa had always dreamed of Padma's big Indian wedding. Surely she wanted her home! She rubbed her hands on her pants.

"Could I go with you, talk to them?" Padma's voice was excited. She could convince them she was still a good girl if she could just talk to them, right? Help them understand what happened to her? Maybe they would talk to the police so they could understand Canadian laws. How she was cooperating to make sure those boys didn't do it again. Her auntie took a drink of tea.

"No, dear. Really. I don't trust your brothers to be civilized, or your other uncles." She took another sip of tea, and looked at Padma, cold, across the table. *What did she need to say to her niece to help her understand the danger she was in from the menfolk in the family?* Looking across the table, she kept her gaze fixed, the words unspoken.

Like a fog lifting, Padma realized the awful truth. Really? They would try to hurt her? It was hard to imagine, but then…she hadn't imagined they'd kick her out either. And Padma remembered the woman at temple, the one who was caught having an affair with a married man. Could they not see this was different?

"Darling, I know you did not ask for this. Things like this have been happening in our world forever. Would it surprise you to know things like this happened to my friends and family when I was a girl, too? Women died. And I know that those boys took something that was not theirs to take, and that you are hurting.

"But this culture of ours has not changed enough. Women are to be a certain way. And I'm sorry your assault was so public that your family can't pretend it didn't happen. I am so sorry. But we must be strong." Padma was shocked. Her auntie had been so loving, caring, and now, this. Would her aunt warm to her again soon?

And with that, Masi Rampreet got up from the table, assured Padma she'd be in touch, took the bill, and was gone. No hugs, no more endearments. It tore Padma up inside.

"Would you like the rest packed up?" the waiter asked, her voice intruding into Padma's sorrow.

"No, that's fine," she said, then stopped herself. "Actually, yes, please do." She'd give it to Taylor and Kenny, thanks for all they'd done. After all, the food was barely touched. She sat for a bit at the table, thinking about her next steps, how much she was going to stick it to those guys, either in court or in the papers. If she was losing her family, she was going to make sure they lost something, too. Their reputation. Education, maybe. She was tired, and sad, but she could feel a steely determination rising.

If she was losing everything, those boys – no, men — were going to pay.

Later that afternoon, Padma dragged herself up the stairs and into the hallway outside her room. Neither she nor Phee had been able to afford the fees for the retreat, so they'd had to share a room, not as a punishment, but because there just weren't enough for everyone to be in a single room…and so they'd offered. She was glad; it had been great having a friend, someone who understood. And let's face it, she'd never had privacy, so she didn't miss it.

As she got near their room, she could hear Ophelia and Dianne talking and laughing, sharing stories. Padma listened from outside for a few minutes. They were talking about Michelle, another participant, trying to figure out why she acted the way she did.

"Can you imagine? She says she can't go five nights without sex, so she had to go to town," Ophelia said, mystified. "I can't imagine *wanting* sex, let alone every day. If she was a guy, they'd call her horn dog."

"I know, honey, and I hope someday you'll enjoy what all the fuss about sex is, but I think Michelle is acting out. She feels valuable, alive when she's having sex. I don't know, really, but I don't think we should judge her." And then Padma heard them giggling again. Padma couldn't wait to be distracted by what was going on.

She opened the door, and they both shot up off the beds and reached out for her when she joined them. How did she get so lucky that these new friends cared more than her family?

"How are you, dear?" Dianne asked, holding her arms open. Padma had no doubt her red-rimmed eyes told the story. "Did you meet your aunt?" Padma wasn't ready to share, so she changed the topic after a short hug. It had been hard enough weeping on Kenny's shoulder in the parking lot.

"What happened with Michelle this time?" she asked. Two nights ago, Michelle had been caught trying to break into the barn next door at the half-way house, and she told everyone it was because she was meeting someone she'd "fallen for" from there. "After all, we're all adults, right?" she'd insisted. None of the staff had seen it that way, and she'd been asked to stay inside after dark.

Well, Padma figured out she'd escaped.

"Last night when you and Taylor were out, she called for a cab to go to town. She was hanging out propositioning guys at the local pub and didn't notice it was across from the police station. One of the servers got spooked by how drunk and forward she was and called over to get her a ride back up here. At least she didn't get sick in the cop car," Dianne said, filling her in. "But Nora and Beth are getting more than frustrated. Kate's trying to keep the peace, help them see this is a symptom of the trauma, I think. Only a couple more days…I hope she gets to stay." Ophelia was chuckling behind her hand. Padma caught her eye and couldn't resist grinning back.

"But it's kinda funny, watching Cook avoid her, and the other guys, too. And who can blame them, right?"

A few minutes later, Padma had shared what had happened at lunch. In the end, she was still sad, but able to calm down enough to work on her homework. She was looking forward to talking to Taylor later. Maybe tomorrow.

Cook. Taylor. Kenny. Ben. Guys she felt safe with, a growing number. Hard to believe.

* * *

NORA, KATE AND BETH

Walking the perimeter of the property, Nora and Kate looked over at Beth. It was a habit they'd gotten into over the years, walking together in the forest. Rules stated the perimeter had to be walked at least daily, and they shared the chore but did it together at least once a week. Gave them a chance to catch up without distractions. Or monitoring.

"How are things going for folks?" Nora asked.

"It's been a relief, actually. I think giving people a day just to do what they need is smart. Some left and met family or did chores. Some took time alone. A few folks hung out together. I'd work it into the schedule again." Nora smiled at Kate.

"How are you doing, Beth?" Kate asked. They walked on a bit and Kate realized she'd zoned out.

"What did you just say?" she asked, not believing what she'd heard.

"I was telling Nora last night I've been a bitch lately to Ben. Angry at Hugh. Fuck Martin. I'm grumpy. And I don't feel well. Tender." Nora kept walking but glanced at her wife.

"Don't say it," she said to the woman she adored. "Women don't like to be asked. Isn't that what you say to Ben?" Beth laughed.

"I don't think it's PMS, but…." Beth just stopped dead on the path. "I don't remember my last moon time." They kept walking in silence, each one afraid to say anything.

Finally, Kate couldn't hold it in any more.

"That's just how I was with Nora when I was pregnant with Brock," she admitted. "And I didn't realize it was the pregnancy at first, even though we were trying. Are you guys trying?" she asked, stopping. Nora stopped with her, but Beth kept going. Ten paces along she stopped and turned back.

"What the hell. We aren't, but we aren't exactly careful, either. So we aren't trying not to be? Does that even sound like a grown-ass woman talking? Fuck. Jesus. God save me from myself and that gorgeous husband of mine," she said. And Kate and Nora laughed.

"That's a prayer," they said in unison, mimicking something Beth used to say all the time.

Completing the circuit around the property half an hour later, Beth had agreed to take a few steps to figure things out.

Visit the pharmacy for a pregnancy test.

Talk to Veronica about what was going on with Hugh and Martin.

Talk to her husband and apologize.

Nora smiled, because she knew now that it was on a list, Beth would get it done.

CHAPTER 22
STRENGTH AND VULNERABILITY

I had a plan.

Yesterday had been good, a day with Kenny and Cook. Brushed some horses, cleaned up their shit. Didn't even mind it. Cooked some casseroles with The Boss, as I'd come to think of Cook. Rearranged his fridge, under careful direction. Sally spotted me a little cash for helping out. I cleaned my room. Even called Marta about getting my ID updated so I could apply for assistance.

I spent an hour or two with Jean in the afternoon to make up for the no-show the night before. She drove us into town, and we went for coffee. I came away smiling, without bruises, and we'd even held hands a bit. Shared a kiss, not that I'd tell. The day felt like a win, all around.

So, the plan.

Arrive early. Eat a big breakfast. Deal with whatever once my belly is full.

I didn't say it was a thorough plan.

Of course, I should have known Sally would make it easy for me. That woman had mad skills for knowing what I needed.

She smiled when I walked in and steered me through the double doors into the domain of "Staff Only." There, like a dream, was a table set for three with coffee, eggs and grilled scones in abundance. Like she'd been expecting me. Like I belonged. And there was Cook, sitting on the far side, enormous hands wrapped around a big mug that said, "Will Cook for Kisses." I hope I didn't cringe, but then Sally kissed the top of his head, and he smiled. Which was hella cute.

"Welcome," Cook said. I ducked my chin and looked out from under my bangs. What was I doing here? Was I in trouble?

"Cook just wanted to talk about this weekend, and past that." Sally winked. "I thought I'd give you a quiet breakfast this morning. A thank you for your help yesterday."

I smiled. "You already paid me," I admitted.

"That's between you and me, remember?" Cook was shaking his head at Sally.

"So, you're gonna help me in th' kitchen?" Cook asked. He still kinda terrified me, which made it hard to figure out what would be expected. I knew I'd disappoint.

"If that's okay," I mumbled. Cook sat back.

"It's better'n okay," he said. "Willing company's a nice change," and I realized he might have "enlisted help" sometimes. I wondered what he was like when you *had* to work with him instead of just hanging around. Kenny'd said he was good, but…really? When had Kenny been stuck in the kitchen?

"I've got some groups to cook for this weekend and next week. Glad for your help." He took a sip of coffee.

"What'd you like about cookin'?" he asked, and I hoped this wasn't a test. I had zero idea.

"I don't really know. Just the idea of making food that tastes good." Then quickly added, "And food that's good for you. Hanging out with you, too," I said. Cook took a sip of coffee and looked at me over his cup. I had to admit his eyes were soft. He took a moment.

"When I started cookin', it was jus' 'cause I was hungry. An' not happy wit' what I was bein' fed," he said. "What I served at first wasn't very good, but I got better," he finished. I breathed out, and relaxed. He smiled at me.

"I know I'm gonna hafta work," I said.

"No problem," he said, finishing his coffee. "We got lots o' time. We'll figure somethin' out," he said. "I gotta do some dishes, and you gotta eat," he said, standing up and walking over to the huge dishwasher. "Come find me once you're all done wit' everything in there," he said, waving at the door to the main rooms. "Sally can help you find your own apron," he added, and I got to eating.

It was nice being welcomed into the inner sanctum. Quiet. Healthy portions. And tons of homemade jam and fresh honey with the most excellent scones.

Five minutes later, Sally sat down beside me, and nudged a full travel mug towards me.

"Cream, one sugar." She really did notice stuff. She put her hand on mine.

"Don't you worry, Taylor. Cook'll teach you all you need, and he won't bite. I promise." Her eyes were sparkling. Really, if Sally liked him this much, he must be okay, right? I took my dirty dishes to him in the dish pit. Grabbing my coffee cup and headed for the circle, I called out a quiet, "Thank you," and he smiled back at me.

What did we talk about in circle that last morning, before heading our own ways?

Kate spent some time talking about sexual assault victims, and how the world judges us based on their past, their behaviour, and how they react to their trauma (including being addicted to all manner of substances and behaviours). It was interesting when she asked us to put a spin on our assaults that would show different perspectives.

Padma shared with the group what her aunt had said about her dishonouring her parents, in effect "asking for it" by attending the party unaccompanied.

"I don't believe it. Really! It sounds like they're blaming you!"

"What the fuck? Your fault? I don't get it. They must not love you like they say."

"Jesus. Trust the patriarchy to come up with that."

"I can't believe your aunt didn't stick up for you. Or your mom."

I tried to catch her eye, reassure her, but she was looking down at the floor. I wanted to defend her family, but however I spun it, the women assembled wouldn't understand. She must have had a shitty time with her aunt yesterday. *Why didn't I check in with her?* I thought. *Oh yeah. Jean.* At last she looked over at me, and I shrugged my shoulders and smiled at her. Kate interrupted.

"Wait a minute. This is Padma's family you're talking about. She loves them. People! This isn't any better than what the press or the public do to others. We, of all people, should know how complicated it is. We have to be understanding, respectful. Even when we don't agree." Kate was firm, and finally the whispers died down. After a bit more discussion, there was agreement that although everyone had a story before their assault, and a story about their assault, there was also an unfolding story *from* their assault moving forward.

"Society has to let those stories evolve, change and grow," Rosie said. Padma sighed, and I was thankful for Kate and the others here who defended her. I hugged her in front of everyone after circle broke up, because I wanted everyone to know where I stood.

Of course, Jean also caught my eye, and winked back a few times.

Then, we got into pairs to talk about what had finally given us the energy to leave. To take control of our lives. Dianne and I walked around the pond and settled down side-by-side on a bench just off the path. Dianne tucked a blanket around our knees.

"Well, for me," Dianne began, "it was when I realized Tommy was going to miss out on university if I didn't do something. He was determined to keep me safe. And keep his little sister from having to take over responsibility." Her face shone when she talked about her kids.

"You're an amazing mom," I said, trying not to sound wistful. "Really. Your kids may have been the motivator, but what actually gave you the energy to leave?" I asked, gently bumping her shoulder. I sounded wise, but I was reading from a card Kate had given each of us. We dropped into quiet. A few minutes later, she answered.

"I think I just finally saw things differently. The fear fell away. He yelled like always, but I'd had enough. I'd been seeing everything through fear for so long…years…and then I saw through it. The fear didn't cripple me any more." I looked over at her, and she kept going. "I wish I could have seen that clearly earlier. I wouldn't have wrecked my kids' lives," she said, wiping a tear from her cheek.

"Wait a minute," I said quietly. "This isn't about regret. You're amazing, Dianne. Strong. Crazy strong. We all had journeys to get where we are now, but you're like…crazy amazing. If it wasn't for you, I wouldn't even be here," I said. I took a breath.

"Before you spoke up for me that first day, no one…not one person… ever spoke up for me. Not my Mom, or a teacher…a social worker…no one. And you took on those crazy scary women you didn't even know." A picture of Terry was pretty clear in my mind, and I remembered Dianne in her lavender sweater set quietly stating her case. "My life is totally different because you stood up for me." I put my arm around her, giving her half a hug. She reached over and patted my thigh, and I tried not to cringe, but she noticed.

"It's nothing. Just pulled a muscle yesterday," I said, wondering which muscle I meant. A couple of minutes later, she said something else.

"Once I started seeing clearly, it's like I couldn't stop. Couldn't shut up, you know? I can't unsee it. I'm not willing to be scared by him again, or maybe when I get scared, I'm going to ask for help. For both *me* and my kids." It was like she'd just realized it. I breathed in quietly.

"I'm really glad. Makes it easier to think of you being brave," I said, grinning. "Your kids are lucky. You're an amazing mom." A couple of minutes later she turned the table.

"You know, Tay, I'm so proud of you I could pop. I wish you could meet Tommy, and Paula. I hope we keep in touch," she said, and then my eyes welled up a little. I hugged her again. "But what gave *you* the strength?" she asked. I started to think about it.

"Well, I guess it's complicated," I started. "Growing up I didn't really know anything else. It's weird to try to explain it 'cause I know how weird it sounds, but back then…well, when it started with Mom, I didn't know it was anything wrong…it was just how things were in my family. She didn't send me to school before I was about eight or so…at first, she told them I was home schooled, and they believed her. But once they knew Mom was working nights, so to speak…well it was clear I hadn't had any school at all. Until school…I had no idea every little boy didn't love his mama like I did.

"Then, when she kept 'loving me,' and I went to school she told me it was our secret and that I couldn't tell anyone. I think I realized maybe something was wrong. It wasn't like my body really reacted bad or anything. I got 'mini-erections,' I called them, but when a kid grows up loving his mama, sleeping and 'cuddling' with her every night…well, when she told me she loved me in special ways I believed her." I sat for a while looking at the water.

"I think I wanted so damned hard to believe her. By the time I was ten I was too embarrassed of her to bring people home. We were different. Mom didn't make meals or keep house. I did the dishes and laundry, changed Jenny's sheets, folded my blankets on the couch…most nights I looked after Jenny, put her to bed. I guess I liked being the 'big man.' If loving my mother wasn't a part of that, I didn't know any better. And by then, we were full-on sleeping together." I sighed a big sigh, and tears dripped slowly off my cheek.

"God, I can't believe how stupid I was. What the fuck? Why didn't I tell people I was being abused?" I wondered out loud.

"You were a child, Taylor! How could you know?" I shook my head.

"I didn't at first, but later, I knew what I did was wrong. You can't live in the city and watch TV and the internet without knowing what sex is. What's sexy. *And* what's acceptable. I'd seen stories about child sexual abuse on the news and heard about priests who'd hurt kids.

"I just didn't want to believe that my family was that fucked up. I told myself that loving within families…it was different." I was picking at a hole that was fraying on my jeans.

"Or maybe a part of me hadn't wanted it to end," I said, the deepest, darkest part of my shame. "I mean, by the time I was really sure it was wrong, I'd made Mom promise never to touch Jenny. And it *did* feel good, some of the time. I was maturing, and sometimes…well, I came. I never told anyone, but when my friends were bragging about conquests kissing a girl, or seeing a breast, I was pretty smug because I was already learning how to satisfy a woman. Or at least please my Mom. Fast or slow, however she wanted it.

"And really, when it's been happening all your life, when do you bring up that you think it's wrong? I couldn't," I finished. Then Dianne reminded me that I was there to talk about why I'd left, and I remembered the boyfriends.

"You know, whenever Mom had a steady boyfriend, she'd leave me alone. And a lot of the time I was glad, but sometimes…you know…I was a little jealous. So I'd act out, and they'd leave. Until Barry." I kicked another stone into the pond and startled something back into the water.

"Tell me about Barry, Tay. What was he like?" she asked.

"Barry was a fat, creepy asshole. I was 14 when he started making moves on Mom. It started out as dating, buying her cheap shit she liked, taking her for dinner. Sometimes she even brought us some food home, but he didn't know about us yet. Then later, he moved in, and was a fat slob. Mom worked nights. I swear, now that I think about it, he pimped her out, and he'd stay home and expect us to wait on him. I was terrified because of the way he looked at Jenny, so I never left her alone with him, and I'd stay in her room after she fell asleep.

"Of course, with Barry in Mom's room, I kinda had to sleep with Jenny. I usually slept with Mom or on the couch, but not after Barry moved in. And staying in Jenny's room also meant I wasn't alone with him, which just felt...smart.

"Once my voice changed and I started to fill out, Barry the Creep started to show an interest in me. He asked Mom to have sex with me in front of him at first. And once or twice I did, just to show him I knew how to treat her well." I started fidgeting, and Dianne distracted me with a bag of trail mix. I dug through the bag searching for the chocolate candies, my face burning, I took a drink from her water bottle. And then there was nothing else to do but tell her.

I'd never told anyone. Never said it out loud. And maybe hadn't really admitted to myself that it'd happened. My stomach hurt, and I was quiet so long that Dianne offered me an out.

"Remember, Tay, you only have to share what you want to," she said. I knew there wasn't any point holding it in any longer.

"Well, Fucking Asshole Barry got worse and worse, and wanted Mom to make me have a threesome with them. I told her I wouldn't let him touch me. It was bad enough letting him watch. I think she was a bit pissed that he wanted to...like maybe there were even limits for her of what was okay. Never knew if she didn't want to share me or didn't want to share him. Anyways, when she was out at night, he'd taunt me. Tell me if I didn't let him, he'd get Jenny involved instead. Shit like that.

"Then, one night, I came out of Jenny's room to get a glass of water, and Barry asked me to bring him one into Mom's bedroom. I did shit like that for him all the time, so I didn't think twice. But when I walked in the room, he wasn't in the bed.

"I stepped into the room and put the glass on the table next to the bed, thinking he was in the bathroom. Before I knew it, he had me from behind, pinning my arms, lifting my shirt, rubbing my chest. I struggled to get away, but I didn't want to yell and wake up Jenny. I just kept struggling while he licked my ears, and rubbed me from behind, with my arms pinned.

"Before I knew it, he had me face down on the bed, twisting one arm. God, I remember the sheets smelled so bad…like rancid BO. He held me by the neck while he pulled down his dirty underwear and my pyjamas. I was begging him to stop. Told him it would be more fun with Mom, but he knew I would never let him. I kept squirming until his heavy body was on top of me and then I just gave up.

"And he tore me nearly in two, forcing me. I just laid there, crying. God, Dianne, it hurt so much." She handed me a handkerchief – soft, delicate. I wiped my tears, but they kept on falling. I looked up into the trees, was amazed that the light was shining through the forest.

"When he was done, he laughed at me. Told me I'd get to like it. It was like a part of me…it was awful. I just got up and left his room. And died a little inside. It hurt! And my body was weird, I'd got hard like I was enjoying it. I went to the bathroom and barfed for like an hour, trying to scrub myself inside and out.

"I'm telling you, I've been wrecked by him. Hard wired fucking wrong now. After I cleaned up, I went back to Jenny's room, and he thought I was in there sleeping, but I was packing my duffle bag, using my phone as a flashlight. I took all my clothes, a couple of books, and my wallet, and Russet, and that picture of Jenny. I left Jenny a note with my phone number, and once I heard the bastard snoring, I left. I thought about sneaking into Mom's room to steal some money from her emergency stash but didn't want to risk waking him up.

"I knew I wasn't ever going to let him touch me again. I guess that's what gave me strength," I said. I probably wouldn't have called it rape before the retreat, but after hearing Padma and Ophelia, and the other women name their assaults so clearly, I knew I'd been raped. And I knew I wouldn't let it happen again.

"Ever," I emphasized. We sat for a few minutes, side by side, and she put her arm around me.

"Tay, you're amazing. You might have had a man's body, but you weren't even an adult and you got yourself out of there. I know you wish you hadn't left Jenny, but really…you had to save yourself. You'll get Jenny soon, I'm sure," she said, and I realized Dianne didn't even know Jenny was missing. I was surprised Phee hadn't told her. Maybe confidentiality really was a thing.

My insides were rotting, I felt so bad. Everyone had convinced me that the only thing to do was try and work with the police, but I knew if I'd stayed home, just been tougher, Jenny would be fine today. I tried hard to keep the bile down.

Dianne probably thought I was just being humble when I couldn't look at her, meet her eye.

Even though Dianne told me I was brave and strong and smart for leaving I didn't feel like it, and still don't. I felt stupid for taking him the water. And leaving Jenny alone after.

I decided after that night if people were going to abuse my body, I'd be in charge. Of who I slept with, how much they paid, and where and when we did it. Never in my car, for example, which was a gift from a regular customer.

And I'm not gay. At all.

Not even a little bit.

CHAPTER 23
WRAPPING THINGS UP

The. Last. Day. I'd made it.

And what was I doing? Practicing my scissor skills again. Picking through magazines and cutting out pictures. Checking the backs first to make sure there wasn't something better on the other side. Laughing with the women who I'd been with for a week, women who knew me better than anyone. Even, maybe especially, my mother.

We were collecting pictures. Things that meant something to us, things that we want to have around us. Dianne's pictures were of cottages, dining room tables with families around them, drives on the open road. Padma wanted to be surrounded by people she didn't know in a lecture hall, learning about science so she could be a doctor. Friends at the beach. And in one corner was a small picture of a bride in a beautiful sari, surrounded by family. Where did she find that photograph, eh?

And we acted like children. Laughing. Teasing. Free to just be with each other. Making art. Some of us beautifully – Ophelia took her photos and curled them to make jingles. She pinned them on her skirt like beautiful dancing regalia for an important powwow. Celebrating. It was pretty and she enjoyed the attention.

"Look at me. Powwow Princess!" I grinned at my new friend.

Terry put all her muscle car pictures into the shape of a motorcycle. Then she started adding pictures of birthday cakes, all lit up, and a beautiful garden, a mountain with a waterfall (those were popular –

what is it about waterfalls?) and the bike took shape. Jean was helping her, because no one else was. I liked that about Jean. Not afraid to be different.

I decided to join them. I was curious about Jean's photos. She wasn't gluing them to her poster board yet, so I leafed through them. She smiled over at me.

There were a few pictures of rooms that were…well, Bohemian? Draped curtains, lots of pillows, some sparkly things hanging. I couldn't see Jean in that space, which was intriguing. Maybe I don't know her after all. There was a theme I called "hanging on the back deck, barbecuing," but all the people looked kind of fake in those pictures. All the rest of the pictures were of cities. Lights. Noise. Cars. Those I totally understood. She had been wearing denim for the past five days, but she was not a woodsy woman.

She came up behind me and smiled at my sorting job. The pile of cityscapes was the biggest pile.

"Looks like you'll be happy to get back to the city," I said. "You must miss it."

"I do, but I'm glad I came. Got to know everyone here." She took her pictures one by one and started to line them up on the poster board like it was a shopping list. "Got to know you. I hope we can get together soon," she added. "I have to get your car back to you." She looked sheepish. "Sorry. I feel kind of weird about that. Just trying to help, though." She went on, lining up pictures in no order that I could see.

"Can I come by later today? I have something for you."

"Sure, we can figure things out," I answered. I didn't want to admit it, but I was going to miss these women. "I have to figure out how to get into Vancouver. I'm staying on at Kenny's for a bit." Jean's eyebrows raised when she looked over at me.

"Really? They think you staying on with these guys is going to help you?" She seemed a little outraged on my behalf, which was cute. "What's he in for, anyways?"

I looked at her sideways and decided to ignore the question.

"Yeah. Cook's gonna teach me some skills. Maybe I'll even be able to get a job in a kitchen!" I was happy and wanted her to know it. A few minutes later I went back to my own scissor work.

I worked hard at my collage. Dream board. Visioning exercise. Whatever you call it. I cut photos from an IKEA catalogue – I wanted to make a home. For Jenny. And I added some teddy bears. Stuffies, she'd called them. I thought about Russet, who I'd hidden in a drawer at Kenny's. It hurt too much to see Jenny's stuffed cat every day but hiding it didn't keep me from thinking about it. Or from hurting, for that matter.

And I had lots of pictures of food. I didn't want to have to explain to the group about Jenny. It made me cry to think about her, and I was still pretty raw with remembering Barry. And how Ophelia had come at me.

Then we shared about our hopes and dreams in circle. We talked about how we were more prepared to face the world now than we were the first day we got together. Some of the women wept with each other. I almost called them girls, but they are all women…I get it now why that's important. Another thing I learned.

We'd clarified our personal plans for dealing with our stuff and had built "Resource Banks" and "Strategy Lists" so that when we were out on our own, we could look at if things went sideways. I kept thinking about that, what I could do if it got bad.

My strategy list looked like "Call Kenny" and "Call Sally." Two people I hadn't even met a few days ago.

Anyways, I finally got a small sense that maybe with what Barry did all I *could* do was leave, and leave Jenny alone. Quite an ending. We reminded each other of how strong we are, and what it takes to be in control of our lives. Teaching us to be even more resilient, in case there's another time we need it. Kate and Rosie were smart.

After lunch everyone started to pack up, saying goodbyes. Some of the women were sobbing. Some, like Terry, were acting like nothing mattered. That was kinda me, too.

And I wondered if I'd ever had a time in my life when I *hadn't* expected good things to end.

I was glad I'd only be heading down the path to Kenny's. No packing, no real leaving…so I hauled suitcases and backpacks down the stairs and outside for the women. Gave Dianne a hug. Ophelia even said she was sorry again and looked sheepish.

"I just forgot that we're all doing the best we can, I guess," she said, shrugging her shoulders. I hugged her, reminded her she was off the hook. I'd figured out why I'd run, even if I wasn't totally okay with it.

Rosie and Kate joined us in the parking lot to remind us that we weren't saying goodbye forever – we'd come back every few weeks for an evening session, until we felt like we'd done enough.

And then, everyone was driving away…and I was walking back down that path to Kenny's with my poster and lists in my hand.

When I got into the trailer, I was alone. I dumped my poster under my bed and hoped Kenny wouldn't find it.

It seemed like I'd been here a lifetime. Every night, when I'd dropped into my dry, warm bed at Kenny's, I'd thought, *Well, that was amazing. Can't see how tomorrow will be better*, and then it was. Better.

Hard to believe that just yesterday I told someone about why I left for the first time. Named it out loud, at least to Dianne — rape. My big secret. And I heard her talk about her secrets, which somehow made mine seem less gruesome. Not worth hiding.

I'd survived, and I think even Marta will agree I gave it my all. I might even be a little better than I was.

I remembered that when I got here I said I just wanted to be fixed. Normal. Able to have a relationship that wasn't screwed up by my past. Normal sex, without cringing or flinching or lashing out.

Nothing's changed. I still want that more than anything.

But what I really *really* want is to get Jenny back. And I'll work with the cops to make it happen. I'm sure everyone around here'll be okay with it, right?

Because I'm all Jenny has. And family sticks together.

The other good news is I'm not going back to living in my car. Which right now I don't even have.

I lay on my bed to rest. I'd exchanged numbers and emails with some people, except I don't have a computer, so I told them not to count on me. My phone is so old and decrepit it only holds a charge for a few minutes. So I'm kinda tethered to the plug, and don't really want to hold up the line talking to other people in case Jenny calls. But I can text.

"See you in two weeks," everyone had called out as car doors slammed and suitcases were loaded. Dianne was so excited to see Tommy and Paula at her sister's. They were planning to move into a new apartment soon.

Padma was moving in with a cousin a couple of towns over and was going to try to get her auntie to talk to the one brother who seemed to be at least mostly human. Not that I think just because people have different cultures they are sub-human. But really…Padma was not to blame for her attack. I knew she really missed her family, but I didn't understand how she could miss people who'd kicked her out.

Or maybe I'd never had family like that.

Maybe I never would. But I wanted to be family for Jenny, more than ever.

Ten minutes later, there was a knock on the front door. And there was Jean, all gussied up for the road. I thought we'd said our goodbyes. Some loaded looks across the parking lot.

"I just stopped by to give you something. I hope it's okay," she said, and reached out her hand through the door.

"I'm sorry. Kenny's not here, so I can't really invite you in," I said, realizing I wasn't sure of the rules but knew I wouldn't be comfortable if Kenny came back and we were…making out or whatever.

"You sure? Just for a minute?" She was looking over my shoulder. *Oh, what the hell,* I thought, and moved aside.

She came in the front door, clearly checking the place out.

"It's nice, eh? For a couple of guys? Bet you thought it'd be a mess," I said. I reached for her hand, squeezed it. "I don't know when he's coming back, though, so…it's not really like it's my place." I felt stupid.

"It's okay. I can't stay. But I wanted to leave you this so we can connect. I know your phone doesn't work really well, and I had this spare one," she said as she handed me a smart phone. Not the newest model, but tons newer than mine (that wasn't smart at all). "I've already programmed my number into it," she said, as she handed over the bag with the accessories.

I actually didn't know what to say. It was sweet of her. And complicated.

I can't afford to pay for a phone. Talk or data.

And I felt just a little bit like I did the first time that pimp tried to buy me over to his stable.

I must have looked confused, because she reassured me.

"Really, Taylor. No strings. It's an old one I had lying around in my car. It's paid for this month, so you might as well use it. Just accept it, okay?" she said, reaching up and touching my cheek. I blushed and bent down to give her a quick peck.

"I'll call next week. We can go out for dinner." And then, she was heading down the stairs. She looked back over her shoulder and smiled at me.

"Or maybe we can stay in," she said.

I smiled, ignoring my gut, but appreciating her tight jeans.

So, is this what a *normal* relationship looks like?

CHAPTER 24
POLICE! – PATTY AND ALYSSA

Patty watched Inspector Derksen duck his head when he entered the "room at the bottom of the stairs" in the detachment. *Why does he always do that? He's not that tall.* She couldn't watch people without asking why, wanting to understand behaviours, patterns, motives. This time, she caught herself. *I have to get into costume, into character,* she refocused. *Ten minutes.*

"Sir. Alyssa is just getting in from school." Her tone said, "Kinda busy here," and he nodded. He crouched over and approached Neil, his brow knit, and head tilted in that universal question, *What's happening?*

"No worries, Inspector. Getting ready to go online, and in case there are photos to be shared, she's getting ready." Gone was Patty's pink and blue hair, and in its place were shoulder-length, dirty-blond braids. She wore a loose, black, Carly Rae Jepsen T-shirt over baggy jeans and sneakers. Mark smiled.

"You didn't recognize me," she said in a little girl voice.

"You just lost 10 years. 15 maybe. Nice touch, wearing Carly's T-shirt. She's still loved in her hometown." Patty smiled and went back to work on the computer. Arun was across from her giving her signals, and they were clearly texting back and forth. The cave was dressed up to look like a teenager's bedroom. Posters, and a bookshelf. Everything looked big, though. Neil signalled Mark to follow him upstairs.

"They aren't on audio chat yet, but could be soon, and we never know when he'll want to go to webcam, so we visited the thrift store and got some clothes and stuff for 'Alyssa' to wear," he whispered, heading upstairs. It was mid-afternoon, and Patty had been text chatting with the suspect for a few days. They were close to asking for a warrant to get his address and other details from the ISP, internet service provider. Arun recorded the live conversations in the hopes that he'd pick up ambient sound from the neighbourhood to help them narrow down a location.

"Thanks for making sure I didn't blow it," Mark said as they entered the empty meeting room. Mark wanted to make sure before he left for the weekend that this crew had everything they needed. The cyber team were putting in lots of hours – taking breaks only during "school hours" and overnight when "Alyssa" would be unavailable online.

"We're learning lots having you here. Anything you need this weekend? I'm presuming we are still days from actually moving in on this guy?"

"Yeah, unfortunately. Probably a few. We'll connect with him tonight. Alyssa is going to be a little more available over the weekend. The main goal is getting him to admit what he wants from her. We've got a warrant to cover recording that. If he says that he wants her to take off her clothes, we can get a warrant to compel the ISP to give up the client's address. Hopefully they do that quickly, and we'll be out of your hair soon, with a small head of this hydra killed off." Mark smiled at the young man across from him. Neil had a way of sharing just the important details, but Mark knew it was a lot more complicated than this. "If we're lucky, he'll implicate others. Or his computer will."

"Okay, but let me know if you need anything. I checked in with the social worker today about Jenny, Taylor's sister. They haven't heard from her and when we sent a car around to check out the aunt's place, it was vacated. It was clear, though, that something internet-related had been going on. Lots of coaxial cable, and electrical infrastructure way beyond what I'd expect for apartment living. These folks didn't want to be shut down by a power failure.

"We did find a blanket that the social worker thought was Jenny's, which sucks. And it doesn't look like they left in a hurry. Things were packed up and moved out. Maybe they got better digs. But Jenny doesn't have the blanket." Neil shook his head, and showed Mark a photo of the blanket on a dirty mattress on the floor.

"I'm not sure if it's them who has Jenny, but sonovabitch, if it isn't, we could ask the team to stay and help find her," Neil said without thinking. Realizing that what he offered was out of line, he tagged on, "if you thought it could help." Mark chuckled.

"I don't want to get too far ahead of ourselves. Let's work with what we learn today, and you and ICE are keeping us up to date. I just wanted to let you know what I learned. I'll tell the Watch Commanders to keep you informed this weekend if anything else comes in. And you've got my number if you need me." As Neil started to walk away, Mark stopped him.

"Everything behind Patty looked kind of big downstairs. What's that about?"

"Well, we've learned that if we blow things up a bit, Patty looks smaller on camera. It's just another subtle way to have him think she's younger than she is. Makeup. Smoke and mirrors. But with simple stuff that little girls like," he finished.

"Thanks." Mark released him and watched the gangly young man head downstairs. *They really have thought of everything*, Mark thought as he stopped by the Watch Commanders' office.

Back downstairs, Neil could see by the look on Arun's face that things were going well.

"Well, I'm home a bit now, but then I'm going to Girl Guides. They let me in a year early," Alyssa was saying. "Then I'm going to my dad's and I'll be home Sunday," she said. A disembodied voice came through the speaker.

"That's great Alyssa. I'll be able to take your photos then. You are going to be a big star!" There was a knock on a door in the background.

They hadn't progressed to webcams yet, but Patty heard the knock clearly, and so did Arun.

"Who's there? Do you have to go?" Alyssa asked.

"Don't worry, just a second." They heard him get up and walk across the room. The door opened, and they heard him shush whoever was behind the door. A small voice could be heard asking something about dinner. Then the little girl's voice got louder.

"But I'm hungry now and I don't want to wait!" The man could be heard whispering again. Then she got louder.

"My NAME IS JENNY. And if you don't feed me I won't...." and the door slammed. Neil saw a text move between Arun and Patty. They waited a minute or two and then Patty started talking to the computer.

"Hey, are you coming back? Maybe I should just forget about this. Who's Jenny, anyhow? You told me you didn't have any models you were photographing right now," and then Patty took a break. She started all over again with the same words a minute later. And a minute after that.

The fourth time she said it, she heard the door open.

"Oh, Alyssa. I'm sorry you had to hear that. Polly is a neighbourhood girl we're babysitting tonight. She's too young to do photography. You heard her, she's immature." The man paused.

"Are you sure? I thought she said her name was Penny or something. Anyhow, I have to go soon. And you have to get her dinner," Patty said, trying hard to make Alyssa sound defiant. She wanted this guy to squirm. Instead he chuckled.

"Ha ha. You know little girls. Her name is Polly, but she's been playing a make-believe game all afternoon with my girlfriend. She's just being silly, calling herself Penny." Arun and Patty's eyes locked over the computer. This guy was swift. She had *definitely* said Jenny, but Patty had planted a seed, and this guy had flown with it.

"Anyways, my girlfriend is feeding her. She just wanted me to eat dinner with them. I'll go soon. Right now, you're more important! You're worth waiting to eat! And you can call me Todd, remember?"

"Well, okay then. What time Sunday should I be ready for you to take my pictures?" Alyssa asked.

"I'll be ready by four o'clock, so any time after that I'll be looking for you. What will you wear? Remember, white shirts don't work very well. And crop tops are really good. Maybe with shorts?"

"I don't have shorts yet. It's not summer. But I have some skirts, if that works," Alyssa said. "And a cute crop top that's got lace on it. Maybe I'll wear that," she continued.

"That sounds great! How short is the skirt? The people funding the photo shoot will want to see your legs," Todd reminded her. Alyssa agreed, asking about how she should do her hair, and if she should use makeup.

"I'll have to borrow it from my sister, but I think it'd be okay," she said.

"A little make up would be okay, but really the clean look is in right now," Todd continued. "I know it's awkward to ask, but do you have a bra? You should wear something pretty if you have nice underwear. It'll help you feel pretty, and then you will glow!" Patty kept up the enthusiasm even though she wanted to launch through the computer and strangle the guy.

A few minutes later, plans complete, Patty hoped she'd sounded sufficiently excited, and Neil called her on cue.

"Alyssa! Supper time!" he called from up the stairs.

A few minutes later, the team was ordering pizza and analyzing what had happened. They were pretty sure that with the tape they could get a warrant, based on the danger Jenny was in, and the comment about the "underwear" but they weren't sure.

Arun was going over the tape, slowing it down and listening for background noises. At one point there was a train whistle, but everywhere in Mission heard the trains. When the door had opened to Jenny, though, there was definite background noise.

"I think that's machinery. Big industrial stuff. I'll check the database of sounds, but it sounds like trucks, and some kind of bigger machine. Like a backhoe or some other diesel engine digging in rocks." For the next few hours, they listened, and created a minute-by-minute transcript of the call, with all the background noise.

Patty held her head in her hand, nausea rising in her throat. Just thinking about Todd with Jenny made her skin crawl.

"It's getting harder and harder to work with these creeps," Patty admitted. Neil tapped his pen on the table.

"I know. Hearing Jenny was hard. She sounded so young," he agreed.

"And way, *waaay* too old, too," Patty added. "I think I'm gonna need to take a break after this one," she said. "I'm getting too jaded. I look at every guy on the street, in a restaurant, and wonder if he's a creeper. And I'm getting…I'm having trouble sleeping sometimes. I always feel like we should be doing more." They didn't look at each other, shuffled papers around and eventually the intensity broke.

"You're okay to finish this one, though, right?" Neil asked. Patty nodded and headed for the back room to change.

They weren't going to wait into the weekend to try for a warrant.

As much as they wanted to put Todd away for a long time, and hopefully find who had distributed the photos and videos, they were really driven by the little girl's emphatic voice they kept playing over and over again.

"My NAME IS JENNY. And if you don't feed me, I won't…." They wondered if Taylor could identify his sister.

And if it would be on the level to get him involved at this point.

JENNY

Jenny clambered up the bed towards the darkened corner of the room when Todd kicked the bedroom door open.

"WHO THE HELL DO YOU THINK YOU ARE?" he shouted at her, reaching for her ankle as she scrambled away from him. Jenny whimpered, kicking at him, trying to get him to let go of her leg.

"DON'T YOU FUCKING DARE, YOU LITTLE BITCH," he screamed. "I TOLD YOU NOT TO BUG ME WHEN I'M ON THE COMPUTER." Todd let go of Jenny's foot, and she rolled further away from him, grabbing her pyjamas and tucking them under her feet. She whimpered into her hands, wiping at the stray tear that tracked down her dirty cheek.

"DON'T YOU TRY TO GET OUT OF IT, YOU LITTLE WHORE," Todd screamed. "YOU ARE TOO MUCH FUCKING TROUBLE." Jenny bundled herself tighter into a ball and dared to answer him.

"But I was hungry," she whispered.

"YOU'RE FUCKING HUNGRY? I'LL GIVE YOU HUNGRY!" Todd stormed out of the room, slammed the door, and Jenny got even quieter, hoping to disappear into the space that gave her nowhere to hide. She wished she had a blanket to curl into.

Ten minutes later, the door banged open again, and Jenny started to apologize.

"I'm sorry. I forgot. I won't…." she stuttered. Todd grabbed her, shouted to his wife for help.

"GET THE FUCK IN HERE AND HOLD HER DOWN!" he screamed. Then his voice got quiet, which made Jenny tremble.

"I am so done with you, you little bitch. I will teach you a lesson you will never forget. You want hungry? I'll get you hungry," he said, holding up a syringe. His wife rushed into the room.

"Oh dear. You don't want to share that with her, do you? She's not really worth it," she said, shuffling around the bed, straightening the dirty sheet with her palms. "I can put her to bed, dear. Just give us a few minutes," she fussed.

"DON'T YOU FUCKING TELL ME WHAT TO DO. THIS LITTLE BITCH NEEDS A LESSON," he shouted. "I told you to hold her." Todd reached across the bed, grabbed Jenny again and pulled her towards him. As he did, her nightgown lifted over her hips and she panicked, trying to pull it down again. Todd slapped her hands away.

"Don't even try," he threatened through clenched teeth. His wife patted Jenny's arm.

"It's alright, dear. I told you to cooperate. Settle down. Just relax. This won't hurt," the older woman said, trying to calm down her young charge. "It's okay, honey. Over in a minute."

Jenny was trembling, fighting to be still, avoiding Todd's meaty hands as she again tried to roll away from him.

"HOLD HER!" he screamed, grabbing her arm.

"Her foot might work better," his wife fussed.

"SHUT UP. YOU THINK I DON'T KNOW WHAT I'M DOING?" He grabbed Jenny's arm and twisted her wrist.

"Don't, please. Don't. I'll be good. No...." Jenny's eyes were filled with terror, unable to look away from the small syringe in Todd's fist. He slapped her arm, trying to raise a vein, unable to see clearly on her small, pale forearm. She tried to pull her hand away, unable to stop resisting. Todd's wife got behind Jenny, steadying her arm for her husband.

"Hush, it's okay. This will help you sleep," she explained to the terrified girl.

"I know what it is," Jenny whispered through clenched teeth. "My Mama.... Make him stop," she begged the woman who had both restrained her and tried to comfort her in the same moment. "Please...." she said, her voice trailing off, her eyes pleading, looking into the woman's.

"It'll be okay," she said, holding Jenny's face to her chest, trying to keep her from looking at what was happening to her. "Just breathe. It'll be done in a moment," she said. Todd stabbed the syringe into her thigh, no longer looking for a vein.

And then it was done. Jenny was sobbing into her elbow, hiding as the heat slowly coursed through her veins, caught her attention, and released her from her captors for the first time.

This is okay, she thought, climbing to the floor between the bed and the wall as she began to nod, feeling a deep warmth and security for the first time in months.

I get why Mama likes this.

CHAPTER 25
COFFEE AND PHONE CALLS

"Come have some coffee. Sit a bit. Humour an old man," Cook said as I added water to the potato pot. Dinner was a ways off, but I wanted to get stuff ready early, save the rush later.

"Just want to get them in water. I'll be with you in two potatoes," I joked. I noticed Cook was moving slowly as he lowered his body into the chair under the window.

"You fail to realize you've entered my domain. What I say goes," he admonished me. I wasn't sure if he was being serious, so I snuck a glance. Truth is, you can never tell with the guys who live here. Half the time they tried to push me around, but I assume they're teasing. The gleam in Cook's eye told me he definitely was.

"Yes, Sir!" I answered. I was thinking about the first couple of days I'd worked at the half-way house. It was weird being a part of the prison system, and it had irked me a little that I couldn't tell who was staff and who was "resident," which is what they called the inmates. Residents. I wouldn't ask, though – Kenny had warned me about not inquiring with anyone about their charges, or sentences.

"I wouldn't ask you about your sexual partners. Think of it the same – deeply personal. And if, at some point, someone wants to share with you, feel very privileged," he'd said over tea the night before I'd started working with Cook. "And decide for yourself how much you believe," he'd finished. That had got to me. And he'd explained that I'd be treated like a "fish," what they called newbies in the prison.

"Because they walk around with their mouths open, looking like a fish," he'd explained. I'd been trying to keep my mouth shut.

I noticed lots of other things, too. Like how *Tide's End* had beautiful wood glowing, carpets designed like artwork, but this space seemed just functional. Unfinished plywood in places, definitely used furniture. I wondered about that. Something else to ask Kenny about. Didn't they care about these guys, too? Or weren't they allowed to make this place beautiful like the retreat centre?

People came and went at all times of the day or night – planting gardens, looking after horses, working at jobs off-site, and working at the facility too, cooking, cleaning, looking after stuff. And people didn't get in each other's faces. Somehow, I'd expected more drama. It was hard to find any even when I was looking for it.

I pulled up a chair and brought my coffee to the table. Cook smiled over at me, and pointed out the window at Kenny, who was tending a big garden. He looked up, waved, and headed in the direction of our trailer.

"That'll be delicious in a few weeks. Lettuce. Radishes. Some herbs," Cook said.

Maybe one day I'd help him in the dirt, but I was loving the kitchen. A couple of minutes later, Sally appeared out of nowhere, a cup of tea in her hands.

"Well, hello, Beautiful," Cook said, and I tried not to look away.

"Oh, stop it." Sally swatted Cook's hand as she sat down beside him. "Have you talked to him yet?" she asked, looking at me. I admit, my eyeballs must have bulged, and I started to sweat. Was I in trouble?

"Nope. Just about to start. He got all defiant and finished the potatoes."

"Did I do something wrong?" I asked. My feet started shuffling under my chair. I hoped my sweat didn't stain my shirt. I didn't look anywhere near them.

Cook put his hand on mine. "Son, it's nothing you've done. It's all good. It's what you're *going* to do. We're gonna figure out your superpower in the kitchen the next few days," he said. What? My "superpower?" I didn't mind peeling potatoes, but "superpower?"

"Got nothin' for yah," I said, again not looking up. My coffee was getting low in my cup, but it had me riveted. Cook chuckled.

"Son, we're gonna figure it out together. I want you to pay attention to what seems easy, what you really like to do. It might be bakin'. Making desserts. Cookin' soup. Putting together a fancy dinner. Makin' comfort food," he said. "Everyone got a superpower. Beth's is bakin' scones. Mine is soup. Kenny makes a mean salad, but you'd never hear him say it. Sally can organize like nobody's business. She orders, an' keeps spreadsheets an' makes sure we don't go over our budget. Everybody's good at something!" He took a swig of coffee.

"Just pay attention," Sally said. "No pressure, 'kay? You're doin' great. Cook is actually taking breaks, and he hasn't grumbled about the help yet. Which is miraculous — he always grumbles about the help. We'll let you know if we need things done differently," she said.

"What's comfort food?" I asked. I loved the meals here, and at *Tide's End*. But I didn't know the definition of "comfort food."

"I think it might be different for everybody. What food makes you feel loved? Cared for? Helps you remember happier times?" Sally asked. Something else to think about. I thought about the cheap pouches of soup and boxes of macaroni I'd made for Jenny on the nights my mom didn't come home. And I think it may have made me feel good only because Jenny was happier when I fed her. Hungry sucked big time.

I didn't answer, though, because Kenny came flying in the back door, with my phone in his hand.

"She called! I answered!" he said, rushing towards us. "Jenny called. I was walking in the door and I heard your phone. I busted into your room and answered. God. I didn't even think about it. I hope that's okay," he said, looking a little embarrassed. He held out the phone for me.

"I told her I'd bring you the phone. She said she'd call back if she could. And I told her lots of us were looking for her, to try and help her. I didn't mention the police," he said, rushing his words. I was stunned. Might have even had my mouth open.

"She sounded scared, but okay, Taylor. She really did. And she said she was glad to talk to me. 'Now I know the phone works, and that Tay's okay,' she said." He looked down. "Maybe she sounded a bit sad," he admitted.

I grabbed the phone from Kenny. Unfortunately, the call number didn't show. I wished I had a different phone, one that automatically recorded that stuff. In fact, the phone I got from Jean had told me she'd called yesterday. I hadn't answered while I was at work.

"Oh my God," I burst out, and almost started to cry. Sally put her arm around me.

"I'm okay. I'm just so relieved she's still okay…alive, I guess," I mumbled. I hadn't realized how afraid for her I was. Sally stuck her head out the door.

"Tom! Find Nora and Beth. We need them in here. Pronto!" she shouted to the fellow in the Sacred Grounds, across the fence. He took off, loping across the field. I held the phone in my hand like a precious thing. Cook put his hand on my arm and looked me right in the eye.

"I get you're worried" he said, and I nodded a bit as tears pooled.

"The cops are helping but they aren't doing enough," I said. "They think she might be in a kid cyberporn thing. First, they said a relative took her. The social worker told the police that it was an uncle that took her from the foster home, but we got no uncles."

A few minutes later, I was still cradling the phone. Beth and Nora had come in, and Sally was catching them up on what had happened. Cook was shuffling around in the kitchen, putting the potatoes on to boil, and the chicken legs in the oven to bake for dinner.

"The rest can wait," he said. Kenny had pried the charger out of my hand and plugged it into the wall. Damn! If only the battery worked, I could have had the phone with me. I hadn't been ready to get Cook and Sally all involved in my problems, and now I'd gone and missed my sister's call. In minutes Kenny was making me tea, and Nora was calling the cops to let them know that Jenny had made contact.

We relocated to Nora's office, so that if Jenny called again I'd have some privacy and a plug for the phone. Neil had arrived from the police station with a brand-new smart phone for me to use and was arguing with the phone company that he wanted the number transferred to this phone.

"No, there is no SIM card. The phone is *that* old. Get it transferred to this phone." He covered the receiver and looked over at me.

"My version of 'Don't make me come down there,'" he said, and smiled. I couldn't laugh back. He was quiet for a couple of minutes, tapping his pen on the desk, waiting to be transferred to "someone who can help me," as he'd made clear. I was trying to distract myself by wondering if I should be in awe or terrified that the police seemed to be able to do whatever they needed to with my cell phone number.

"Just a second. He's right here." A moment later I was on the phone with them, guessing my account passwords, and telling them I was okay with it. I asked if I could transfer the phone number back later. I knew I couldn't afford this expensive phone. Neil started nodding his head back and forth frantically. I put my hand over the bottom of the phone, not sure where the mic was.

"Are you going to pay for this phone after? Because I can't," I said. Neil assured me he'd work something out. I decided to go along with it because I needed a new phone anyways – the old one sucked.

A few minutes later we hung up, and Neil reassured me they'd "make it okay" once they were done with me and Jenny. It was so weird to me that the men at *Just Living* were helping me *and* the police.

A moment later, the fancy phone rang, and my heart started to pound. I answered but it was only Arun from downtown, checking to see if the number worked yet.

"This is the number Jenny has, so it's working. I can trace any calls that come in. Thanks for letting us do this, Taylor." I couldn't believe how quickly everything was moving along. But it was late, and I was tired and starving and I really hoped Jenny was in bed, sleeping, dreaming about school tomorrow. I kept the phone on me though.

Sally stuck her head in the door.

"Come back when you can, Taylor. I've saved dinner for you," she said.

Sitting in the kitchen at the little table, eating an enormous plate of mashed potatoes with melted cheese, baked chicken legs, and a huge salad, I started to imagine that this could be *my* comfort food. If only I was sharing it with Jenny. If only Jenny would call back.

Inspector Derksen walked in with a fancy, clear plastic bag full of stuff for my phone – a headset, and charger, a manual and stuff. I stood up when he came towards me – my mom taught me manners. And the Inspector of the local police station was someone to be respected. Or feared. Either way, until Jenny was back, I would stand when he came into the room.

He sat down across from me and smiled.

"Really, Taylor, eat. This has been quite a day!" And he told me about the phone – that it was a special one police use, but he'd be sure to replace it when they needed it back.

"I can get you a year's coverage, with a phone as nice as this. As long as you don't want too much talk or data!" he laughed. I couldn't believe it.

Then he went on to remind me not to lose hope. He told me about a "possible encounter" they'd had with Jenny on a web chat. "She seemed quite feisty. I won't try to convince you she's okay, because I don't really know, but she wasn't taking any guff from the man on the web chat. If it was her.

"I have a recording of the conversation. Would you listen to it and let us know if you recognize her voice?" he asked. Would I? Try to stop me!

He pulled out his phone and started a recording. And it was her! I'm almost 100% sure – I told him 85%, because it's been a long time since I've heard her, but I think it was her! She did sound feisty. I was glad she was sticking up for herself, getting food when she was hungry. She'd grown up a lot since I'd last talked to her.

Then he showed me a picture taken at the last place they had on record for her.

"Is this her blanket?" he asked. I teared up. There, tied, dumped in the corner, was the pink baby blanket Mom had brought her home. "Do you know why she still carried it with her?" I sniffed.

"Yeah. She wrapped her stuffed cat around in it. The last time I saw her she gave me her cat. It's in my room. And she told me she'd keep the blanket until we were together again, and she could wrap Russet in it again." I noticed tears pooling in Sally's eyes, and Cook headed to the pantry for some cookies. I heard him blow his nose in there, which set me off as well.

A few minutes later, Inspector Derksen'd gone over all the features of the phone with me and reminded me that any conversations I had on the phone would be overheard by law enforcement.

"I won't let anything be used in other cases. I just want you to remember that." He stuck a small RCMP sticker onto the face of the phone. "This is to remind you. I don't want you getting into trouble for anything just because you're helping us," he said. Maybe this guy was okay.

I was glad I'd broken it off with my old clients when I decided to try to get custody of Jenny. I knew I couldn't be doing that shit with my little sister and Social Services around. So far, I didn't think any had called me, but if I heard from them, I'd shut them down.

A few minutes later, everyone was sitting around the table in the dining room, sharing warm apple pie and ice cream. I was starting to feel stuffed, and tired. I didn't know if I'd sleep a wink tonight, though.

I kept the new phone on the table in front of me, hoping it would ring and hoping it wouldn't.

Neil had told me the only thing I had to do if Jenny called was keep her on the line if possible. I wasn't to mention police, just be her big brother.

I'd decided, though, that I was going to try to figure out where she was. She had to have noticed something about where she was living, right?

Fuck. I really needed to get it together. I had to.

I wanted to be the best big brother around.

I decided I had to go looking for her. Enough of this shit.

CHAPTER 26
PLANTING SEEDS.
GROWING FUTURES.

Three days later I was sitting in my bedroom at Kenny's, pretending to think about cooking, and figuring out my "superpower." Truth? I was a little obsessed with how much the "right amount" of cologne was, and how my jeans – washed, but really old – looked on my butt. I had plans to go to town with Jean that evening, and while I wasn't totally sure what she meant by "get together," I wanted to be prepared. Kenny and I had laughed about whether "picking up my car" was a new frame for "getting lucky," but anyhow, he'd told me to use his scent. I found the least offensive one and I'd tried to figure out how much to apply. It wasn't like when I was on the street, trying to cover up my skankiness, and attract the attention of the passing men.

And I'd decided to drive around the Downtown East Side, look for my mom and my sister. She was probably closer to me, but maybe my mom knew something about relatives in the Valley where Jenny'd been sent. I planned to spend some time searching once I had my car back.

I was doing some kitchen planning for later in the week and figuring out my superpower. First step, according to Sally, was thinking about food. I had lots of practice conjuring meals — but I realized that this was different from what I'd done as a child. It was like dreaming — fun, even — when you had lots of ingredients available, and there wasn't an ache in your belly. Or your sister's.

Kenny and I were hosting a dinner party for Beth's birthday in a few days, and it was kinda like my coming out – I was pretending to be a foodie. God. Pretentious much? Kenny and Nora had invited some people, told me to plan to cook for ten. I had to make sure it was perfect.

And whether the cologne for tonight was too much. Maybe I would have time for another shower before Jean came to get me. Had I overdone it?

Back to planning for dinner. I was trying to figure out how to keep all the guests happy. "Don't. Just don't," Sally had told me. "Pick one or two people and cook for them. The rest will feel the love…and enjoy the food." So, I'd decided to focus on Beth and Ben, even though I didn't know their favourites.

Were the bruises on my leg totally healed? I'd gone from literally black and blue to shades of green and yellow. I hoped it wasn't noticeable any more, because I knew Jean hadn't meant to hurt me that day on the bench. She'd just been giving me a covert squeeze. Not her fault I was such a wuss.

Focus on Beth. I knew she worked incredibly hard for *Just Living* and *Tide's End*, running programs, finding work for the men off-site, inviting youth from the Friendship Centre up to do sweats and other ceremonies with the Aboriginal Brotherhood and about a million other things.

The menu planning…the shopping list…it was all feeling a bit like a test. And a little like an adventure. Like tonight with Jean.

"Let me come get you so you can pick up your car," Jean had said. "We can have dinner together if you want." I definitely wanted. It was embarrassing to admit, but a few nights this last week I'd gone to sleep, and woken up, wondering about what Jean looked like under her fancy denim. And once, I'd even dreamed up the taste of her. She was the first woman I daydreamed about. Late bloomer?

Tomorrow, I'd pull up some recipes on Kenny's computer and work with Cook and Sally to figure out my shopping list.

Did I have a longer T-shirt that would cover the holes in the butt of my pants? Lots to think about. Including my "date with Jean" jitters.

I'd have to ask permission from Kenny to fire up his ancient computer…and go on the internet. I didn't understand all the regulations around here, but I knew enough to not presume going online was okay.

Ten minutes later, I was scanning Kenny's cookbooks, thinking about casseroles with vegetables and light sauce…and had I brushed my teeth? Did my breath smell okay? Then there was a knock at the front door.

Was Jean early? Do I answer it? I was *not* going to ask her in. That would be too awkward, her wanting to neck, me wanting to get out of the trailer, because, well…not my house. Or her security level. And then I heard a voice.

"Taylor? You in there? It's Beth. Do you have a few minutes?"

All kinds of alarm bells rang in my gut, but honestly, I had no reason to say no. It was still about an hour before I expected Jean at the parking lot at *Tide's End*, so I opened the door.

"Hi Beth. Kenny's not here." I hoped her visit wasn't about me.

"Well, that's okay, because it's you I want to talk to." Dreaded words. I invited her in, and we sat at the counter. I didn't even think to offer her a glass of water, because, well, the only thing worse than getting bad news is waiting for it.

"Taylor, some of the guys, including Kenny and Cook, have been raving about you, and talking about how helping you feels…well, good to them. Like they have a chance to make a difference. How are you finding things?" I think my mouth dropped open. Really? She was checking how *I* liked things? My eyes darted around the trailer, trying to think of one thing to say that was honest without being totally gush.

"Are you kidding? Coming here is the best thing that's happened to me. Really. Like, in my life. I love it here, and Kenny's been great. Has he had enough of me?" My voice squeaked.

I knew there had to be a problem following good news. I'd gotten used to the "shit sandwiches" that foster care parents and social workers usually delivered.

"If you have bad news, remember to start with something nice, and end with something positive, too." They all did it. I prepared for the shit next.

"Taylor, having you here has pushed a neat project forward. I've been working on it for a year off the side of my desk. Now it's getting real, and I wanted to run some ideas by you," she said. I squirmed. Looked over her shoulder, under the table, anywhere but at her. I wanted to make this as easy for her as possible, because, heck, they'd already done more than anyone needed to.

"I get it if you need me to push off now," I said. Beth looked up at me, startled.

"Um…no. Not that at all, Tay. I need your help with something." She looked down at some papers in her hands. "Something I hope helps you, and Kenny and Cook, too.

"I've been trying to put together a plan for a new place in downtown Mission. The soup kitchen there closed years ago, and lots of people still struggle for food, especially younger people and families. Kenny and Cook have wanted to open a 'pay as you can' food place down there for a while, but the funding is…well, it's hard." I breathed deeply, the scent of my cologne distracting.

"A while ago, the college in town that trains chefs talked to me. They want a live commercial kitchen to run their students through, one that feeds paying customers. Cook wants to work with the students and thinks you could help. He thinks you could help him connect with the younger folks — maybe some street kids. At first, we'll invite them to come and eat, but if they want, they'll be able to learn to cook there, too." I glanced at the clock on the stove, and my leg started to bounce up and down.

"Kenny wants to get more parolees involved in growing stuff to support the project and he keeps planting more of the fields for veg. Only the horses seem concerned about more gardens, but I think they're just curious. They already have lots of space." She smiled, and I presumed she was trying to joke, so I smiled, too. Still expecting a thud from a different shoe.

"Are you interested? At first, you'd get training and certification in food prep, but your help with the project would pay for your training and your room and board here, even a little fun money. Eventually you could work there if it takes off." She looked over at me, and my face must have been blank. "Or not." She paused.

"If you decided to, after your training you could move back to the city and get a job there. No pressure." She snuck a sideways glance at me and laughed.

"Really Taylor," she giggled, "It's all good. Honest. No problems."

"Holy fuck," I said, and then blushed. "Would I be interested? Um... hell, yes...oops, sorry." I blushed.

This was more than I could have imagined. *This* could be a way to train so I could get Jenny back. Hallelujah. Things just kept getting better. And the day wasn't over yet....

I just hoped I could trust it all, that maybe I'd find her downtown.

We made plans to talk at the dinner I was going to cook. (She confirmed she loves salmon, so a nice light casserole was in her future.) I thanked her again at the door while I hurried her out.

I had a ton to think about. Including figuring out if I had to shower to maximize the potential for the rest of the evening.

Beth turned on the steps on the way out and called out to me.

"You smell great, Taylor. Honest. Whoever they are, they're lucky," she said, and I started to sweat just a little bit more. I waved and blushed again.

CHAPTER 27
MINIMUM WAGE –
DIANNE AND TOMMY

As the bathroom door quietly clicked and locked, Dianne turned and started the shower. She peeled her sweaty, black socks off. The throbbing in her feet intensified and she started to sob. Her feet were swollen, a deep ridge above her ankle from those socks, a part of the polyester uniform that came with the job she'd taken last week. She grabbed a towel to wipe her tears, then rubbed her feet. Sitting so she didn't fall over, she started peeling off her stinking clothes. She tossed them outside the bathroom door, not wanting to share another minute with them. She'd have to remember to wash them before she headed to bed, so she could put the damned things on again in the morning. She couldn't remember ever being this defeated.

In the shower, she scrubbed away the smell of grease, and grabbed the back wall to let the warm water pound her body. Her head hung. Her sobs grew, and she wondered, for the thousandth time if she'd made a huge mistake tearing her kids from their home and running from what had been their life. Her bruises had healed, but her heart and her wallet kept hemorrhaging. Damn! She wanted to rent her own space, but everything was so hard!

The water started to cool at the same time as her body lost the energy for more tears. There was a knock at the door, and she could barely hear the whisper over the water.

"Mom? You okay?" It was Tommy. "I got Paula to sleep for you." She grabbed a towel and turned off the taps. She was afraid to speak just yet, not sure how her voice would sound. Tommy knew her way too well.

"Mom? Sandy needs to shower tonight. Are you okay?"

"Say sorry to Sandy. Just lost track of time. Be out in a minute." She'd tried for sing-song chipper but out came high-pitched panic instead. Dianne knew she wasn't fooling her son, but maybe he'd pretend, like they'd both been doing for the last week.

Dianne shuffled into the kitchen, wrapped in her bathrobe.

"Thank you for getting Paula down. I'm going to have to make it up to her tomorrow. I'm surprised she agreed to let you read to her after I'd promised I'd do it. That's the fourth night in a row."

"You know I don't mind. And neither does she. You really don't have to do it all, you know." Tommy put a mug of chamomile tea in front of her, and she wrapped her hands around it. "Give me your foot," he said, pulling up a chair beside her. He rubbed it through her socks, and Dianne sighed.

"Oh my God. Thank you. How did I get such an amazing son?" she asked. Tommy kept up the foot rub and smiled.

"I guess *you* raised me," he said. A couple of minutes later, Dianne had her head in her hands, and was starting to yawn.

"Mom, I did something today and you have to hear me out," he said. Dianne's eyes sprung open.

"That doesn't sound good!" she said, waiting.

"I got a job at a gaming store. They've offered me 30 hours to start and promise I can have more hours and responsibility in the fall. Really. And they're paying me more than you're getting." Dianne couldn't believe it. She wasn't getting 30 hours a week yet!

"But what about school in the fall?" she asked. "Besides, it's great that you want to work, but that's money you'll put away for college," she said, as if it was decided. "I'm proud of you for wanting to be responsible, but really, Tommy, you have to trust me. I can manage this." Dianne didn't even believe herself. They sat for a few more minutes while she drank her tea, and Tommy finished her foot rub.

Standing, Dianne took the mug to the dishwasher, and loaded it. She heard the shower going.

"I have to get my uniform in the wash," she said. "We can talk about this tomorrow." Tommy chuckled.

"It's already spinning. I saw them outside the bathroom door and tossed them in the machine. I'll stay up and put them in the dryer. Don't worry.

"In a couple of weeks, you're going to quit that job. Really, Mom, it's gonna kill you, and Paula misses you. Go to bed."

They talked for a bit about finding an apartment. Dianne had little in savings for down payments, and furniture, and food. How was she going to do it when it was time to move out of the transition house? She was getting pressure from the other women because Tommy made them uncomfortable. And now this…he acted like an adult, so it was hard to convince them he wasn't.

When did he get to be so capable, so assured? It reminded her of what had attracted her to Tommy's dad years ago. He'd been so confident. He'd looked after her. Tommy wanted to help, but it was Dianne's time to get her life together and become self-reliant. She had lots to prove to the world, her ex…and herself.

They'd talk about it tomorrow.

The next day after work, Dianne headed to the shower, and realized she didn't feel as wrecked. After reading a story to Paula, she headed to the kitchen to eat. Her cell phone rang in her pocket, and a quick glance told her it was Padma.

"Hey girlfriend, how are you?" Dianne loved that the younger folks from the retreat just presumed she was one of them.

"I'm good, Dianne. What are you up to tomorrow night? Can we meet for dinner or something?" Dianne could hear the tightness in Padma's voice.

"Sorry, I can't meet for dinner. I got a job and have to work until after nine. How about now?" Dianne didn't want to leave her new friend hanging; she knew Padma didn't have many people to talk to. She heard Padma sigh, and let some silence hang on the line. They had all night. A moment later she could hear Padma walking.

"Just give me a minute, I want to go outside," she said. Dianne had no idea where Padma was living, or what her circumstances were. And that made her stomach hurt.

A few minutes later, they were chatting, Dianne with her hands around a mug of soup.

"So, you remember I was meeting with the cops to talk about the guys who raped me and sold the film to an internet porn guy? They wanted to offer the kids lesser charges if they helped nail the cyberporn guys?" Dianne reassured her she did.

"Well, I've been staying at my cousin's place. She has a small apartment off campus. And we've been talking. I need to talk to somebody about her ideas, and I thought of you," she said. Dianne's stomach had started to relax, but soon it knotted up again.

"You know I'm here. What is she suggesting?" Dianne asked.

"Well, she's a law student, and works with a student society that helps people with cases that aren't covered by legal aid." Dianne didn't see the connection; as a crime victim, Padma didn't need a lawyer. Couldn't have one in court.

"I'm so glad you've got a good place to stay." Dianne asked, "Is it nice, or is it hard staying so close to campus?"

"It's great, except I don't really have a room. For now, I'm glad to stay in the living room, and her roommate has been great. I just don't know what I'm going to do next," Padma admitted.

They talked for a bit about how hard it was to find good accommodation, and the money to pay for it when they were still working through their stuff.

"Anyway, Nasreet thinks I should consider something else, once the criminal case is over. The police think the guys will plead guilty soon," Padma said. "Within the next three months, certainly by fall. Then sentencing and it'll be all over." Dianne heard Padma take a deep breath, and the sounds of traffic.

"Nasreet thinks I should sue them. In civil court. Get compensation for what they did to me. She says it won't be hard to prove how I've been affected, and she knows some of the guys' families. Says they have money. And that with their confessions, it'll be easy." Dianne almost dropped her phone. *Of course* they should pay financially!

"That's amazing, Padma. What do you think?" she asked. More silence.

"Kind of dirty. Like I was letting them off easy with a plea deal to a lesser charge so I could sue them," she said. "It feels kind of slimy." It was Dianne's turn to take a moment.

"Padma, what those young men did to you was horrid. They drugged and raped you, and they filmed it. Then someone sold it, and that *will* affect you for the rest of your life.

"Remember how much you lost? Your studies. Your family. Your home. Your peace of mind. Your friends. And now you have to figure out a whole new future. *And none of that is your fault.* I don't think what your cousin suggested is slimy at all. It's the fairest thing I've heard.

"And I get why it's not clear. It's complicated. But you sound hopeful…and you should. Maybe this is your chance at a new start! A way to rewrite the ending!" They talked a little more about it and made plans to get together soon.

"Thank you," Padma said, and Dianne smiled.

After hanging up, Dianne thought about her life, and getting it back. She started a list. She'd go by her old place and pick up her car. It was hers, after all, and she deserved it. Thank God she'd registered it in her name. And the house...a part of that was hers. The furniture, at least. It'd be hard to get any equity out of it unless her ex (yes, she was starting to think of him that way) agreed to sell it, and she couldn't imagine he would. How would she figure out what was hers? She should talk to Padma tomorrow about seeing Nasreet's lawyers about how to go about getting a separation agreement.

She felt courage rising up, encouraging her to stop apologizing and take what was rightfully hers.

Maybe there'd even be child support.

What a difference a day made.

* * *

BETH AND BEN

Beth chased Adam and Bruce out to the soccer fields they'd be playing on for the next hour. She'd helped the boys change into their uniforms in the car, and Ben was waiting beside the field to help them tie their cleats. Yes, Adam and Bruce in cleats. *Terrifying*, Beth admitted.

This had become their Saturday morning ritual. It gave their mother, Donna, some down time, and it got Ben and Beth out of the house early. And Beth loved these boys, whom she'd cuddled since infancy. Even though they were still in elementary school, she could see her late friend Glenn's mannerisms in his boys, which made her smile.

Ten minutes later, the boys were running around kicking the players on their respective teams (they seldom connected with the ball), and Ben wrapped his arms around his wife from behind.

"Aren't they amazing?" he asked. Beth nodded.

"They're doing so well after the rough times they've had," she said. Ben reached into a bag and handed Beth a tea.

"A little milk," he said. "Just for you." He grabbed his cup of coffee. "Maybe one day we'll have one or two boys of our own," he dreamed.

"What if we have girls?" Beth asked, smiling.

"Oh, wow. I'd never thought about that. I don't know much about girls," Ben admitted. "But I think I'd like that, too." They kept watching the boys, sipping their drinks. Ben sometimes got a little too enthusiastic cheering on the boys, but this morning Beth just smiled at him.

She had something to share with him, and now seemed as good a time as any.

"When do you think you want kids? A baby?" she asked. Ben stopped short, looked at her.

"Really? Are you ready?" he asked. "Now? Soon?" he said. He couldn't believe it. They'd talked about having babies, but Beth always delayed, said the time wasn't right.

"Well, not today, for sure," she said, smiling.

"When?" he asked, still not understanding.

"How about seven months?" she asked. He looked down, counted on his fingers.

"I guess if we started to try in late fall, we could expect a babe in about a year? A little longer?" he asked.

"True," Beth admitted. "But maybe we just wait seven months and see what happens," she said, reaching down and putting her hand on her lower belly. Her eyes sparkled as she looked into the eyes of the man she adored. He could be so daft! Marrying an ex-monk was like that. "Not terribly worldly," Nora had called him.

A few moments later, the lightbulb went off for Ben.

"Oh my Grace!" he exclaimed. "That's why you haven't been drinking coffee!" He spun around slowly, hands over his face, trying not to spill his emotions onto the other parents watching. He started whispering at his wife, wrapping his arms around her shoulders.

"How long have you known? How did it happen?" he asked. "I presume we aren't telling everyone yet." Beth turned and looked at him.

"How did it happen? I thought I explained all that to you already. Did you forget?" she teased. They put their foreheads together.

"I found out this morning. Nora made me promise to take a test a while ago, and I kept postponing it. I couldn't figure out why this stuff with Martin was bugging me so much. We talked. She and Kate suspected. I didn't. So I waited awhile, but I'd promised." Ben was beaming at her, grinning from ear to ear. She put her palms on his cheeks.

"You don't mind?" she asked.

"Are you kidding? This is the best adventure with my favourite person I could imagine." They agreed to just keep it between themselves for now and redirected their attention to Adam and Bruce.

After all, they already had children they had to look after, even if it was just on Saturdays.

Later, after dropping off the boys, they took a walk around the grounds of the abbey nearby, and kept dreaming out loud with each other, glowing.

"How long before we tell everyone, do you think?" Ben asked.

"Let's wait awhile. I want it to be just for us. At least until we're through the first trimester," Beth suggested.

"Does that mean you're gonna make Martin wait to tell him you're okay with forwarding the boxes to the boys? Or do you want to tell Hugh earlier?" Ben asked. When Beth stopped short and put her hands on her hips he realized he'd made a bold assumption.

"What are you talking about? I'm still not okay with it." She walked further down the path away from Ben, turned back. "I'm pregnant. Not mentally ill. I might feel things stronger right now. But I know what I know. It's not okay to ask kids who lost their dad to murder to have stuff in their house made by the murderer. Listen to that. Just listen to how that sounds. I can't even imagine." Ben cocked his head to one side. Walked towards his beautiful wife.

"Oh Beth. I never really thought about it like that before. I just kept seeing Martin wanting to do something nice. Symbolic. Something good for them. And him." He reached out his hands, hoping his wife would take them in hers.

"Exactly. Like the whole fucking system, *you* were thinking of *him*." She took his hands and squeezed them.

"Which is why we have to be brutally careful when we think about Adam and Bruce. Until they're old enough to make decisions for themselves." She kissed him on the cheek. "Not to mention…who would tell Donna?" Donna was doing well mothering the boys. But she was still angry that their father had been killed.

They strolled back towards the car, and Ben squeezed his wife's hand gently.

"Wow. I hadn't even thought about Donna," he admitted.

I know. Just think about that. And don't *ever* suggest that because I feel stuff strongly, that I'm…flaky because of this pregnancy. Or hormones. Or anything else female."

Ben put his arms around his beloved and pulled her in close for a tender kiss. Resting his forehead on hers, he couldn't help but smile.

"How did I get so lucky?" he wondered out loud. "Thank you for putting up with me. You know I love you, right?"

Beth hugged him back and whispered in his ear.

"I sure do, Daddy."

CHAPTER 28
GROWING UP. AND GOING OUT.

I stuck my hands into the warm suds in Jean's sink and realized that I had no idea what I was feeling. Relaxed. (Like when I was alone.) And excited. (Like I have no idea when.) The smell from the curried dinner hung in the air, and I looked out Jean's windows at the North Shore mountains. Life looked very good from where I stood.

Jean had excused herself to change "into something more comfortable" a few minutes ago. Yes, she'd actually said that, and I hoped I knew what might happen next. My whole body hoped.

Dinner had been easy. The drive out had been easy. The kiss in the car had been easy.

And I'd never spent any time with a woman – or a man – that was easy. I'd always tried to figure out what they wanted or needed. To get them to want me or leave me alone. Sometimes, if I was really on the ball, I was trying to figure out how to get what I needed. Food from Mom. Or quiet from Jenny. Money from a trick…or how to make someone a repeat customer. Be left alone by a cop. And yes, sometimes the lines between cop and trick were blurred. Both men and women cops…it was all so complicated.

So when I'd found myself laughing at dinner, without even trying, and thought about the drive out and my stomach didn't clench, I was chill. Except where I was very hot indeed.

I finished up the few dishes Jean and I had used for our take-out, wiped the sink and polished her shiny taps when I felt her hands on my shoulders and jumped. How could she be that stealth? I liked to think I'm pretty aware, but maybe I'd been daydreaming....

"You okay?" she asked. "You didn't have to clean up." I smiled and turned in her arms, wiping my hands on my clean jeans.

"No problem. Really. I've been smiling the whole time." When she reached up for a kiss, I ran my hands down her sides to her hips and pulled her in. Her silky robe felt warm, and sleek. Slippery, almost. I moaned, holding my forehead to hers. I looked down, and she loosened the tie around her very tight waist, and I groaned again, my body tightening up. What she didn't reveal had me on fire.

Jean might be older, but man, her body behind lace looked hot to me. And my body was showing her. She smiled up at me, and opened her legs just a little, to straddle my thigh. I just about lost it.

"Do you want something to drink?" I asked, trying to buy my body some time. Savour the moment. I reached into the rack for a couple of tall glasses and pulled away to get ice from her fridge. She smiled back at me.

"As long as I'm clear about what follows a drink," she said. "Just water for me, thanks." She headed to the bookshelf and put on some Ed Sheeran. And wow, did I love the shape of her.

We sat on the couch, and her sips of water didn't help cool my imagination. Somehow her tongue on the glass was pure...distraction. I held my cool glass to my forehead, and the condensation felt great.

Then I was lying on my side on the couch, with Jean beside me. My body felt a lot less relaxed than I was trying to act...meandering caresses, gentle kisses. Her hand creeping up my thigh wasn't helping. I started getting more direct with my caresses and she actually purred.

"Let's move this to my bedroom," she suggested, and I agreed. She stood and reached for my hand to help me up. Which was useful, because I was a little light-headed. She started a new playlist – some easy jazz she said – and suggested a glass of wine.

"Am I driving home tonight?" I asked.

"Only if you want to…." she answered. My mouth dried, and I was glad for the wine.

Several hours later, Jean slept naked beside me. Her nightgown and robe were pooled on the floor beside the tangle of my jeans and T-shirt. My mind raced, replaying the last few hours. I worked to keep my hands off of Jean and wondered if I'd ever sleep again.

So this was what good sex was about. Soft skin, gentle caresses working towards pounding climaxes. Yes, plural. Lips and tongues exploring one another. My heart pounded just thinking about it. And I don't think I embarrassed myself. At least, not for long.

This kind of loving was the best there could be, I was sure, and I was determined to stay awake, just feeling Jean's closeness, the crisp but slightly sweaty cotton sheets. Breathe. The scent of us in the air….

And then, the sun was streaming in her bedroom window, and Jean was making noise in the kitchen.

"You want coffee, sleepyhead?" she called to me. My mouth felt dry, and my skin decidedly slimier than it had last night. Left-on sweat did that to me.

"You bet," I called back. "Be there in a minute. Just give me time to shower," I added. Before she could argue, I slipped into her bathroom. And judging by the steam on the mirror, she'd already cleaned herself up. She'd even laid out a new towel for me. I caught a glimpse of my grin in the mirror and surprised myself.

Ten minutes later, I'd finger-combed my wet curls and run my hands down my T-shirt to flatten the wrinkles. At least it didn't smell. Or rather, it smelled vaguely like Kenny's cologne and Jean. Good, in other words. We ate breakfast at her table looking out another window. Jean didn't live in a high-rise, but even at the fourth floor the views were great. I had my phone in my pocket, like always, but wasn't tempted to glance at it.

"Hey, want to get together tomorrow? Or even tonight?" she asked. Boy, did I ever, but I needed to work with Cook. And to go look for Jenny.

"I have to work lunch today, and breakfast tomorrow, so I can't. I can call, though?" A scowl passed over Jean's face, like the shadow of a bird you barely notice. "We have a conference this Saturday at *Tide's End* and I'm working the kitchen with Cook. And Friday night, Kenny and I are having some people by for dinner. Lots of prep to do," I explained.

"You know, I bet you could get work if you moved back to Vancouver," Jean said. *Right,* I thought. Clearly, she hadn't been a young homeless guy living on the streets here. Jobs sure didn't chase you down. "Think about it."

"I like what I'm doing at *Just Living,*" I said. "I'm learning a bunch. Maybe after the weekend I could drive out and cook for you. Make it up." I was floundering. It felt like a wall had gone up between us. I reached over to put my hand on hers, and she pulled away, grabbed the cups and plates and headed for the kitchen.

"It's okay. I get it. You're busy," she said. *WTF? I just had some things to do. Hopefully she'd get over it.* "And now that you've got your car back, maybe I'm not needed," she tossed at me over her shoulder. Now I was really confused. Hadn't I just offered to cook for her? I followed her into the kitchen and put my hands on her shoulders this time. I brushed my lips on her neck and felt her melt a little.

"Really, Taylor. Don't start what you don't have time to finish." I pushed her hips against the counter with mine, wanting to show her just how much my body wanted her. Again.

"Who said I don't have time?" I said, reaching my hands under her shirt and caressing her breasts through what could only be described as half-a-bra. Literally…her nipples were right there. This wouldn't take long, right? I wanted to look for Jenny and Mom downtown before I headed back to the Valley, but how long could she take? Her nipples were hard. And she was gasping, bracing herself with her hands on the counter.

A few minutes later, I unzipped her pants, and reached down into them…and a few minutes after that, I thought I was bringing her close, but then, no. While she was red-faced and panting, she kept squirming, getting close and moving away. I got it. I had to show her how much I wanted her, appreciated her, and not just for fixing my car.

"So…I hope I get to do this again and again, for a long time," I whispered into her ear. "You're beautiful, you're interesting, and God you are sexy." Again, she was close, and then far. I carried her over to the couch, and decided to unwrap her, give her some close kisses. And then, she couldn't squirm away, and then, she was crying out, lifting me up and holding on with her arms around my neck. She rolled me onto the couch, her body on top, and she melted into mine.

"Oh God," she panted. "I've forgotten how good it is with younger men…." She was squeezing her thighs around mine again and again, milking her climax. And I was throbbing, but aware I had to go. How would I get out of here? Cook was expecting me.

A few minutes later, she had my jeans around my knees and she was riding me slowly, up and down, rocking her hips. I didn't last long, but it was deep, and thick and fucking amazing. And I was moaning, even after I came inside her. She brought me a cold, damp cloth and I cleaned up, packing myself away as discreetly as I could.

Soon, we headed for the parking lot so she could give me my keys and send me on my way. But she didn't let me go without thoroughly kissing me first, in front of the binner in the alley, and her neighbours caught the show out their windows.

"Call you tonight?" I asked. She smiled at me, and I swear I saw a blush.

"I'd like that," she said.

I was whistling as I drove out of her parking lot. My car looked and drove great — I could have eaten off the console, something I'd never said before. Not that I would, of course. I headed for the DTES, determined to look for any familiar faces who'd known Mom. I parked my car, and walked the alleys for a while, and met up with a couple of old friends of my mom's. They hadn't seen her, or Jenny, for a couple of years. Shit. Not what I wanted to hear. I headed back to my car, head down.

And then I saw the clock on the corner of a building. Fuck! I was at least an hour later than I should've been to give Cook full support for lunch. I headed down the road but didn't speed because I couldn't afford the ticket. I did practice my apology. I'd never been late to his kitchen before, so I hoped he'd be okay with this time.

I felt like I'd been on a roller coaster. I started to think about all the ways I was fucking up. Big ways like with Cook and looking for Jenny. I needed to get back on the street and ask tougher questions.

And small ways like I'd have to buy condoms. I didn't want to be caught without again. I presumed Jean couldn't get pregnant at her age, but really. What if she was carrying something?

Or I was?

CHAPTER 29
COMMITMENTS

The days flew by, and I decided that even though I still fucked up, I was getting better at being on track. I'd planned and cooked for Kenny's and my dinner party. Learned a ton, like don't just add flour to warm salmon chowder to thicken it. Picked every lump out by hand. And don't try to be the cook and eat with guests. I didn't enjoy either enough.

I also had another session with Ben. Appreciated his support. And called Marta to keep moving stuff forward, left a message on her machine. Maybe adulting was just about trying and persisting.

I thought about all of it as I drove out of the Valley towards Jean's. We'd had some wicked phone calls and she'd invited me back to her place. I'd packed my car. Food for dinner. Check. Condoms. Check. Smile...you bet, window open, sun shining, driving through forest.

And then my phone rang, and I glanced at it. Pulled over to answer. It was Inspector Derksen.

"Taylor, we've received the warrant for the ISP, and expect to have the data to the team this weekend. We haven't had contact with Jenny since that one time, but there's no reason to think she's been moved. Patty tried to get him to answer some questions about her, but he deflected. At least he's still pushing Patty for chats." I tried hard to sound enthusiastic, but really, what was taking so long? I was counting days, and they were adding up.

"Yeah, thanks Inspector. I guess it takes the time it takes," I said.

"I get every day must seem like forever, but this isn't extraordinary. We're doing our job. The good news is that no images of Jenny have been found online." I wasn't soothed. I'd heard about the depth of the dark web. Just because they hadn't found video didn't mean Jenny wasn't being taped. And it didn't mean creeps weren't watching her. I knew creeps. Fuck. I needed to do more. My stomach lurched. I swallowed the bile.

"Okay. Thanks for calling. I appreciate it, really." Whatever. "I'm heading out for a cooking gig. Gotta go," I said, wondering if cooking for Jean really counted as a "gig." But I'd promised I'd be there by six, and knew that with traffic, I'd be late.

And then traffic had been bad, and I was later than just a little late.

Jean wasn't very forgiving. Good thing I'd spent some of Sally's money on that wine. I'd tried to kiss her when she'd answered the door, but she wasn't having it.

"What the hell? I'm here. Alone." she'd said turning and walking away. I froze. Didn't put the bags down. Was I leaving? Her arms were crossed when she turned back to me. "I'm waiting for you, and you can't even call? Text? I gave you a phone." I'd wished she'd shouted, but her voice was tight. Steely.

"I was hurrying. Sorry." No response. I put my bags down. "I don't text and drive," I'd whispered. Not the right thing, clearly. She'd spun so fast I was half expecting a kiss and was stunned when she slapped me. Small, quick, but she'd hit my cheek hard and it'd stung. I didn't move to rub it, because no one ever saw me hurt. I tightened my jaw instead, trying to decide if it'd really happened. I steadied my breath, and she walked away.

"I'll go cook," I said, and headed for the kitchen. I kept on deep breathing for a minute or two, running water, getting pans onto the stove, and putting stuff in the fridge. Then I poured her a glass of wine and headed back into the living room.

"I bought this for us," I said, watching her from the doorway. She was looking out the living room window, ignoring me. *Great*, I thought as I walked closer to her.

"I brought this for you. I'm really glad we got together, Jean." She didn't move. "And since I don't have to drive tonight." She finally turned, took the glass and sipped. It was like a switch was flipped.

"Thank you. I guess I'm hungry," she said. "I just wish you'd be here when you say you would." I headed back to the kitchen to grill the salmon and veggies, glad the rice was already on the stove, second guessing my menu, my technique, everything. "It'll just be a few minutes," I called to her. I didn't mention that *she'd* been the one who'd told me to be there so early. I'd told her that with work and traffic, that I'd be later.

Soon I served dinner to the table I'd set, and Jean had thawed out a bit. Maybe the wine had been a good idea after all. She stopped me before I could sit down, and a few minutes later things were much warmer between us. Steamy, in fact. Then, we made love on the couch. In the shower. On the bathroom counter. So much for hungry. Or maybe I'd just tried to feed the wrong craving. The woman was…well, let's just say I felt good when she moaned.

The evening turned out to be lovely. The fish was good – even reheated – and the company was awesome. Yes, Jean was still pissed that I worked so hard. Yes, she let me know it.

"If you lived in Vancouver, you could get a job that didn't have so many hours," she'd said. "It's just that I care!" *And live where?* I wondered. *Back in my car?* Then we argued a little when I said I really *did* need to get some sleep. I tried to make it up to her with the promise of a date in Mission the next time she was out.

"Group is happening next week. Maybe we could go out after?" I asked.

"Maybe we could be daring in my car, if you can't invite me home. I used to love the back seat," she said. I cringed.

Yes, I'd neck a little. But I *really* didn't need Mission RCMP finding me naked and fucking in a steamy Lexus. With an older woman.

"Or we could get a room," I said, tickling her. "I want to love you with clean sheets, and a bathroom nearby. Really. You're worth it." I was trying to keep it light, but it hadn't really landed well. And I didn't have any money for a room, so I didn't push it.

"Are you embarrassed of me? Don't want us to be seen in public?" she asked. There was no winning.

"No, I'm embarrassed how horny I get around you. And I don't need people watching," I said. "I hope my days of car sex are over, Jean. But I'd love to take you out for a meal before our meeting, or coffee after." Everything I said seemed to bug her a little. And then I looked at my phone. Which also bugged her.

It'd taken some more loving (and less sleeping) to convince her I wanted her, but at least when we fell asleep it was on good terms.

The next morning, I was looking out Jean's window and still smiling, thinking about the dinner I'd made for her. I noticed the rising sun over the mountains to the northeast as I stole a look out her bedroom window. I shut the bedroom door as quietly as I could and slung my duffle bag over my shoulder. I'd planned to head back to the DTES to talk to some people in the shelters to see if they'd seen Mom. And Cook had been great, but I hated being late and didn't want to make it a habit when I stayed at Jean's.

I headed into the kitchen to pack the knives and a few leftover ingredients I'd "borrowed" from Cook's kitchen. Last stop before heading down to my car. The smell of last night's dinner was starting to stale, so I cracked the kitchen window.

Time to get out of here. And next time, I seriously had to work on more sleep.

But I was young, right? At least that's what Jean said when she wanted more of me. More time, more cooking, more loving.

As I headed for the door, I reminded myself that Jenny was *the* most important thing. Looking for her and learning to cook. And I really didn't know where Jean fit into that equation, but in her defense, I hadn't told her everything about Jenny yet. She'd generously fixed my car. And given me the phone.

I just wish I'd noticed her in the doorway before I'd bumped into her.

"Mmmm…sneaking out?" she asked, looking sleepy.

"No! I just wanted to avoid traffic, and thought I'd let you sleep," I'd said. I put the duffle down, my mind racing to find a quick exit strategy. "But this is even better," I said, wrapping her in my arms. "I love waking up to you."

An hour later, I was running down the back stairs, duffle in hand, heading for my car. I knew with the traffic I'd be lucky to get to the kitchen before morning break even without stopping at the shelters. Fuck. How was it the sex could be so good, and the relationship so complicated? I'd fucked up again. Shit.

I pulled over at a rest stop to clean up so I could head right to the kitchen, and that's when I noticed Inspector Derksen had called again. When had my phone been put on silent? His voicemail asked me to call him, and by the time I'd done that and headed back to the highway, I knew it'd be lunch before I got in. I texted Kenny and told him I was needed at the police station. Something about "complications" with some data.

Like I needed more complications.

CHAPTER 30
GETTING OLD - COOK

Cook folded his meaty arms and laid his head on them. His enormous body quietly rose and fell with his breath. *Steady,* he told himself. Staring at the table, he closed his eyes. Could he really do this? It seemed every time he got involved in something good, it went sideways. He sighed as the timer buzzed and he knew he had to open the oven before the scones burned. He smelled the raisins and the butter, sweet and delicious.

"Relax, Cook. I'll check them," Beth said, walking into the kitchen. He lifted his shiny head, rubbing the stubble above his ears.

"Sorry, Mugwump. Jus' catchin' my breath. Sometimes I wonder if I can do this," he said. "I can't worry Sally, but sometimes I do wonder." He sighed, slumping back in the chair. Beth looked over, and thought he looked tired. Old.

"Do what? You're amazing. The meal Taylor put together for us on Friday was delicious. He's learning lots. The meal plans you submitted for the classes are affordable and will teach the students some real skills. Why the worry?" Beth grabbed a tea towel and lifted the scone trays from the oven. Cook smiled. She danced in the kitchen, like she was born to bake. "And where's Taylor? Wasn't he scheduled to help you this morning?" Cook leaned his head back against the wall, sending up a silent prayer as he decided to get real with her. For about the hundredth time.

"That's a part of it. Taylor was so keen. He was always on time, stayed late, came back and did prep after dinner. But then, somethin's shifted and he's been late. And distracted. I don't know what's changed, but maybe I was expecting too much. I don't really know what I'm doing, gettin' all high-falutin and bein' a mentor. I keep telling Sally that."

"And what does Sally say?"

"Well, she reminded me I don't really know what's going on with him. I get my kitchen, but a young guy like him? Who knows? Not me." Cook looked out the window, caught his thoughts. "Says maybe I should ask." He sighed again and used his arms to push himself out of his chair.

"I didn't realize how much I'd come to depend on him. But I'd better start thawing some soup for lunch," he said. "Was gonna make somethin' fresh, but I just don't have the energy today."

"You get the soup. I'm going to track down Taylor. Or maybe Kate. I want to know what's changed. Someone will tell me – I really don't think you did anything wrong, Cook. He's young, remember. And he has a lot on his plate," Beth said as she ducked out the back door. Cook headed for the walk-in freezer. Luckily there was always something on the shelf to feed the many bodies at the half-way house. The raisin scones would make up for chicken soup that wasn't fresh.

Ten minutes later, Kenny stuck his head in the back door.

"Hey, Cook…Taylor just texted me. He's late because he had to go by the cop shop. Something about his sister, 'kay?" Kenny was covered in dirt from the garden, and Cook was glad he wasn't bringing it into his kitchen.

"Jus' a sec. Time for a break – wanna drink?" he asked.

"Wouldn't say no to some juice," Kenny answered, smiling. His heart swelled at the old man who cared so much for all of them.

Cook pulled up a chair to the small table outside the kitchen door and handed Kenny a cold glass of orange juice.

"How's that boy, anyways? He's been kinda scarce around here," Cook asked.

"Well, seems he's got himself a girlfriend from the group. A woman named Jean, maybe? I didn't get to know the participants except Taylor," Kenny admitted. "Anyways, he seems to be smiling a lot. Sometimes seems rushed. I think Beth's looking for him to talk about being 19 and responsible, so I let her know about his text."

Cook looked down at his glass, wishing he could dismiss his worries as quickly as Kenny seemed to.

"Jean. Jean. She's the older lady, right? Seemed classy, maybe over-classy." Cook said. Kenny shrugged, looking at his garden.

"No idea, but he's spent some time in Vancouver at her place. I wouldn't say he's juggling everything well, but it's not like he can bring her to my place," Kenny reminded the old man.

"I guess it's been so long, I've forgotten what it's like," Cook said, and sighed. "I jus' worry, I guess. He was so focused on gettin' trained at first. Maybe I'm wantin' too much," he finished. He collected the glasses to head back inside. "Will there be any greens for dinner? Or should I use the ones I bought?"

"Let's use the ones in your fridge, and mine can grow a bit bigger." Kenny started walking back over the lawn towards the garden. He turned and looked at Cook.

"Hey, Cook, I'll look out for him, 'kay? He always talks about how great you are. He appreciates you. He's a good kid, with lots on his plate." They shared a knowing look. "Maybe he thinks he's more experienced than he is. I'll get him to report in…have a talk with him. At least she got his car running for him, right? He's got wheels…." Cook looked up at the blue sky and pointed to the eagle soaring on the warm air currents. He didn't need to use words to underline how important he thought their conversation was.

"See you at lunch." He opened the door and walked back into his kitchen.

After lunch was cleared and the guys had brought the dishes through to the wash station, and Beth had helped move the few leftovers to the fridge, Cook took off his apron for his after-lunch break. Nap, really. Then he saw Kate, hanging around the dining room door.

"Hey, Cook, can I talk to you?" she asked. "I'm a bit worried about you…."

"And I'm worried about this plan for the cookin' school. What if I'm jus' too old for this? What if it's too much?" He wasn't above using Kate for good advice….

"What support would make you feel more comfortable with it?" she asked. She never told him what to do, he realized. He thought about it.

"I think we need a bigger team. I don't wanna jus' rely on Taylor when he's so young. What'll I do if he takes off and I can't do it in September? Or he gets a better offer? I don't want to be a burden on him…he's gotta be free to go if he wants to."

Sally and Kate's eyes connected over Cook's shoulder. They loved this big guy to bits and remembered the year when his "ticker" had nearly failed him. They didn't want a repeat of that.

"Okay, let me think about it," Kate said. "I'll talk to Nora and Beth. We can't have the whole plan hinge on one young man. You're right. It's not fair to him…or you. Much as it did seem like a good idea. Don't worry, Cook. We'll find a way. And that soup was wonderful!" she said, ducking out of the dining room.

"As usual, my man, you've named it. I love you," Sally said, heading back upstairs with his dirty apron in hand.

And then the back door opened, and Taylor shuffled in, his head hanging.

"I'm sorry, Cook. I'm gonna get better at this, I promise. Really."

"Awww, damn, Taylor, you weren't oppose' to hear that," Cook said, realizing the screen door to the back porch had been all that stood between the teen and their conversation. He wondered when Taylor had started listening.

"No…I think I was. I can't be distracted. I've gotta focus on this chance you're giving me, and Jenny." He tied his apron around his waist and headed for the washup sink to scrub his hands. "Do I chop some veggies for dinner? I thought we'd roast them to go with those burgers." Cook smiled at "his kid," as he'd come to think of Taylor.

"Sure," he said. "But honest, Taylor, we can work out a schedule so you have some time to do other stuff," he said, grinning as he headed upstairs. "I'm goin' for my siesta. Maybe think about makin' some fruit crumble with some of last year's fruit in the freezer." No point in totally letting the kid off the hook.

Cook paused in the doorway, one foot on the bottom stair.

"What did Inspector Derksen want?" he asked. "If you don't mind tellin' me," he qualified. Cook's stomach tightened. He always felt like he was walking a tight rope between MYOB and caring.

"Just some stuff about my mom. No big deal," Taylor answered. "Nothing new, not really. Sorry it made me late." Taylor knew he was stretching the truth, but the cops had offered an excuse too good to sidestep.

"Well, any time you want to talk about it," Cook said, "I'm here."

As the old man shuffled upstairs, Taylor thought about what he'd learned.

Yes, no surprises.

But it wasn't easy to hear your mom probably wasn't ever coming home.

CHAPTER 31
GETTING REAL

Beep.

"Hey, Marta, I want to be prepared if the police find Jenny. I mean, when they find her. I think it might be soon, and I want to be ready to get custody. The cops are pretty sure Mom's…uh…dead, so…I guess I'm the closest family. Only family." My voice trailed off, rising at the end like a question. Beep. My stomach clenched, and I left my phone number again. I couldn't even master leaving a phone message.

It took her days to get back to me. Long, frustrating days. Apart from my date with Jean, I used the anxious energy to clean the trailer, learn how to braise beef bones for soup, and focus on some baking techniques that Beth was willing to share. It's hard to follow a recipe when you don't know what the hell they're talking about. Knead. Punch. Beat. Combine. Stir. Fold. Cream. But once she showed me, I got it quick. Feels good to learn stuff that I will actually use. I'm setting a goal – learn to make flaky croissants so I can make them for Jenny when we've got our place. They're like the most special bun I can imagine. Pretty. Soft. And yummy. They feel so rich. Jenny will love them.

Mostly I thought about my little sister and leaving her behind. Like every minute, I thought about Jenny. When I cleaned my room, I moved Russet onto my bed again. Because not having the damned cat out wasn't helping me to not think about Jenny. And sometimes, when I was tired, or frustrated, I could cuddle it, and if I cried a bit, Russet didn't mind. Russet didn't judge.

I hope Jenny doesn't either.

I finally got an appointment with Marta for the next week, and Kenny offered to drive me in. I was glad for the company. He agreed to check the shelters with me, too.

On the way, we talked about my mom, about what Inspector Derksen had wanted that day when he'd called me in.

I told Kenny about stopping by the detachment, and how it was weird to be invited into the Inspector's office. My stomach had clenched. Just being in the building made my blood freeze. He had swung the detachment door open, waved me in and led the way through a maze of desks and hallways, past cops in uniform, some people in regular clothes. There were computers, and copiers and other weird machines everywhere. It wasn't my first time inside, but it was the first time I was summoned by the boss.

I tucked my head down and kept his heels in my view, following close but not crowding him. Were they as curious about me as I was about them? I didn't catch anyone looking at me, but I know they have way more experience in covert....

The Inspector steered me into a corner office. No surprise there, I guess. He is the big cheese in this little town. There were some windows, but up really high on the wall so you couldn't really see out of them except to trees and sky. Or clouds. It rains a lot.

Then I told Kenny, "You couldn't peek in either, I guess. He invited me to sit across from him. His big desk had piles of papers and files on it, but I couldn't actually see any of them. I just sat there, perched on the edge of the chair, hoping this would be quick. My stomach hadn't stopped hurting since I'd left Jean's...Vancouver." I didn't tell Kenny that my stomach always hurt around cops. I suspected he and I shared that. Then I told him about what Inspector Derksen had said.

"Taylor, we put out some enquiries into the whereabouts of your mother." My head had snapped up and I must have looked startled because he put his hand out to reassure me. It didn't.

How did my mom's whereabouts become a police matter?

"I spoke with your social worker, and she gave me some information on your mom's last known whereabouts. I put out feelers, and I think we have some news." He'd started shuffling papers on his desk, straightening piles. I was pretty sure that it wasn't good news.

"You didn't have to do that. I'm used to Mom coming and going. I just wish we could get Jenny back, so I could look after her. I'd be good at it," I said. Really. That's what I said. I cringe now when I think about it. *Good at it?* WTF?

"We think your mom might be a part of the Missing and Murdered Women Investigation. It looks like she may have gotten tied up with some of the men who are on trial now for murdering women like your mom." My head had snapped up.

"My mom's been murdered?" I asked. Although, even as I said it, my stomach settled. I think I knew.

"We aren't sure, but we found some remains down by the river in the Downtown East Side that might be hers. The coroner asked if we could help with the identification. That's why I asked you to stop by.

"You're her biological son, right?" I nodded. *Who the fuck would let a junkie prostitute adopt?* I thought.

"Would you take this form and go to the hospital for a test?" he asked. "They just need to swab your cheek and then they can match the DNA from the woman's remains to your DNA. Then we'll have an answer." I had a million questions. Including, *Do I want to give my DNA to the cops?* But it was like he anticipated that.

"The reason we're asking you to go to the hospital is that we won't keep the results on file. It'll just be to match you and then they'll discard your sample," he said. He reached into his top drawer and pulled out a piece of paper. Gave it to me.

"Just head to the lab in the hospital. They'll know what to do. You've got a car that works now, right? Don't need a ride?" I was glad my car would start, so I declined. I was trying to figure out if I was sad or happy I might not see my mom again. Or if I actually felt anything. A few minutes later, I was heading up the hill to the hospital, and I decided to just get it done even though I was late for Cook.

I should get the confirmation in a week or two, but I was pretty sure Mom was dead. It made sense. I hadn't heard from her for almost a year, and she'd kept in touch better than that before, even if it was just to ask for money.

So I told Kenny I'd been waiting for the results, that I'd gone to the hospital that day, just to get it over with. Talking to Kenny about it helped. He never pretends to know what to do.

"That sucks, Taylor. I'm sorry," he'd said. I admit, just his saying that helped. I hadn't told anybody else, and it was weird knowing that other than me, the only people who knew were the cops. I wondered who else he'd tell. A few minutes later we parked and headed into Marta's office. I was glad Kenny was going to be there with me.

I'm not gonna pretend it went well. Marta brought us into a room with a door. I got the impression she didn't have an office but that this was a room lots of social workers used to give people horrible news. Does good stuff ever come out of this office?

It didn't take her long to crush my plans.

"Taylor, we don't think you're the best candidate to look after Jenny. We have to think about what's best for her," she said. That was literally how she started. Fuck. Don't hold back, Marta. Don't let me down slowly, or anything. I started to argue. I might have used the word "fuck" a few times. Like, "I'm her fucking brother. No one else will care about her like I do." Stuff like that. It might not have helped.

Anyhow, Kenny took over from there.

"So, you kind of led Taylor to believe he'd be able to apply. What's changed? What does he need to do?" he asked. *Good questions,* I thought. I breathed in, reminding myself I didn't want to get kicked out of the office again.

"Oh, he can apply. Of course he can. But right now, I don't think I'll be recommending him as a guardian." She turned to me. "You just aren't ready, Taylor. Think about Jenny, what she'd need." She looked down at the papers in front of her.

"I know you feel bad because you left her at your mom's. You did get yourself out, which was really good. But there's lots of other stuff you need to take care of to make a home for Jenny. One that will work for her." She started to stand up, like we were done. Ready to go.

I wasn't.

Kenny took over again and got the laundry list of what I needed to do to have even a chance of getting Jenny. And he even thought to ask about alternatives.

"Where else will she go? Somewhere near Taylor? Can he at least visit and help her?" he asked. She agreed to consider his questions, but just to get us out of her office, I think.

Like they'd let Jenny stay near a half-way house, I thought.

Kenny led me out of the building and we set off to look for Jenny. We stopped by a women's shelter, but they told us they don't allow kids to stay, even if they're on the street. They suggested a couple of other places to try. I insisted on leaving them my number in case they saw her.

And then Kenny made sure I got in the vehicle to head home because I was bruising for a fight, bouncing into people on the sidewalk, and swearing at everyone.

"Hey, settle down," he said, steering me towards our ride. "I can't afford more charges, so you're on your own," he joked.

All the way home I just stared out the passenger window and listened to the rain pounding on the hood of the truck. The raindrops running down the window matched the tears flowing down my cheeks. I felt like a part of me was dead inside. *Was there really any point in trying? Maybe*

I should just move in with Jean, go back to work on the street, I thought. I kept thinking about what Marta had said to me.

You aren't ready, Taylor. If you think you are, then show me by having a space for you guys to live. A way to make money. The ability to get Jenny to school, and stuff. Think about it. Are you ready for that? Do you really want to take all that on? You have to show me. Because you can't take her on and then change your mind

I had to show her I could take care of my little sister. I was trying to convince myself that I'd never ever give up on Jenny again. And I was taking care of me, right? Just like Marta had told me I had to. Now there was new stuff. More stuff.

Just give me a month, I thought. *Maybe two. I'm gonna get this together.*

CHAPTER 32
LEGAL WORK

The next day Kenny and I were sitting around the kitchen table, whining about our love lives. I'd cooked pancakes and brewed coffee, and we were both enjoying a morning off. We didn't see each other that much any more, what with my working for Cook in the evenings, and his working the gardens during daylight. So we'd decided we'd have "trailer meetings" — which really meant sitting around eating and laughing, I guess.

"It *is* nice being…I don't know, having a girlfriend? I mean, I've never had one before, so it's nice and all…but I never thought it'd be so hard. So much work."

"I guess that's the price of regular sex," Kenny teased. My face turned red.

"I just thought it'd be easier. You dating anyone since Carson?" I'd heard him on the phone with some guy the night before. It'd sounded… angry.

"Nah. Too much bother, really. I have enough drama," he said, and I laughed.

"Me too," I said. "Some days I wonder if it's worth it. How long I can keep it up? At least I'm getting on better here with Cook. I think we've found shifts that work. I hope he's getting some rest," I said.

"Oh shit!" Kenny slammed his fork and knife down. "What time is it?" I pulled out my phone – it was 8:45 and I told Kenny that.

"You have to get over to the half-way house! Beth wanted to meet with you at 8:30 and I was supposed to tell you. Shit! You get over there, and I'll call her and let her know I forgot." I grabbed my jacket off the back of a chair.

"Good thing I never hang this up," I joked, and flew out the door. It felt good when I heard him laugh as the door slammed behind me.

I stumbled towards the retreat centre, my sneakers catching on the uneven path, but I didn't slow down for a breath. Truth was, Beth kind of scared me, and I still felt like I could be sent on my way at any time. Everyone told me that wasn't going to happen…but everything here felt too good to be true.

I flew in the door to the room off her office, and stopped short, put my hands on my knees and tried to catch my breath. My lungs were on fire.

"Can I get you a glass of water?" Beth asked, leaning on the doorway to her office with a smile on her face. "Really, you look like you're going to pass out." She walked across the room to the sink, and grabbed me a glass, brought it over. She brushed her hair behind her ears and beckoned me into her office.

"Sit down, Taylor. Catch your breath. You forget we've all known Kenny longer than you. He's quite OCD about his space, but a complete scatterbrain when it comes to remembering messages. And time. I was just about to call him when he called me.

"Thanks for coming." She sat behind her desk and pulled out some paper to write on. "Don't know if Kenny told you why I wanted to talk to you, but here it is." I loved that Beth got right to it.

"So, I've been talking to Cook about some possibilities for *Tide's End*. We want to encourage the community to use the space, as long as what they want it for is in keeping with who we are and what we value, so I talked to him about what offering catering over there might look like." I nodded my head and thought about all the nights I walked past the place towards the trailer, and the windows were dark and cold. So different from the first night I saw the warm firelight through the windows.

"That's a great idea. Is there money in that work?" I asked. "Because maybe some of it could be used to support the victim and survivor retreats."

"Well, that's the thought. At least, keeping it in use gets the name out in the community about the work that's being done here, which helps.

"Anyways, Cook said he doesn't really want to take on more kitchen management but thought about you." I must have gasped. I was so not ready to take that on.

"No, no…not to run and manage everything, but to be his 'go to' guy for getting stuff done. If you suggest menus, and what would have to be ordered, he can make sure it makes sense. Sally would help with the budgeting and ordering. And yes, we are still going ahead with the plans for the school in the fall. This is to get us through the spring and summer.

"What do you think?"

And think I did…for more than a few seconds. How would this help me get Jenny back? I needed to get a job, get a place in town… volunteering here wasn't going to help all that. But what a chance to show what I could do!

"I'm excited! Thanks for the offer, but I don't know how long I can stay here, volunteering. I have to get money, work if I'm going to be able to help Jenny," I tried to explain. Even to me I sounded ungrateful. And I knew what I was trying to say.

"Well, that's the best part of this plan, I think. If this works, Cook has offered to decrease his hours and pay. We expect more income, so we'd be able to pay you. It isn't much to start, but as the work expands, I think we'll be able to expand your pay. And if we get the grant money for the cooking school downtown, I think we could make it full time." I couldn't believe it. Money. Paid for cooking…not hooking? Maybe that should be my tag line. I must have been grinning, because Beth reached over and shoved me in the shoulder. I looked up.

"Holy. You're kidding, right? You would pay me to make soup and wash dishes? Order some greens? Do I know enough to help?" My stomach was already clenched thinking about all the ways I'd let Cook down already, and all the new ways I could fuck up. I almost said no.

But then I pictured Jenny, and Russet and what she was enduring. *If I need to work to be her brother, her guardian, then it wouldn't be adulting if I turned down the first legal work offered to me, now, would it?* I thought. My grin grew. Cook was the best teacher ever, and I really wanted to make him proud. And Sally too.

"When do I get started?" I asked, and almost toppled off my chair when she told me.

"Well, Friday evening we have a small appreciation dinner to host for our community members and volunteers. We thought we'd do it at *Tide's End*, a simple meal with some gift giving, a few speeches and a whole lot of love. I'll be there with Ben, and Nora and Kate will come. Some of the men. Tom, who I think you've met. Kenny. And about 15 guests.

"Do you think you can come up with a simple dinner for about 30 with 48 hours' notice? If you're going to go lavish, make it on the dessert. Small portions, but special, okay?" My mind was doing cartwheels, coming up with ideas.

"Could I ask someone to help?" I asked. "Volunteer, of course." I thought I'd check in with Padma and see if she had Friday evening off. She'd serve the guests much better than me. I'd rather hang out in the kitchen.

"Let me know who," Beth said. "Someone I know? And they must be an adult, because of some of the guests," she finished. I didn't want to say what my idea was in case Padma was working. Or didn't want to help.

The next two days were a whirlwind of busy, planning, checking with Cook and Sally for budgets, and decision-making. I was trying to keep it as much of a surprise as possible.

Soon enough it was Friday night, and 30 people were sitting around tables in the dining hall of *Tide's End*, enjoying my soups – tomato basil bisque and chicken rice and vegetable – and eating my rolls, warm from the oven, with fresh butter from the dairy across the bridge. Simple, inexpensive. And good.

Dessert was ice cream – again, organic and fresh from the dairy – in either chocolate or vanilla – with warm raspberry sauce drizzled on top, and a fresh gingersnap cookie. It looked fabulous, and Padma and I had fun trying out different "plating" ideas and tasting everything.

"How can I help?" Cook said, poking his head into the kitchen. I should have known he couldn't stay at his table the whole night. I looked around the kitchen – it wasn't too disastrous. Some soup in each pot that I would put in the walk-in fridges for tomorrow's lunches.

"Hey – how was it?" I couldn't help myself. I had to know. Padma punched my arm.

"I told you they were groaning over your buns," she said, giggling a bit.

"The soup was good. Real good. Maybe the chicken could have had more corn," he said. I smiled. There wasn't any corn in the soup, but Cook liked corn, and in the Fraser Valley, it was plentiful and cheap, so there was lots in our freezer.

"Next time – corn chowder!" I said, grinning.

"D'ya think the tomato soup had enough seasoning?" he asked, teasing. I liked to pretend he was Gordon Ramsay, going on about seasoning things. I kept working on putting the ice cream into the bowls – a scoop in each – and Padma followed behind, drizzling the raspberry sauce and adding the cookies just so. There were eight on each tray – four of vanilla and four of chocolate. She was going to have to get them onto the tables quickly.

"You could help Padma get these out to the guests," I suggested. "Tactical error – the warm sauce is going to make a puddle of the ice cream, and the effect of the fabulous plating will be lost if the cookies are just floating on a hot mess," I said. Padma giggled again.

"Come on, Cook, follow me. Bring a tray. I'll serve, you just restock me." Cook looked relieved.

Five minutes later, the desserts were out, and I put the soups in the fridge. Cleaned some pots. In 20 minutes, other than the dining room dishes, I was done cleaning. I wiped down counters, listening to the speeches come to an end. Soon I could turn on the loud dishwasher, and we'd be finished in no time. The door swung open.

"Taylor – come on out. There's a few people I want you to meet," Beth said. I couldn't really say no to my new boss, so I changed into a cleaner apron and headed into the dining room. There was applause.

"Friends let's give a warm thank you to Taylor, who planned and cooked our entire meal tonight. He had one instruction – make the volunteers feel appreciated. Without spending too much money." Everyone started to clap, and my face was burning. Padma was grinning and making sweeping motions and bowing in my direction. I really didn't know what to say, so I just stood there wondering how long before I could head back into the kitchen to do the dishes.

Beth put her arm around me and steered me over to a table where Nora and Kate and two other women were sitting. I'd seen one of them before, helping Kenny in the garden. Ben pulled up a couple of chairs, and I sat down. So much for escaping back to the kitchen.

"Taylor, I want you to meet Claire and Veronica. They've volunteered here for years, and I want you to meet them," she said. I looked up, eyes wide.

"Veronica lives in the neighbourhood. She's the one who offered to take you in when we realized you couldn't stay here during the retreat." I remembered hearing her name. "And this is Claire. She's a retired schoolteacher who helps around here," Beth continued.

"Hi Claire. Good to see you again," I said, still trying to figure this out. "We weeded together one afternoon," I explained.

"Good to see you, too, Taylor. I had some of each of the soups, they were good!" she said. I smiled at her.

We sat and chatted for a bit. Beth had warned me that I might have to hang out with the volunteers, so I was happy to pretend for a bit. I was still surprised at how many nice people there were who helped out around here. But then I heard the dishwasher running in the kitchen. I looked up, startled.

"Hey – I need to clean up!" I said, my mind a jumble.

"No need," Padma called from the kitchen door as she came towards us. "Cook and I made fast work of the dishes – did you know you can clean like 30 plates in one minute in that machine?" she asked. I remembered how amazed I'd been the first time I'd used the commercial dishwasher. "We even cleaned the big pots you soaked," she said. "All done. Sally and Cook said to say good night." As Padma reached the table, Ben pulled another chair up.

Padma slid a dessert in front of me and hit the back of my hand with a spoon.

"Hey, you…eat up. Last one," she said, and I grinned at her. This would be like my fifth one tonight, but I hadn't eaten anything else. I dug in, starving now that the dinner was over.

Before long, I was driving Padma home, and planning to get together the next week before the Follow up Gathering on Wednesday. Thinking back over the evening, my heart swelled.

Things were happening at a fast pace now. Inspector Derksen thought it'd be less than a week before they located the house where they thought Jenny was being held, and we had to get plans in place before then. I had the Follow Up Gathering next Wednesday. I had to think about getting a bank account. Maybe fit in a date with Jean. This adulting stuff was taking a lot of energy, but I smiled. Maybe I *could* do this.

For the first time in a long time, I believed it might even be possible that I'd be able to be Jenny's big brother again.

Looking at big picture stuff, I still worried about getting a place for myself where she could visit. Hell, she wouldn't even be able to *get to* the half-way house, let alone visit. I wondered how far my small paycheck would take me, in terms of renting a space, and paying for my car insurance.

I saw a light, but I knew it was still a very long tunnel.

CHAPTER 33
SOLID GFS – TERRY AND JEAN

The champagne-coloured Lexus coasted to a stop in front of Terry and Barb's apartment. *She'll be out quick, if she knows what's good for her,* Jean thought. It never occurred to her that she needed to parallel park; for years, she'd double parked in her neighbourhood wherever she damned well pleased. No one would dare report her. Or ticket her. Within seconds, Terry was walking down the sidewalk towards her, hands thrust into her jean jacket pockets. Jean leaned over and popped the passenger door.

"Hey, how are you?" she asked.

"I'm good. Not sure about these reunions. I guess maybe I got what I needed out of the group," Terry admitted. Jean smiled at her friend.

"At least I get to see Taylor tonight. He's been kinda scarce. Not as available as I'd like."

"Maybe he doesn't know how lucky he is." Terry grinned at her friend.

"If he only knew," Jean answered. "I can't believe you're feeling done. This is only the first one, right? I kinda like seeing where everyone is. Three weeks is a long time! I wonder if that little brown girl's been offed by her brothers." Terry looked over at her friend, surprised. Jean was casually merging onto the highway, glancing over her shoulder.

"Padma?" Terry's voice was a little strained. She'd liked the little kid, felt sorry for her. Why was Jean so weird about it?

"Yeah, I guess that's her name. Poor kid." Jean looked over at Terry, slouched in the leather seat next to her.

"Well, that's family for you. Do you want some heat over there?" Jean asked, reaching for the button for the seat warmer. Terry smiled across the console.

"That's nice. Thanks for driving me. I guess I'm just not used to the whole 'murdering the women' thing." Clearly Terry wasn't going to take Jean on, but her face flushed when she thought about how close she'd come to killing her husband.

"You got plans with Taylor after the meeting?" Terry asked. "Barb's gonna come get me when she's done at work, so you don't need to worry about driving me back."

"Yeah, we're planning to go get a drink together. Maybe more. Taylor's been bad, and I want to show him just what happens when he's bad." Jean was leering, and Terry laughed. She glanced over at her new friend, wondering if she'd ever be as cool on the outside as Jean was. Like a cucumber.

"Oh, he's young." Jean caught the look from the younger woman. "And strong. He'll learn that one of the advantages of having an older woman is that she isn't afraid of him." Jean's eyebrows wagged up and down, which made Terry snort a little. "And that can be very fun indeed." Jean shimmied in her seat. Terry flinched. TMI. She knew about the occasional use of handcuffs. Wondered if Taylor did…or was teaching him a part of what Jean described as fun?

"Well, clearly you know the value of a good lesson or two. I hope he's a willing student."

A few minutes later they stopped for a coffee at a drive-through, and Terry pushed restart on the conversation.

"So, the retreat really helped Barb and me. She's glad I'm telling her about stuff now, communicating. How's it going for you?" It bugged Terry that Jean hadn't opened up in circle, when she, a tough nut, had cracked. Jean smiled over at her motorcycle-loving passenger.

"Well, it helped me sort some shit out in my own head. I have quite a story, and I was tired of it haunting me," she said. She shot a quick glance at Terry and was glad to see her looking out the window. A few seconds later, she asked.

"Did you want to hear a little about it?" Jean asked. Terry nodded, staring out the windshield. She knew any time she looked Barb in the eyes when they were sharing, Barb shut down.

"So, a while ago, when I was just out of school, I was on the street, and hooked up with a guy…Johnny…he took care of me. We were together a long time, but things got rough. I really wanted to have a baby, and he wouldn't let me. Kept telling me I had to stay on birth control. I guess if his friends were sharing me, he didn't want me off it. I just wanted him to stop handing me around, but that's not how things worked in the club. Beat me up over it. More than once.

"Then he started moving younger women into the club, and sharing them around, too. I was getting older, and knew I wouldn't be welcome for much longer, so I got another guy to help me leave. I think maybe Johnny was okay with it, because it gave him an out. I'd been cranky… Johnny had been moving some young guys on the street, and pimping them, and he treated them like shit. Sometimes I called him on it.

"Anyways, I got out. Stole a little money and set myself up in an apartment. Soon, I was like the mom on the street to these young guys. Started bringing them food, making sure they had somewhere to stay when they were done working for the night. Helping them out, you know." Jean took a sip of coffee, savouring the warmth.

"Somewhere along the line, they gradually started aligning with me, and I built up a good business, got them off the streets and into a rooming house so they were safer. Moved them downtown where they had a different clientele. Let's just say before I retired, I built up enough that I won't have to work again.

"I keep my head down, though. I was careful not to move into Johnny's territory, but I don't think he was real pleased I was working the business and doin' okay. Anyhow, once I retired and had some time on my hands, I realized that some of the stuff that had happened to me was keeping me up at night. Stuff I'd seen, been forced to do.

231

"I thought the retreat would help, and it did. Really." Jean took another sip. Jean didn't mention that she'd been caught pimping the boys, and when she'd cried trauma from her assaults, the prosecutor suggested she attend the retreat. Actually, made it a condition of her plea. So she went.

"Well, I'm glad it helped you, too," Terry said, looking at the trees passing by her window. "We're almost there. We made good time," she said, in passing.

"Yeah. And I got to meet Taylor, who's been a great distraction. That's helping, too. He's never really been romanced. Or been able to romance. We're having a little fun. And he's a quick learner, if you know what I mean." Jean looked at Terry and flashed her beautiful white teeth. Terry chuckled.

"No doubt. I bet he's lovin' it too," she said.

"Yeah. If only he'd move back into the city, give up some of the drama at *Just Living*. I'd set him up in an apartment." Jean turned off the highway, heading up the rural road into the forest towards *Tide's End*. "Anyways, I appreciate that you're getting a lift home, because I'm hoping to have fun tonight. Show him how I roll." Jean smiled as she lowered the driver's window and flicked her empty coffee cup into the ditch.

Terry didn't know what to say, surprised at her disgust. Jean knew it wasn't okay to litter, right?

And she did know that Johnny had been her pimp, and not her boyfriend, right?

But had she figured out that Terry knew?

Terry smiled and pretended it didn't matter.

CHAPTER 34
ROUGH RELATIONS

Padma met me on the path walking over to *Tide's End*. I was really looking forward to seeing the other women, grateful that Padma and I had stayed in touch.

"Tay, I have a favour to ask." She kicked a stone off the path. "I have to move out of my cousin's and get my stuff from my parent's place. I've found a place with a roommate and I started a job. I'm hoping I can make it work." She hooked her arm through mine as we walked towards the reunion.

"I'm kinda excited, and mostly a bit scared. Can you help me get my stuff? I'm a little afraid of how it might go. And I need your wheels." I saw her side-glance me, checking out my reaction. Of course, I would absolutely help her, and I let her know. Might as well be helping someone, 'cause I wasn't being much help to Jenny. My nightly calls to the shelters and soup kitchens hadn't turned up anything.

"There isn't too much. I'm trying to find a bed, other furniture, but that's not what I'm talking about. It's just my stuff. Some schoolbooks, some music and clothes out of my room. And the stuff from my cousin's where I've been staying fits into a couple of garbage bags." I remembered the garbage bag luggage of my childhood – back and forth from foster homes, or even when we had to move quickly after Mom fucked up paying the rent again. The torn duffle I had now I'd taken from a rich kid in the group home, and it was old then.

"Do you want me to ask Kenny to help, too? Two guys are stronger than one," I said. "And he's pretty friendly. Good at diffusing any shit. If it's on the weekend, we can probably both get some time off. Maybe even get a truck from here." Was I allowed to offer? "If they'll let me," I added.

"Do you think he would? Really?" Padma asked. "It's next Saturday. If that works. I could do it Sunday, I guess. But I want to get it done." She gently squeezed my arm as we rounded the corner towards the big door that I hardly even noticed any more.

"Well, things are going good for me," Padma told the circle. "I have a job in an Indian restaurant, and I'm moving in with a roommate Saturday. Taylor's gonna help me." I admit, I cringed when I saw the look on Jean's face. I would've liked to tell Jean first, because I'd promised the weekend to her. She shot daggers at me over the circle…I was in trouble. Again.

Whatever. I'd decided I had to talk to her. Let her know that I'd be focusing more on getting to work in the Valley so that when Jennie is ready, I can try again for custody. Maybe Jean and I *weren't* supposed to be. Having a girlfriend was more complicated than it seemed in the movies.

The evening went quickly, and it was good to hear from everyone. Rosie let us decide what to talk about, and the group couldn't agree on anything. I realized we're less connected, that we've kinda grown up. And apart, but also it feels good. We agreed to have one more meeting, and then decide if we want to keep on going.

Around a table during break, Ophelia, Padma, Dianne and I decided we were going to keep in touch, even if the meetings stopped. Ophelia and I are going for tea next week. She lives nearby so we can go out after work, which is great. No big commute, or gas bill. I need someone like her who tells me like it is…no bullshit. And she lives close.

Dianne invited us over after the next meeting.

"I'll cook," I offered.

"Only if I get to buy the ingredients," she replied. "After I get into my new place. I'll let you know if we need dishes!"

"I've eaten off of paper plates before," I reminded her. "And worse." We shared phone numbers to plan together, and I asked her if I could call her sometimes.

"Of course, Taylor," she said, her eyes all lit up.

Something else to plan for! I like dreaming about making the perfect dinners for people. Maybe I can make enough food that I can send some home with Padma. And, I'm curious about Dianne's son…maybe I'll get to meet him.

After Ben joined us and talked about setting up 'individual support plans,' we were hanging out in the parking lot saying goodbye, and Jean grabbed my arm in her sharp fingers. Hard.

"Are we still doing tonight, or do you have other plans like Saturday?" she said, her voice quiet, clipped. She'd leave bruises on my arm, so I lifted it up and spun it onto her shoulder in an old move I used with clients who manhandled me. If I didn't bend my elbow too much, I could keep her at arms length. She gasped, just a little.

"Give me a moment to say goodbye, and we can head out," I said, hoping she'd wait to yell at me. I liked these people. They didn't need to see Jean and I fighting. "Unless you don't want to?" I almost wished she'd drive away.

"No, I planned for this. Let's do it," Jean growled at me from beside her car. "Grab a few things and meet me at the hotel in town, I'll be waiting." She moved in close to my ear. "Room 314," she whispered. But it was a harsh whisper, the kind my mom used when she wanted me to behave when the men were "visiting."

I ran home and packed a quick bag. Told Kenny I'd be back in the morning and forgot to ask him about helping Padma. No sense keeping Jean waiting…a hotel room! She did love to surprise, and I didn't want to disappoint her any more than I already had.

I opened the hotel room door and tossed my old duffle inside.

"Jean? Where are you, babe?" I asked, seeing the bathroom door closed. A minute later, she came out, and her silky nightgown was… inviting. My body sure felt invited, anyways. She was holding a glass in her hand, sipping what looked like white wine.

"Pour yourself a glass, Tay," she said, motioning to the small tray sitting on the bar fridge. I ducked into the bathroom.

"Just let me wash up first," I said. I was still a little amazed that this beautiful woman wanted to be with me.

"Be quick. I've waited too long," she called out. Maybe she'd calmed down. I washed my face and hands, made sure I was presentable, and stepped out of the washroom and into Jean's arms.

A little while later, I came up for air. We were undressed in the huge bed, doing what couples do. Clean sheets. A gorgeous woman who knew how to love me. And my body responded over and over. I was grinning from ear to ear…life was rockin' right now. But it was time to talk about the weekend.

"Hey, babe, I'm sorry about Saturday morning. I can come out Saturday night, and stay until dinner Sunday, if that works for you," I said. "Padma asked for help moving, and I'm going to get Kenny to help, too, so it won't take too long. She wants us around in case any of her relatives get crazy." Jean didn't say anything, didn't even look at me. "I'll make it up to you, promise," I said, hoping she was okay with it. I tried to kiss her neck, but she turned away. I could feel a chill come into the room. Into the bed. I sighed.

Jean swung her feet onto the floor, and headed for the bathroom, wrapping the top sheet around herself. She didn't exactly slam the door, but I heard the force behind it closing. Controlled but pissed. Fuck. *Now what?* I thought as my stomach braced itself. I sat up, pulled on my pants. And then things got weird, even for me.

Jean came out angry.

"You are so fucking selfish," she spit at me. Quiet, but pissed. "I go out of my way for you and your precious job, getting this hotel room. You just don't appreciate me.

"You don't even have the decency to check with me before you change our plans." She turned and headed back into the bathroom. I heard the tap running, so I got up and poured her another glass of wine. Took it in to her.

She grabbed it out of my hands, dumped the wine down the sink and slammed the glass onto the counter. I was glad it didn't break.

"What the hell, Taylor. Why do I bother? I give and give and give. You cost me a fortune. Hotel rooms aren't cheap you know. Even in shitty little towns like this one." I backed away, headed for the bedroom.

I swear she went on for about five minutes. Maybe ten. And she didn't yell, but her cold, clipped voice was worse. I tried not to cringe, sitting on the edge of the bed. Words were fired at me, and it felt like gun shot. I just shut up. Took it, like I had when Mom's boyfriends lost it. My body felt charged, like it had when Barry came after me. Or when a trick got nasty on the street. I glanced at the door, trying to remember where my phone and stuff was, my duffle, in case I had to make a quick exit. And Jean saw that, I guess.

She grabbed my shoulders, threw me on the bed and started kissing me. Hard. I struggled to get my arms out, but she pinned them. Stared at me.

"You can't treat me like that, then just think about cutting out. I mean it. Own it like a man, treat me like a woman." A minute later she was slapping my chest, kissing me, hitting me, gouging me with her nails, and the loving and hurting were getting all confused in my brain. But parts of my body liked it, that was for sure.

Jean grabbed my crotch through my jeans and wasn't gentle, manhandling me until I was hard. Chafed even. But her anger hadn't drained at all. What was going on? It was like she was making me pay in waves, slapping me, then kissing me and apologizing. Then she'd calmed down a bit, and before I caught my breath she'd start punching and scratching me again.

Unfortunately, it was giving me a raging hard-on. I kept trying to hold her, wrap her arms into mine, but it just made her madder, so I stopped and just dropped onto the bed, decided to take what was coming.

That seemed to settle her a bit, and slowly the intensity of the hitting, the anger drained away, replaced by an intensity of passion I hadn't felt with her before. With anyone, really. I rolled her over on the bed, got out of my jeans again, and tried making soft, gentle advances, stroking her cheeks, pulling the blankets over us so she wouldn't get cold when the sheen of sweat she'd raised started to cool. I entered her slowly, murmuring apologies. She let me rock into her, slowly increasing the pace.

She seemed to be enjoying it, but then I felt her temper slowly rise again. I tried to pretend it wasn't happening, that we were just making love, but something was different.

And when I started to come without her, she let me have it. Pounding on my back, raking nails down my sides, grabbing my hair and pulling it. I lost track of all the ways she was hitting me, hurting me. But my body didn't stop climaxing, even when I pulled out. I'd felt it before. The horror. When Barry had raped me, when clients had forced me to do things I didn't want to do, but my body climaxed anyway.

I felt dirty. Small. I wanted to crawl under the bed and disappear, wait for her to leave the room so I could gather myself and leave.

Then, like another switch tripped, she calmed down and started to kiss me.

"I'm sorry, Taylor, but you brought this on. You make me a little mad. You've got to treat me better. Let me know what's happening. Make me feel special." Each explanation, each plea was punctuated with a kiss, a murmur. I didn't understand, and was too tired to try, so I just gave up. Gave in.

"Really. Sometimes I feel so much when I'm with you. And then I get jealous when I find out you'd rather be with that little girl. Scared, maybe, that you'll pick her. I know I'm getting old," her voice trailed off. I heard her excuses, but I was spent. And there I was again, sitting on the edge of the bed, trying to pull myself together, aware that I didn't want to piss her off again.

"It's okay, Jean. Really. I get it. I'm gonna go get some water," I said, ducking into the bathroom. When I turned on the light, turned on the tap, I caught sight of myself in the mirror. There were a few scrapes on my arms, more on my body, but I wiped the blood off them, and once I pulled my T-shirt back on, you could hardly tell. I didn't think I'd have too many bruises to explain.

I dressed and headed back into the room. Jean was tucked into bed, sitting and watching TV. She patted the bed beside me.

"You don't have to go right now, do you?" she asked. I agreed to stay for a little while and tucked my arm around her. She sighed, putting her head on my shoulder, her hand on my thigh. I felt our bodies relax into one another, just hanging out.

A few hours later, she was asleep, and I snuck out the door, leaving the TV on to cover my exit. I left the key in the bathroom where she'd be sure to find it. I was glad I didn't have a paper or pen to leave her a note, because I hadn't figured out what to say to her yet.

As I snuck back into the trailer, Kenny whispered out of his bedroom.

"Hey, you're home early. Or late," he said. And I just chuckled.

It was really good to be…home.

CHAPTER 35
TOO. MUCH. EXCITEMENT.

"Hey, Taylor, got a minute?" Kenny asked me.

I was cleaning up after dinner in the big kitchen at *Just Living*. I'd given Cook the night off since he'd offered me Saturday and Sunday to move Padma and spend time with Jean. I was putting leftovers into the fridge for the weekend, and kinda humming. I liked the kitchen after everyone had left – puttering, cleaning. It felt like maybe I *could* be responsible and look after things. And then Kenny ducked in the side door off the dining room.

"Cook around?" he asked. I waved him in.

"He and Sally are in their room, I think. Gave him the night off."

We sat down at the little table under the window, and I got us some juice from the fridge.

"I'm going out tonight, but I'll be back to help with Padma in the morning, okay?" he said. I nodded, watched him fidget.

"It's all good, Kenny. I know you'll be there," I said. Kenny's eyes jumped back and forth between the kitchen and door to upstairs.

"Yeah, well, I have to go see a guy. I'll be back in lots of time, though. Just want to touch base with Cook first, let him know I'm going." He stood in the kitchen and pretended to smell the air. "Are those gingersnaps?" he asked.

"Yeah, I baked some more tonight while I was cleaning up, because everyone loved the last ones." I grabbed a few from the pantry, and put them on a plate to share, then put some in a paper bag to take home.

"A few for now, and some for later. We ate the rest last night," I said. He smiled and headed upstairs towards Cook and Sally's suite.

Last night, he'd seen my bruises and scratches.

He'd made tea.

"What's with that?" he'd asked, putting the gingersnaps on a plate and pointing to my arm. "They don't look like love bites," he said. His quiet voice told me he wasn't teasing. So, I told him.

"Yeah. I don't get it. One minute she's all great, and I'm happy, and the next she's losing it. Like, really losing her shit on me. I don't think it's worth it," I'd admitted out loud. It was the first time I'd really said it. Meant it. I breathed easier, like sharing my idea made it possible.

"I'm kinda scared to tell her, you know? But I need to be free to focus here, look after things if I'm going to get Jenny. Anyhow, I'll tell her soon," I said, a plan forming.

I'd wait until I was at her place tomorrow night, or maybe Sunday when I was leaving, to break it off. I was man enough to talk to her right to her face, even if my heart pounded and my mouth went dry when I thought about it. How much worse could it be? Besides, I needed to get my things from her place, give her back her phone. Maybe I could borrow some money from someone to pay her back for my car repairs.

Kenny and I laughed, wondering if it was something in the trailer water or the tea that made us dating failures. I took the mugs from the table over to the sink. They'd wait for the morning to be washed up. I locked up the door, turned out the lights, and headed back to our trailer.

As I opened the door, all I could hear was quiet. I turned on the lights in the hallway and smiled, put the bag of cookies in the cupboard, and turned towards my bedroom. I put my dirty clothes in a laundry bin Sally had given me, and looked around, smiling. My stomach didn't hurt. My body was warm, and dry. I was actually tired from work, not from stress.

I felt like maybe I could be an adult after all. I could work towards getting Jenny, being a role model.

I kissed Russet and settled into bed, listening to the boughs of the evergreens blowing in the wind as the rain fell on the tin roof of the trailer. It was the best sound ever, knowing I'd get to sleep through the night. This sleeping alone was something I could get used to, I thought, spreading my arms wide in my clean sheets. Life even smelled good.

About nine o'clock the next morning I started to worry. Kenny hadn't come home, and I was a bit squirrely because he'd been so clear. I grabbed my wallet and phone and headed for the trailer door, glanced back at the cell phone Jean had given me and decided to leave it behind. *Soon enough!* I thought.

I found Beth in her office.

"Beth, Kenny had arranged for the truck so we could move Padma today, but he's not home. Can I still use it?" I'd always let Kenny get keys and stuff. Drive, even.

"No problem, Taylor. Not sure where he is, but you'll be okay moving Padma on your own?" she asked. It sounded like she trusted me, and my chest puffed a little.

"Yeah, she doesn't have much stuff. A couple of garbage bags full, a few other things. You don't happen to know of some boxes we could use instead of garbage bags, do you?" She told me to take any from the carport, where the produce boxes were stacked.

"You haven't heard from Kenny, have you?" I asked as I headed out. "His phone goes right to voice mail," I told her.

"Well, the weekend is his. I'll ask around, but we hang back once men become staff here. It's their lives, after all. I'm sure he's fine," she said.

I'm not so sure, I thought as I carefully backed out of the parking lot and headed to pick up Padma.

Spending the day with Padma felt great, except for the scary bits. First, we went by her parents' house, but her brothers' cars were there, and her mom wasn't home. Her cousin called us, told us to come to her aunt's place first. On our way I went through a drive-through and splurged for a coffee and donut for each of us. It felt good to have a little cash. Sally paid me a little every week for helping in the kitchen.

"Everybody deserves some fun money," she'd said. So, I was having fun. Padma had the tunes loud, and we were singing along, heading down the highway. Before long, we pulled into her auntie's driveway.

It only took a few minutes, and we'd loaded her stuff into the boxes. Padma and her cousins were laughing, packing stuff up, talking in Punjabi, and I just smiled and hefted the boxes to the truck. We were just about to head out when her aunt came screaming into the driveway.

"Oh, Patheeji, I'm so glad I got here," she called out, flying out of her car and gathering Padma into her arms. "You can't go there yet. Let's have some tea first," she said, herding us back into the house. We had tea and sandwiches, pretending everything was normal, laughing and joking. But something seemed off.

"Patheeji, you can't go yet to the house. Your brothers are still there. Uncle is going over to get them out, but until he texts, you should stay here. Maybe we should make some food together," she said, checking her phone. Again. I settled in for a longer visit, and realized we were behind schedule. I knew I'd be in trouble with Jean, but Padma needed me.

About an hour later, her uncle arrived, and we sat down to eat a feast. With friends like these, I'd never be hungry. Around seven o'clock, Padma's uncle announced he was going with us to the house.

"Just in case," he said. It was sinking in that Padma's brothers had planned an ambush, had meant to really hurt her. It was hard to believe.

Yes, my family hurt me. A lot. But I don't know that they set out to do it. It just seemed to happen. We headed for the vehicles.

Padma's cousin, Ran, made a wall between Padma and me in the truck. Not a screen, but a wall, he was that wide. Big smile, too. The way he inserted himself between us, without any discussion, told me just how comfortable the family was with Padma sitting close to me. Not. Her uncle, aunt and two cousins led the way in their car.

When we arrived, the cousins and auntie went to the door, and told us to drive around the corner and wait. I admit, my heart was pounding. Auntie and Uncle had walked up the path with a big soup pot from our dinner, and everyone except Padma and I moved right into the house. The cousins, I heard later, had headed for Padma's room "to play some music." Padma and I kept waiting, sitting in the truck, getting more and more cold and tired.

"Hey, move over here," I said, and pulled her beside me. Take that, Ran. "Use this blanket to keep yourself warm." I tucked her under my arm.

"What do you think you'll miss the most, Padma?" I asked in a quiet voice. I didn't know if it was good to talk about it, but so many of us from the retreat had had to leave our lives that I couldn't help but wonder. She didn't hesitate.

"Birthdays. Family parties. But mostly festivals and weddings. When everybody gets together and is kind and generous. And it's beautiful." I thought about the stories I'd heard about weddings that lasted days, and festivals and big party tents I saw pictures of, set up on driveways in suburbia.

"Wow. Yeah." I breathed in and out. "That would be hard." I am so not profound, but really, when I say, "I can't imagine," I really can't. She must have noticed my quiet.

"What about you? Will you miss birthday parties?" she asked. I coughed. Remembered how big Jenny's smile was when I'd show up in her bedroom after dinner, hiding a small candle burning brightly stuck in a Joe Louis or Swiss Roll I'd lifted from the corner store. Sometimes I'd have a small toy I'd found, something like a keychain or a little toy like the machines at the grocery store gave rich kids with a dollar. One year I'd even saved up and we'd bought one for her.

"Sometimes I tried to do something for Jenny on her birthday. We'd have our own little party," I said. "I'd forgotten about that." I was smiling, felt warm inside. Different, having happy thoughts about Jenny and home.

Silence fell between us. Padma patted my leg and laid her head on my shoulder, and soon her breathing settled, evened out. But I wasn't going to go to sleep, just in case I had to get out of there quickly. My nose curled at the smell of rain mixed with car exhaust, and I realized I might not be a city boy any more. I knew that Padma was good for me, sharing her stories of family and reminding me that even when it all looked perfect from outside, family was what we made it. I hunkered down in the truck to wait.

Then the cousins came running around the corner with their arms full of stuff. Boxes. Suitcases. Posters. I jumped out of the truck and opened the back. Padma moved back over to her side of the seat.

"Quick!" Ran said. "I don't know if they saw us, but we've got to get this stuff into the truck. Then you guys can head out. My mom will drive us home."

Minutes later, we were heading to the highway, my heart pounding. I looked over at Padma and she was wiping her cheeks with her sleeve. I glanced in the rearview mirror. There was a car following us.

"I can't believe it. They really wanted to hurt me. I'm so glad for my cousins," she added. She put her cheek on the cool window, looking out into the rain. The car was still behind us. I went around the block. My heart started pounding. As we merged onto the highway, I slowed down. It pulled up beside me, but I couldn't see anyone inside because the windows were black. I sped up, and it got behind me again. I was glad Padma was distracted, even if it was because her heart was hurting. I tried to lose the car, but every few miles I looked up and there it was again. Shit.

"Padma, what kind of car do your brothers drive?" I asked about ten minutes later. I'd had my hand on the seat between us, and Padma had put her knee against it. It felt good to have even that small connection. Her tears had slowed down.

"A black Honda Civic and a Charger. Why?" she asked.

"Because one's been behind us for a while, and I've woven in and out of traffic a bit. I don't want to go to your place if it's your brothers." Padma twisted around in the seat, trying to see which car I was worried about.

"Shit. It's them, I think. How did they find us?" she asked.

"They've been with us pretty much since we left," I admitted. She pulled out her phone and started texting her aunt.

"Auntie says they were pissed at us and ran out before she could stop them. She was hoping they didn't catch us." I reached in my pocket and handed her my phone. I didn't want to take my eyes off the road, because the streetlights on the rainy surface made things harder to see. Maneuvering the big truck was taking all my concentration.

"Here. Open my messages, and text my cop friend. He's there under Derksen. He knows Patty and Neil. Tell him what's going on and ask him what we should do." My hands were getting sweaty. I'd never thought of calling the cops for help before, but I knew Padma was in danger. I was trying to keep my eyes on the road and keep track of the car behind me because I didn't want to crack up the truck that wasn't mine. And from time to time, I couldn't help but wonder where the fuck Kenny was. I'd love it if he was driving right now.

As we approached the highway exit, my phone buzzed.

"He says to hang tight and just exit the highway. He'll have a car pull my brothers over for a routine traffic stop, and that'll give us time to get away. God, I'm glad I know their vanity plate," she said. I smiled. Such a simple solution.

"That's the Inspector in Mission," I said. "We keep in touch because of Jenny. Patty hopes they'll be moving soon on her case," I confessed.

"Taylor! You didn't need to help me today with all that going on," she said.

"It's okay. You've been a great distraction today. And I've had fun. Except for this part." I realized I was smiling. Padma grinned back at me.

A few minutes later, the red and blue lights in the back window told me we should make a few turns and head back towards Padma's new apartment. We were there in ten minutes, and I parked in the back and hid the truck under the building's overhang. I really hoped that after their run-in with the cops the brothers would give up.

A half hour later all Padma's boxes were in her new place, and she was unpacking the stuff her cousins had grabbed for her.

"They even got my brother's Bluetooth speaker!" Padma shouted, opening box after box. There were clothes, and kitchen stuff from her aunt. Books, some university texts. A sleeping bag. They really were looking out for her.

Soon we were listening to Bollywood music, laughing, and she was ordering pizza. It felt so good to be with her, just hanging out and helping her unpack.

A few minutes later she showed me some Bollywood dancing from online movies and pulled me up to teach me some moves. Did I mention I have two left feet? The smell of pizza, the pink and orange of the bright wall hangings her cousins had thrown in the boxes, and the great music made me forget about getting to Vancouver that night.

And then, when I remembered, I decided to ignore it and stayed with Padma. Was that relief I was feeling? After all, I couldn't even text Jean. About an hour later, I texted Beth to let her know I was okay. She told me Kenny had come home and suggested I might want to come back and hang out with him.

"He's in rough shape, Taylor," she said.

I was on my way.

CHAPTER 36
THE PAST NEVER DIES - KENNY

Kenny looked out at his former crew mates, and a few new to the gang, from between swollen eyelids. Blood trickled into his left eye, and he realized he must be cut. He shook his head, trying to keep it from blocking his sight. His wrists were zip-tied together, and he could hear what was going on in the other room. Yes, now he knew he was stupid to agree to the meeting, but he hadn't expected an ambush. What the fuck did Ink, the guy he'd served time for, expect? That, after this beating, he'd happily rejoin?

He was pissed that he'd been sold out, was scrambling to figure out how to get out of here. And the asshole hadn't even had the decency to be here when Kenny'd arrived. The other young guy who'd also shown up? He was being beaten too, as a way of welcome. *How fucked up is that?* Kenny wondered, remembering his own initiation.

Just shut up, asshole, Kenny thought as they beat up the poor punk in the next room. *Take your beats quietly and they'll leave you alone.* It'd been going on for hours, on and off. Beat Kenny. Beat the other kid. Rest for a while. Threaten to force Kenny to beat the young kid. Repeat. Apparently, they were waiting for some epiphany from the two of them. *Just take it and shut up. It'll be over sooner,* Kenny thought.

Thug One sauntered back to the kitchen, a two-bit fuckup with attitude.

"What the fuck happened? You were legendary. 'Kenny took the rap for everyone,' they told us when we joined up. All you had to do was come back and take your place." Kenny knew the whole time he was locked up that he'd have a place back with these guys, but he'd decided to leave. Grow things. Be free of law enforcement. Maybe even fall in love again.

He'd been thinking about Carl all night, his first real love who'd killed himself because of drugs, and addiction, and prison. Mumbling under his breath, he apologized to his dead lover.

"Damn, Carl. I didn't see this coming. Thought it was over. Shit. Should have known better. You would have, if you were still breathing." The young punk thought he was talking to him.

"What the fuck, man? What're you on about? We ain't gonna kill you or nothin'. Just come back. Work with us," he said. "The boss's on his way." Kenny cringed. He didn't want to explain himself to his old buddy from high school. He knew Ink wouldn't understand leaving the life, the money, the women behind. But then, Ink — Jas as he'd been called then — had never *really* known him.

How the fuck am I going to get out of here? Kenny wondered. He knew he was well overdue at home and half hoped Taylor or Cook would somehow save him. Because he was fucked otherwise. He really didn't want to be here when Ink arrived. That could end with a needle in his arm, and he'd seen that train wreck in too many lives. He just wanted to be back in his garden…he could smell the soil, imagine the tired muscles in his shoulders when he closed his eyes. He tried to send up a prayer.

And then there was a commotion in the hallway. Banging on the door.

Shit, he thought. *Just like him to arrive with chaos behind him.* Kenny's heart pounded; his mouth went dry. Maybe it was time to give in.

"Let us the fuck in or I'll fuck wit' you hard!" He heard the voice at the door, and a moment later the door frame broke where the chain had once been.

Thank God for short screws, Kenny thought, smiling. The door banged on the back wall as the young kid was bounced out of the way. Next thing he knew, Tom and Cook were literally dragging him out of his chair, and out the door. Picking him up by his biceps, they kept the pace down the hall. Trying to keep his feet under him, he stumbled, but they dragged him faster, out the back door, arms still tied together. Who knew Cook could move so fast when he needed to?

Moments later they shoved him into Cook's truck and tore out of the alley. One guy came bouncing out the back door. Kenny looked back again and was glad the guy'd headed back inside. Kenny's head was racing, spinning, taking in everything.

As they rounded the corner, Kenny ducked his head onto Cook's lap. He could smell trouble, and just wanted to get away. Last thing he needed was to be spotted now. He thought he heard sirens far off.

"Holy fuck. Thank you," he croaked, barely able to believe he was free. Except for his arms.

"How the fuck did you guys find me?" Kenny asked.

"Someone's got a potty mouth," Tom scowled. "What the fuck were you thinking going alone? Seriously." Cook coughed, and his gut bounced up and down, Kenny's head bouncing with it. Kenny laughed, and Tom barked, his pulse rising.

"Fuck. You think it's funny? You don't get it. What if we'd got caught in there?" Kenny's relief started to fade.

"It worked. That new kid, Jeremy, said it would, and we didn't believe him! Maybe computers can be useful," Cook admitted. Kenny had no idea what they were talking about, but his heart rate started to even out, and Cook got control of his cough. They propped Kenny back up and explained.

"We found your computer, and Jeremy hacked it. You gotta get new passwords, man. Carl4Ever is just so lame. We all know it." Tom paused to merge into traffic, and Kenny said a short prayer.

Thank you, Carl. You keep on looking out for me. I still miss you.

"Well, seems not changing my password is workin' for me," Kenny said to his friends. He was trying not to grin from ear to ear, feeling sheepish about dragging his friends into something that could land them back in prison.

"Anyway, the kid located your phone on the screen. Some connection between it and your computer. He told us where to go, and there you were. Just had to figure out which floor. Luckily you were behind the first door we broke down." Tom was shaking his head, and none of them could believe they'd pulled it off. Cook cut the strap from Kenny's arms with a pen knife, and soon they were flying down the highway, making good time on their way back to *Just Living*.

Kenny looked out the window and realized the sun was setting. *Where the hell did the day go?* he wondered. A comfortable silence had settled over the truck.

"Hey guys, should I call the cops? I really think that young kid could die if I don't," Kenny said.

"Already done, my fren'." Cook's voice was soft. "Imagine us, callin' in the po-po. We did it when we drove up. Jus' in case we really fucked up. Anonymous, of course." A couple of seconds later, he added, "Not that we need to go tellin' anyone 'bout that." Kenny sighed and rested his head on the back of the old, hard bench seat in Cook's truck. *Look at us,* he thought. *Not long ago I'd have rather died than call the cops for some asshole. Tom'd only have called the cops to an ambush.*

"Thanks for coming," Kenny said for the tenth time, his eyes closing.

"Thanks for letting me drive," Tom said, pulling Cook's chain. "We'd still be on our way if the old guy had driven," he added.

Soon, Kenny's head had fallen onto Cook's shoulder and he was dozing. Next thing he knew, he heard the creak of the passenger door opening. He smelled the rich, clean air of the cedar forest around his trailer, felt the rain in the air.

The best feeling of home he'd ever had.

Thank fucking God for these men, Kenny thought. *Thank fucking God for this life.*

He couldn't help but think of how many vegetables he was going to grow for these guys next season. And all the other ways he planned to say thank you. Remind them that he was grateful to this place, and the life he had landed.

And that they were along for the journey.

"Hey. Did Padma get moved?" he asked as they parked Cook's truck.

"All moved and settled. And the kid didn't even crack up Beth's truck," Cook answered, patting Kenny's leg. "Now let's get you into your place to clean you up before someone important sees you and freaks out."

As they helped him up the stoop to his trailer, Cook finished the thought for them.

"And gets us all into trouble."

CHAPTER 37
ADULTING

"Come on in, Taylor. Put your stuff on the counter in the kitchen here," Veronica called to me when I got to her place that afternoon. She'd hired me to cook a meal for her book club, based on what I'd cooked a few weeks back for the volunteers at *Just Living*. I ducked through the laundry room, and into a recently renovated kitchen. Granite counters, gleaming appliances, clean hardwood floors, dark blue cupboards...with lots of cooking tools dotted around the place. Warm sunlight streamed in the window over the sink. And there was another one. Two sinks. A double sink on the big counter, with a view of a gorgeous backyard and forest, and a smaller one on the island. Three sinks! *Yes, this will absolutely do.*

My first paid gig, and I had an amazing space to cook. I hoped I wasn't the weak link in the plan.

"Can I just put this stuff in the fridge?" I asked, anxious to see its insides. I'd lain awake last night worrying that Veronica's place would be a dump, like all the places I'd lived in with Jenny. I dreamed of giving her this kind of place one day.

"Sure," Veronica declared, throwing open one door on the stainless steel appliance. "I emptied space for you. Let me know if you need more. The sauces you asked for are on the top shelf." A clean top shelf, I noticed. The whole fridge was sparkling. "Make sure you give me the receipts from your shopping," she added.

"Oh no!" I said. "The ingredients I bought are included in the price I gave you." She chuckled.

"You'll never make enough to live that way, Taylor. The client foots the bill. I can afford it." I had a ton to learn about pricing meals, and making sure clients were clear about costs, and stuff. I had had a moment in the grocery store debating if I could afford to feed Veronica's group when I saw how expensive high-quality produce and meat were. But I was ready to pay for my mistakes in quoting my first cooking job ever. And here, she saved my ass.

I put the groceries in the fridge, and took off my coat, hung it over a kitchen chair. I started to wash up.

"Take a second, Taylor. There's lots of time, right?" I knew there was because I'd brought the cake already decorated for dessert and had snuck a peek in the truck when I'd arrived. It had travelled just fine. I took a deep breath and tried to get my shoulders to drop.

"Sure," I said, not clear what she wanted. I admit, my mind was always preoccupied, wondering if everyone was secretly interested in getting down and dirty with the boy toy. It *always* went there.

"Can I give you a tour? It's always a good day when I have guests" she admitted. She pulled at the bottom of her sweater and looked at the floor. *What?* Was she lonely? This was the nicest house I'd ever been in when not with a rich john. My eyes got big when we rounded the corner into the living room.

"It's way too big for just me," she said, showing me the living room that her book club members would be more than comfortable in. My living rooms had always had old mattresses and dirty sheets as furniture. Hers had two comfortable old leather couches and a fireplace.

"Here's the dining room. I set it up for tonight, but I eat in the kitchen for every day." Imagine having *two* rooms to eat in. Then I saw at least five bedrooms, and three bathrooms.

"You have a lovely home," I told her. I wasn't sure how to really say thank you for this chance to feed her friends. I decided to cook the most amazing meal, so we headed to the kitchen.

An hour later, there was a spaghetti sauce bubbling on the stove in the soup pot I'd borrowed from Cook's private stash, and Veronica was cutting vegetables on the kitchen table for salad. We'd been chatting, and I realized I'd grown comfortable enough to ask her a few questions about her life. I wasn't stupid enough to ask about her husband. I'd heard he'd been murdered in a grow-op bust or something.

"Well, I don't know what you've heard, but I have three kids. Two sons, and a daughter. You'll meet her tonight. My boys are different – not two peas, that's for sure. One is a bit of a beach bum. The other is an accountant. Only one of them approves of me," she said giggling. *The accountant,* I thought. *Always the accountant.*

"Let me make you some tea," she said, standing up. "That sauce smells delicious. I'm glad you said you wished you'd had fresh herbs – because my garden has lots. Surprised you didn't take some from Kenny," she said. The fresh oregano, basil and thyme smelled glorious when I'd added them to the organic onions and beef, and cremini mushrooms, I admit. I asked if I could get a little more thyme to add to the garlic butter I'd whip up after our tea, and Veronica assured me there were blankets of thyme growing in the back yard. I wondered what that was like, having so much space you could grow blankets of herbs. And what it'd be like to be able to ask Kenny for anything I wanted.

Soon, Veronica's book club started to arrive, and I melted into the kitchen to prepare and plate their dinner. Veronica took it out to her friends, who were laughing and teasing each other.

I was putting the last pots in the drying rack when Veronica started bringing empty plates and cutlery into the kitchen.

"Just put them down on the counter. I'll load the dishwasher," I said. I'd already cut the cake and put it on plates on the kitchen table, each one with a few mint leaves. She made a couple of more trips, and then I heard the energy in the other room get bigger.

"They want you to serve the cake," she said, bringing the last of the plates. "I tried to tell them you were shy." She smiled at me, but I don't think she was as sorry as she looked. The twitch at the corner of her mouth gave her away. I tried to resist, but she wasn't having it, so I found myself carrying a couple of plates and heading into the dining room, still wearing my splattered apron.

"Here he is! We thought she was keeping you secret!" one middle-aged woman exclaimed. My head ducked – I couldn't help it.

"The meal was amazing, Taylor. Can you come next month, too?" a woman at the end of the table said.

"Taylor, meet my daughter, Brenda," Veronica said. I smiled at her, nodded and put a piece of cake in front of her. "Glad you liked it," I said.

Applause broke out, and I admit, I squirmed. Applause from seven or eight women isn't loud, but they meant it. I smiled at them and said, "Thank you."

Only one woman wasn't really smiling at me. Claire. She was also a volunteer at *Just Living* and lived in town. She helped out at the high school where I hoped Jenny would attend sometime. But she wasn't smiling at me, so I made a point of smiling at her, saying, "Hi."

She actually looked away. *Whatever*, I thought, ducking back into the kitchen. The conversation seemed to get back on track, and they took hot drinks to the living room to talk about the book. Finally, everyone was gone, and the house got quiet again except for a little background music Veronica had on.

Washing up and putting my dishes and empty bags to go out to the truck, I was humming. Everything had gone really well, I thought. Well, except for that thing with Claire. That was a little uncomfortable.

Veronica came back into the kitchen.

"Well, it was a huge success. Everyone loved your dinner. Spaghetti Bolognese, garlic toast, a huge salad. Chocolate espresso cake for dessert. They were moaning in appreciation." She tucked an envelope in the clean soup pot. I smiled, ducking my head. It *had* been good.

"I put the extra sauce in containers in the freezer for you," I said. "Labelled them, and I think I dished out portions for about two people."

Well, that was awkward. No judgement about living alone. It just seemed like single portions were kind of sad.

"Thank you! You should think about cooking real food for people like me who are tired of cooking." I couldn't imagine what that was like. "Raising my kids, cooking for Bob, it was what I did for…well…decades. I'm so done," she said, and I started to get it. I took a couple of trips to the truck and returned to hug her at the door.

"We could talk about that, Veronica. I'd love to cook for you sometimes," I said. She sent me off, her eyes a little damp, and I backed slowly out of the driveway while she waved from the garage.

I liked the rhythm I'd gotten into since that crazy meeting with Marta, the social worker. Really. It'd only been a few weeks, maybe a month or two since deciding to go to the retreat but I felt like I was growing up.

Lately, I'd been working with Cook more, in the kitchen, but also planning for the cooking school. We'd been talking about what I'd learned, and what he'd teach, and when. Beth set me up for some certificates, and I passed my Food Safe, and Kenny talked me into doing Market Safe, too, so I could help him sell veggies and food at the farmer's market. Passed first time! Studied hard, and worried tons, but mostly I knew it going in. God, my stomach had hurt for days before the test.

Maybe I can do school after all. It feels good to know stuff, so I don't hurt anyone with my cooking.

Driving home down the windy, rural streets between Veronica's place and our trailer, I got to thinking about life. I decided I needed to do more to find Jenny. I was done with waiting. Maybe I could troll the Downtown East Side in person and ask more questions, this time about online porn, pedophilia and stuff. Could I do that while I kept my life on track?

It'd help if I freed myself from crazy Jean. I had seen her once since moving Padma, but not for very long, and she hadn't been happy with me. At the time I'd decided it wasn't the right time to try and break up. She was already angry enough.

But then I got thinking about other stuff. I had an honest income. Small, but honest. I had a friend in Kenny who I wanted to be around for, so hopefully he doesn't get beat up again. I hummed, even though my stomach still hurt most of the time over worry about Jenny. I'd made one big mistake, and she was still paying.

I resolved to head downtown this weekend if the cops didn't get her first.

Tonight, I'd made my first honest money from a gig I managed all by myself, and Veronica's envelope had included a healthy tip. Honest work – and even though the pay wasn't huge, and I was tired, I could see that with a few nights a week like this and a small income from working with Cook, I could make a go of it.

Baby steps to adulting, I thought, singing along to a CD. *Steadily forward towards better things,* as Kate always said. *I got this. To getting things right. And living with Jenny.*

I called Jean, as much to hear her voice as to share about my day. I wanted make a plan so I could break up with her, but I ended up telling her about feeding all of Veronica's book club.

"Really. I don't know how much she paid you, but I won't pretend to like that you chose to stay in the Valley to hang out with a bunch of women tonight. And what did you say about cooking for her regularly, maybe? What the hell, Taylor. What am I supposed to think?"

"You know I only cooked food tonight. And ongoing gigs aren't a sure thing. I just think she's lonely, but I don't think of her like that." I paused a second or two. "Not like you. Maybe I can come up soon to see you." I was clearly fishing for an invite, but she wasn't biting. It felt like the nights I'd beg my mom to stay home with Jenny and me.

"Oh hell, Taylor, I'm not waiting on you." She chuckled and we said goodbye.

What the hell, I thought heading up the driveway. *Why doesn't she think of me like Ben thinks of Beth?*

Clearly when I have the warm fuzzies going on I'm gonna have to learn to think before I dial.

I was proud of how the evening had gone. A new feeling.

Now to warm Claire up. Because that lady was as cold as a nun's tit.

And to rescue Jenny. Soon.

I had to get on that.

CHAPTER 38
JUST FRIENDS

"I'd like to see Inspector Derksen, please?" The front counter was worn where people had rested their arms trying to peer through the window separating me from the detachment. This was the third person who'd asked what I wanted, why I was at the police station. I didn't think I was moving up the food chain towards the Inspector, either. Clearly it was different showing up here without an appointment. I sighed, turned away, jamming my hands in my pockets.

"Whatever. He told me to drop by any time. I thought he meant it." I reached for the door, trying to decide how I'd track down Patty. Maybe I could call her. Had she given me her card? Number? Was she "in the phone" already? Head down, I put my back to the door, braced for the wind and rain.

"Taylor?" I looked up. It was Neil, poking his head around a wall. "Is that you?"

A few minutes later, I'd passed some test of worthiness, and was headed into a lunchroom with Neil.

"Mark's not in right now. I think that's why they weren't being clear. Really." I felt a little better. "Just wait a second. I'll go get Patty," he said.

"Did Jenny call you?" It was Arun who got into the room first. It took me a minute to figure out what he was talking about. I shook my head, disappointed. They didn't really want to see me. They just wanted any "evidence" I could give them.

"I thought you guys were going to be busting this dude this weekend." My voice was terse, sharp, even to me. "Don't you even know where she is?" Neil and Arun sat down as Patty arrived.

"He hasn't heard from Jenny." Arun brought her up to speed. "Mark's not around. I'm not sure what we can tell him, but…." His voice trailed off, and Patty took control.

"Okay, Taylor. Thanks for coming by. You're worried about Jenny. I get that." The words sounded sympathetic, but I could tell Patty wasn't all warm and fuzzy. "Here's where we are." She stopped, and spread her arms out, running her hands across the table.

"The guy, calls himself Todd, has been moving around. Not sophisticated or anything. Just chatting with me as Alyssa from a bunch of different places. We know it's him, but his ISP is changing so we don't have a clear address. Yet."

"I thought you were going to get a search warrant on the ISP last week," I pushed. I was having trouble following all the technical stuff, but I had to try. "I expected you'd have Jenny by now." They kept me talking, not telling me anything except it was going to take a little more time. Really? Tell me you guys care about my sister. A few minutes later I was frustrated and knew I had to get out of there.

"So, the bottom line is, you guys are no closer to finding Jenny. She hasn't called me. You don't know where this creep Todd is…but you say you're getting closer?" I was picking at the lint on my pant leg, trying to figure out how to get out, and who else could help me find my sister. WTF? I knew I shouldn't have trusted them.

Patty put her hand on my shoulder, and I jumped.

"Tay, we're trying. Believe me. I'm on web chat with this guy almost every day now, but he's moving around. He's been at the same location three times, though. Once when your sister talked to us. That's what we think is the home base of the operation, but we have to be sure or we risk all this work and won't end up with anything. No arrest. No charges. And the creep'll just set up shop again somewhere else, and other little girls like Jenny will be forced to get involved." I was having trouble breathing. I focused on not screaming, like I used to when a john got weird. Because I was just rational enough to know yelling in a cop shop somehow wouldn't work out for me.

Or for Jenny.

And they want me to trust them. With my little sister's life.

"You look like you're not sure," Neil said. I snorted.

"Well, between the social worker telling me they lost her, and you guys saying you're close to finding her, Jenny's been in the hands of some guy you say has been raping kids and selling porn online for at least four weeks. Probably longer.

"And you've done nothing for my sister, but you tell me you're looking out for her, will rescue her soon. That you're more worried about the next little sister that could get involved than you are about my little sister. But that I should leave it up to you." I took a breath, looked at the floor between my feet.

"Tell me again why I should trust you? How exactly are you helping her?" I was whispering. "Tell me," I said, looking into Neil's eyes. The room was so quiet I could hear the meeting going on next door. Patty tossed her head at the wall.

"Briefing," was all she said. Like that'd make me feel better.

Ten minutes later they'd told me all they knew (again), all they were doing (again) and promised they'd let me know if anything changed.

"We really do expect to be moving on this by next weekend," Patty said as she showed me out. "I'll get Inspector Derksen to call you. But we do really appreciate all you're doing, Taylor. I don't know why you aren't hearing back from Jenny, but I'm hoping soon, okay?" She put her hand on my shoulder and squeezed.

I was dismissed. And sitting in my car, I decided I didn't want to be alone, so I called Padma and headed to her place.

"Sure, let's have tea!" she'd said, sounding happy that I'd invited myself over.

I ran my hand through my hair, brushing the curls on the top of my head back and forth. Padma sat across from me in her living room, smiling at me trying to be clear on the phone. She'd talked me into calling Jean to break it off.

"Jean? Jean? I just want to come by and get my stuff." We'd moved pillows from Padma's room onto the couch. The colours were bright, but they didn't clash. It made me think of bright-coloured saris surrounding us.

"No. You can't tell me this is working. You've been nothing but mad at me for ages." The woman was going a little crazy. Surely, she can't think I'm just going to be okay with her shrieking at me? Like, that's attractive?

"Yes, I remember last week. And you chewed me out for working." I listened for a couple of minutes, but then I'd had enough.

"Jean, I'm done. I don't know why you can't just bring my stuff next week to the next gathering, but I get that you're pissed." I let her scream in my ear again while I caught my breath.

And then she told me Jenny was just "another two-bit sex worker," and that I'd never get custody. And that did it.

"I'll come by next Wednesday afternoon, before the group. You need to see me? I need my stuff." My voice was hard. I hung up on her while she kept on shrieking. Padma applauded me.

"Way to go, Taylor! If you want, I'll come too," she said. I shook my head, as much to clear the voice from my brain as anything.

"Nah. Don't worry. I'll get that stuff. If I hadn't left the photos of Jenny and me with her, I wouldn't even go back...like my toothbrush matters? But she isn't going to keep those pictures of us. Even if they're just copies." I'd lent them to her because she wanted to "ask questions" for me with some of her "colleagues." It had slowly occurred to me that Jean was still involved in shady business, and I really needed to put some distance between us. Besides, I needed to return her stuff – the phone, and some other "gifts" she'd given me.

I figured I'd go in to work early to get the snacks ready for the gathering that night, and then drive into the city before traffic got really bad. A week later I really wished I'd taken Padma up on her offer to come with me.

"Tell me again about what you talked to Beth about," Padma said, stuffing her food in her mouth. We were giggling, watching movies, and feasting on nachos. I'd never gotten along with anyone like I did with Padma. If this was friendship, I liked it.

"It was great!" I told her. "We talked about this space she's rented for the cooking school, and how if I work with her and Cook, she'll let me do prep for private gigs at night, and stuff. Like without charging me, when I use my own ingredients. Like I did for Veronica.

"And she's going to pay me, so it's a real job!" I was so excited about the meeting with Beth. "I'm also welcome to stay with Kenny, pay a little rent. If I can save enough, I'll pay back Jean for the car repairs.

I wanted to know about her life, too.

"How are you doing, anyways? Did you hear from the lawyer yet?" I asked. We talked for a while about her case.

"Yeah…they're starting to prep for the trial, but I still don't really believe it's going to happen. I think they're negotiating. The Crown counsel tells me they won't take the plea we offered, but I'm still hoping. I think their families want them to fight. They might even get off. I can tell." We laughed for a while, sometimes sad laughing, convinced we knew better than to trust the system. Soon, though, she steered the conversation back to me. This time I talked about Jenny, even though I didn't really have a plan.

"If the cops don't move this weekend, I'm gonna see if I can figure out where she is. My car's running. If I can learn where he is, I'll just hang around the house or whatever until I see her, and then get her. She'll come with me. I don't care about charges against that old man. Jenny's safety should be number one, and I'm done waiting!" I punched my fist into my hand and Padma laughed.

"Just try to keep you down!" she said, laughing.

Driving home, I got to thinking about things. Even if I wasn't sure about how to find Jenny, I'd figure it out. I could look young, and I'd offer to pose for photos if I had to.

But first, I'd be cooking for Padma and Dianne and Ophelia, right after the Survivors Gathering. Maybe our last one.

Something else to look forward to.

CHAPTER 39
NIGHT TERRORS

Fuck.

Five minutes ago, I'd piled into my car, dumped my bag, and thought, *whatever*. I'm done with her. Luckily.

And then I reached in my pocket and found the cell phone she'd given me. Fuck.

I decided to give it back to her, just get it over with. I'd torn back up the stairs and went to knock on the door and realized it hadn't closed when I'd pounded out a few minutes earlier. Guess it hadn't really slammed after all.

I'd thought about what to do. Go in, leave it on the counter, and get the hell out…but from the hallway I heard Jean's voice.

"I don't know, Terry. I don't think I can come. I can't believe I fell for him." She was on the phone to someone. Someone from group? Did she say Terry? She was sobbing. And then I heard her tear her shirt. WTF? She'd been mad, but not crying when I'd left her.

Looking down at the hallway carpet, my vision tunneled, and I listened hard. I wished I could hear Terry's half of the conversation. Was Jean really upset with our breakup? I held my breath, considered closing the door and propping the phone against it. Then I was glad I didn't.

"No…I'm scraped up. Sore. I feel dirty. I never thought he'd do that to me. I'm thinking I should call the cops." I took a shallow breath, afraid she'd hear me. After a pause, she went on. "No, I never thought of that.

The hospital? You think? A rape kit? You think? Maybe you should come over." Fuck.

Running down the stairs, I dropped her phone between the railings, and heard it tumble, banging off the concrete on its way down.

I spun out the door, banged it closed and sprinted to the car. My ears were roaring. And I had not one fucking clue what I should do. Except.

Rape? Rape! She says I raped her? She hit me, threw me onto the bed. She fucked me. Hard.

One more time. For old times' sake, she said. And I bit the hook. But then she got really dark.

Got me to hit her, wanted me to choke her.

I just wanted to get out of there.

Get my stuff.

She told me if I'd do her hard, I'd be free of her….

Fuck. But I did hit her. Not like hard, but she screamed at me to hit her.

My head was spinning, and I was trying to figure out what next. What do I do? How do I escape this?

I am so fucking stupid.

But I never dreamed she was such a sicko. How could I have been so dumb?

Driving down the highway towards home, I was having trouble thinking. I turned my body, trying to shoulder check to get onto the highway, and winced. My back, my right side, pulled from where Jean had dug her nails into me. I kept flashing back to her, on top of me, driving herself onto me. Begging me to hit her. Get rough with her. I'd gotten mad, frustrated, and the meaner I got, the more she moaned. Fuck. I tried to breath. Focus. What next?

I couldn't involve the guys. Not Kenny, not Cook. The women couldn't save me. I'd made a serious fucking mistake. All because I wasn't man enough to tell her to fuck off. All because I wanted an easy way out.

All because, maybe, there was just a small part of me that wanted to show her. Be hard. Rough.

I got off the highway, headed up a back road, and stopped. I needed gas. First smart thought I'd had. Didn't know how long before the cops'd be looking for me. Headed back into town and filled up. Paid with cash. Kept my head down at the pumps.

The smell of the gas, the bright halogen lights made me nauseous. I was able to keep from puking till I was out of town, but on the road towards *Just Living* I pulled over, let it go. Heaving, again and again, all the time thinking about Barry, about all the johns, my mother, about Jean. Afterwards I felt slimy. Wished I had some water to clean myself up. Take a drink. I couldn't even break up with a girlfriend. Freak.

I was so stupid I didn't deserve any better. I got back on the road, tearing towards the trailer. *Slow down. Don't get stopped.*

I didn't have a plan, but I knew a next step. I had to call Padma, give her an excuse. No way I was going to the circle tonight. I had scratches on my neck. My back. Hell, maybe even my face. I tried to look at myself in the rearview mirror, but the darkness, and almost driving into a ditch made me stop looking. Focus. Drive. The trees were flashing by, my headlights shining up the road. Again, I pulled over. Called Padma.

Her phone was ringing. Fuck. Should I get her involved? The only friend I'd ever had? This was stupid. She'd see it was me. I couldn't hang up. My heart squeezed. I started missing her.

"Hey, Tay. What's up? I'm just heading out the door. Ophelia's picking me up."

"Yeah. Padma. Hi. Just wanted to let you know I can't make it tonight. Something came up last minute." I wished I'd thought more about what I'd tell her before I'd called.

"What? What are you talking about? Something with Cook?" I agreed with her assumption, and then got off the phone. I might have said I'd call her later.

Then, for the first time since the cops had given it to me, I powered off my phone. If they could find "Todd" or Jenny with a phone, they could find me with the one that was theirs. A few minutes later, I was at the trailer.

"Hey, Taylor," Kenny called out as I bounced in the door. I shouted, "Hey," back to him as I raced to the bathroom and shut the door. Fuck. I looked worse than I thought I would. Blood on my face, my knuckles were beat up from banging through doors and rounding concrete corners. I peed, washed my face and hands, tried to tame my hair and look decent.

"Just washing up for group," I called out. "In a rush." I pulled off my shirt and saw the claw marks Jean had left. Peeled off my jeans and jumped into a quick shower. I felt so gross, seeing her marks on me, smelling her.

I scrubbed myself, and then grabbed a dark towel. Didn't want to leave a blood trail. My head was racing, still just thinking through to the next step.

I bounced into my room and shut the door. I didn't want Kenny to actually see me, but the next moment he was outside my door, talking to me.

"Taylor, I'm heading to Beth's. Nora got some money for plants, so we're planning some fruit vines and trees. Beth'll be with you at the follow up. See you later!" he called out. And then I heard the door slam. Finally, a break. Quick.

I threw on my old clothes, grabbing the ones from my bottom drawer, the ones I'd hoped I'd never have to wear again. Some T-shirts. I put on a couple more layers, grabbed my old sleeping bag and my duffle. Shoved my stuff in it – mostly what I'd brought with me, but I admit I took a couple of things Kenny'd given me. An old fleece jacket. Some socks. The T-shirt layers I'd added. Then I thought twice, and grabbed my clothes out of the dirty laundry, and the ones Jean had torn. No sense leaving anything behind to make them wonder. Or for the cops to seize.

I went into the kitchen and emptied a few things into my bag – some crackers, granola bars. Took a big bottle from the recycling and ran water into it. Took a load of stuff out to my car, then came back for a few more things from my room.

Finally, I put Russet, Jenny's stuffed animal, on the counter. My face turned red thinking about what an asshole I was, believing I could look after her. I took out the cell phone from the RCMP, turned it back on. Left them on the counter with a note that just said, "Thank you. And Sorry."

And I ran. Ran into the night, just me and my old car, and headed up the highway, away from Vancouver. Headed past the prisons, past some farms, and well into the next town. Opened my window and let the pelting rain drive the memories away. At least for the moment.

Was running the right thing? I kept wondering. I'd always thought it was cowardly, but I really couldn't see another way. In fact, it felt right. I wasn't going to jeopardize everything until I knew it was the right thing to do. And driving into the darkness, this felt…okay?

I kept going until I found an old road with an underpass that went under some railway tracks. A train bridge over a river. I parked the car and turned off the lights, found myself hidden in the shadows. No one would see me here until morning.

Hopefully by then, I'd have figured out a next step. I couldn't help but notice the irony that I was staying upriver from where the tide ends, where the brackish water turned to clear mountain stream water, and the pounding of the waves didn't exist. But I didn't feel calm. So much for tide's end.

I'd run far enough that if the cops were looking, it wouldn't be Mission cops who found me. So much for adulting. I couldn't believe I'd been so stupid.

I climbed out of my car, took a leak on a trestle. Pulled out my sleeping bag and climbed into the back seat just like old times. Said a few prayers to Grandma trying to calm myself down. For now, I was fine.

I prayed they'd find Jenny, that someone would help her.

I'd never get to look after her now. Probably wouldn't even be able to see her.

I burrowed under my duffle and sleeping bag. *They will never see me here*, I hoped.

Sometime later, I fell asleep.

CHAPTER 40
GASLIGHTING – THE CIRCLE

Rosie called the women to circle and stood in front of her chair, holding the talking piece. She was resplendent in her quilted skirt, hues of blue and green and turquoise. Jewels, embroidery, and some quills outlined the patterns. Dianne, Ophelia and Padma took their seats together, watching the other women in a group by the front door.

"He's not coming," Padma whispered to Dianne, who'd asked about Taylor. "I think he's with Cook helping out." Ophelia shushed them, then looked at the gaggle of women at the door.

"C'mon, ladies. Rosie's called the circle," Ophelia barked. *Respect,* she thought. The women hung by the door, whispering to each other. One of them, Mary, came flying in the front door, her cell phone at her ear. She hung up and apologized.

"Sorry, I was just checking for something," she said. "Jean and Terry are coming, but they're gonna be late." Rosie nodded, and Kate emerged from the back office with Ben.

"Let's come together," Rosie said. "We've invited Ben. Have a lot to cover. And I want to hear how you're all doing!" Her voice was light, inviting. Whispering to each other, the women slowly moved towards the circle.

"We shouldn't have ever let him stay," one said.

"I knew there was something off," her confidante whispered back.

"I didn't expect that, but I can't say I'm surprised. Men!"

"Are you sure? Really?" Padma heard them but couldn't figure it out. Were they talking about Cook? Ben? WTF? She looked at Dianne, who shrugged.

Rosie invited Ben to speak. He encouraged them, "Think about the waves that continue to carry us around. Some knock us off our pins, others lift and hold us if we float. Think about how much control you have, where you watch for waves, where you can step out onto a beach. What pounds at you without stopping, like the tides." A few of the women nodded, but it was clear that many were distracted.

After another round to touch base, the women focused, and settled in to listen. Ben reminded them what they'd shared during the workshop.

"Sometimes, looking back after you're away from a bad situation, you can wonder how you were so stupid," he started, looking at several women who'd talked about how they'd gained some perspective. Dianne squirmed.

"People who are aggressive, or who have power or control can make you doubt yourself, your memories. They might tell you you're exaggerating, or that you remembered wrong. Or that you blame them for hurting you when they were just looking after you or trying to help. And at the time, it's hard to argue with them." He let that sink in, invited them to share their experiences. A couple of them talked about how their men had tried to woo them back.

Padma shared a little about her discussions with the lawyers. The accused were trying to reframe what had happened, tell the police she'd wanted it, welcomed it.

"Except I was out cold on the video. The doctors said I'd been a virgin. I don't get how they can even try that stuff," she said.

As the women shared one after another, Kate smiled. *They're realizing how crazy their attackers are to try to tell them it didn't happen. They're so strong now!* She wondered if the retreat and circles were what helped. *We'll have to survey them anonymously, tell the funders about this.*

Rosie asked if it was time for a break, and Ben asked to speak again before they did.

"There's a name for what you've experienced. It's called 'gaslighting.' I'm telling you this because there's lots in the media about it right now.

"Sometimes stuff may happen to you, further down the road. You might meet someone who *is* just trying to be nice, take care of you. You might have to talk to the person you've broken up with, because of legal reasons, or children. And it might start to happen again. Or you might think it is.

"If you want to talk to someone, we are available. Or you can look up online stuff about gaslighting and see what you think. Knowledge will help you figure it out.

"Did you just hear yourselves this evening? You are all so much stronger. And you may have noticed – some aren't here tonight. That'll start to happen, and it's good. It means, hopefully, that you're moving on with your lives.

"You probably won't ever forget what happened to you. But you'll learn to make sense of it, and you can have a great life as you move forward. I know it's hard to believe right now, but Rosie, and Kate – they've been victims of some very serious crimes." Rosie nodded silently.

Ben went over some more resources, and then thanked the women again for welcoming him.

"Before you break, I want to say goodbye. I'm going to head out now. Leave you to have an open circle for the second half. To talk about your plans. Dream a little," he said. "It's been a privilege." He waved as he left, and the circle broke for snacks.

Padma turned towards the kitchen, and there was Cook. *Wasn't Taylor supposed to be with him?*

"Wonder where Taylor is?" Sally had said to Kate as she turned to go back into the kitchen. "I expected him to be here." Padma overheard them and grabbed Dianne and Ophelia, along with some of the oatmeal cookies and cinnamon rolls Sally had announced were becoming "a

Taylor specialty." If they'd looked up, they'd have noticed that all the other women were huddled together around the door, that Mary had left with her cell phone once more to her ear.

Padma, Ophelia and Dianne headed to the table they'd often sat at during the retreat. "So where's Taylor? Even Sally's wondering where he is." Padma looked down, her forehead creased. "He said he'd be with Cook, but Cook's here. I don't get it." Her hands were wringing the paper napkin she'd pulled out of the holder.

"What do you mean, he said he'd be with Cook? Cook's in the kitchen, I saw him." Dianne reached over and took the napkin from Padma, put her hand over the young woman's. "Slow down, let's figure this out together. I'm sure there's an explanation." She was trying to be reassuring, but her stomach was starting to clench, too.

"I don't know! And where the hell is Jean? I thought Mary said she was on her way with Terry? I don't see them." Ophelia didn't like surprises.

"I know! I'll go ask Sally where he is," Padma said. "Maybe I'll find something out."

"No. Wait," Ophelia answered. "You'll blow it. Give away too much. Let me try. They'll know where he is." She didn't wait for an answer before heading across the room.

"Hey, Sally. Where's Cook? He busy tonight?" Ophelia asked. "Taylor must be working hard for him."

"Cook's pretty tired tonight, so we're visiting in the kitchen. That's why Taylor baked the cinnamon rolls for him early this morning and set out the cookies. Got everything ready. They've been working pretty hard making plans and orders for the cooking school. Getting application forms ready. It's a lot of work for an old man." Sally smiled. "He's grateful for Taylor," she said.

"Yeah. Tay's awesome. That's why it's strange he's not here," Ophelia said, turning away. "We were just wondering where he is." She snuck a peak at Sally before heading back and saw surprise on the older woman's face.

"You don't know where he is either?" Sally said. "Hmmm…Let me call Kenny." Ophelia nodded and headed back to the others.

"What exactly did he say?" Dianne was asking Padma.

"I'm not sure. Let me think." The young woman looked down for a moment. "I don't think he said anything straight out about Cook. He said he wasn't coming, something came up at the last minute, and I said, 'Like what? With Cook?' and he just agreed. Where is he?" Padma's eyes darted around the room.

"Not with Cook. Or for Cook. Sally has no idea, she's checking with Kenny," Ophelia told them. Their eyes grew wide as they looked at each other.

Mary came bursting back in the front door, announcing loudly that Jean and Terry would just be a few minutes. She was frantically looking for Kate and Rosie, who she found at the kitchen door.

"Jean needs our help," she said. "Terry said she's been hurt, but she wants to see us. Can we wait for them?" Mary asked the group leaders. Looking at each other, concern in their eyes, they reassured her that they would.

That's when Taylor's friends turned and started to hear what the other women from the group were saying. From the corner came snippets of "we never should have let that guy come" and "I don't know about this." "Poor Jean. Little fucker, I'll get him." Dianne's face turned pink, and she grabbed Padma's arm.

"Wait," she said. "We don't know what's going on."

"We sure as shit don't," Ophelia whispered. "And I don't trust nobody."

CHAPTER 41
BELIEVING THE STORIES – THE CIRCLE

The circle was settling back in, with Kate and Rosie encouraging everyone to hold some silence. And then the door opened and in came Terry, with her arm around Jean.

"It'll be okay. They'll understand if anyone will," Terry said, loudly enough that the women heard her from every corner. They moved towards the two chairs that were open and joined the other women. Jean winced as she sat down, using her hands to lower herself gently into the chair. Several of the women gasped watching her.

"I'm okay," Jean said. "Now that I'm here." Terry patted her hand, and she smiled at her friend.

"You are so strong," Terry whispered, but everyone heard.

"It's okay," Jean answered. "You tell them."

"Well, earlier tonight I got a call from Jean. She needed my help because Taylor came to her place to get his stuff, and the little prick took *way* more than his stuff," she began. "I took Jean to the hospital, and the doctors and cops took all the evidence that we'll need to prove it." Michelle smiled, and Mary let a small fist-pump go.

"Should'a left with Ayesha," she said under her breath.

Twenty minutes later, Terry'd told them all what had happened, and the circle was restless, whispering judgement. Soon, Terry deflated, and Rosie took over. She reminded them that when people have been hurt, especially at first, they need certain things.

"It's not up to us to judge anyone here," she started. "But Jean, we will listen to you. And in this circle, tonight," and Rosie's voice got steely, "you will be believed. And you can tell us as often as you need to," she said, her voice trailing off. "And what is said here will not be shared beyond the people in this room." She paused. "Under any circumstances." Kate was clutching her clipboard, settled a little at Rosie's words.

Padma tried not to cringe as Jean told them, again and again, about how she'd told Taylor it was over, and asked him to come get his stuff. How he'd come earlier than she'd expected, pounding on her door, demanding to see her.

"And then, when I told him again it was over and tried to give him back the stuff he'd left at my place, he got mad. Slammed the door. Pushed me. And then forced himself on me." She took a breath, shuddering, working hard at not allowing herself to smile. *They really believe me,* she thought. *Tonight, it will be all about me, and I'll show that little shit a thing or two.* Her tears pooled as she looked at Terry and smiled a little.

"Thank you," she whispered, but the whole circle heard her.

Padma tried to keep her face blank, but she growled just a little under her breath. Dianne squeezed her knee. Hard, and Padma gasped. Rosie's look was piercing, and Padma straightened in her chair, her backbone becoming rigid, her face neutral.

Dianne smiled at her young friend. *That's better,* it seemed to say. Glancing at Ophelia, Dianne wondered if the girl had moved her chair away from Padma, or if she'd never really been that close to them. *What have you done, Taylor?* Dianne wondered silently. Her stomach hurt, thinking about her young friend. *I wish I believed you couldn't do that.*

"It was horrid." Jean shuddered. "He came at me. More than once," Jean sniffed, and looked at Terry. "Then he finally left, and I called Terry, and I'm really glad. She took me to the hospital, where they scraped and swabbed and pushed me around. Plucked my hair. Took my clothes. They think they've got enough to get him." A tear rolled down her cheek. "It was fucking hard," she said, wiping her nose with a tissue. "Sorry, Rosie. But it was awful." She took a shuddering breath.

"I talked Terry into letting me come here. Now I feel safe." Mary handed Jean her packet of Kleenex, and the others were whispering back and forth, words of encouragement.

Ophelia snorted a little.

"Do you have a question?" Rosie asked the young First Nations woman.

"How can you feel safe when Taylor was supposed to be here?" Ophelia asked Jean, looking right at her, showing nothing in her face. *Good for you,* Dianne thought. *That does feel wrong.*

Terry answered. "We talked about that on our way out of the hospital. I called some of you and asked if Taylor had come. Mary told me his car wasn't even on-site." Ophelia looked around the room and saw several women nodding. Everyone except Padma.

What the.... Dianne thought. *They knew what was going on?* Ophelia crossed her arms and turned her shoulders just a little away from the others. *It's like she wants out of here,* Dianne thought.

"Jean just wanted to be in circle tonight," Terry explained, hanging on to the Talking Piece. "You don't have to believe us," she finished. A few minutes passed, and the circle continued, the support and caring for Jean pouring out of these women, who had all been hurt, who understood like many others wouldn't. *This is solidarity,* Rosie thought.

The Talking Piece came around to Dianne.

"I hope you get whatever it is you need," Dianne said. "We've all had horrible things happen, so we know what that's like," she said, handing Padma the talking piece.

"I'm sorry, too," Padma said, wondering if she should cross her fingers. Mostly she was sorry she didn't know where Taylor was, what had really happened. She wanted leave to go find him but knew that wouldn't help. Soon, the group decided to end things early so Jean could get back to the city before she was completely exhausted. Kate and Rosie looked at each other, and Kate left the circle to call Beth.

Twenty minutes later, Jean and Terry'd hugged their friends twice, and promised to be in touch with Rosie or Kate. They climbed back into Terry's car.

"I can't go home. The police said so," Jean said, thinking to herself that that had gone better than she'd imagined in her wildest dreams. During their goodbyes, the women had wanted to hug her, wish her well, let her know they would help her. Jean had flinched as they hugged her, and thought, *for once, it actually works to hate being touched by these flakes.* She turned to Terry, not sure how much longer she could keep up the charade.

"Can you take me to a motel or something?" she asked Terry. "The cops can call me tomorrow when they come by to gather evidence. They don't want me to go back there before then." She didn't want to do anything to jeopardize the investigation, after she'd worked so hard to stage the chaos left at her place.

"No way," Terry said. "You're coming home with me. Honest. Barb won't mind,"

"As long as we can just go to sleep without telling Barb all about it again. I'm just so tired," Jean negotiated. And so, it was settled. Jean would sleep in Terry and Barb's spare room, and Terry would drive her home in the morning. They'd wait together outside for the police.

Padma raced for the kitchen when the circle closed. She was afraid she'd burst into tears and didn't want to show those women her frustration.

Besides, she wanted to find out what Sally and Cook knew. Kate stopped her at the door.

"Hey, the kitchen's closed. Wanna come over here to talk?" she asked. "I'm just waiting on Beth," she said, leading Padma into the office where she'd first talked to Taylor. When the door quietly latched shut, Padma burst into tears.

"I don't think he's okay," Padma blubbered. "In fact, *I know* he isn't." There was a quiet knock on the door, and Dianne and Ophelia were outside. Padma waved them in, her sobs growing. She couldn't help but remember what Taylor had said about breaking up with Jean and looking for Jenny. Was all of that somehow tied up with what was going on with Jean?

"Remember, what we say can't go beyond us, if we're talking about the circle," Kate said. "The integrity of the circle trumps everything."

"*What* do you know that makes you so worried, Padma?" Kate was determined to figure out where they'd gone wrong, how they'd jeopardized the women's safety by letting Taylor into the circle. The whole program, their funding, their future depended on figuring this out, and showing how they'd do things differently next time. Her mind was racing.

She was grateful that Padma shared it all with her. The phone call, Taylor's voice and how weird he sounded. That he'd been uncomfortable going to Jean's, just wanted Jenny's photo back. A few tears fell, and Dianne offered her a Kleenex.

"I don't necessarily believe Jean," Ophelia said, arms crossed. "But I don't really know Taylor either. I do know that woman is a dragon. I get that something happened, but that's just her side of it," she said. Dianne nodded, and Padma pulled her hand away.

"Yes, Phee. That's true. But we don't know, so we all have to stay open for now. Let them figure it out," Dianne said.

"What do you mean, a dragon?" Kate asked, wondering just how street smart Ophelia was, her heart sinking when she realized the young woman probably knew exactly what she was saying. In Chinatown, women who ran escort agencies were sometimes called dragons. They weren't to be poked.

Ophelia just gave her a cold stare. Before Kate could remind them about their agreement to believe Jean, Beth was there.

"I went into the trailer. His stuff is gone. Fuck," she said, and Padma bristled, not sure what that fuck meant. "Kenny's out, but I called him. He said Taylor was going to town today to break up with Jean, but he has no idea where Taylor is now. Taylor didn't mention plans to leave." Kate patted Padma on the shoulder.

"It's okay, we'll get to the bottom of this, and make sure we know... we really need to talk to Taylor, find out his version of events. Really," Kate assured them, sighing as she left the room with Beth. "We've got to check in with Rosie and the others," she said as she closed the door behind them. Phee snorted.

"Yeah, I get it. Circle the wagons. Cover your asses," she said, dismissing them. "I'm heading out. I've gotta work tomorrow, and this is enough drama to last me a month." Dianne just nodded, her face revealing her confusion, and Padma glared.

Well, I believe him, Padma thought.

No way the Taylor I know would do any of that stuff.

CHAPTER 42
ROUSED

Crack! Crack! Crack!

I jumped at the noise, my heart pounding. Pushing my sleeping bag onto the floor of the back seat, I struggled to sit up. Why the fuck was it so bright? I shielded my eyes, trying to figure out what the hell was going on.

Fuck! It was cold in here, almost cold enough to see my breath.

With that bright a light, it was likely a cop at the window, but with the dawn sun peaking from behind I couldn't see past the brightness to be sure. My stomach hurt in a way that it hadn't since arriving at *Tide's End*.

Knock! Knock! Knuckles, not a billy stick this time.

"Open your window," he called out. Definitely a man.

Fuck! I rubbed my face, and realized he'd seen me. I scrambled, and glancing at the window saw a badge pushed up against it. Fuck.

I rolled the window down a crack, hoping like hell it'd go up again. Of course, it was the leaky one.

"Uh…yes?" I asked. *Was this it? Was everything about to collapse around me?* The guy lowered the light a little, shone it around the car, taking it all in. My eyes started to adjust, and I saw the dark uniform with the tell-tale yellow pant stripe. Gun belt. *Yup. Cop.* My heart raced. What did I need to cover up? Other than who I was, of course.

"ID Please. What are you doing here out under a bridge?" The constable's voice was gruff, but not angry. Looking around the car, I knew it didn't look good. I had no idea where my wallet was. Luckily, the cop didn't wait for me to answer.

"You drunk? Sleeping it off?" Mind racing, I tried to figure out the options. Is it better to be drunk than caught for rape?

"No, officer. Umm…I just got tired last night and didn't have anywhere to sleep. Decided to pull over and rest rather than get into an accident…." I was still trying to remember where my registration and stuff was. Had I even seen it since I got the car back from Jean? Was that a smile on his face?

"Okay, son. Would you mind getting out of the vehicle for a minute?"

Okay, I thought, here it comes…I hope he doesn't hurt me too bad… but then when I got out, he just tried to catch a whiff of my breath. I brushed off my jeans, stood up tall.

"Can I check my glove box for my registration?" I asked. He nodded, and I got the papers, saying a silent prayer of gratitude that Jean hadn't taken them. That would've fucked me up. I shook my head.

Jean had already fucked me up bad.

"Can I grab my jacket? I think my wallet's in the pocket," I asked. It was chilly out, and I didn't want to shiver in front of him.

"Sure, go ahead," he said, taking my documents. I reached back into the car, trying to grab my jacket from the front passenger seat without uncovering anything of consequence.

Then I realized I didn't *have* anything of consequence in the car. No drugs. No cash or stolen goods. No address books full of names I didn't want found. Not even any beer or liquor…wow. I shook my head, smiling, as I pulled it out of the car, slipping on my coat.

"There a problem?" the constable asked.

"No, sir. Just thinking about how the only thing I have in my car you might be interested in is some baking I made at work last week." I smiled at him as I said it, and reached into my jacket pocket, pulled out my wallet and a plastic bag with a couple of scones. I opened the bag and held it out to him.

He smiled back at me.

"That's okay, son," he said, handing me back my documents. "Just don't stay here, if you know what I mean. We don't let people camp on roads here. Best you find yourself on your way, now, okay?" I swallowed. Really? I just had to keep on going? He hadn't even called in my plates.

"Where you heading?" he asked. The cool air had my brain firing faster than I'd expected.

"Was heading to visit friends in Osoyoos," I said. I'd never been there, but thought the place sounded like fun.

"Okay, son. Drive safe," he said and headed back to his car. Then I noticed he hadn't even put his red and blue lights on. Maybe luck was on my side. I decided to wait for him to leave before thinking about where I'd go next. Where could I lose myself for a bit, until I figured things out?

And how the hell was I going to figure things out?

CHAPTER 43
HELPING OUT – POLICE

"Antoni! Hold up a sec!" The uniformed officer stopped and looked at the young dispatcher. The Afternoon Watch was breaking up and heading out.

"The Commander just gave me this. I thought you might like it," the dispatcher said. "Vancouver wants us to go pick up a fellow from that half-way house up the Valley. The one that housed that murderer a couple of years back." Antoni hated the ex-cons and had complained about them for years. "Bringing down our property values," he'd said. His parents owned an acreage up north of the small town, and Antoni didn't like having ex-cons in his parents' back yard.

"What's the guy wanted on? Parole violation? New charges?" Antoni asked.

"Not sure. He's a person of interest in a sexual assault, I heard. Your fave." Antoni's lips curled and face twisted at the mention of "skinners."

"'Kay. Thanks, I guess. Me'n Brad'll look into it sometime tonight," he said, heading out the door to his favourite patrol car. *We can hit that place after dinner, when the civilian staff are gone home,* he thought. *Bunch of do-gooders.*

Bang! Bang! Bang! Beth's feet hit the floor at the same time as Ben's. *What the hell was going on?* she thought.

"I'll get the light and go down the back stairs. You go down the front," he said, pulling on his jeans and grabbing his "dog collar." Sometimes the priest's garb could diffuse a situation. Beth jumped into her clothes as she started to hear the doors in the hallway slam open. The men were pouring out of their rooms in various stages of undress, some dead quiet and others hollering.

"What the fuck? Who's waking me up?" they mumbled. Beth felt a hand on her shoulder and was glad to see Elder Hugh pulling on his robe.

She smiled at the old man whose presence settled her.

"Go on down, Beth. I'll talk to them," he said, pointing with his chin at the men in the hallway. Beth hurried down the front stairs after reassuring Hugh that Ben was already downstairs.

"Can I help you?" Beth asked, sticking her open hand into the space between the constables in the doorway, and Ben. "Let's just step outside to talk," she said, forcing them onto the covered porch. Ben joined her outside, and they shut the door behind them.

"I'm Rev. Beth Hill, the Director here. This is my husband, Ben. Can we help you?"

"Yes, Ma'am. We've been asked to come by and pick up one of your men. A fellow named Taylor Smythe? He's wanted for questioning in Vancouver. Is he inside? Can you let us in?" the older cop asked.

Beth wrapped her sweater around her shoulders.

"Taylor doesn't actually live here in this residence. He's been staying with one of our staff members in a trailer nearby. I don't think he's here tonight." She took a breath and looked the older cop right in the eye. "He's an adult and he's not under warrant, so we don't keep track of him." Beth didn't share any real information about where Kenny's trailer was, Ben noticed. So did the cops.

"That's interesting. I'd have thought you'd keep a closer eye on the men here after that incident with the Indian a few years ago," the old cop said. The look Beth gave him made him take a step back. She just kept staring at him, daring him to say something else. Ben exhaled slowly.

"Well, I guess we're the experts at re-integration, and you're the experts at law enforcement. You might want to chat with Inspector Derksen about that," Ben said, hoping his wife could catch her breath. *Really?* he thought. *Like you think we'd ever forget what happened?* Ben knew Beth had struggled to believe she could do good here at *Just Living* after that time.

"So, would you mind pointing us in the right direction?" the younger cop asked.

"If you want, I can walk you over once I get ready. You can wait out here with Ben or in your car." Beth could hear the men moving around in the foyer behind her. Inviting cops inside wouldn't help. A moment later, Hugh stuck his head outside. Ben almost laughed. He'd messed up his hair, and his glasses were off-kilter on his face.

"Beth? You good?" he asked, in his "harmless old Indian" voice, as he called it.

"I'm good, Elder Hugh. Thank you. Have you met these police constables? Ben's going to keep them company. I'm just going to get dressed and take these men over to Kenny's place in a minute. They're looking for someone who's not there," she said. "You can tell the other men," she said as she put her arm around his shoulders, turned and went back inside, closing the door behind them.

The men slid glances out the window, checking out who was on their porch. As Beth ran upstairs, she could hear Hugh telling them what was going on.

"Just a couple of cops wanting to talk to Taylor. He's not home, but Beth'll take them over there. One of you might want to call Kenny and let him know who's coming," Hugh said.

Ten minutes later, Beth put on her headlamp, and stomped out the front door, making enough noise that the officers heard her coming. Ben was sitting on the bench outside the front door, looking over at the pond.

"It's a beautiful moon reflected there," he said to his wife, who stopped long enough to look at her husband.

"That it is," she said, putting one foot up on the bench to tie her laces. "Let's hope peace prevails tonight." She handed him his cell phone she'd grabbed from beside their bed. "I'll text if I need you or the men," she said, and headed towards the police car. Ben watched her give them a few directions, pointing down the road towards the highway. Clearly she was going to walk to the trailer, and was sending them the long way around on the road.

"Would you like me to join you?" Ben asked, coming up behind her as she leaned into the police car.

"No, it's alright," she said. "I've walked that path many nights. The officers are going to drive over, so they have their vehicle," she said. She turned, kissed Ben just a second longer than he was comfortable with and turned towards the trail.

"You vixen," he whispered after her.

"Just giving the officers a show. Anything to confuse them," she whispered back.

"Well, that went better than it might have," Beth said to Kenny as they walked back towards *Just Living*. "Inspired, really. What made you think of doing that?"

"I got thinking – if they believe he's an ex-con then they don't really know much about him. So, they probably don't know he's working with Inspector Derksen. I just decided to pretend that's why they were here." He grinned as they reached the front porch of the residence, Ben greeted them.

"Everyone's inside waiting for you, they want to hear what happened," he warned them. A few minutes later, they were sharing tea and cookies, ones that Taylor had made. They'd left the lights off in the living room and the moonlight streamed in a window. Ben had lit a candle.

"So, when Tom told me the cops were coming, I decided to meet them on the porch. I don't know where Taylor is, but there's no sense in telling the cops that." He grinned at his fellow ex-cons. "I put the phone he left behind – the one from Inspector Derksen – into an envelope, and added a note to the outside. 'For Inspector Derksen – thanks for this.' And when they drove up, I handed it to them and said, 'I bet Inspector Derksen sent you to pick this up from Taylor. He left it on the counter for Mark. Thanks – it saved me a trip.' They didn't know what to think.

"They asked me if I knew where he was, and I told them I hadn't seen him since yesterday morning. That he often stayed overnight in Vancouver." Kenny took a bite of the cookie. "Didn't mention that I'm l looking for him, too. I expect we'll hear from the detachment tomorrow. Taylor mentioned he thought the raid was going to happen sometime soon. Maybe he's waiting somewhere nearby for Jenny."

Beth looked down and sighed. She wasn't going to tell anyone else she didn't think so....Taylor might be in trouble. She had to figure out what to do about it, how much to involve the men. It was complicated, and she already felt overwhelmed by how much trouble their program might be in.

Had they invited a sexual assault at a gathering of vulnerable participants? What would their funders think? She dragged her fingers through her hair, already planning to meet with Nora and Kate the next day. How could they spin this, learn from it, minimize the damage?

And more important how do they make sure they are always working within the principles of *Just Living*? She looked up at the words on the wall plaque in the kitchen and was reminded that safety had to be their first priority.

Just Living is a home, a community and a way of life.

At *Just Living* we ask:

Is it safe?

Is it just?

Is it compassionate?

Is it honest?

Is it responsible?

We support people to make meaningful change,

be accountable as their best selves,

and live together with dignity

in the aftermath of crime and tragedy.

We are *Just Living*.

"Tomorrow, guys. We'll talk tomorrow. Right now, I've gotta get back to bed, 'kay?" she said, heading to the kitchen to put the mugs in the washup area. She reached back for Ben's hand, and they headed upstairs together. The men stayed downstairs, and she heard Kenny head back out into the night.

"In the morning I have to talk to Nora about this. We'll have to figure out how to make sure everyone is safe, including the men here. This is too much to be bringing around here," Beth said to Ben as they headed into their room.

"Yeah," Ben agreed. "I don't know what happened, but I don't feel great about any of it, and I don't have one clue about what's going on. As usual." Beth smiled as she got back into her pyjamas.

"I can't help but think Taylor and Jenny might still need our help." She smiled at her husband. *Always supporting,* she thought. "Jean, too, of course. They're both our clients. But I'm too tired to figure this out tonight." Of course, Ben agreed.

Beth ended up telling him her worst fears. About Taylor running away after Jean accused him of rape. About Jean engaging the cops in a manhunt. About Taylor running, and jeopardizing his chances for custody of Jenny. Heck, even chef training. She told him he couldn't share with anyone because of confidentiality of the circle. They'd always listened to one another, shared and debriefed the good and difficult. It was good circle practice for the facilitators to work together, and Rosie and Kate had assured her it made sense to include him.

"Because," she said, "sharing joys and sorrows…that's the best part of being married. Almost."

Ben wasn't sure what she was alluding to, but he'd take it. Sex? Nah… she wouldn't. Would she? She chuckled and kissed him goodnight.

"Yes, lover. I meant that. We're married, remember?" She smiled in the dark. "Love you, Ben. Don't ever change," she said, "and I love being able to surprise you."

He kissed her back. God, he loved this woman.

CHAPTER 44
OLD WOUNDS –
BETH AND VERONICA

The next afternoon, Beth knocked on Veronica's door, and was glad she'd thought to bring some scones. Veronica welcomed her into the warm kitchen and put on the kettle. She smiled when she saw Beth's gift.

"You know you're always welcome, but I won't say no to baked goods. Ever," Veronica joked. "Now what couldn't wait until we get together at *Just Living*?" Beth gently ran her fingers over the woodgrain of Veronica's table while she found her words.

"I need to talk to you, but I don't even know what I want to talk about. Except I'm feeling bad about my reactions to something." Veronica poured tea and sat beside this young woman she admired.

"Well, I guess you can start anywhere because…the order doesn't really matter." She took a sip of tea and waited. It didn't take long.

"So, a month or so ago Hugh met with me. Told me Martin had carved some toy boxes for Adam and Bruce. Asked me if I'd be a go-between to share them with the boys." Veronica already knew about the complicated situation – Martin, in a rage, had killed Beth's colleague and friend, Adam and Bruce's father. They were forever connected. *Trauma bond,* Veronica called it. She let Beth keep going.

"And the minute he asked, it felt wrong, but I've been trying to figure out why." She looked up at her friend, a woman who had conducted herself with such grace and care in the time since her husband was murdered. She cocked her head. "I just know every time I think about it, I want to punch someone. So far, I haven't, but Ben's received a few beastly comments and angry looks in the past few weeks. It's time." Veronica smiled at Beth.

"I remember when the police called me and told me they'd arrested Roger. And they asked if I'd come down to the station to meet with the Crown prosecutor and I was feeling overwhelmed and I asked for a drive." Veronica took a sip of her tea, thinking about that day years ago.

"They said I lived too far, that I would have to drive myself. Not 'Could I drive myself?' but that I'd have to. I lost it, and quietly hung up on them. Not sure what snapped, but I can tell you it was the beginning of something." Beth looked at Veronica, who radiated love and understanding.

"Really? They'd pick you up now, though, right?" Beth asked, jarred by how that upset her. Veronica smiled at her, broke off a piece of the scone and savoured it. Beth waited, her ideas zipping inside her, stirring her up.

"I don't really know. And whatever treatment I get now would be different than a new victim. Someone who doesn't know how to ask, who isn't afraid to 'take it up the ladder,' so to speak. But that day, I was too much trouble.

"I made myself tea, much like we're having. An hour or two later, the police called back. I pretended like I didn't know they were waiting for me. Strung them along because I was still angry, said I'd try to come sometime. Finally, after a minute or two of back and forth, the cop said something about arresting me for not cooperating. And in an inspired moment, I knew what to say.

"'Would that get me a lift to the station?' I said, and then hung up again. They came and got me, but it took me a long time to figure out *why* I was so angry."

The women just sat, each lost in their own memories of the days after they were on the living side of murder.

"I think I'm pissed because Hugh and Martin would even ask. Like another thing I have to do for Martin. Who's already being taken care of by Hugh." She rubbed her thumbs on her mug of tea, looked out the window at the birds at the feeder and smiled.

"I know it doesn't make sense. I can talk to Hugh any time I want. But no one, not even Ben, asks me how I'm doing. If I need anything. I have to ask for help." Veronica chuckled.

"It doesn't have to make sense. Really. It's still valid. And I do understand. It's why I'm so glad *Tide's End* is happening." Beth remembered that Veronica had shamelessly fundraised from her friends for the retreat centre for crime victims. "Nothing really prepares you for murder. Assault. Victimization. And so, how do you know what you'll need?

"Right now, you need to not be thinking about Martin. Didn't you ask Hugh for a break?" Beth nodded at Veronica.

"And he was really careful, but he still asked. I guess because I look like I've got my shit together. And I do, mostly. But...I guess in that moment when he mentioned the boxes, I was overwhelmed. And angry. Why should I have to talk to Donna about it? Do they ever really think about what they're asking?

"I get that it's good for Martin to be doing something...making art, contributing in some way. But really? How does that play out?" Beth had forgotten about the tea, and the birds out the window. Something in her core ignited.

"So, I ask Donna. If she says no, she looks like a bitch not willing to help Martin. Okay, sometimes I think Donna doesn't mind looking like a bitch. But what does it do to *our* relationship?

"And what if she says 'yes'? How the fuck does she explain that to people? Or worse, to Adam or Bruce?" Beth shook her head back and forth. Veronica didn't even flinch at the F-word any more.

"What if she does tell Adam and Bruce? How do they even say yes or no to something like that? A nice box, good looking. Probably one of the nicer pieces of furniture in their apartment. And when people find out where it came from? WTF?" Beth took a deep breath and looked out the window again.

"I think I get it a bit now," Beth joked. "Wow. It's just crazy that people would even ask." A minute or two passed. "But I think we do ask victims to do outrageous things all the time. Even us at *Just Living*, who pretend to care. That we know better. I feel like I should go back and rewrite all the policy to make sure we are…I don't know. Really paying attention. What they should and shouldn't be asked to do. Fuck." Beth kept thinking of other things they did at the half-way house that just presumed that crime victims were somehow magically looked after.

Veronica chuckled.

"You guys do okay, mostly. But now that you've seen it, I think you'll notice it more," she reassured the young manager. "Kind of like you can't unsee it." She poured them another cup of tea. "And I will let you know, if you want. But you do pretty good. Of course, at the dinner last month, I heard the men from the institution got a ride to your place to help with landscaping. The attenders at the dinner didn't get that offer," Veronica poked. Beth shook her head again and laughed.

"Never occurred to me," she said. "But I bet it would be kind to be asked."

"Yeah, even I was a bit thrown that evening. Wondering what Bert would think of me working with criminals. Not all of my kids approve." She waited a moment. "I might have taken a lift. Or, burst into tears and cancelled. But it would've been nice to be asked."

As they washed their mugs, Veronica asked Beth a question.

"What do you think I'd have done if Roger had wanted to give my kids toy boxes?"

"Out of the blue? You'd have probably told him to burn the damn boxes!" Beth said.

"Yeah, you're right. Or to sell them and give me, or some victims group, the money."

On the way out the door, Veronica asked for permission to change gears.

"Hey, I was thinking about Jenny. If they find her. Taylor said he doesn't qualify to have custody. Do you think he'd be interested in me helping out with her? Maybe with fostering? Claire and I were talking about it." They agreed to talk about it later, but Beth knew it was more complicated than she'd let on. She couldn't tell Veronica what had happened between Taylor and Jean.

But if things worked out, it was a great idea that Beth kept mulling about in her mind on the drive home.

When she wasn't worrying about how to manage the crisis from the group who'd just finished their retreat.

CHAPTER 45
BREATHING SPACE

I smelled the damp air and tasted the cedar on my tongue as I stepped out of my car. Breathing deeply, I opened my eyes wide. The light was magical as the sun rose above a mountain, and the smell of forest calmed my heartbeat. *Breathe, Taylor,* I told myself. Over and over and over again. Slow in. Deep breath. Slow out.

After the cop woke me, I'd bundled up my stuff and driven to a rest stop. Washed in the sink, used the facilities. I even washed the socks and underwear I'd taken off the night before and then draped them over my back seat to dry.

I wanted to get off the road quickly – my red car was like a beacon, and I'd already been spotted once. The cops could be looking for me, and that fellow who'd let me go – he'd be embarrassed. For sure, he'd be looking. If there was a bulletin. Even if I hoped I was unimportant, I couldn't help but be cautious.

I took another deep breath and headed into the run-down café I'd seen from the road. It was off the beaten path, on a back road heading towards a small town. I had a little money left and hoped I could make it last. It was hard to tell if the ache in my stomach was from thinking about how quickly my food and money would disappear, what it would be like in prison, or if the rumbles in my gut were just from hunger. I hadn't felt like eating last night, running from my life. I swallowed as I opened the dirty glass door into the café.

"Two eggs, over easy, whole wheat toast, sausages," the waiter confirmed. Tammy was middle-aged, kinda round, wearing jeans, a T-shirt and an apron. No uniform here, but I smiled. She reminded me of a younger Sally.

"And coffee," I reminded her, tipping my cup towards her. I'd been looking out the window, checking out the traffic. Lots of SUVs, with lots of gear on top, heading into the woods to hike, cycle, kayak, maybe camp. It gave me an idea. When she returned to fill my cup, I took the opportunity to ask a favour.

"So, I want to spend the day up in the mountains. Everything I own's in my car, so I'm a little worried about leaving it parked at the trailhead. Is there somewhere near here I could park it off the road?" I told her I could pay a little, that I wasn't looking for a free ride. After a minute or two of chatting, she told me to wait a minute, she had an idea. Did my eye twitch when I smiled and said I wasn't going anywhere? God, I hope she didn't think I was winking at her. She left me alone with coffee and a paper she'd brought me. Yesterday's, I noticed. I'd already read it in Cook's kitchen. God, how my life had changed. My stomach clenched again, and I put the paper aside.

A few minutes later, my eggs arrived, and Tammy gave me my answer.

"I asked John, the owner, if you could park it behind here, and he said you could but just for today. No leaving it parked for weeks, because the garbage trucks come the day after tomorrow, and he needs it empty by then." I grinned. Perfect.

After I'd nearly licked my breakfast plate clean, I headed to the cash register to pay my small bill. Big tip, small bill, I thought as I dropped the $10 on the counter. I poked my head into the door of the kitchen.

"Thank you for letting me park here," I said. "I'll be gone after today, for sure." John was middle-aged, clean enough, like his kitchen. He was struggling to bring a couple of boxes in the back door.

"Here," I said, taking them from him. "Let me help. Least I can do." I spent the next ten minutes helping him receive his supplies and put them away. I even put the new produce carefully behind the older stuff in the walk-in fridge. He noticed, like I'd hoped.

"You worked kitchens before?" he asked, shaking my hand.

"A few. Here and there," I said, making sure I was telling him nothing. "I like the pace, the variety. It's honest work, feeding good people good food." I'd thought about that sentence the whole time I'd been eating his eggs.

"I like how you included the tomato on the breakfast plate, for example. Just enough to clean up the egg yolk and it tasted fresh while I was doing it. It's the small stuff." It had taken a bit of work to find something to mention about the boring breakfast.

"What's your blue-plate special tonight?" I asked. "I'll have to eat before I head home, after my hike. Maybe I can look forward to it," I said. A "blue-plate special" – comfort food that's on special in these old diners, Sally'd explained. I missed her and Cook. John smiled at me.

"You decide. Spaghetti, or meatloaf?" he asked.

"Mashed potatoes and gravy? Meatloaf, every time," I said. I shook his hand again as I headed back into the diner. Ten minutes later, I'd parked my car around back, put my pathetic duffle bag on my back, and was heading down the road.

Great, I thought. *Now I've got nowhere to go until dinner time, and nothing to do.* I decided I could do worse than hiking and walked in the direction of the trailhead about a kilometer down the road.

That afternoon, sitting just off the trail, I ate the last of the food I'd taken from Kenny's place. Our place. And started to wonder if I'd ever find another home I could relax into like I had there. Maybe I wasn't meant to be an at-home kinda guy. I closed my eyes and tried to imagine where I'd end up. An apartment? In the city?

I didn't think so. I'd been so much calmer since living in the trees. Perfect world? It'd smell like this, I decided. Veronica's was like this. Kenny's too. Lots of damp earth smells, some tree smells. Water from a creek. I'd hoped I'd get to sleep in the bedroom at Kenny's again. I opened my eyes, headed back to the trail.

Who was I kidding? I'd be spending my next few years in jail. I had to figure out what to do to make that as good as possible…but realistically, that's where I was heading. It was Jean's word against mine. I knew I hadn't raped her, but when I imagined her telling everyone I did, it just sounded so possible. Imagining her voice, her woundedness, *I* was starting to believe her.

Who had she told, beyond Terry? The circle? Would they trust me? Padma? Kate? Dianne? How about Sally and Cook? I walked on, the trail taking my attention.

This is crazy steep, I thought. Puffing, my body was definitely getting a workout. It was surreal, being in the mountains, heading upwards towards I didn't know what. A little further on I met some guys coming down the trail.

"Just another kilometer, maybe," they said. I nodded. My face was red, and my heart was pounding. I stopped to catch my breath again. Like every 100 steps. I was getting close to I didn't know what. A few minutes later, the vista in front of me opened, and I could see the whole valley below me. The river, the train bridge I'd parked under, the town where I'd gotten off the highway.

Hope, B.C. Hope, like I had any. After spending some time taking in the view, and letting my breathing come back to normal, I headed down the path again. It took me longer to get down than it did going up.

Because really, what was I climbing down to? *Meatloaf,* I thought, and decided to follow Sally's advice.

"Just worry about doing the next thing well, and the rest will take care of itself," Sally'd reminded me for the hundredth time last week when I started to panic about getting orders placed with suppliers, and receiving a delivery, all while I was supposed to be working on the cooking school application forms. I smiled.

God, I'll miss Sally when I'm in jail, I thought later that evening. I smiled at John when he asked me how I liked it.

I was so hungry that cardboard would have tasted good, but I didn't tell him that I thought some seasoning would help. It paid off when he invited me into the kitchen to talk about menus for the week. I pitched in on dinner cleanup, and he waived a hand at me when I tried to pay for dinner.

This'll work out okay for a bit, I thought later driving away from the diner. I'd promised to stop in for breakfast, after telling him I'd be hiking the next couple of day in the area. He told me about some old train tunnels I was going to check out.

Lying in my car that night, wrapped in my sleeping bag, I was still thinking about my situation. I kept asking myself *why* I'd stayed with Jean so long after I'd wanted to leave her. *The sex,* I told myself. The sex, the affection, and the whole damned love story.

And I guess maybe because of Mom? I'd only started to understand the fuckup that I'd become because of the abuse I'd suffered. *Was it the abuse from her that had brought me here? Was I that stupid? How the fuck would I ever get over this without blowing my own brains out?*

I'd begun to believe my own make-believe about being in a relationship with an older woman who loved me, who took good care of me, my car, my phone, about being able to look after Jenny, working for Cook, training street boys to become chefs. I shook my head.

You are a hustler, a little boy toy, and that's the only trick you'll ever have to survive. Jean was just one more hustle, one more way to make ends meet. This one you just felt better about, I reminded myself. I hadn't really done the work Rosie had told me I had to do. I wasn't facing the world with courage, being daring in my healing, taking the difficult path towards wholeness. I was scum, and had wasted the best chance I'd ever get, I told myself. My gut hurt. *What did Jean really give me that I didn't already have?*

Because I knew I'd truly fucked up by staying with Jean longer than I should've, just because it'd been easier than confronting myself.

I still smiled when I thought about Jenny. *Maybe I'd made things better for her. Hopefully Mark, and Patty will look after her.* Now sleep. *One good thing.* Ah Sally. I love you.

The fresh air, big walks and comfort food finally had their effect, and soon I could feel my muscles relaxing and my breathing settling down.

You just need to find a new hustle away from this trouble. Get yourself gone, boy, I thought as I drifted off, saying prayers to Grandma for my new friends and Jenny.

I thought about that while hiking the next day, and the day after that. And the next one.

And then I remembered I needed to move towards something instead of running from stuff. And I had to stop just waiting for life to happen to me. I couldn't just stick around on the edges of my old life, hoping for some White Knight to rescue me. *Not gonna happen.*

I'd worked out an unspoken agreement with John. I did some prep work and baking for him, and he fed me. I'd even tried making a few croissants, and they weren't bad. I parked my car at his place during the day, tucked behind the restaurant. Every night, I'd parked somewhere different, on a quiet street. He and Tammy pretended like I was on vacation.

But the hole in my gut just kept getting bigger when I thought about Jean, and Jenny and how I'd had to run out on everyone at *Just Living*. So far, I'd gotten away with just disappearing. Lucky, I guess. I knew that couldn't last and started to spend my cold nights thinking about where I could hide.

Northern B.C., I decided. Oil patch maybe. Not as a worker, but to offer service to the workers? *For how long?* I asked myself.

As long as it takes, I decided. I couldn't risk looking back, and no one was going to save me from who I was. I'd lived under the radar before. I knew guys who'd done it for a lifetime.

Not the life I'd dreamed of, but the life I've created, I told myself, thinking about how Ben had told me I was building something better. *I'm just a boy toy taking advantage of my assets and running from my troubles. Nothing changes,* I reminded myself. And I wondered if it ever would.

The next morning it all changed in a flash at the diner.

CHAPTER 46
LAYERS OF INTEREST –
BETH AND THE INSPECTOR

The soft light shone into Beth's office, and she smiled. Her morning was going well; schedules were being written, and a report for a funder was almost complete. She'd talked to Kate and Nora, and they'd come up with a strategy to deal responsibly with what had happened in the group. All by 10:30. Her phone rang and she smiled when it was Inspector Derksen on the line.

"Hey Beth. Heard you've had a little excitement up there," he said. "We've had some down here with Taylor's sister's case, and I'd like to talk to you about it all, if you have some time." Beth knew "some time" meant "not on the phone." When Mark wanted to talk on the phone he always asked if she "had a minute."

"Where? Up here?" she asked. "I've got time this morning, or even early afternoon." She let that sit for a moment.

"Cook will be serving lunch at 12:30 if you want to come," she added. She heard Mark chuckle on the line.

"No, I think it's best if we meet off-site, if you know what I mean," he said. They arranged to get together in a small café on the outskirts of town.

"I ordered you the usual," Mark said as Beth slid into the booth across from him. "Tea and pie."

"Don't you dare tell Cook I eat pie when I'm away from the house. He thinks I don't like it, but I just find his crust a bit tough. Taylor's doing better at building a gentle crust, though," she said, smiling in her teacup.

"Is he around? Taylor, I mean." Mark looked at Beth. "I'm presuming not since he sent me his phone?" Mark took a bite of his giant oatmeal cookie. "Off the record, of course." The two were used to "off the record" conversations. The agreement was that they would share information if either thought it would help keep the community safe, both at *Just Living*, and surrounding it. They also agreed to deny those conversations.

So far, neither of them had had to, but lots of hurt, a suicide or two, and a little "criminal code" behaviour had been prevented.

"Nothing illegal in the prevention," Mark always said to explain his actions to the men at *Just Living*. No charges had ever been laid, so they'd grown to trust each other.

"No. Taylor left last week, and we don't know where he is. No cell phone, so we can't reach him. I'm worried, Mark." He smiled, knowing she wouldn't give him any information if she didn't need to. But he already knew.

"Yeah. I'm worried too. He seemed like a good kid, trying to find his way, focused on helping his sister," he said. "Hard to understand what happened that made him a person of interest in a sexual assault case," he added, laying some of his cards on the table.

"We're trying to figure that out, too. Kenny doesn't believe it, just so you know, and I have zero idea. We're having to rally around the situation, though, and figure out what it means for our programs. If you asked me from a gut place, I trust him. Might be because I know Taylor better than Jean. She never really connected with me. Or Kate." The lemon meringue pie arrived, and Beth breathed it in. "God, this smells so good. Only one better is rhubarb meringue, but I only ever got that from my Nana Beth." A few bites later, Mark shared what he knew.

"Well, Jean is known to police. She's believed to be someone who runs a group of young men for profit. And she's stirred up stuff with some unsavoury organizations around where she works. Has a reputation for being very tough, and quite persuasive. She's had charges she ducked in recent years, and I know some colleagues would be interested in trying to catch her at something. Knock her down a few pegs, if nothing else." *Wow,* Beth thought, *he really is laying it all out here.*

"If Taylor got in touch with us, big if, should I ask him to connect with you? I *really* can't be seen turning him in." Beth took a bite of pie, a sip of tea. "You're gonna have to give me something to tell him. If he's arrested, the men will turn on me like vipers." She took another bite. "And I wouldn't blame them." Her look was piercing, clear.

Mark finished his cookie and coffee, and sat, rubbing his temple. A minute later, he ran his fingers through the top of his thinning hair, and Beth knew he'd thought up a plan.

"I was trying to get hold of him yesterday because we're planning to raid the place where we think Jenny is being held. I wanted to give him the heads-up, and it's interesting that even knowing he's a POI, I still want to do that. My gut tells me there's a solid kid under the crap he's survived," he said. *Step one,* Beth thought. Mark took a breath.

"I have nowhere to get hold of him, but if I did, I think I'd be safe to say the colleagues downtown who are wanting to talk to him would put Jenny's wellbeing over rushing a conversation with him. And they told me they really don't want Jean to find him.

"So, if either one of us locates him, do you have somewhere private you could stash him where we could talk off the record?" Mark knew Beth and Ben had a remote cabin that few people knew about. He'd only been there once, a couple of years ago, for a picnic and hike with the younger couple. A special place that they protected. It would be perfect to stash the young man. He kept going.

"I would have to check with my colleagues, but I'm sure I could convince them he's an asset, as well as a suspect. It might open creative ways to investigate Jean, at the very least."

"I might know of a place," Beth said, smiling. "If he calls, of course. I wouldn't arrange anything with him until you had an agreement, though," Beth said as she finished her tea and sat back. "I could talk to Ben about it. See what he thinks," she said, and they understood they had other people to check in with.

"Anyways," Mark said as they got ready to leave, "the raid is going to happen tomorrow, as far as I can see. I talked to the social worker in case we need some place to stash Jenny quickly, and they mentioned something about Veronica maybe qualifying?" he finished.

"Yeah, she told me she'd like to help out...her and Claire, maybe? I talked to her about it the other afternoon, and she's pretty keen. She's getting a visit this week from Social Services." Mark shook his head in disbelief.

"Does she ever stop giving back?" he asked as he gathered his jacket and hat. After settling up, he left first and drove away in the marked car before Beth left the restaurant.

"Inspector," Patty said as she trailed Mark into his office. "I wanted you to know. I was online chatting with the target this afternoon. He's looking forward to seeing me tomorrow. Anyhow, Alyssa asked if I'd 'get to see Penny or Jenny or whatever.'" The young-looking investigator used air quotes to let the detachment boss know she hadn't jeopardized anything in asking. "Wasn't happy with what I heard. Arun recorded it, and I think you should listen." Mark put down his files, hung his jacket on the back of his door.

"What was it? I'll come down later and listen, but just give me the gist of it." Mark knew he had paperwork to catch up on.

"Well, when I asked him, he told me he said something like 'Don't worry about her. She's becoming a bit of a pain. That's why I'm looking forward to meeting you.' I asked what he meant, and he said he's thinking about getting rid of her. 'She whines a lot. Uses drugs,' he said. Might have called her a 'fuckin' addict' but I'm not sure I understood him. Pretended not to, of course." Patty looked down to the carpet in the Inspector's office. "I don't think we've got much time to get her out of there, if that's where she is. Tomorrow can't come soon enough," she said. "I've arranged to meet him after school tomorrow, at the park. While he's out, the team is ready with warrants to go in." Mark slowly shook his head.

"You're right. I'm glad you've played this so well, Patty, and not a moment too soon. Everything ready for tomorrow?" he asked. She nodded her head.

"I just hope it goes off without a hitch," she said.

"Let's get an ambulance or two standing by, just in case we need the support," Mark added.

"Good idea. We're going over everything one more time, and we'll head out early tonight, spend some time at home. Might be it for a while." Both cops knew that the night before this kind of raid, everyone was jumpy, even when things were as prepared as they could be. And that there'd be loads of stuff to process, reports to write after tomorrow.

"Try to get some rest. I'll come down in the next hour and check in, then you guys can head out." Patty headed for the door.

"Patty?" She turned back to the leader. "Thanks for everything you do. I know it isn't easy, but it really matters. Your team has been great. We'll miss you around here," he said, knowing that after tomorrow, they may not have another moment like this one.

"You're welcome, sir," she said as she tapped the door frame with her hand twice. "It's been a tough slog. Not sure how much longer I can do this, so this may be my last for a while," she said and headed towards the back stairwell.

"Shit," Mark said under his breath, rubbing his hands over his face again. "Jenny Smythe, hold on. We're coming," he said, sending a prayer up for the little girl. He put in a call to Veronica to give her a heads up about their plans.

NORA AND KATE

Later that evening, Nora and Kate sat in their trailer drinking their coffee and watching their little boy tumble on and off the couch. He jumped down, rolled onto the cushions he'd stacked on the floor, then clambered up to do it all over again. They smiled at each other.

"Who could have dreamed this would be us, eh? God, I feel so lucky," Kate said to Nora, touching her hand. "I didn't know I could be this happy." The phone rang in the kitchen, and Nora offered to get it.

"Hello," she said into the receiver.

"Hey. Is Kate there? This is the number she gave me," a voice said on the other line.

"May I tell her who's calling?" Nora asked.

"It's Terry. From the Survivors Circle." A moment later, Kate was on the line with her.

"Terry! What's up?"

"Well, I hope it's okay to call. I didn't know what else to do," she said. "I'm looking for Rosie. I want to see her, maybe have a conversation, if that's possible." *Wow,* Kate thought, *I've never heard Terry sound so... frazzled.*

"Of course, it's okay to call. I told you to do just that if you needed us. Just a second, I'll find out about Rosie." Kate held her hand over the receiver, and asked Nora when they were expecting the Elder.

"Terry, it sounds like Rosie will be in tomorrow afternoon, and then three days after that. Can you come in one of those times? Or do you need her sooner?" Kate asked.

"Tomorrow would work. Can I see her at *Tide's End?*" Terry asked. They planned for the two women to get together, and Kate hung up.

"She sounded upset," Kate said to her wife, "and that's unusual for her. I hope she's okay." Nora was heading down the hall with Brock, their little man.

"Wanna come get wet in the bathroom with us?" Nora asked, just as the phone was ringing again.

"I'll get that. Could be Terry again," Kate answered.

Ten minutes later, Kate hung up the phone and headed towards the bathroom where squeals were pouring out from under the door. She slowly opened it and peeked around the edge.

"Is it safe to come in?" she asked, smiling. She wasn't sure who had more bubbles on their heads, Nora or Brock. It seemed to be a competition to see who could have the tallest pile.

"Five more minutes," Nora declared, standing up and putting her arms around Kate, who laughed.

"We don't have to share bubbles!" Kate laughed. Brock was trying to put his face into the water, but he wasn't quite that brave yet.

"Everything okay?" Nora asked.

"Oh yeah. Another of the participants. Padma. Worried about Taylor. *She* doesn't believe Jean, wanted me to agree. I reminded her we don't have all the facts, and have to put safety first. First Kenny. Now Padma, and she says Dianne is with her, too. I listened, thanked her for her opinion, told her I don't know anything new. And reminded her that I need to support Jean, of course. She did say she understood that, even asked how Jean is doing." she finished. "Anyways, I told her I couldn't share about him or Jean if I knew anything, but we promised each other that if either of us heard from him, we'd ask him if we could let the other know. I told her he's still wanted by the cops, though, and we have to cooperate." A few minutes later, Kate was wrestling her son into his fluffiest pyjamas, and the three of them were piling onto his bed for stories.

"Six," Brock declared, holding up three fingers.

"Lots," his mothers agreed as they tucked each other under the blanket and got down to the most important thing at that moment.

"Stories," Nora said, and kissed her people.

CHAPTER 47
CHANGING PERSPECTIVES - ROSIE AND TERRY

Rosie carried her mug of tea through to the counselling room at *Tide's End*. Sally had told her Terry was waiting outside the office and had sent a plate of Taylor's cookies. "We're running out. I really want him back home soon," she'd added. Rosie smiled at Sally.

"I know. It's hard," was all she said. *Damned right,* Sally thought, even though she admitted she wasn't sure exactly what Rosie meant when she said that. *It's all hard,* she agreed. She wiped her eyes with her apron and breathed in as she headed back to the kitchen. *I have no idea what's happening with that boy,* she thought, *but even if he's done wrong by Jean, I will help him. God damned, he deserves better.* Cook hadn't wanted to talk about what was going on, but she knew her man was missing the youngster, too. He was slow to trust, and slammed things around a bit whenever she'd tried to talk with him.

"Hello Terry. It's good to see you," Rosie said and welcomed the woman into her space. "Let's light a little smudge, sit for a bit." Rosie opened her bundle on the table between them, pulled out an abalone shell and some ground sage, lit it. The smoke danced towards the ceiling. Rosie breathed, as Terry had seen her do before. She sighed, smiling, and sat down across from the old woman whose palms were held up to the sky.

Man, I wish I could look so calm, Terry thought. Rosie opened her eyes and when she looked closely, she realized Terry was close to tears. *Hmmmm…*she thought as they sat in silence for a few more minutes. *That shield of anger…is it cracking? Will the hurt little girl inside show herself?* she wondered.

"How are you doing?" She put her hand over Terry's, who flinched just a little.

"I'm a little freaked out. And confused," she said, looking out the window. They sat watching the birds dart back and forth between the pond and trees.

"Spring," Rosie said after a few minutes of silence. "Birds are busy." Terry turned and looked at her.

"What do you do when you want to believe somebody but it's really hard?" she asked the Elder.

"What do *I* do?" Rosie crossed her ankles, tucked her feet under her skirts. Thought for a moment. "I ask myself why it matters if they're telling the truth. If it doesn't really matter, I just decide to believe them." She helped herself to a cookie and waited. A couple of minutes later, Terry squirmed in her seat.

"What would make it matter?" she asked. Rosie nodded. *Good question.* She took a deep breath. Talked slowly. She was still thinking about it.

"Well, is someone gonna get hurt because of the truth coming back to bite them? Or are they telling a story that'll get someone else hurt?" she asked. "I think that's what I think about." She patted her skirt. "Then I ask the Creator what to do." She breathed. "It's complicated," she said, and Terry's eyes snapped towards the Elder's face.

"What do you mean? What do you know?" Terry took a drink from the water glass in front of her. Her fingers drummed on the table between the women, rocking the abalone shell.

"Well, you're here, and something is bugging you. It's different, seeing you upset. Maybe I've never seen it before." Rosie tugged on one of her braids. "You know I'm here for you. I'll listen. And won't tell anyone anything unless *we* decide we have to." Rosie poured tea, sipped the fragrant brew and blew over the top to share the fruity scent. "I love this berry zinger. Zinger. What a funny word." Terry let out a big sigh and leaned back. Looked right at Rosie.

"Okay. So here it is. I don't know any more if Taylor raped Jean. Her story seems to keep changing." Rosie glanced at Terry, looked up at the ceiling. She'd decided some time ago that that young man was a good young man, and she didn't think he would hurt someone without a good reason. *Some people who've been hurt, they lash out. But Taylor…well, he's a good boy, even if he hurt Jean,* the Elder had decided. She knew it in her bones, but she'd still help the tough woman figure out what she had to do. Finally, she spoke up.

"We know it isn't black and white. That hurt people sometimes remember things out of order, or wrong. Maybe one piece, but not another. But in time, the story comes. Maybe that's what's happening…." Rosie looked down at her fringed shirt, worked to straighten the fringes, knowing this would take the time it took. But Terry kept right on talking.

"I know. I remembered that. And it's why I asked Jean to clear up some differences. In a not-shitty way, you know? Like 'I believe you, and one time you said Taylor did this and then you said that. And I'm just wanting to figure it out before you have to talk to the cops because they'll grill the shit out of you, girlfriend,'" Terry said to her.

"And she fuckin' lost it. Got all pissed at me, which is fine, people been pissed before, you know? But then she said 'About time some guy had it stuck to him. Maybe he deserves it. For all the times no one got charged.'" Terry looked at Rosie, shrugged.

"Made me think, ya know? Like did Taylor really do it? Fuck. I really want to believe her. But I don't want her to wreck his life. Or his sister's."

Rosie gave her a sideways glance, and poked at the sage, relit the smudge.

Oh shit, Terry thought. *Respecting the medicine includes no swearing.* Terry started to apologize. Rosie patted her hand and sighed. She looked right at Terry. Smiled. *I see you struggling,* she thought.

"Well, let's think about it. Like the cops would. If Taylor didn't do it, why'd he run? People will ask that, right?" Rosie was smiling softly at Terry. "He didn't come around, didn't stay. What would you say to cops who pointed that out?"

"Shit, of course he ran." She flinched. "Fuck. I'm sorry. I keep swearing. I'm trying," she said, rubbing her hand back and forth through her short hair. "We're a bunch of rabid women who rose up like a bunch of jackals. Did you see us? Everyone just got disgusted with him, wanted to hang him." Rosie chuckled. "He had to know we'd react that way," Terry added. "He just knew. And he knew the cops would never take the side of a young street hustler." Rosie sat back, took another sip of her tea.

"Maybe we got mad because we wanted to get mad at *all* the rapists. Maybe at our own. And maybe everyone getting mad was what Jean needed right then. Maybe we knew what she needed. What we needed." Rosie reached for the plate of cookies, offered one to Terry.

"Cookie? Taylor made them. I don't know if that makes them taste better or worse for you, but I thought you should know." Terry brushed a tear from her cheek and accepted a cookie. She hated crying but wrote it off to frustration.

"The kid was okay, you know? When I think of it, it's hard to believe he'd have the guts to hurt Jean. She always seemed the one driving that relationship. But she was so messed up at the hospital, you know? I don't know what to believe." Terry crossed her ankle over her knee like a middle-aged trucker, then picked at the cuff of her jeans. "I'd feel shitty if Taylor's life is ruined over this," she said, looking up at Rosie again.

"So, it's complicated." Rosie smiled, and sighed again. "It often is. I'm glad you came to talk to me about it." She brushed the smoke upwards towards the small vent in the ceiling. "Carrying our good thoughts," she said, watching the smoke leave the room. Terry looked up, too. Sighed, and slapped her hands onto her thighs.

"Is there something I should do?" she asked. "I hate not knowing what to do." The words hung quietly between the two women.

"Since Jean talked to you about Taylor, is there something you want to do? Other than talk to me?" Rosie waited, let that sit for a bit. "Is there someone else you want to talk to?" Terry got up and started pacing the small room.

"I don't know. What to do, you know? If I tell someone that I don't believe Jean, she'll shit on me. Furious. I don't even know what she'd do." Her eyes darted around the small room. She pulled off her jacket, threw it on the chair.

"But fuck," her eyes shot to the smoking smudge shell and she looked over at Rosie, a small shrug, "Sorry," and went on. "If Taylor goes to jail for something he didn't do…if he can't help his little sister…fuck. That would be awful, too. I shouldn't have even come here. I don't know what to do. I am NOT a rat. I won't do that." Terry's voice was loud, sharp. Rosie took Terry's hand, patted it, encouraged her to sit down.

"Take a breath. There's no rush. Relationships are complicated. Especially when friends or family hurt each other. They never show this part on TV. Sometimes with these assaults, it's not clear what happened or who's to blame for what. And everybody remembers different stuff."

"I know." Terry was quietly fuming.

"I bet you're used to being real clear," Rosie said, chuckling. "It's either wrong, or right, right?" Terry chuckled back, and something shifted. She smiled at the old woman.

"You could do something to try to figure it out," Rosie said. "What would help you decide? You'll know it when you know it. And no one will ask you to be a rat." Terry thought about it a moment, again rubbing her hands back and forth through her spiked blond hair.

"I can't grill Jean. That won't work. She'd sniff that out a mile away. And I'm not ready to talk to anybody else." Terry looked through the light tendril of smoke dancing upwards to Rosie. "But maybe I can just hang out with her. Support her. Maybe it'll be okay. Maybe I'll know."

"You will, when it's time. And Terry, if you're wanting to call me again, I'm okay with that." The Elder snuck one more cookie into her pocket. "They're so good," she giggled. "You're being real smart. And I see you caring, even when you try to hide it." Rosie smiled. "One more question. Did you want me to talk to anyone about this? 'Cause I don't have to, but I'm happy to take some heat if you want. Don't have to disclose my sources," she said, grinning.

Terry got up and started putting her leather jacket on. "Nah, that's okay. But it's something to think about. I'll let you know. Right now, I'm just glad you'll talk to me," she said. "I don't usually get involved. But I just keep thinkin' about Taylor's sister." As Terry straightened her sleeves, picked up her helmet, she asked, seemingly as an afterthought.

"Is he around, do you know?" she turned, one hand on the doorknob.

"No, we haven't seen him since that night. No phone either, so we can't find him. His sister is still missing, though. I know that from Beth. She's been talking to the police because some of the guys here wanna help the little girl if she's found. Not in person, of course," Rosie said, giggling behind her hand. "That would be funny," she added, but Terry didn't ask why. She didn't even want to imagine what the men here were doing time for. It wasn't funny to her.

"Can you let me know if he does check in? Maybe it'll help me," she said.

"I can check with him, what he wants, for sure," Rosie said. Terry turned and looked at her.

"Right. Because I'm not the only one who gets to share with you privately," she said, nodding.

"Right," Rosie said. "I'll hold your conversation close until I hear from you," Rosie said. "Which I will do, right? Soon?" Terry agreed to reach out again to the Elder and let herself out.

Sally was sweeping the lounge floor when Terry walked through on her way out.

"Hey, Terry. Hope everything is okay," she said, offering the woman a hug.

WTF? Terry thought. *Only Barb hugs me, but Sally just does without even asking. People here are weird.* She hugged the woman back, and smiled, surprised when her eyes teared up unexpectedly.

"Yeah, I'm good. Rosie's helped."

"She has that effect. For everyone," Sally said. "She even makes Cook feel better when he's missing me, or life is hard. And he's a tough guy. So don't feel bad." Sally patted Terry on the sleeve and opened the door for her.

"Don't be a stranger, eh?" Sally said as Terry left the room. Rosie chuckled from the hallway.

"You don't stop, do you? Everyone gets a hug," Rosie said to her friend. Sally helped Rosie into her coat, wrapped her shawl around the Elder's shoulders.

"You too," Sally said, and gave her a big hug. "Thank you, Rosie. For carrying all of it."

"Time to go to the Sweat Lodge," the Elder said. "Gotta let go of some of it. Not mine to carry," she said. As she turned at the door, she called back. "Just doin' the next thing good," she said, winking at Sally, who laughed back at her.

"One good thing after another," Sally called back, waving at the Elder as she shuffled out the door.

"One good thing after another," Sally said under her breath as she turned out the lights and started locking door. "I hope this gets turned around. Sending love to Taylor. And Jenny. And Jean. All of you," Sally said to no one in particular as she followed Rosie down the path towards the rooms she shared with Cook in the Residence Lodge.

But her step was a little slower, her heart heavy.

It was hard when you cared so much about everyone, and they were struggling.

Time to go get Cook to do some baking for that little girl she hoped would be home soon.

Since big brother Taylor's cookies were almost gone.

CHAPTER 48
THE NEXT GOOD THING

I was sitting pushing my eggs around, adding jam to the dry brown toast, and mostly angsting over when *exactly* to leave and where *exactly* to go when a bird hit the window over by the door. All eyes in the diner were drawn to the THUD. Tammy rushed out the door to try to help it.

Looking over, my eye caught the news story on the TV hanging in the corner. It was an old TV, small, the thick kind with a tube, and it was on a shelf in the corner where Tammy could watch it from the cash register. I'd never noticed it before.

The flashing red and blue lights on the screen grabbed my attention. The words at the bottom of the screen were what kept me watching, though.

Arrests made at house in Mission. Child pornography suspected.

The sound was off, and I was too startled to ask to have it turned up. I kept watching what was happening...had happened, I reminded myself...on camera. One person was being led out of a house and into police car. He looked big, his arms were thick and he was wearing jeans. At least I presume it was a "he." He had his jacket pulled over his head. Then more were led out. Two. Three. One was definitely a woman, wearing an old cotton dress. Heavy set. The last couple of people I saw before the camera panned to the lights of the police car were smaller, probably teenagers, no idea if they were girls or boys, but my gut told me they were girls. Everyone had a coat or blanket over their heads. Before

I could really put it all together, the news reporters were on to their next story.

Was that the guy they thought had Jenny? Was this the raid, finally? Were one of those people my little sister? They'd all seemed so tall, but I knew it had been three years since I'd seen her. Was Jenny that big now? My brain was exploding with the images it'd just seen. I was looking back and forth around the diner. Why was nobody else watching? I wanted to stand up, shout, point at the TV, but everyone else had gone back to their breakfasts.

I caught my breath, slowed down, finished my food. I thought about where to go for more information, who to ask. The bell over the door rang, and Tammy came back in.

"Just a sec. Gotta go wash my hands. That bird'll be flying nowhere but heaven," she added, heading to the washup sink in the back. *Maybe she'd help.* A minute later she was doing the rounds of the tables with a coffee pot in her hand.

"Hey Tammy, if I wanted to check some local news, where would I go to do that?" I asked. "I'm feeling out of touch, and before I get back on the road, I just wanted to catch up." *Shut up,* I told myself. *Too much sharing.*

"Well, if you want the internet, the library has some computers. Just a block past main street. You can't miss it." She poured me coffee, and I added enough cream to preserve my gut. "You need an account, though, to go online. Let me get you my number," she added. *Fuck, she's nice,* I thought. People generally were. *Where were these people before?* I wondered. *Why did I only meet assholes when I was on the street?*

Five minutes later, I was heading out the door, with her number and password on a slip of paper. I'd said my goodbyes to her and John. I just had to find out what was going on in Mission before I got on the highway and headed the other way.

Soon, I was sitting in the library with three browser windows opened in front of me. On the inside, I was pulling my hair out. On the outside,

I was writing a few notes on a piece of paper I'd gotten from the librarian with one of those short-assed pencils they leave around.

I'd watched three different 15-second videos of the same bust in Mission and was convinced this was the one I'd been waiting for. My brain was racing. Was Jenny found? Was she okay? Was she even *there?*

I tried to slow myself down. Looked out the window at the rain through the trees. *Think of three things you're grateful for. Three physical things to ground yourself.* I could hear Ben's voice in my head. *Next good thing.* There was Sally. *Whatever you're having a feeling about, it's okay.* Rosie joined in the group hug I was listening to. All good advice.

One thing to be grateful for? These were better voices in my head.

Second thing? That Tammy had a library account and gave me the number.

Third thing? Hmmm…that was harder. I thought about it for a minute. *The life of that bird, sacrificed on the altar of glass, so I would notice the TV, maybe.*

And now I had to think about next steps. Next good thing.

Do I head north, trust them to look after Jenny? Get out of her way? Would she be better off without me?

Was there harm in just finding out about her before I left? I thought about that for a bit, and realized I was overstepping my "30 Minute Limit" on the computer. I glanced around. No one was waiting. Did this thing time out, or something? I didn't want to get up and leave the computer station, because I didn't know if there was a limit to how often Tammy could go online in a day.

Questions. Questions. What do I need answers to?

I knew I didn't want to call 911 and ask for Inspector Derksen. *Who do I call?* I sat back and tried to imagine what Sally would say. Rosie. Ben. Kenny.

Each of them added a piece to the answer. Sally – *Who would know?* Rosie – *Who do you trust to give good information?* And I knew she what she meant by "good information." Stuff that comes from the heart *and*

the head. Someone who considers the history of the Ancestors. Ben –
*What is daring? Who will challenge you to step up in a way you will be proud
of?* And Kenny – *Just fuckin' do it, man. Get on with it and stop worrying
so much.*

I called Kenny. Because truth is? I knew his number.

It ended with GRO-WEED – something he was really proud of. He
loved growing weeds, making beauty out of them.

And he'd bragged that he'd kept the number out of the hands of some
two-bit dealer.

I found out where a pay phone was from the librarian and headed
out.

"Hey Kenny. It's Taylor. Sorry for running out, man." My heart
started racing when Kenny answered the phone. In person.

"Taylor! I was hoping you'd call! I miss you, man," he said. A little
more awkward back-and-forth, and then I asked about Jenny.

"So I saw a bust on the news this morning. Do you know if Jenny's
okay?" There was silence on the line, and my anxiety started to spike.

"Hey man, I don't really know. I'm sorry. I don't know a lot and I
haven't heard anything except something went down. But if you can give
me some time, I'll go ask Beth." My turn to be silent.

"Hey," I said, risking all. "I don't know what to do, man. I was just
going to head north, you know, 'cause, well, Jean…I didn't want to deal
with it, you know?" I took a deep breath, looked over my shoulder and
saw a big, black bird circling above. I chose daring.

"And now I don't know what to do. I want to see Jenny. You know?
But I don't want to just show up…for the …." I shut up for a minute.
"Not that you've gotta take my shit on," I finished.

"Hey, I get it. It's complicated. I didn't listen to much of what people
were saying. Whatever. I don't know where you are, but why don't you
drive in this direction? Call back in about an hour? I'll see what I can find
out." I promised to call back around lunchtime and headed for my car.

334

It took me more than an hour, but I drove back down the Valley, towards my sister. I found a pay phone outside a liquor store, and decided it was as good a spot as any.

"Hey Kenny. It's me," I said when he answered on the first ring. God, it felt good to be in touch. This *was* the next good step.

"Hey Taylor. Thanks for calling back." I heard him talking to someone in the background. "Wait just a sec, okay?" He laughed, and I smiled. "Beth wants to talk to you. She's been hoping you'd call. Is that okay?" he asked.

"Yeah, but I want to talk to you after," I said. I needed to hear his voice a bit more. Seconds later, Beth was on the line.

"Hey Taylor, you okay?" she asked.

"How's Jenny? Did they find her? Is she okay?" I had a million questions jumbling out.

"They did find her. She's in the hospital right now. They're looking after her," she told me. I let out a big breath I hadn't realized I was holding. For days. Months. Maybe years.

"Shit. Oh God. Thank you…thank you. What a relief." My voice cracked. Tears welled in my eyes. I wanted to shout to the universe. "Jesus, that's good news, Beth. Thank you. I'm so glad. God that feels good." My smile was a mile wide.

"Taylor? She's not doing great. And you aren't here. We don't know what all's wrong, but she's struggling. Medically. We're all picking up the pieces for you around here, and I won't lie. Feelings are mixed." I nodded, then realized she couldn't see me.

"Oh man, I am so sorry." I was swinging back into worry again at the same time as I was running out of steam. What a roller coaster!

"Will you come back? Maybe see Jenny? Talk to Mark Derksen off the record?" Beth froze for a moment. "Will you think about it?" I breathed out. My gut clenched.

"The cops are looking for me?" I asked. Was she asking me to turn myself in? In exchange for seeing Jenny? But why was she offering to hide me then? I couldn't figure it out.

"Well, Mark told me you are a person of interest in Jean's investigation. I don't know what went down, but it's in the hands of the Vancouver Police. Mark wants to talk to you about Jenny. He wanted me to ask if you'd consider it." We both started breathing into the phone, like a standoff. She broke first. "So you know, he's never laid a charge after agreeing off-the-record to me. But he doesn't control the VPD."

It's remarkable how little you can pace when you're stuck on a land line. My legs were burning to move, get out of there. Everything in my brain and body were telling me to run. Except the part about Jenny.

"Does she need me?" My voice quavered. My breath came in puffs. My stomach clenched.

"Give me a minute." I again looked up. This time a seagull was flying overhead. "Is there a warrant out there on me?" I took a step away, then one back to the phone. I heard Beth sigh.

"There *isn't* a warrant. I checked with Mark. You're a person of interest. They just want to talk to you. Mark wants to talk about Jenny. Thinks she'd do well to see you right now. Help her want to get better." My brain started filling with images of my little sister, her recovery. And dealing with the awareness that her big brother had abandoned her again. A minute later, Kenny was on the phone. I had no fucking idea what to do.

"Hey, bro. How are you doin'? A lot to take in," he said. He was quiet for a bit, and my body calmed down. I breathed out, looked up the street to a tree. Big bright leaves, just starting to grow. Kenny had taught me to notice. Spring. Promises of life. That helped calm me down, too.

"What is she asking me, Kenny? She wants me to hide at *Just Living* and talk to the cops? So I can visit Jenny? I don't get it." I said to my friend.

"No, she's got a place lined up where you could go off-grid and stay with me and Ben overnight. Alone. A nice place. Mark'd come out to talk to you. And now, I think, if you come, she's figuring out how to get you in to see Jenny. On the lam. No cops," he said. "Kate used to be a nurse, and can help, maybe?"

"Why?" I wondered. And I guess I'd said it out loud.

"I think they're worried about Jenny. People are all over the place about what happened between you and Jean. I won't say it hasn't had an impact here. Some are ready to kill you. But most of the guys around here are like, 'I don't know, man. Shit happens.' They aren't ready to judge you." Kenny took a breath.

"Oh man! In case I need to say it, you gotta know I believe in you. Why would you…you know… when you wanted to just be done with her? Sorry. I didn't think I needed to say it. But I do." I could hear Beth in the background. "Not that an ex-con's opinion really counts…." he added.

"Kenny? What do I have to do? Like to make it okay. Short of ratting, you know?"

"Awww, Taylor. You'll know. We've all been in dodgy places around here." No easy answers. *Fuck, he didn't really say whether he thought I'd done it.* "Beth wants to talk to you again." He handed the phone over.

"Hi Taylor. So you know, what I said to Mark was that I had no idea what happened between you and Jean. Over the past few days, people have been calling to ask about you. Padma. Dianne. They care about you. And want to know you're okay. But I want you to be safe. And I want you to be able to see Jenny. For her sake, as well as yours. And I think coming in might be the best way to work towards that.

"You don't have to decide now. But let us know before the end of the day, 'kay? Ben and I need to know whether or not he'll be driving me home, or heading out with you and Kenny." Ever practical Beth. I could feel the bile in my throat, though. All I could think about was, *No promises, not the VPD, no idea what happened.* She wasn't siding with me, that was for sure. But did I have a choice?

"Yeah, I'll meet them. I don't have anywhere else to be. I have to see Jenny if it'll help her." I kicked a piece of gravel towards a garden. "Tell me where and when to meet you guys." A few minutes later, I had my instructions. Where to stash my car. Where to meet them. They'd bring me a backpack, to carry my stuff.

We were going hiking.

And believe it or not, my stomach was a little less sore.

Even though I knew I might be arrested.

Fuck it, I thought. *I'm almost out of money, but unlikely I'll need a lot of gas where I'm going. Might as well have a good last meal.* I headed into a grocery store, bought myself some real fruit and veg to eat, a little cheese, and drove into the forest to hide out until it was time to meet up.

When I thought about Jenny being safe, my smile was wide enough that it'd light up a whole intersection.

And then when I thought about her in hospital, I felt like a shit again.

CHAPTER 49
QUESTIONS OF EVIDENCE – JEAN AND TERRY

Jean looked over as Terry jumped into the passenger seat of the Lexus.

"There are very few women who can pull off black leather, but you're one," she said to her friend. "Nice jacket. Do you want to stop for coffee on the way?"

"Oh. I thought they were expecting us right away?" Terry replayed the phone call she'd gotten from Jean less than an hour ago. The police apparently wanted to talk about the case, and Jean had said she wanted a friend along.

"Yeah, they're expecting us. But making them wait a bit won't hurt," Jean answered.

"No, I'm good. Let's just get this over with." Terry knew that coffee would burn a hole in her stomach. She just wanted it done, in part because it was dragging up all kinds of shit from when she'd dealt with the cops after she'd been assaulted. Had assaulted her husband after he'd assaulted her. Although it was more than a decade ago, she still nearly teared up when she thought about what it was like being a dyke and grilled by the guys in uniform. Who were clearly homophobic. And didn't find her attractive.

And therefore, couldn't believe that her ex-husband, the rapist, had wanted her. As if it was sexual attraction that made a man rape.

She hoped things went better for Jean.

Ten minutes later, they were ushered into an interview room in the Vancouver Police Station.

"I'll go get the investigator who called you," the young officer said to them as she closed the door. Terry looked around and sat on the side of the table where the chairs weren't bolted to the ground. Then got up and moved to the other side. She looked at Jean leaning against the wall by the door. Somehow, and Terry couldn't figure out how she did it, Jean looked smaller, timid even. Maybe it was her shoulders curling in, her head hanging a little. *Is it real?* Terry asked herself, and then felt her face turn red for even thinking that.

"Are you okay?" Terry asked. Jean sniffed into a Kleenex.

"I'm good. Just not sure about this. You've warned me. Dianne warned me. Ophelia. And Padma. Especially Padma. Maybe I shouldn't have pushed." Terry tried not to gape, but she couldn't help but wonder *Why now, Jean?* Luckily the investigator came in before she could think any more about it. He dropped a file folder on the table and looked at Terry.

"Jean?" he asked. "Jean Tremblay?" Terry nodded no and pointed at Jean against the wall.

"That's Jean. I'm her friend, Terry." The man looked up at Jean and took her in. His look said, *Well, aren't you everything they warned me about.*

"Jean. Have a seat," he said, pointing across from him. Jean sat and started chewing her thumb nail. "You had some questions?"

Jean took a deep breath and started to talk, then hesitated.

"Take your time," the cop said. She did. Even Terry was getting a little uncomfortable, so she put her hand on Jean's shoulder.

"Yes. I do. First, is that recording?" She pointed to the camera in the corner.

"It is recording, just so you won't have to keep answering the questions again and again. It could even save you from having to testify in court."

"Okay. I'm wondering when you guys are going to arrest the man who hurt me?" It was the same question she'd posed over the phone almost every day.

"We're still talking to people." The investigator glanced at the file. "Mr. Taylor Smythe is out of town. We'll know more when we speak to him. But we have a few questions for you, if that's okay?" Jean's piercing eyes looked at him across the table.

"Questions? I guess…." she said, leaning back on the chair, her arms crossed. The fellow looked up at her with his pen and notepad ready.

"Okay. So can you tell me again what happened between you and this young man on the last day you saw him?" Terry felt Jean bristle and patted her arm. Jean took a breath and began.

"So, like I said before, Taylor called me and said he wanted to come and talk. Things hadn't been good with us, and I told him he was spending too much time in the Fraser Valley and didn't seem to want to come to Vancouver, even to see me." Jean took a sip of water, pursed her lips. "He told me he wanted to make it all up to me. I think he knew I was going to break it off.

"Anyways, when I heard the doorbell, I threw on my bathrobe and answered it. I wasn't completely ready for our 'date.' He came through the door with some flowers and a bottle of wine. I think he was hoping to woo me. I was caught a little off guard, but he breezed by me. I went to my room to finish getting ready, and he put the flowers in water. I think he'd cut them in the gardens where he lives, because they looked ragged. Kind of cheap.

"Next thing I know, he'd poured some wine, and had followed me into the bedroom. He wasn't real happy when I told him I wasn't interested in getting physical, and that's when he got violent." Jean put her Kleenex to her nose and looked off into the corner. She started to sob a little, and Terry reached out and put an arm across her shoulder. Gave her a quick hug.

"Then she called me, and I came and got her, took her to hospital." Terry finished the story for her friend. "You must have those reports," she said. Jean thanked her and turned her head away from the police officer. He let her gather herself before he continued.

"Can we go?" Terry asked, squirming.

"In a minute. Just a couple of questions," the officer said.

"First, what did you do with the wine glasses Taylor had poured? We thought we'd send them to the lab but couldn't find them." Jean looked up.

"I must have washed them and put them away while I was waiting for Terry. I don't really remember much after I called her."

"I understand," the officer said. "Is the bottle around? We didn't find a bottle with any wine in it." He shuffled some papers in his file folder. "It's just that glass would be great for holding prints. You know," he said, looking down. He knew his buddy was watching him through the window, and he didn't want to look at him. He also didn't want to set Jean off; he'd watched some of her interviews and she could go ballistic in a heartbeat.

"I must have poured it out. Put it in the storage room with my empties," she added. "Shit. I'm so stupid. Why didn't I just leave it all alone? I needed to do something," she said. "I straightened the living room, too."

First I've heard of the living room? Terry thought. She looked at Jean out of the corner of her eye. *Shit,* she thought. *That story's changed again from when I heard it.* The cop didn't seem to notice.

"One last thing, and then you can go. And thank you for cooperating so much. It really is helping us get the evidence we need," the officer said, bringing something in a plastic bag out of the file.

"This piece of paper. Have you seen it before?" he asked.

"I don't think I've seen that one. But it's a receipt from the shop near me. Maybe Taylor stopped there and bought the flowers he brought me. Did he drop it?" she asked. She looked coolly at the cop across from her.

"Well, the interesting thing is that it's for flowers, from the day Taylor came over. But according to the shop, you paid for them with a credit card. The officer who went to collect your bedding for testing found it on the floor in the bedroom and thought it might be relevant. She picked it up for us."

"Did you buy flowers for someone else?" he asked. "We're just trying to get a clear picture of what happened. And we know sometimes it's hard to remember. Is any of this making things clearer?" And that did it. Jean flipped, and stood up, shaking off Terry's arm.

"What the fuck are you talking about? You have no idea. None. What it's like to be raped. Used. Treated like shit. It happened, and that little…. Well, he isn't going to get away with it." She paced back and forth in the room.

"Am I free to go? I can't fucking believe this. No wonder women don't come forward. You bunch of pricks. Lying pricks." Jean stormed over to the door and reached for the handle just as it opened. Terry stood, not wanting to be left behind. An older man with a lot of braid on his shoulders and cap stood holding the door.

"Thank you, Jean. We'll be in touch when we find the young man and interview him. If you think of anything else in the meantime, please don't hesitate to call the office." He moved slightly to let her pass, looming over both women as they left the room. He invited her to walk clear through the office with his outstretched hand. "If you can clarify any of this, just call and we'll get back to your case," he said, effectively dismissing the women.

"Inspector! I should have known you'd be tied up in all of this!" Jean's voice was cold, her words barely controlled.

"Come on Terry. Never trust a cop. Fuck. You. All," she said with just enough volume and emphasis that the whole squad room stopped and looked. She marched out, head high, and Terry scurried after her.

The silence in the car was deafening as Terry drove back to Jean's. Terry was confused, worried about her friend, and wasn't sure if she should even say anything. *If* Jean was throwing Taylor under the bus, what would she do to Terry? She looked out the side window, not wanting to glance over at her friend.

"Well, spit it out. What are you thinking?" Jean said, almost under her breath. Terry inhaled slowly.

"I'm wondering how you knew that cop, the flashy one. Why he talked to you like that."

"He was a vice officer years ago. Let's just say he got up my business way too often. I can't stand him." Jean pulled the car out of the parking spot and accelerated quickly away from the curb. "Let's just say we can't stand each other. He's the reason they're backing down," she finished. She was speeding towards Terry's place to drop her back home.

"Oh." *I wish I had one solid hint about this,* Terry thought.

"I don't know why I'm so mad at Taylor. He *did* take advantage of me." Jean accelerated down the road, speeding up to run a yellow light. "I don't like being taken advantage of. And maybe because I don't think he really gave us a chance. We could have built a dynasty, working together. Better than some fucking cooking school. I was willing to give him everything. A place to live, good love, even an allowance." Terry was surprised to hear Jean sniffling and looked across the car to see her looking out the window.

"I thought he loved me. I'm not sure I've ever really felt anything like that before. It was nice. I guess I'm wrong for thinking I deserve a relationship with him, after I helped him. It's not fair." Terry cringed. *Was there an assault?*

"I'm sorry," was all she could muster. "I guess it wasn't meant to be."

Fuck, she thought. *What the hell am I supposed to do now? Call Rosie? Don't call Rosie? And what the hell made this my problem?*

"Don't worry," Jean interrupted her thoughts. "I don't know what I'll do, but I guess I'm done with the cops." A few blocks passed by, and soon they were driving up in front of Terry's apartment building.

"I bet I could still spin it though, to try to get him back," the older woman said as she parked the car. "So don't think about ratting me out, okay?" The piercing look she left with Terry stopped the biker in her tracks.

Man, that woman is cold. Calculating.

Terry shoved her hands into the pocket of her leather jacket.

Fuck that, she thought.

And when she got in her door, she took out her phone and dialed Rosie.

CHAPTER 50
AT RISK – HUGH AND COOK

Hugh walked into the kitchen at *Just Living* carrying a tray of coffee mugs and a plate of crumbs from scones. Sally rushed to take them out of his hands before anything dropped, and the sag in his shoulders and the shadow on his face told her he could use a friend.

"Hey, Mooshum, thanks for bringing that in from your office. You know I'm happy to collect it, though, right?" Sally asked, welcoming him to sit down. He chose his favourite chair by the window overlooking the back fields; he loved to watch the horses graze in the pastures beyond the garden fences.

"I know. But I wanted to talk to Cook about something. He around?" the Elder asked.

"Yeah, he's lying down, but he'll be here in a minute or two. He's been upstairs a while." Sally bustled around the kitchen, making them some more tea. A few minutes later, Cook appeared.

"Hey, friend, how are you?" he asked Hugh, leaning on his shoulder. The two men had known each other for years, and over that time, they'd leaned on one another, back and forth, until their friendship was solid.

"Gettin' by," his friend replied. "Gettin' by." Hugh sipped his tea and put down his large mug. "Spent the afternoon with Rosie." He shook his head in amazement. "That's some woman," he said, and looked out the window. "She's better than I'd ever be with some of the women in those groups," he said, telling Cook nothing, and everything.

"We shared our worries until the tea was cold, and our minds were clearer," he added. "She thought I should come talk to you because… well, sometimes I think she believes you're smarter than I know you to be." The Elder smiled, put his braids over his shoulder and looked at Cook.

"Well, I get that," Cook answered. "Because you've never been a quick one to notice smarts when you're around them." Sally snickered at the two men, bantering back and forth.

"I'm heading upstairs for a bit. There're cookies in the jar if you need them," she said, taking off her floured apron. "I'll be down to help with dinner. You guys be nice to each other," she said, her eyes sparkling at Cook.

"Would you mind hanging out for just a minute or two?" Hugh asked, and Sally turned, her hand on the door frame, and looked at the old men at the table.

"You sure?" she asked, not wanting to intrude on their time together.

"Oh, yeah…I'm sure," Hugh said. "This is one of those times we need all the old brain cells to make sense of things." Sally joined them at the table, worried about the news Hugh had to share.

As Hugh looked out the window, watching the tall grasses blow in the breeze, they settled in. They knew Hugh would share when the time was right.

"So, Rosie and I, we sat and talked about all the things on our minds," he began. "You know we still wrestle with knowing when to share something we've been told, but this time we think we need to. And we decided that you two will know what to do. If anything." He took a sip of tea, and even Cook held his tongue, understanding when to tease.

"Someone from the Survivors Retreat came to see Rosie last week. And called her this weekend. It seems the older woman doesn't always tell the truth." Hugh looked down, swinging his head slowly from side to side, the weight of her deception lying heavy.

"That must be hard on her," Cook agreed. "Always hard to keep up untruths."

"True," the Elder shared. "So, this woman was pretty clear that your young friend is at risk of being hurt from something he didn't do." Cook's breath turned deep and calm, and he worked hard at not smiling. Sally, on the other hand, held nothing back. She slapped the table and pushed up.

"Well, you're telling us stuff we already knew. Taylor might make a rookie mistake with a woman, but he's not violent." She sighed. "When will that boy come home?" she asked, not expecting an answer. Cook put his hand on his woman's arm.

"I never trust that my believing something will help anyone, so I'm glad someone with a better reputation has spoken out. I can't imagine how hard that was. I'm glad she told you." He shook his head. "I think it'd take a lot for someone to speak out on a victim. Especially someone in that group."

"No doubt," Hugh said, shaking his head back and forth again. Cook knew that these things – talking about what had been shared in confidence – were hard for the Elder. But the people at *Just Living* had a difficult ethic they had decided on together.

Caring first.

If someone was at risk of hurting themselves or someone else, they had to talk about things. Figure out how to lessen the harm. Prevent the pain.

Care first. And sometimes it backfired, but mostly people were warned when they attended a circle, moved into the half-way house. Talked to the Elder.

Trusted the wisdom.

Another pot of tea, and they'd decided what to do. No names had been mentioned, and weren't shared, except Taylor's. It stayed that way. But Sally would talk to Mark Derksen and let him know that they had a source who might be willing to talk to the police, that the complainant in the case had indicated to this person that her story wasn't...trustworthy. They agreed it was the next good step, and Hugh asked one last question.

"Do we involve Beth right now? Or Nora?" he asked. "Beth's kinda busy with figuring out the stuff with Martin. They're sharing letters back and forth. He's answering questions. She's asking a lot of him. It's… thick. Never easy to figure out the right next steps in a situation like that. But I might have asked too much." It was Cook's turn to shake his head back and forth. Hugh was referring to letters exchanged between crime victims and those who were responsible for the hurt.

"She's a brave and fierce little thing. Living so…true…carefully after what happened with Martin. It's hard work," Cook said. Sally put her arms over her man's shoulders and kissed him atop his bald head from behind. "I say we keep it between us unless Mark asks for more information. Done?" he asked, looking at his mentor.

"I agree. She *is* brave and fierce. And we can carry this one." He pushed down on the table, reached for his walking stick. "But we have to tell her soon. She'll be a spitfire if we keep it from her for too long," he said.

"Good idea," Sally said, gathering the mugs and putting them in the washup area, to wait for the dinner dishes. "I'll go call Mark and get back to you."

Later that night, Sally called Hugh.

"Guess what. Mark just got back to me. When he called his contact at the Vancouver Police, the man said, 'You mean Terry Germaine? She came in two days ago and made a statement.' Apparently we have old news, but they were happy to have it confirmed, to know Terry's story is consistent, from a different source." There was a chuckle at the end of the line.

"Tell Cook we're so slow I'm behind the folks I'm helping," the Elder answered. "I guess we made the right move. I'll tell Rosie what Terry did," he answered. Sally hung up the phone and headed upstairs.

Cook would be happy to hear all was well for his boy.

CHAPTER 51
JOINING A CLUB

I'd never joined a sport. Belonged to a club. Been a Boy Scout.

But sitting by the wood stove, mug of tea in hand, I imagined this is what it felt like. And also…I thought priests and nuns and stuff were supposed to be poor? Now I'm hanging out with people who have amazing secret cabins in the woods they don't talk about? Who is that lucky?

Ben and Beth, I guess. Perks of being tight with The Man? *Does* God reward his "good servants?" 'Cause he sure doesn't seem to care much about the children on the streets. All I knew about priests before *Just Living* I learned from gay priests who were still closeted. Not always nice people, but sometimes so ashamed even *I* cringed on their behalf.

Kenny'd met me at a parking lot where I'd stashed my car.

"Ben's up ahead lighting the fire. Maybe he'll even cook us some grub," he said as he helped me pull my stuff together. He had a pack full of food. After a drive we'd hiked for about a half hour, and then we were in a field of wildflowers, sun going down, looking at this ancient cabin. The flickering of light in the windows made my heart hurt a little. It was what I imagined a nice painting would look like.

An hour later, we were sitting around the wood stove, eating beans, wieners and the best bread rolls I'd ever tasted, and drinking tea that Ben had brewed. And I was thinking that this might be how it felt to belong to a club.

"So, what do you know about Jenny?" Kenny asked. I couldn't tell if he didn't know anything or was fishing for what I'd been told.

"Not much. That she's in hospital. Inspector Derksen wants to talk to me. He said he thinks she might get better if I go see her." I hung my head, reminded of my sister. Here I was drinking tea by a fire like a posh asshole. I hadn't been the one to find her.

"That's about what I know," Kenny said. "Beth told me she's sick. I knew she couldn't tell me more." We'd both looked at Ben. *Maybe she'd told him more,* I'd thought. He held up his hands in front of him.

"Sorry. She didn't tell me anything except I should bring lots of food and show you the hot springs. Which is her way of telling me she trusts you, and she thinks that either things have been hard for you, or they're about to get hard." My heart jumped and squeezed, I swear to God. Beth trusted me?

"Or maybe she thinks things are hard now, and will be later, too," Kenny added.

"Mark's coming tomorrow afternoon to talk," Ben said.

"Can we go to the hot springs in the morning then?" Kenny asked. He seemed eager to make sure we didn't miss out on that. "As preparation," he said, which scared me a bit.

What the hell was Mark gonna say to me? I wondered all night.

Because apparently, sleep is still optional.

Fool. Meeting with cops.

The next morning was grey, and drizzly, so when the other guys got up I wondered if we'd still go to the hot springs. It felt easy to be around these guys. Ben's hair clearly wasn't cooperative, and Kenny was yawning and scratching his belly. This was definitely "guy" habitat, and I grinned.

Nothing was keeping Kenny away from the hot springs, though. After a big bowl of oatmeal and some excellent caffeinated brew, we packed our water bottles, and towels and Kenny asked if I had good hiking shoes because…well, hiking, and rain, and mud, and stuff.

"Um…are these okay?" I said, holding out the old runners I'd worn up the day before. "They're all I've got now."

"They'll have to do – the ones I gave you are still at home I guess?" he added. Home? My heart jumped. Again.

They had both reassured me that going naked in the pool was normal, so I didn't need to worry that I didn't have a swimsuit. Or underwear, for that matter. I hadn't been able to keep mine clean.

After much twisting and turning along what they called a "trail" that seemed more like bushwhacking, I heard waterfalls. One or two more turns, and we were there. I gasped.

The clear, fresh water thundered down a rock face and became a stream that ran by the cloudy pool, and it was amazing. We stood around the steaming water, silent, and it felt weird and right at the same time.

I could see Ben's lips moving while his eyes moved slowly up and down, praying? I looked up to the sky, grey between the cedars that were dripping with moss. A couple of minutes later, Ben crossed himself, and they turned and looked at me.

"Cool, eh?" Kenny said in a quiet voice.

"Or hot, depending on your perspective," Ben whispered, his eyes smiling.

"Yeah," I said back, trying to keep my jaw from dropping. Ten minutes later, we were sitting, crouched in the warm water, soaking up to our shoulders. We were leaning back on these rounded rocks that were covered in moss around the edge of the pool. I found out later that Ben and a friend had built the whole thing from a spring that emerged after an earthquake. It was amazing, and weird. Kinda smelled a little, but not like me after a week on the street or anything.

The steam rose up around us, reaching the cedars above, and then the water dripped back down on us. Like cool rain even when it wasn't raining.

"Mark's coming today," Ben started. *Here we go*, I thought. "Anything you want to be sure to ask him? Maybe if we talk about it a bit now, Kenny and I can help you remember when he's here." Kenny chuckled.

"I know I clench up around the cops still," he reassured me. So, I talked it out with them.

"I don't really know what's going on with Jenny, which is why I came back, but...whatever she's been through? It's...well, I don't even know what it'll take for her to get better. Or if she caught something...it happens," I said. "And I guess I'm kinda thinking she'll hate me." There. I'd admitted it. But I couldn't stop.

"And I think I might have really fucked up with Beth and Cook."

"Don't," Kenny interrupted. "Cook misses you and wants you back." Which made me blush.

Future reference? It's okay to blush in hot springs, because my face was already red.

"Let's face it. I really want to see her, but will I be any help if I just end up getting arrested?" I asked. Kenny and Ben listened. And Kenny shook his head in agreement at a bunch that I said. A few minutes later, I couldn't help it, and words just tumbled out.

"And I can't forgive myself."

"For what?" Ben asked. "For getting yourself away from a bad situation?" We sat a while, and I tried not to think about my shame. Kenny chuckled.

"We've all struggled with that one. For sure. Think about it, Taylor. We're all guilty of shit," Kenny said.

"And we all struggle to forgive ourselves. Every. Fucking. Day." Whoa. Apparently, monks swear.

"Well, I'm having trouble getting over it," I admitted. "I may need to talk to you about it again. And again."

After a while we got out of the water and drip dried. Naked. It was weird to be with other guys like that with no agenda.

We got back to the cabin, and Ben started heating soup for us. Kenny cornered me in the loft while I changed into cleaner clothes.

"Hey, Taylor?" He came up behind me whispering, and I jumped. "Yeah?"

"If you wanna get out of here before Mark gets here, I'll understand, and cover for you." I smiled.

"Thanks. But I gotta do this." I smiled, putting on my pants. "Like I'd ever find my way out'a here, anyways." He chuckled.

"You're amazing. And you underestimate yourself," he said, heading down the ladder to the main floor. I stayed upstairs, watching out the window for Inspector Derksen, thinking about what I'd say when…if…I saw Jenny the first time.

And then he got there, and it was time for lunch. I hardly ate because my stomach was tight, but I knew what I had to do. I headed down the ladder to see him.

"So, Taylor, thanks for agreeing to see me," Mark said while we were sitting around drinking more tea. Who knew the guy club involved so much tea? Kenny and Ben were cleaning up from lunch and packing up the kitchen. I guess the plan was to head out soon. Mark had asked me about ten times to call him Mark, so I was starting to think of him that way. I shrugged.

Reaching into his pocket, he gave me back my phone.

"It's yours. Like I said, I'll switch it out for one that we won't monitor once we're all done." I was smiling as I wrapped my hand around it. Now I had everyone's numbers again.

"You didn't have to see me, so thank you. I wanted to let you know everything I know about Jenny." He pulled out his phone and started scrolling through a few emails until he pulled up a picture. Handed me his phone.

"There she is. As you can see, she's really sick."

I don't know what my face did, but Kenny reached over and grabbed my shoulder. I hadn't even felt him sit down. My first thought was that Mark was mistaken. That young woman, stringy hair, hollowed cheekbones, all those machines and tubes, this wasn't my little sister. My body flooded with relief, and I lifted my head to say something. But I hesitated, and looked a second time at the photo, used my fingers to zoom in on the face.

Fuck. I took a deep breath and felt my chest collapse.

I looked a third time and saw her precious face – the same one that had looked up at me night after night, sleeping, while I studied and watched over her in our bedroom. Somewhere in the body of that wired outcast was the soul of my little sister.

And my heart broke, and my mind shattered.

There she was. Beautiful. Older than I expected. Tied up to IVs and machines with numbers on them. She didn't look very alive. I felt desolate. Unanchored. Mark spoke first.

"She came in completely out of it. They think she'd overdosed, according to the doctors. She's struggling, for sure." He rubbed his palms down his thighs.

"But the main doctor thinks seeing you – hearing your voice – might help her try harder to get better. She thinks Jenny needs a reason, and we're hoping you're it." Which made me think about that. I broke my silence, holding on to the phone still.

"I really want to see her. I wish I hadn't left her behind years ago." I finished my tea, put it down and took my blue enamel mug to Ben to wash. It gave me a minute to think about how complicated it all was. Then I realized for the twelfth time that there really was no choice. I turned and faced the cop.

"I'll do anything if it'll help her. Anything."

"Okay. Beth and Kate were coming up with a plan to get you in as a hospital worker or something, because right now she's got cops there the whole time watching her door. We don't want to alert the uniforms that you're here yet. Does that work for you?"

"Why Kate and Beth?" I asked and found out they both used to be nurses. Seems everybody had a life and a half around here. We all had pasts, but theirs were reputable and I wondered why anyone would give up a really good job.

We talked a little about the details, how someone would drive me to the hospital the next day, Kate probably, and we'd go in together. I couldn't believe it was going to happen that quickly. I was nervous, and scared.

"Thank you. Really. I get you're sticking your neck out for me," I said. I counted the boards from the ceiling to the floor – 14 – and swallowing, I continued. "I know if I've gotta go from there right to the police station, I still want to try." Mark wasn't making eye contact with me, so I kept going.

"It's okay. I get it. You want her to wake up because whatever she remembers will help your case." I knew all about hidden agendas. Now *he* looked startled, took a deep breath.

"Nooo…that's not it," he said exhaling. "Your seeing Jenny isn't tied to turning yourself in. At all." I almost laughed watching him squirm. He just kept on, digging himself in.

"I promised a friend at the Vancouver Police that I'd ask you a favour," he said. *WTF,* I thought. *You think I'm an idiot?*

"They have some collaborating reports that lead them to believe it's possible Jean isn't telling the truth about what happened that night with you. They need to interview you, obviously, but wanted to talk to you about working with them to get her to admit it while they listen in." My head snapped up, and so did Kenny's. Ben just turned, wide-eyed and looked at us.

"What are you talking about?" Ben asked. "That sounds like it might be risky."

"I suppose there's some risk, but they'd work to make sure it was as safe as possible," he said. "I don't think Jean has a history of being violent," he added, and I actually snorted out loud at a cop.

"Maybe not to you," I said, trying hard to not sound like a snotty kid. The bruises were gone, but my body remembered.

"Well, she's ticked off a few of my colleagues over the years, and I think they'd like to lay a few charges on her for wasting their time. And yours," he said. "Not her first charges."

"If I can see Jenny, I'll help," I said. It was really that clear. I didn't care if Jean got to scratch or slap me again. Small price for my little sister.

"No," he said, as Ben started to pack our stuff to the door. Kenny'd already rolled up my sleeping bag. "I meant it before. One really doesn't depend on the other. I just promised my colleague I'd talk to you about it. And you don't have to agree now. Think about it.

"We want you to see Jenny. And we'll keep letting you in if it helps. I'm not going to call and tell them I've seen you until Jenny's getting better," he said.

We locked up the door and headed down the path. Kenny got between us, which I was grateful for. Gave me the walk to think about things.

At the cars, I thanked Mark for setting this up, and Ben for the cabin. Kenny was going to drive me back to my car, and I started to tell Ben I'd see him at the trailer. Mark stopped me.

"Don't tell me where you'll be. We'll just be in touch through Beth, okay?" he said. "And one last thing." He looked at me with piercing eyes. "Before I came up here, I saw the team that helped break Jenny's case. They were packing their stuff at the detachment, and Patty said to tell you that what you told them made a big difference. Not just a little difference, but a big difference. And Arun agreed. Okay?" He put his hand on my shoulder.

"What you did mattered. It helped us get to Jenny before…well, before things got even worse," he said. "You're a good brother, and if you were my son, I'd be proud of you," he said, and my eyes might have welled up just a little. I looked down at the ground and mumbled thanks, kicking some gravel around with my old runners. I struggled to figure it out. Did I rat Jean out?

I threw my stuff in the car, and started to get in. Ben came over and gave me a big, silent hug. Man, I hope I get a chance to hang out with him more.

With the huge lump in my throat I didn't risk saying anything out loud, but I smiled and turned towards the window.

And I wondered…is ratting wrong if I did it to save my ass?

What about if I'm saving someone else's? I knew the guys at the half-way house would have an answer.

But was it *my* answer?

I cried a little on the way, thinking about my sister all alone in that hospital bed.

Her all alone at that house.

And being left all alone with that bastard who raped me.

Because I deserted her.

Fuck, I thought. *I hope we can actually help her now.*

CHAPTER 52
NURSING CARE

Kate and I were dressed in scrubs, me with running shoes from Kenny, heading down the corridor at the hospital. I couldn't believe that no one stopped us at the nursing station just based on my pounding heart.

"Hi Kate," a voice from behind the counter called out. "Here's the IV for the patient in 4021." An older woman with grey hair and glasses, she handed Kate an IV bag, and a package with some tubing and stuff in it. "She's the only one in there. Just change the bag. Thanks for the help today," she said, perhaps just a little too loud. Here was Kate, being a nurse, and I was working out how to walk without tripping in my new rubber-soled shoes. My knees were actually knocking together.

"Thanks, Lila. Not a problem. Always willing to help out," she said, putting the bag in the pocket of her top like she'd slipped IV bags onto her person every day for the past ten years.

Wow, I thought. *Kate really is comfortable in the hospital. No wonder she kept telling me not to worry, that she had my back.* And then I started to worry again about Jenny. I was going to see her in just a minute or two, and I couldn't believe it.

Last night, Mark called me and updated me on Jenny's condition.

"She had some blood pressure issues at first, and the doctors were working to make sure it stayed up. She's on oxygen and has a couple of

IVs. She's hooked up to a BP machine all the time. She hasn't thrown up since admission but has had trouble breathing. Fentanyl is a terror, and it'll do that to you. They have no idea what else she's been on; it'll be a few days before the tox screen comes back from the lab. She was in a coma at admission, but the Naloxone has counteracted some of that. Honestly, they don't know about ongoing brain injury. They've been using the Naloxone sparingly because it can drive patients into horrible withdrawal.

"They say she should be conscious by now, that she's not showing classic signs of coma, but she's not responding to either voice or physical stimuli, and they can't figure it out. That's where they're hoping you come in. Sometimes the voices of family help.

"Be prepared to stay there for a while. They'll sneak food in for you, once we get you past the guard. I'm just clearing up things with the cops; technically there's still a bulletin out to pick you up.

"We can talk later if you're still willing to help them with the situation with Jean. I'm in conversations with them now." We'd shared our goodbyes, and I'd thanked him again for setting this up.

Nothing Mark had said to me prepared me for what was next, though. Kate shared a hello with the guard outside her door.

"The doctor wants us to monitor the patient much more closely, so the student will stay," she said, and I nodded at the man. Who clearly wasn't really paying attention to us. Entering the room was like a sucker-punch to the gut.

I struggled to recognize my sister. Kate put an arm around my shoulders and squeezed.

"Stay strong," she whispered into my ear, leaning towards me. "She needs you now, big brother." I pulled Russet from my bag and put it on the table beside her. I was hit with a wave of nausea.

"Hey, Jenny Henny, I'm here now," I said, my gut squeezing. God, I was so late. Too late, maybe. Kate moved up the bed beside all the machinery, took out a pen and paper, and started recording numbers. Then she pulled out the IV bag and actually changed it!

"Keep talking to her. Pull up a chair. You can hold that hand. It all helps," she said. "Sing her songs, tell her stories, whatever you guys did before." She didn't say anything about the tears trickling down my cheeks.

Jenny looked emaciated. Her arms looked like toothpicks, and I wondered how she looked bigger and so, so small at the same time. Even her shoulders were bony. My eyes travelled up to her face, where her eyes looked shadowed. There were dark smudges under them, and scratches on her cheeks. Her hair was stringy and black, and at first, I was shocked. It didn't look like Jenny's at all, but then I noticed the roots were growing out – there was the light brown hair I was used to. I wanted to grab her and hug her, maybe run away with her, but she was pretty attached to machines, and it was all so much to take in. I sat down beside her, and took her hand, kept talking, saying nothing and everything.

"Hey, Jelly Belly, I'm sorry it took me so long, but I got here as soon as I could. I love you baby. Really. And I know it was horrible, but nothing is going to hurt you again, I promise. I'm here now, and I'm gonna stay as long as it takes." I took a breath, wiped my face on my scrubs.

"I'm sorry it took so long, but I had to grow up, figure some stuff out. Some of it hasn't been really good, but I'm better now. I love you." It all came spilling out, and I just kept stroking her hand, up her arm. There were black and blue marks up and down them, and her skin felt like paper. "Can I touch her face?" I asked Kate.

"That should be fine. Just stay away from her eyes. They've put some goop in them so they don't dry out. If she stays unconscious much longer they might put goggles on her with liquid in them, so her eyes don't get damaged," she said. It seemed like every part of Jenny was at risk. I put my forehead down on the bed, hiding my face, and had a quiet sob. Kate came around the bed once the IV was changed and rubbed my back. She leaned over and whispered in my ear.

"Now, Taylor, precisely now is when you need to be strong for Jenny. I don't know if you noticed, but when you were talking to her, her heart and respiratory rate went up a bit. She's hearing you. It's okay to cry with her, but don't you dare let her think she isn't going to get better. Because that's just not true. She's already come so far. She's off the ventilator." Kate pointed to a big bandage on Jenny's neck. She stopped whispering.

"That was where her trach tube was. She's breathing on her own now. She's starting to twitch, which is good. She's going to continue to get better. You have to know that.

"This is a strong, and brave, young woman who's seen some horrible stuff." I looked at Kate and realized now she was talking to Jenny as much as to me. "She's got so much going for her, though. Her heart is strong, and I see from her chart that her blood pressure keeps recovering to normal. She's actually sleeping some of the time, according to her vitals. She's probably hungry, so they're giving her calories through this tube." Kate held up the IV. "She's going to feel so good when she can eat popsicles and drink cold lemonade and orange juice. What were some of her favourite foods?" she asked.

"She used to love it when I made Kraft Dinner, with ketchup. That was a good week, when we had enough that we both got to eat big bowls full. I have boxes for us now, Jenny. Cases under my bed in my trailer, and we can eat as much as you want." I put my hand over hers and could have sworn it jumped.

A few minutes later, Kate showed me where to write numbers, and where to get them off the machine, and she left me in the room. I sang to my sister and remembered some stories from when I used to make them up to help her sleep.

"Hey, Jenny Penny…remember when you used to give me a word and I'd make up silly poetry? Like when I sang about the Princess Unicorn Hair?

Henny was a little girl with hair so mean
She worked so hard to make sure it wasn't cleaned
Because shampoo hurt
Much more than dirt
And never made her scream."

The lights gradually got dim out the window, and the room got darker. I sat back in the chair, and looked at her, smiling. She was my sister, and we were together. It felt good.

And scary.

An hour later, Lila came by to check on us. She looked at my charting and snickered.

"Man, you're better than some of the first-year Med students who do this work. Every ten minutes like clockwork. You don't have to keep that up all night, but even charting from time to time tells us a lot." She pointed to some numbers. "See here where her breathing evens out? She's likely asleep right now." That explained her quiet voice. "She's been sleeping on and off since she came in, but she's had more and longer awake times. She is improving. Honest." She left me a dinner, and some snacks. Reminded me I could use the washroom in the room, and that the nurses would be coming in hourly to check on us.

"Use that blanket," she said, pointing to one on the end of the bed. "You can sleep in this chair. It reclines." She shuffled around the room a bit more, checked Jenny's machines, pushed some buttons and alarms went on and off, and then she looked right at me.

"You're a good brother, Taylor. Kate told me about how much you wanted to come and look after her.

"It's too bad, what she's seen. She's been hurt, but not by you. I hear you helped catch the people who hurt her, and now they can't get to her ever again. That makes you an amazing big brother." I couldn't tell if she was telling me or Jenny, but I knew I'd need to hear those words a few more times before I believed them, and I wasn't sure Jenny ever would.

She patted my shoulder, picked up her papers and pen, and we were alone again.

I stayed beside Jenny for a day and a half before Kate convinced me to take a break, head home for a shower, new scrubs, and some "real food," as she called it. I was at home waiting for Kate to drive me back to the hospital when my phone rang.

"Hey Mark, what's up?" I answered. I was still a little startled every time I spoke so casually to a cop. A head cop.

"Well, Taylor, the hospital called to let me know Jenny's waking up. I thought you'd want to get there before my guys who'll interview her tomorrow. I'm sending a guy around to drive you there now. And if she's awake, don't talk to her about what's happened to her, okay?" I couldn't believe it! I hung up and ran out the door, then ran back in and grabbed the bag I'd packed. My phone rang again.

"Holy Mark! I can't believe it! Thank you for sending someone for me! Kate said she'd be home to drive me back in an hour or so, if that works better for you guys," I told him, thinking he'd called off his driver.

"Two things. Just found out you aren't a person of interest any more. The Vancouver cops know you're coming and the guard there is expecting you." I smiled.

Turns out the Vancouver cops wanted to meet me the next day to talk to me about helping them catch Jean in a lie. Something about putting some pressure on her about a young man who was missing from her area.

"I think if you ask Kenny, he'll drive you," Mark said. "A birdie told me your car isn't insured right now. Don't worry Taylor. I'm sure you'll have a steady income soon," he said, and I felt a little kick in my gut. I knew it was "the responsible thing to do" when I'd parked my car. I was hoping things would settle down with Jenny and I'd be able to get back to work, a paycheque, and wheels that moved. Mark and I made some plans to talk the next day, and Kenny agreed to get me to the hospital.

It was a short drive, made shorter with his help. I couldn't stop saying thank you to him.

I just wish he'd stuck around to get me where I wanted to be.

CHAPTER 53
LITTLE SPITFIRE

"I'm sorry, you can't go in there." It was hard to change direction, both literally and not, when I was going full throttle towards my sister. The cop's voice made it clear he wasn't letting me by. I hoped I didn't end up in handcuffs.

I paused mid-stride, saw there were medical staff going and coming from her room, and I heard Jenny's voice quiet, raspy. I couldn't make out what she was saying, but the charge nurse moved to shuffle me off to the lounge. I didn't budge.

"Wait. I'm her brother. I have to get in to see her. The police asked me to come." Funny how quickly I aligned myself with cops when I wanted something. I tried to brush by the woman in scrubs, but the cop outside Jenny's door stood up and took a step towards us. I stopped, with a heavy sigh.

"Why can't I see her? I'm Taylor, her brother. I was here earlier. I've been waiting for days to talk to her, just went home to clean up." I was confused but followed a nurse down the hall into a corner of the visitors lounge.

"Your sister is waking up, it's true. You heard her. She's being seen by lots of medical and support staff right now and they asked you to wait in here." The woman, Connie on her badge, started to walk away.

"Wait. Who asked me to wait in here?" I asked.

"Jenny did. We told her you were on your way, and she asked us to give her some time before she 'had to see you.' We told her she didn't have to see anyone except a social worker," Connie explained. Her words felt like a gut punch.

Turns out, awake means you're allowed to say no to visits. Apparently, Jenny'd specifically said she didn't want to see me.

I dropped my backpack on the floor beside me and slumped in a chair. Staring at the floor between my feet, I sat there for a long time trying to figure things out.

Did I piss her off when I was visiting before?

Was it something I said?

Was she mad at me for leaving her at Mom's?

Did the cops tell her something about me? The crap with Jean, maybe?

What the hell had made her say no to me now? I knew it could be anything. Even something I hadn't thought of yet. But I had all night, and I wasn't leaving.

I sat there, alone, vaguely aware of the few people around me.

Every visitors lounge seems to have one person – either a patient or visitor – who sits staring at sports on the TV, unaware of what's going on around them. Luckily, this guy kept the volume down.

There's also always a family sitting in the corner, trying to keep a child entertained, waiting out their turn to visit a grandparent. Tonight, it was a quiet Southeast Asian family, visiting a grandmother. People trickled in and out of their group, which never got smaller than six or eight. Tea arrived, and they complained about drinking it out of Styrofoam.

I blended into the corner. After a couple of hours, the nurse came to see me, let me know Connie had gone home, rotated off shift. Jenny was doing well and was settling in for the night.

And still didn't want to see me. I thanked the nurse but didn't move from my chair. At one point I got up and refilled my water bottle, went to the washroom, but I would stay for however long it took. I expected to get kicked out at some point, but they didn't try. I guess having a sibling come out of a coma came with privileges, unlike if you're homeless looking for a place to crash. Don't try to sleep anywhere in a hospital, I'd learned years ago.

As the evening wore on, I decided I had to talk to somebody, and decided on Kenny. I'd promised to let him know what was going on. I took a stroll down a hallway and into a stairwell, put my pen in the door to hold it open, and climbed down a few flights.

"Hey, roomie, how are you?" he answered.

"I'm okay. Hanging out here at the hospital. Just wanted to let you know I don't think I'll be home tonight." It still made me happy to think of our trailer as "home."

"That's okay. How's Jenny?" And suddenly I could hardly speak. I didn't want to sob in the echoing stairwell and thought a dam would burst if I opened my mouth. All that came out was a quiet *gasp, gasp, sob, gasp.*

"Awww, Tay, I'm sorry. Isn't she doing well? I heard she was waking up. We're all prayin' for you'n her, buddy." I felt like a little brother when Kenny called me "buddy," but in a good way. I sniffled.

"She...she...she is. Getting better." Tears were flowing now, but I was still keeping it quiet. "She's awake. I can hear her talking on and off. But she won't see me," I confessed. And then I just put my hand to my mouth and let the silent sobs come. Kenny got it.

"Awww, buddy. I'm so sorry. Fuck. That sucks so much. But you stay there. Stay strong. Awww, shit. That is so hard. You are being such a good big brother." A few more minutes, and there wasn't anything else to say. Kenny'd commiserated and sympathized and apologized, and I felt a little better. He'd even wondered out loud if she was embarrassed, which gave me something to think about. I was trying to figure out if he meant she was embarrassed or embarrassed of me. I crept up the stairwell, snuck back through the closed visitors lounge door, and settled in for the night.

About an hour later, the night nurse brought me a tea, and told me that if I wanted to, she'd sneak me into Jenny's room for a bit. My sister was sleeping, had been sedated so wasn't likely to wake up.

"The social worker called a while ago, Marta something, and said that she'd encourage contact between you. So I don't see any harm. If Jenny wakes up, just sneak back in here, okay?"

And that's how I got to see her for a bit.

It was a long, miraculous and heartbreaking night.

I thought about Ben, talking about "the dark night of the soul." Was that what this was? Jenny's little-girl-ness collided with her street-ness, her hair softly lying on her pillow, her chest rising and falling, I realized someone had washed her hair, and cleaned her up, and she had fewer machines attached. Someone had brought her a nightgown with a stuffed bear on it. Russet was still on her bedside table, and in the soft glow of the machines she looked like an answer to my prayers. Honest to God.

The night nurse came in from time to time and checked on her. Once, Jenny woke up, and started talking. I melted into a shadowed corner.

"When can I get out of here?" she asked.

"Not for some time, dear. There are people coming to talk to you, people who want to help. But first, you've got to get well. Strong. How are you feeling?"

"I just want to get out," she answered, and I saw her fingers worrying the edge of the blanket. *Oh shit, I've seen that before. She's wired. She's gonna start really jonesing soon. Or maybe she already is.* I wondered if her nurses had figured it out.

"Taylor went home, I guess," she said, sighing.

"Nope. He's around, waiting. That brother cares about you a whole lot," the nurse answered, and I shrunk a little more.

"Well, that's fine. I don't want to see him." She turned her face into her pillow, and I thought of what Kenny'd said.

"Yet," the nurse answered, and she tucked in my little sister after giving her another pill. On her way out the door, she looked right at me and winked. My sister was already heading back into dreamland.

Good for her, I thought, wishing her only an easy time coming down from whatever. After a few minutes I crept out of the room and went to the nursing station.

"Did you give her something to settle her down?" I asked, presuming the nurse would know what I was talking about.

"Yes, we are sedating her, like I said," she answered.

"That's good." I tugged at my T-shirt, looking down at my runners. "I think she's in for a rough time for the next few days. I'm guessing you know what I mean," I said, looking up at her. The nurse smiled and touched my arm.

"Yes, Taylor. We're monitoring her. Fentanyl…any narcotic, really… well, it's hard to get off them. Harder still to stay off. And we don't know what else she's been on. Your sister's in for a tough ride. She's lucky to have you, right?" she said, challenging me. I realized she was asking how I'd support Jenny's rehab.

"Yeah. I've helped a few friends kick it and I've watched some try, and not make it. Lucky for me, it's not a path I've had to walk," I said, trying to emphasize my good character. What a joke. "I will be there for her, for sure.

"Thanks for letting me stay in her room for a while. Really. I appreciate it. I'll head back to the visitors lounge now, if that's okay," I said, checking in with her.

"Sure," she said. "You could go to the cafeteria for an early breakfast if you want. The doctors won't be around for an hour or so, but I'll make sure to let you know when they're here," she said. I thanked her and headed to wash up. I didn't have enough money to buy cafeteria food, but I'd grabbed some bars and muffins from home, and they were still in my bag. On my way back into the lounge, the nurse called out quietly to me.

"Hey Taylor, what do you take in your coffee?" she asked, holding up a big mug.

"At this point, anything you've got," I said, grinning. I walked over, and thanked her for the mug, dressed with lots of cream and sugar. She pressed a small box of cookies in my hand.

"I found these in the breakroom. Just going stale. Help yourself," she said, and I smiled, holding back the tears. Sometimes angels wear scrubs.

It had been a long, long night, but the sun was rising. I'd slept a little, and surprisingly, didn't feel like shit. I guess all those years of sleeping in my car had prepared me for getting enough rest just about anywhere.

Jenny wouldn't see me yet, but I wouldn't let that stop me. I called Kenny and let him know I was coming home to wash up. Maybe she'd see me tonight.

It had to get better, right?

CHAPTER 54
DAY TERRORS - JENNY

The dark creature grew, extending arms that seemed to erupt talons as it reached out and chased her off the ridge and into the cave. She scratched her way along the surface of the slimy walls, watching the bugs crawl both away from and towards her. She wanted to scream, but was terrified to open her mouth, afraid of what might try to suck out her brains. Or her breath. Scratching at her arms, she felt the welts rising, blood starting to flow. The creature seemed to smell the iron tang, and rushed towards her.

She scrambled further into the dark cave, frantically trying to see what was beyond the next corner, but the darkness was thick, squeezing the breath from her lungs. *Taylor! I need you! Why don't you see me? Come and help me?* The sobbing began again, and she started to wonder if this was how she'd die.

Whimpering, she glanced up and saw a small piece of sky above her, drawing her forward. She started to scramble up the wall, looking for fingerholds, but she could feel the beast grabbing at her clothing, trying to pull her backwards. The cool breeze from the hole above caressed her face while at the same time the heat and darkness crept towards, then seeped into her limbs making her slow, drowning her. *Taylor!* She screamed in her mind, knowing that he wasn't coming, had never come before. *Taylor!!!* Where was he? Couldn't he hear her? He'd said he'd be there…but the small flicker of hope inside her was struggling.

The beast was screaming at her, shrill, insistent, and it began to wrap itself around her, stopping her from moving even one step higher. The hole to the sky started to fly away from her, but when she wanted to reach towards it, her arms were pinned to her sides, prickly, on fire.

Losing all hope, she started to scream, trying hard to drown out the beast that she knew would consume her.

And then, she felt its talons. Darkness consumed her, and she gave in to it.

Later, a group of medical staff surrounded Jenny's bed while she slept. A young woman in a lab coat started to speak.

"Jennifer Smythe is a twelve-year-old female, who presented with a Fentanyl overdose brought in by police from a raid." The young intern glanced at her notes on the small sheet of paper in her pocket. She blinked, trying to steal a glance at her new boss. "She was intubated and ventilated upon arrival and was managed first with Naloxone and vasopressors, and now with tranquilizers. She has shown signs of severe withdrawal and overnight began to suffer from psychoses. Anti-psychotics are being given round the clock, and it is expected that as her vitals continue to stabilize, she will gradually improve. She has been conscious for 24 hours and is eating well on a soft diet. She's asking for solids. She is able to bathroom herself with assistance." She took a breath, and the nurse smiled at her.

"She has no parents and was under the care of Social Services. A social worker is working with us to try to find her a stable living situation when we discharge her, hopefully within the next week. Upon admission, there was extensive evidence of sexual assault." She checked her notes and stopped when interrupted. She looked up anxiously at the group of lab coats that surrounded the young woman in the bed.

"What evidence of sexual assault? Could it have just been activity?" a resident asked. The intern bristled. Jenny's nurse inhaled sharply.

"She's twelve years old." She glared at the resident, who flinched.

"Consent is not possible from a twelve-year-old." The attending physician's voice was stern. "Continue," she said to the intern while also glaring at the resident.

"She has an older brother who visits regularly and wants to re-engage with her more permanently, but he is not, at this time, a suitable caregiver. He has only recently had a stable address and has limited prospects. She has resisted his visits, and it is not clear if their relationship is healthy."

The young woman looked down at her notes again, fidgeting with the nametag around her stethoscope that hung around her neck.

"Thank you. Well done. When was her last dose of Risperidone?" the older woman with grey hair asked.

"The resident on call ordered a shot overnight when she began hallucinating. We are wondering about adding some Ativan, as needed. Also, we weren't sure if you wanted us to continue with a regular dose of Risperidone?" the nurse asked the medical staff. The young woman was sleeping peacefully.

"Okay. Thanks. We'll order the Risperidone – chart that Serge – and add the Ativan prn. Give her food, such as it is. Is her brother around?"

"No, he went home to rest, should be back later today. Her social worker is asking if she can have stable visitors – some potential foster care providers want to meet her."

"Fine. We'll talk to the brother when he returns. If he's in before I'm in clinic, page me." After a short physical exam that didn't wake the young woman, the medical team hurried on to their next patient.

Jenny pulled the twisted sheet over herself, tying her IV line into the mess in the process. Her body felt heavy, her brain fogged. *Why am I so sweaty?* she wondered, and had a fleeting memory of darkness, and being chased.

"Shit," she whispered under her breath.

"It's okay, let me help," Christie, her young nurse, offered. She untied the line, and soon had Jenny's bedding straightened over her. "Do you want to sit up? I'd like to help you change, maybe wash up a bit," she said, handing Jenny the controls for the hospital bed. Soon, Christie had Jenny sponged off, and helped her into a clean gown. She changed her sheets and bundled and tossed everything into a bin. As she finished taking Jenny's vitals, Jenny fell back asleep, and Christie hoped it would be a peaceful rest.

She never wanted to find a little girl tied up in her blanket in the corner screaming ever again.

CHAPTER 55
PROMISES OF HOME - JENNY

That afternoon Jenny was enjoying several cups of jelly and fruit salad when four women knocked on the door.

"Jenny? It's Kate." Kate came in, wearing her usual jeans and T-shirt this time, and introduced the patient to the other women. Jenny looked up and smiled.

"You're looking so good! I'm glad you're starting to feel better." Kate gave her a small hug, and patted the bed, straightening the sheets around the young girl. She wished Jenny's colour was better. *Time,* she thought.

"This is Marta, you might remember her. She's still your social worker. And this is Veronica, and that's Claire, the women I was telling you about earlier." They came in, tossing their sweaters and bags on a chair, and gathered around Jenny's bed, shaking her small, bruised hand one after another. Jenny tried to plaster a smile on, but it was a bit stiff. *Who are these people, and what do they want with me?* she thought.

"So, Jenny, once you're feeling better, and the doctor says you're well enough to go, we're going to get you settled in a new place. Maybe with Claire while you're at school, and Veronica, on weekends?" Marta said to the young woman. Jenny's eyes shot up to Kate's.

"I thought you said I'd be with Taylor most of the time," Jenny said. She started to straighten her blankets, smoothing the fold over her torso again and again with her hands. She couldn't even look at Marta, who was standing at the foot of her bed.

"Jenny?" Marta tried again. "I know you don't know these people, but that's why I brought them to meet you."

"You said Taylor'd look after me," she repeated to Kate.

"Yup. I did, and if you'll let him in to see you, you can talk to him about it," Kate said. "For now, though, he's not settled well enough to look after you full time, but he's working on it. Veronica has lots of room at her house for both of you, though, and she's agreed to put up with you and your big brother," Kate said. Jenny glared at Kate, snorted.

"Like anyone really cares," she said. *Well, there goes trust,* Kate thought.

Veronica smiled and patted the bed.

"We'll see what will work for you. Let's talk about it. We haven't even told Taylor yet in case it doesn't work out. You can come and see my place soon," Veronica added. "Taylor said he'd bake for you when you come visit. He's got some real promise as a baker and cook, so he'll feed us well," Veronica said. "He's in school and working to be a chef. I've been impressed by him. He's working harder than my boys did at his age and really wants to see you, Jenny." Veronica reached into her purse and brought out a bag of Smarties. "Whenever you're ready, of course. He asked me to bring these to you. Said he remembered when you liked them," she finished, reaching out to hand them to Jenny.

Jenny didn't look at the woman, ignored her offering.

Fuck you, she thought. *It takes more than Smarties to buy me back.*

"Well, you just let me know if you want them or not. I'll give them back to him if you don't." Veronica put the bag of chocolate treats on a table beside Jenny's bed. Kate handed the young woman a cup of water, anticipating Jenny's need for distraction. Jenny looked up — her eyes filled with anxiety. *Save me,* they seemed to say. Kate moved closer, bent over and whispered in Jenny's ear.

"Just a few more minutes and I'll round them up and kick them out. Marta had to see you today. Sorry," she said, brushing Jenny's hair from her forehead. Jenny had told Kate yesterday that she was feeling self-conscious about her looks. Her roots, her bruises, her broken nails. All of it was hard. Not to mention the twitching.

"Jenny, this is Claire," Marta ploughed on. "She's got a bedroom in her house in Mission that she's offered you for when you're ready to head back to school. We'll have to arrange for your records to be transferred." Jenny snorted again. Like there were records from her last school. She'd attended what…two weeks? They'd never even tried to find her.

"I've already started the process. Don't worry, it won't take long," *When will that bitch shut up?* Jenny snuck a peek at the older woman standing to the side of the room. She was heavy set, wearing baggy pants and an old cardigan. Her shoes were like granny shoes, and her hair was shaggy, and she seemed old. *She looks like she's never had a mirror,* Jenny thought. *What the hell would that old hag know about raising kids?*

"Veronica's house is too far for school buses, so you can stay at Claire's during the week. Then you and Taylor can head to Veronica's for the weekends. And I bet Taylor will come visit you and take you to dinner and stuff whenever you want."

Marta realized she was trying just a little too hard to sell this whole situation to Jenny. Which was stupid, because really Jenny didn't get any say about where she'd live and was so out of it, she wasn't sure the girl was paying attention. Marta felt guilty about what had happened to the young woman, but all she could do was try to give her the best placement she could. She was surprised her boss, Paul, had left the file with her, but he said doing anything else could raise suspicions, something he wasn't willing to invite.

"Anyhow," she continued, "your job right now is to get well. If you want to see your brother, let us know. Kate, maybe, can get hold of him. Then, when you're getting closer to being released, we can go for a visit so you'll at least have a picture of where you're going. These are good homes, Jenny. Talk to your brother about them, if you want.

"And just so you know, that man who hurt you, there's lots of charges against him now. He's in lots of trouble with police." Marta didn't want to elaborate, but it looked good for charges that would stick, and apparently the guy was cooperating with the police and sharing information about who he'd sold the files to. The cops wanted the ring of distributors. It would likely take years for the investigation to head to court, though, so she didn't want to promise too much. She reached into her bag.

"Here's something we found of yours from your last place, Jenny. I wasn't sure if you'd still want it, but I washed it and brought it back." Jenny's eyes glistened at the sight of the pink blanket that Taylor had said was made by her grandma, whom she'd never met. Marta put it on the table in the corner.

Jenny wiped her cheeks, and started picking at the tape that held her IV tubing in her arm. Her eyes were flicking around the room, never settling on anyone's face, but she was definitely trying to keep track of it all.

"Hey, you," Kate said, moving in close to the young one. She gently took Jenny's hand and started softly stroking the bandages. "It's okay, lots of time, no changes now. I'll come back to talk this afternoon, if you want. You get to be the boss of everything that goes on while you're in here, okay?" Jenny latched onto Kate's sight, and looked pleadingly at the one woman who seemed to understand what she was going through.

"Please?" Jenny said, sounding almost like a squeak.

"Of course," Kate said. "Anytime. You've got my number in your phone, remember? And if you want to see Tay, or not, let me know. He's still waiting. And he asked me to tell you he's in no rush. He's got lots of daytime TV to keep him occupied." Jenny's eyes pleaded with Kate, who knew she'd had enough of these visitors.

"Okay, ladies, off you go," Kate said. "I'll meet you in the lobby in about 30 minutes. "We can make plans from there," she said, dismissing the trio.

"Sweetie, you can't just decide where you go," Kate reminded Jenny for about the hundredth time. *Like you can keep me anywhere,* Jenny thought. She remembered how easy it was for Taylor to get away.

"Unfortunately, even though Social Services 'fucked up,' as you so eloquently put it, they're still in charge. But this time, your brother is in a much better place to hang out with you, help you stay safe. I know starting school again seems stupid since you've missed so much of the year, but maybe you'll meet a couple of people to hang out with over the summer.

"And I can help you if you want. Anyhow, no rush. Let me know when you want to see Taylor, okay?"

Jenny was getting tired. The nurses came in, left a tray with soup and a pathetic-looking sandwich, and some meds. Kate recognized the sedatives, so wasn't too surprised when Jenny started to drift after taking them.

"Maybe later today, okay? You can let him know. Tell him to bring pizza. This shit is almost worse than what we ate as kids," she said, rolling the tray table away from her. "Warm milk and cold soup just don't appeal right now." Jenny started to gag a little and was again picking at the tape on her hand. Kate grabbed a roll off the trolley by the door and came over to her.

"Hey, I'll let him know. Do you want me to change that tape, so they don't know you've been at it? I can leave a piece on your pyjamas to fuss with if you want." Kate knew there was no point in telling the young woman to stop picking at the tape; the alternative was the scabs on her arms, or her face, or anything else she could scratch. Tape seemed a small price.

"In fact," she said as she tore off a piece and cleaned up the tape on the IV, "here's the roll. Hide it. You can stick it anywhere you want and fuss away at it. Just don't stick it to Russet. I think it'll pull off the wool holding that poor kitty together." Kate smiled, and Jenny latched onto the tape with her fist.

Note to self, Kate said. *Bring a few things to occupy her hands.* Kate gathered up all the stuff that'd been left around the room, straightening for the staff. She held up the Smarties. "Stay? Go?" she asked.

"It's okay, you can leave them," Jenny answered. *Score one for Veronica*, Kate thought. *And Taylor*. Finally, the room was put back in order, with the things Jenny would need within reach, and Jenny actually smiled at

Kate. *I don't know where Taylor found her, but she's different,* Jenny thought as sleepiness fogged her brain.

"One last thing," Kate added. "A friend of mine, Ben, said he'd be happy to talk with you about what happened. He's a great guy, and he doesn't have to report to anyone. Not schools, Marta, Taylor or me. Usually he's really expensive, but for you he said he'd counsel you if Taylor kept baking cookies for him." She winked at Jenny. And she headed towards the door to see Taylor.

"Your brother really is that good a cook," she said. "Think about it. No rush." She dimmed the lights, and Jenny put her head back, looking tired.

"Thanks," she said. "Say hi to Taylor for me. Later, okay?" Jenny mumbled.

But Taylor wasn't in the visitors lounge when Kate went to find him. *Where are you, little man, when I have good news for you?* Kate wondered, picking up her phone to text him.

After dropping everyone back at their cars, Kate headed for *Just Living,* and the dining room where she hoped Cook would still have some dinner for her. She poked her head in the door and found Cook, Sally, and Rosie sitting around the table. The place was spotless.

Darn, too late, she thought.

"Hey, just wanted to see how you all are doing," she said. "Anyone know where Nora is?" she asked.

"She just headed out to your place with a plate full of food for you," Sally said. "But if you've got a minute, we'd love to pick your brain." Cook headed to the stove and poured a fresh cup of tea for Kate, stopping for a bit of honey off the shelf.

"Here you go," the big man said, putting the mug down beside her. "That should keep you going until you get home."

"Sure," Kate said, patting Rosie on the hand as she sat. "Hello, Auntie," she greeted her friend.

"Hey, lady. How are you? How's that little girl?" Rosie said, wasting no time.

"I'm good. Looking forward to good food, and my little boy," she said. "Hopefully he doesn't eat it all. And Jenny's getting stronger every day. I worry though. She's got some big problems she's not talking about. She reminds me of some of the street kids I used to see. I'm worried about her." Kate took a sip of tea, and the folks around the table were all sighing, looking at one another.

"That's too bad," Cook said. "Gonna be hard for her. An' her brother." The old man took another scoop of honey and added it to his tea. A reaction to stress, Sally thought. "I miss him. Real bad."

"It'll be okay," Sally said, reassuring her man. "We're all going to look after them," she added. "He'll be back working soon."

"Yeah. And we should talk to someone smart about what we can do to help a guy like that," Rosie said. "Maybe you can ask that smart man, Ben, to talk with us. Build us one of those plans he's always talking about." Kate smiled, tears welling in her eyes.

"Yes, I will do that. They do need a plan," she said. "And we're just the people to build one for them. It'll be a little complicated, but maybe we can get permission for Jenny to come on-site, like we do for those young folks from the Friendship Centre," Kate said, already thinking of some steps they could take to build support. "They're gonna need all the help we can muster, I'm afraid. But that's one of those things we do really well."

"Well, that's true. And sometimes the government can meddle. Especially with the little ones. We're gonna need to have a real good plan, maybe help from the youth workers at the Friendship Centre. All my relations," the Elder emphasized, and Kate smiled at her. *No doubt, it'll be tough*, Kate thought. *And those youth workers are savvy about how to keep the government and law enforcement at bay. Good idea, Rosie.*

She finished her tea and set her cup down in the wash tray. "Now, I'm going home to find my wife and hug my son and eat a fine dinner before I lay down my head," she said, collecting hugs on her way out the door.

If only Taylor would message me back, she thought. *Little bugger.*

CHAPTER 56
TEAMING UP

Getting out of the shower, I heard the phone ring, and dashed to get it. *Maybe Jenny's asking for me!* I thought. No such luck. It was Mark, calling to set up the meeting with the cops from Vancouver. Including Patty. It felt like weeks since I'd seen her, and I wanted to thank her for finding Jenny.

I asked Mark to give me some time to find wheels. I was seriously going to have to get work so I could renew my insurance. I might risk driving to the hospital with expired tags but wasn't stupid enough to try that when meeting cops. Luckily, Kenny lent me his truck.

We met at a run-down Chinese restaurant, easily located by the horrible neon sign out front. The parking lot was full, usually a sign of decent food at least.

The restaurant was dark, but Patty stood so it was easy to find them. We ordered, and the conversation got going. Patty introduced us, told Yousef and Andrea, the detectives, that I was the one who'd helped with the investigation into the cyberporn case last month, and they started lobbying for my help. Yousef was a crusty old guy who kept raging about "that woman, if you could call her that." Andrea helped keep the focus on the nuts and bolts of the planning. At one point, Yousef made my ears burn when he raged about the young men who'd been disappearing from her area. Apparently, *she* was a person of interest in some of the cases. And my ears were burning because I was trying to get my head around how badly I'd misread her. *Why* did I have to find older women attractive?

Once I agreed to help them the plans took shape quickly. I'd try to get an invitation to Jean's place. In the meantime, the younger cop, Andrea, was going to take me clothes shopping. I needed a shirt with a button or two so they could swap them out to put a camera on me like James Bond. It'd have the capacity to send footage directly to them. Once I got permission to visit Jean, we'd set it up so they could be outside in a van, keeping me safe from Jean's anger.

Like that was possible.

After lunch and clear instructions on how to do what they needed, Andrea and I headed to shop. I wanted to be done with Jean as soon as possible, hopefully within days. Maybe I could get Kenny's truck again, if Jean was willing to see me. I was wary of going over there, but it was a small price. How would I get her to admit what she'd done? Would it be enough to get me off? What if I couldn't make it work?

This being a rat for the cops wasn't as straightforward as I thought it'd be. I was scared it could all go wrong, and I'd end up in jail or on the registry, and never see Jenny again. And I wasn't stupid. I also knew the guys at *Just Living* were unlikely to keep supporting me. Walking to my truck, I got Patty's attention, and she came over to me.

"Hey. Is this gonna work? Am I gonna end up with a record?" I asked. "I'm still willing, you know, but I just want to prepare myself going in."

"What? Taylor! Of course, it'll work out. Didn't they tell you? They don't have enough to charge you. In fact, they really want to go after Jean because she clearly set you up. And Yousef is pissed at her for wasting their time and putting you at risk. Shit, I thought you knew that. You were still willing to do this?" She pulled down on her sweater.

"You need to look after yourself here, Taylor. Don't risk your reputation just for us, okay?" I nodded. A few minutes later, Patty'd heard all about how Jenny was doing, and Andrea and I were heading to shop. I was spooked by how everything was falling into place too easily. No set up should go this smooth. *Is this how easy it is to become an informant?*

Andrea convinced me to call Jean before I headed back up the Valley. I worked hard at making myself seem devoted and…well…obedient. Andrea recorded it on my phone.

"Jean!" I sounded surprised when she answered on the first ring. "I thought you'd put me to voicemail. How are you?" I was surprised she didn't hang up.

"Why aren't you calling me on the phone I gave you?" she asked, suspicion creeping into her voice. I realized she hadn't known it was me.

"I know. It broke when I dropped it. That's a part of why I'm calling… not because I deserve anything after running away from you, but because I wanted you to know I'm sorry, and to cancel the phone service. I hope you haven't been trying to get a hold of me." I'd decided to keep to the truth. "Anyhow, I wanted to let you know that, and to thank you again for everything you did for me. I have a little something for you, and wanted to know if I could drop by tomorrow with it?" There was silence on the phone.

"I understand if you don't want to. It's okay," I said, sounding like a lost puppy in my own head. "I hope you're doing good. Real good, 'cause, well, you know. And thank you," I finished, but didn't hang up. I could hear her breathing on the other end, and it reminded me of Mom being exasperated with Jenny and me. I waited for the explosion. I didn't have to wait long.

"Damn, Taylor. I don't know what to do with you. You're crazy. And you make me crazy too." She sighed. I softened my voice.

"I know, eh? Me too," I agreed. I chuckled, real quiet. "How are you doing?" I asked, my voice like silk. Who knew I'd be good at this? "I've been in and out of okay," I admitted. And then shut up. Silence. Time went by, then she finally spoke.

"I'm doing okay. I'm done with the group at *Tide's End*. Probably with everyone. Are you still seeing them?" she asked, clearly fishing.

"I only saw them this week because the cops finally found my sister. She's doing okay, still in hospital. Which is why I have some time to see you, if you want. I'm couch surfing right now, to be near her," I added. I wasn't paying rent at Kenny's, so I guess that was the truth. "Why don't I stop by later in the week and talk? Just talk." I said. "We can figure this out...you know...even...with all the chaos...there's a part of me that feels like I...I still need you. To see you."

We made plans. She said not tomorrow, but maybe the next day. Or the day after that. By the time I was off the phone, Andrea had sewn the camera buttons on my shirt, reminded me not to wash it, and I was heading down the highway. Kenny'd told me to go straight to Jenny. He'd pick up his truck at the hospital later.

Driving back to town, I knew the only place I wanted to be was with Jenny. Bolting wouldn't have been possible. Good to know I'd done the right thing.

An hour later, I entered the visitors lounge, hoping to catch my breath and settle down. Maybe find some food. I had a lot to think about...including what to say to my sister, if I ever got to see her. *That'd calm me*, I thought, which was ridiculous because I was yawning. It was days since I'd slept well, slept in a bed even. I was bone tired, but knew I'd rest better if I could see her, even for a bit. Kate had been texting me, but I'd ignored it while with the cops. *Maybe she's still here*, I hoped, but the nurses at the station told me she'd left.

There was an old First Nations guy sitting in the corner of the waiting room, and he waved me over.

"Taylor?" he quietly called. "Come sit here by me." He patted a chair next to him. I was so glad to have someone tell me what to do that I just did it.

"I bet you don't know me but Cook asked me to drive Rosie here. She's talking to your sister, and Cook thought I might be good company for you. He thought you were having a rough day." He reached into his bag, and brought out a sack of food Cook had sent.

"Rosie's friend! She talked about you." I felt like an idiot, taking the sack and stashing it away. I knew there were protocols for when you meet an Elder, but I had no idea what they were. Do I shake his hand? Hug him? From a chair? I just sat there, feeling every bit a fool. Luckily, like Rosie, Hugh was okay with just hanging out. A few minutes later, I asked how Jenny was.

"I think she's okay. Rosie's been in there a while. They're jus' talking. Kate suggested she come, talk to her about life. And Rosie…well, she's Rosie. You know." I did. Because Rosie had admitted to us that she'd used lots of drugs but was clean now. I doubt Claire or Veronica had experience with being wired. Hugh didn't say anything directly, though, and I respected him for it.

"I'm glad she's here. I'm worried about Jenny. I think she maybe used more drugs than the hospital knows. I almost wish she was at a downtown hospital." The suburban hospital we were in must have had some experience with drug use, but not like the folks in Vancouver.

"It's here too, unfortunately. We can only try to help, and trust," Hugh said. I sighed, looked down at my feet.

"I know. I just want her to get better so bad." He put his hand on mine.

"She hasn't had it easy, but I hear you haven't either." I almost started to cry. *Get a grip,* I told myself. I just kept looking down, and Hugh reached beside his chair and into the big bag he had with him. After a couple of minutes shuffling through stuff, he came up with a large, shiny, black stone, and handed it to me.

"Warm this up. Hold onto it. A piece of the earth," he said. I felt the cool rock in my palm, wrapped my fingers around it. "Just keep holding on," he said, and I did. Somehow, I felt calmer as the rock warmed up in my hands.

"Don't worry, son," Hugh said after a long time. "You've been given a lot to carry. It's heavy. And it might even get heavier. Who knows?" He took a breath, fussing a stain on his jeans.

"Sometimes you can find someone to give your burden to, and it'll help them and you to share it." He patted my knee next, and I smiled at him. "Can you carry that for an old man? Even just for a while?" he said, grinning at me. "Not only crazy white people carry rocks around. Someone gave me that one, and I just couldn't put it down. Now I know why," he said. I chuckled.

"Thank you," I said. "I do feel better." I took a bottle of water out of my bag.

"Well, just ask when you need help. Lots of folks around *Just Living* speak well of you…I think they'd feel better if you let them help," he told me.

"They are helping. Kenny puts up with me. Lent me his truck. Cook has taught me so much. And Sally…." My voice trailed off. He chuckled.

"Yeah. That's some woman," he agreed. We sat for a while, just hanging out. I couldn't stop rubbing that stone back and forth between my hands. "By the way, you make good cookies," he added, and I smiled at him.

"Jenny's not a burden, you know. I just wasn't old enough to look after her before," I blurted out. Hugh chuckled.

"Yup. Family ain't a burden," he said, nodding his head slowly. His braids moved a little on his shoulders. "But that other stuff you've got going on? Sally told me how you're helping," he clarified.

Jenny wasn't a burden, but damn, those buttons, the cops, my plans with Jean…all of it was so…much. I shook my head, realizing how much

I wanted all this over. I brushed the tears from my eyes with my fingers. I was so tired I could hardly think, but decided to risk it all.

"I think I've probably blown it with the guys at *Just Living*," I admitted. "I've agreed to work with the cops on something. I know that won't be popular." I looked down at my shoes again. The old man looked over at me again and caught my eye.

"Hey, Taylor. Don't worry so much. If you're doing the right thing, it'll be okay. Really."

I decided that for now, I would just believe him. I drifted for a bit. Hugh took his blanket from around his shoulders.

"How about you rest a bit?" he asked and waved at the couch on the other side of the room. It was getting darker, so we moved over there, he covered me up, and within minutes I was pretending to sleep. Hugh was snoring in the chair beside me. *Weird,* I thought. *I want to trust this guy. Cook. Sally. Kenny. Kate. Beth. Ben…that's a long list of people I trust.*

Why couldn't I see that Jean wasn't someone to get involved with?

Or did I know it all along?

Moments later, I drifted off.

CHAPTER 57
BUILDING PLANS

I woke up when I heard some rustling next to me, and Hugh started grumbling about being disturbed. The weird light from the parking lot was streaming in the window across the room. My mind scrambled to figure out if it was still night while trying to rise out of a deep sleep. Deeper than I'd felt in days. I sat up, shook my head trying to clear it. Rosie was leaning over Hugh.

"Hey, old man. Stop your grumbling." She shook him gently and giggled at him. "You are such a bear." She sat down beside him. "Okay, Grumpy. I'll give you a few minutes." I smiled at them.

"Hey, friend. How are you? I hear things are a bit rough," she said. Where to begin?

"I'm doin' okay, I guess. Glad Jenny is here, found." I took a breath, smiled thinking about it. "I'm really glad." I looked right at her.

"Missed you that last night the group got together. But I understand. You okay?" she asked.

"I think it's gonna be okay. I've got some things to do first, but…I've got people helping me."

"Well, some of the group members have been asking about you. Maybe call your friends, eh?" she said, smiling. "And I was talking to Kate yesterday. And Veronica and Claire. We thought you and your sister might do well with a bit of a plan. They want to offer her space to stay with them. So that, and support plans and stuff. She suggested a circle."

What? Jenny might be able to stay in that amazing house with Veronica? Rosie was picking a bit at the fabric of her skirt.

"Are you ready to get back into a circle with me?" she asked. I couldn't tell if she was feeling vulnerable, but I knew I was. Maybe we both were…. Circles are like that.

"I should call Padma. Dianne even. I feel bad…. I've been out of touch for a bit." I smiled at the Elder, who was patting my leg. "What you said about Veronica looking after Jenny? That's amazing. And I think a circle is a good idea. As long as I get to say who isn't invited." She slapped my leg.

"No worries, Taylor. Everyone in the circle gets to be comfortable. I'll check around and see who should come. What do you think? Veronica, Claire, Kate. Maybe Beth and Cook and Sally and Kenny. This old man here." She patted Hugh's knee. "What about Padma and Dianne? Ophelia?" I nodded for all of them.

"What about Ben? He's been a big help for me, someone to talk to," I suggested. "And of course, my sister." Rosie grinned at me.

"We have a next step, then," she said. "If only I can wake up the old man." She reached over and shook Hugh again.

"I'm up, give me a minute," he grumbled. He started rubbing his face. "Jeez, you people. It's nighttime. Why you waking me?"

"Well, I thought your wife might want you home tonight, so I thought I'd offer to drive you," she said. "She is my friend, after all." Their teasing was so…good natured. They had so much to be angry about, both of them, but they were so…gentle. I smiled, hoping one day to be more like them.

"So, Taylor, we'll leave you here, for the night, eh?" Rosie said, putting her arm through Hugh's. "Kenny said to tell you he got his truck. The old man left some snacks from Cook."

I touched the sack beside me. "And, oh yeah…Jenny said you should visit her in the morning. If you've got the time." Her eyes were sparkling, and I grinned. Hell, I smiled so wide I thought my face might crack.

396

"Really? She said she wants me to go in there?" My heart raced, thinking about what it'd be like to talk to my little sister. God, I hope she's okay.

"Yup. Almost forgot to tell you," she said, clearly lying to me. She seemed as happy to give me the news as I was to get it. "Just be yourself, and don't worry about what's happened. Or what's gonna happen. Just be there, 'kay?" I nodded as they left, tears trying to get by the lump in my throat.

I had to tell someone, so headed to the stairwell again. Padma answered after just two rings and I realized I'd been holding my breath.

"Hey. How are you?" I asked.

"Oh! Taylor! I'm great. I bought the most amazing jeans yesterday, and a smashing little top to go with them. With the right sweater, I'll be able to wear them at work!" I swear she sounded like a bubble-blonde Valley Girl from 20 years ago.

"Nice," I answered, baffled.

"What the fuck, Taylor! You ghosted me! ME! Do you know what that does to a friend?" She was back. And real.

"Yeah…I'm really sorry about that. I ran. I disappeared. And I didn't have a phone…." I let my voice trail off, not sure what else to say. "I'm really sorry. Does it help if I admit I didn't plan for any of it?"

"No kidding, dipshit! Like you wouldn't want to reach out to your friends for help or anything…where have I heard that before?" I may have, once or twice, told her she had to rely on help from friends to get on her feet. She was pissed.

"I'm good?" I had no idea how to have this conversation. All I was really good at was running. I could hear her sigh at the other end.

"I did hear from Rosie that you were okay. Thank God for that woman. Kate wouldn't tell me anything. And I'm glad, but I'm still pissed." What could I say? I was wracking my brains, trying for something to deflect when I heard Rosie's voice in my head. *Just tell them the truth when you're not sure what to say.* It seemed like good advice.

"Hey, I really am sorry. I was so scared when Jean came after me…I heard her talking on the phone to Terry, and I knew she was crying rape. I just panicked and ran. All I could think about was staying away from the cops, because with a record I'd never get to help Jenny. And I didn't want to wreck all your lives, too." I just let the silence get calmer between us.

"Yeah, I get it. But damn, now that I know you're okay, I'm pissed. Give me a minute. I'll get over it," she said, chuckling.

"Can we go for dinner or coffee or something? I'm at the hospital with nothing to do until morning, but I don't have wheels either. Jenny said she'd see me in the morning. I'd love to see you, catch up. In my defense, I've never really had a friend before." I laughed. "Man, that sounds pathetic." She chuckled again.

"Okay, I'll come and get you. Give me 20 minutes." We arranged where to meet, and as I was signing off, I figured I better come clean.

"Oh. And Padma? I don't really have much money," I said. She laughed at me.

"Maybe I'll call Dianne. We can drop in on her and let her feed us," she suggested.

That, I decided, would be perfect, and I told her so.

Soon I was taking a shower in Dianne's new apartment. She was washing my clothes, and she and Padma were visiting. She'd left out her son's robe for me to wear.

"Come on, Taylor. Dinner's ready," she said. It was almost ten o'clock, but she'd insisted on cooking for us. I dried off and joined them. Over pasta, the questions began.

"So, where did you go?" I told them about living in my car up the Valley for a while, working in a greasy spoon. I didn't provide details, and they didn't push me. They told me about Jean coming to circle that night, telling everyone that I'd sexually assaulted her. And they told me, over and over again, that I should have called them, asked for help.

"I know, but I didn't have a phone, or your numbers, for that matter. And, I knew Jean would be telling everyone I was horrible. I didn't know what to do."

"What made you come back?" Dianne asked while she added to my plate, more pasta, then garlic toast and a simple salad. It all tasted so good, so I didn't bother to protest.

"One morning in the diner I saw on the news that the police had raided a house in Mission. I had to find out if it was the place Jenny was, so I called Kenny. He told me she'd been found.

"Then we made a plan, and I decided I had to come back, turn myself in if I was ever going to get them to let me help her." I looked down at my hands, again feeling the terror I'd felt that morning. *What if coming back had resulted in being arrested?* I couldn't swallow.

"Don't worry. It all turned out okay," Dianne said, patting my arm.

"Wow. I guess I forgive you this time," Padma said. "That would've freaked me out, too." We drank tea and caught up while my clothes dried.

"Dianne's doing fabulous. Working. Tommy's doing great, in school, and working to help out. Paula's back in school. Isn't this apartment great?" Padma was a proud friend.

"Everything's just great!" I teased. "How about you?" I looked at my friend, Dianne, the woman who had listened to me so often during our retreat.

"Padma is doing amazing stuff. She's working and following up on the court cases. Her family tried to shut that down, and she didn't let them. It hasn't been easy, but you've been amazingly strong." Dianne reached over and grabbed Padma's arm. She tilted her head.

"Who knew that when we decided to be strong so much chaos would follow us, eh? Thinking about that first time in circle, we were all so timid. Not any more!"

It's true, I realized. *Everyone except Jean seemed shy that night. Everyone – even Terry – seemed tentative about being there. Maybe that's why I found Jean so attractive,* I thought. Not that I'd confess that to my friends.

We talked about doing a circle with Rosie for Jenny while we did dishes. They both decided it was a really good idea.

"If only to make sure you don't run again," Padma teased, snapping at me with a tea towel. "I'll call Ophelia and tell her about it. She'd be a great help," she said, and it was decided. They'd touch base with Rosie in the morning.

It felt so good to hang out with them, and I told them so again and again. Before long, Padma begged off to go home. "Work tomorrow!" she said. They'd decided for me that I'd sleep at Dianne's that night.

After saying goodbyes, Dianne made up the couch and offered to drop me back at the hospital on her way into work in the morning. I got a little teary thinking back on the day as I tucked myself in. Man, I was lucky. Good friends. Jenny was getting better. People who wanted to help. Life was improving.

I slept like I was sedated. It was so good to be safe, and warm, and cared for. I decided again that I wanted more of that in my life.

CHAPTER 58
BLACK WIDOW - JEAN

Jean hung up the phone and rubbed her temples. *Well, that changes things.*

Yesterday, she'd spent a good part of the evening trying to reconnect with the boys in her neighbourhood; they seemed to be running scared from her. The damned retreat had been a colossal waste of time, other than meeting and spending time with her little boy toy. *I thought I'd get credibility with the cops if I went, but that doesn't seem to have worked.* But then Taylor called.

Maybe there's a way to pull this off…maybe I can use that little shit after all. She saw Taylor in her mind, and mentally rubbed her palms together, thinking about how best to take advantage of this opportunity.

That's the difference between me and the other assholes in this business. I know how to capitalize on opportunities, she told herself. She pulled a wineglass from the cupboard and poured herself some wine. Gazing out the window to the streets below, Jean played out scenarios, looking for ways to gain advantage with her stable of boys out there. Last week she'd heard from a competitor, Jag, that they'd be looking to shut down her income soon, luring her boys over to their management. Fuck Jag.

If I could just get them fighting among themselves, she thought. *I need to come up the middle and create security for myself. Learn something about them. Catch one of them ripping off the other. Stealing workers. Something big.* She got up to pour another glass of wine and caught a glimpse of herself smiling in the hall mirror.

They just have to think I know something, she thought. She knew she'd figure this out.

An hour later, Jean picked up the phone.

"Jag. Good to hear from you." She ignored his laughter at the other end. "I have a friend from that half-way house who's coming to see me this week. He's got some info about that other Indian friend of yours… Pra-something? Praneev? You know the one. Something about some kids who work with him." Jean smiled when she heard Jag's laughter stop.

"Really? He does, does he? I wonder if you are leading me along again, old lady." Jean's eyebrows rose at the slur, but she didn't let her voice show her irritation.

"Well, we shall see. Let me know if you're interested. You know I'd rather work with you even if this time I've been a little slow with the payment," she said. "I just want to be left alone to make a bit to keep me going." They made a little small talk, Jean stroked his ego talking up how pretty his girls were, and they hung up when she agreed to call before the weekend. She headed over to the stereo, put on some slow jazz, and poured herself another glass of wine. She had more thinking to do.

That'll work! Jean grinned as the pieces clicked together in her mind. *I'll show these punks,* she thought as she picked up her phone again.

"Kev. How are you? How's your boss?" she asked, reaching out to a guy from the North Shore. She'd heard good things about him, thought he might be moving up.

"So, I've been thinking about you, and wanted to solidify things here. I'm interested in building some friendships. I've been learning a little about some punks that Jag works with, and your boss's name was mentioned. Jag said they were messing with some of your young men…." She'd said enough and just waited. She could hear Kev cover the phone, and he mumbled something to the guys at the other end. A minute later he was back.

"Where'd you say you heard that?" he asked. *Smart boy,* she thought.

"From some boys up the Valley. Some guys who've spent some time inside. Just thought you'd like to hear. Anyways, if you want to connect, just call me," she said, getting ready to hang up.

"Who?" Kev asked. "Where, again?"

"Just a young punk who's been hanging with some guys at a half-way house. *Living Well,* I think it's called. He's been working for them. And me," she said. "Anyways, let me know if you want the details this weekend. Unless you want to go work for Jag," she added, trying for a dig. She hung up, confident that he would call back.

She tossed her phone on the couch and, arms stretched, wineglass in hand, she spun into the kitchen.

Damn, I'm good, she thought, reaching for the fridge door. *One more glass, and then I'll head to bed. This old lady hasn't lost it yet!*

Closing the fridge door, she turned when there was a knock at the door. Walking over, she put down her glass and looked out her peephole. One of her more reliable young men was on her doorstep.

"Jimmy! How are you?" she asked, opening the door wide and inviting him into her hallway. "Come in, come in. What can I do for you?" she asked.

"I just wanted you to know what I heard," he said, looking at the floor. When he peeked at her face, Jean just raised a single eyebrow and tapped her toe.

"Well?" she asked. "Don't be shy...."

"You know I don't want him to get in trouble, but I thought you should know I heard those two new guys talking to someone from over the way. That dark guy. They were giving him something. Money I think. I just thought you should know." Jimmy's voice trailed off, and his eyes were darting back and forth between his feet and the door.

"Jimmy, you don't have to worry. Thank you. One of Jag's guys? Is that what you mean? The two I introduced you to this week?" Jean put it all together and didn't like where this was headed. Things were worse than she first thought. Maybe her moles were talking to her direct competition. Fuck.

She held out her hand to Jimmy, and he thrust a little money into it.

"That's all I got today. Remember? It's my girlfriend's birthday so I didn't work much," he said. Jean counted the meagre sum and peeled off a couple of bills to hand back to Jimmy.

"That's okay. I can't give you your usual cut, but here's something to share with your girlfriend." Jimmy's hand was on the doorknob, and he was letting himself out.

"Jimmy?" Jean called out. The young kid with the blond spikes turned towards her, a hopeful look in his eye.

"Thank you," she said, taking the door from his hand and closing it after him.

Fuck, she thought again. *I need to figure this out. What the hell am I going to do? What have I done?*

By the time she climbed out of the shower, Jean had convinced herself that all was well. She'd planted a few seeds but committed to nothing.

Her plan could still work. She was still in control and knew how to use it. First, Taylor. Then these little punks.

I'll get that little fucker first. Then I'll get all of them, she thought as she slid between the satin sheets.

CHAPTER 59
VISITING HOURS

I woke up early, hungry, and anxious, so I decided to get up and cook for Dianne and her kids. It's hard to cook a good meal without making a bunch of noise – especially when you don't know where stuff is – so I cooked a simple breakfast from food in the fridge, with pots that were clean on the stove. Then I searched for the flour and made pan biscuits to go with the frittata I'd put in the oven.

"What are you doing?" Dianne stumbled into the room, rubbing her eyes, and it felt good to surprise her. "You didn't have to!"

"You didn't have to let me sleep over. Or wash my clothes. Or feed me. Besides, I decided this morning that doing stuff for people is the best feeling ever." My new motto.

"Breakfast in ten minutes. I can hold it if you want," I added. "No rush." Dianne poured herself a coffee, and another for Tommy. She went down the hall to wake her kids up. Some mothers just do that, I noticed. Help their kids.

Maybe I can be that kind of a big brother, I thought, and started to set the table and wash my prep dishes. No help to Dianne if I left the kitchen a mess.

A half hour later we'd fed ourselves and were piling in Dianne's car. When she dropped me at the hospital she jumped out of the car and gave me a quick hug.

"Good luck today, Taylor. You really deserve it. You've worked hard to get to here." She really did get me. Friends. Who knew?

I stopped at the nursing desk, and Connie told me the doctors had just been through.

"They said they thought Jenny won't need to be in the hospital much beyond the next few days. There's little they can do for her medically, but there aren't many rehab spaces available. You might want to talk to Marta about it," she said. "She mentioned she has foster places set up for Jenny, but I think she might benefit from some more time in a space focused on her rehab. What do you think?" she asked.

Hell yes, I thought, but I didn't say it that way. It was weird to be asked about Jenny's care, but that's what I was signing up for. When I barely felt able to take care of me. *I'll get to that right after I get a job, and car insurance,* I thought.

"Thanks. I'll look into it, 'cause I think you're right. She's gonna need support, and foster parents can be great people but not…set up for rehab, I don't think. Shit, I thought we'd have some more time. Actually, I didn't think about when she'd be released. Sorry for swearing." Clearly, adulting was hard this morning. Involved more than cooking for friends.

"Anyways," Connie said, "Jenny asked when you'd be in. We'll give you guys some time."

As the distance to her room got smaller, my heart beat faster, my palms got sweatier and my feet slowed down. *Fuck. This is it. What if she hates me for leaving her…or maybe how much does she hate me?* I knocked quietly, pushed the door open a bit when I heard her quiet "Yes?"

"Jenny?" I said. As if someone else could be in the room. "How are you?" I am a walking cliché. *She's in the fucking hospital recovering from a nightmare, you idiot.*

"Taylor?" she answered. She tried to hide behind her blankets when I walked towards her.

"Yup, it's me. Finally," I answered. I was going to make more excuses, but I heard her sobbing in her blankets, and I couldn't get to her quickly enough. I wrapped her in my arms and held her close, whispering dumb shit in her ear while she clung to me, sobbing. I just kept petting her head, holding onto her. I slid onto the bed beside her, wanting to get to her level. She cried, and I let her. It seemed like forever, but after a while her wrenching sobs turned into hiccup sobs.

"Hey Jenny Benny, I'm here now. I'm not going anywhere. I'm so sorry. I love you. You are so strong, Jelly Belly." Around and around the words kept going, and at some point, it occurred to me that *it wasn't about me any more*. I tried to just be with her, thinking about Rosie's parting words. "Just be yourself, and don't worry about what's happened. Or what's gonna happen. Just be there, 'kay?"

A few more minutes, and Jenny started to wipe her face on the sheets. I stood up, got her a damp facecloth from the bathroom, but when I handed it to her, she started all over again. I opened my arms again, and she dove back into them. It was like she'd been saving all her tears since I left her. My heart was bursting with happiness and weeping with heartache, and I held her on and on while my shoulder got wetter and snottier. It was more than I'd hoped for. And it was awful.

About an hour later, there was a knock on the door. Connie had arrived with a mid-morning snack, and some water for Jenny.

"You go take a walk for ten minutes, Taylor. I have to change Jenny's bed, and she can get washed up." I let Jenny go and looked right at her.

"You want me to go for a bit? I won't leave the building, and I'll come back as soon as Connie says you're ready." She nodded at me, wiping her face again, this time on her hospital gown.

"Hey, Russet is back in her blanket!" I noticed the stuffed cat was wrapped up on the windowsill.

"Yah, Marta brought me the blanket. I'd lost it at one of the places." She smiled at me, her eyes watering again. Heading out, I grabbed my water bottle but left my backpack.

"You'll take care of this for me?" I asked. I didn't know how else to reassure her I'd be back. "Help yourself to whatever's in there," I added, grinning. Yes, my wallet was in my back pocket, my phone in my jacket. I'm not stupid.

I spent the afternoon listening, reassuring, smiling, crying and occasionally answering questions. She wept and fidgeted, and sometimes we laughed when we reminisced about how fucked up our life was before all this.

"It took me a bit to realize not everyone had a mother who was a hooker when I got to school," she admitted, laughing. "By then, I just didn't fit in. I kept saying the wrong shit." Her face got sad. "Kept hoping you'd come back for me...for a long time, Tay. Prob'ly longer than I should have. Did you think about me every day?"

"I did think about you, Jelly Belly. I was pretty fucked up at first, then trying to figure out how to survive. But I did think about you a ton and felt like a shit for leaving you."

"I thought about you every day," she said. My heart broke a little more, and I gave her a hug, tears on my cheeks.

She was getting tired, picking at her blanket, at the tape on her IV. Connie came back in, and changed her IV bag, hung something new. Brought her another meal. She grimaced at it.

"Hey, big brother, how about you go get some pizza for your little sister? Looks like she wants real food," Connie suggested. I still had 20 bucks from Sally, so I knew I could. I looked over at my sister, who looked hopeful.

"Why don't I let you rest. I'll be back before supper." She told me what she *really* wanted (greasy burgers – the really crappy kind), and I made sure it was okay with her for me to go for a bit. I left, feeling lighter than I had in a long time, and enjoyed a walk in the rain to a burger joint. *I'd happily spend my last 20 bucks on her smile, again and again,* I thought.

I spent a day and a half with her, giving her breaks now and then to rest, sometimes because she was tired, sometimes grumpy. I called Jean, but she said she hadn't decided anything yet. I told her I still wanted to see her, that I missed the feel of her. She was quiet for a long time, and I think that time I got to her. I agreed to wait another day for her summons.

Over those first days, Jenny and I talked about everything, and nothing, for a couple of hours at a time. Then she'd get anxious, jonesing, and the nurses would show up, give her something to help. She'd sleep, and it'd all start over again. Mostly we just caught up with each other. I found out that she'd been in a couple of foster homes that she complained about at the time, but it turned out they were okay in comparison to where she'd ended up.

"In my kid head I thought that if I kept complaining, Marta'd let me live with you. I didn't realize she didn't know where you were. I thought she knew everything.

"Then that bitch showed up. Said she was Mom's sister-in-law or something…and convinced Marta to pay her to look after me. It got really bad after that."

"Yeah…sounds like that was around the time I *did* try to get you. I was done with living outside, under bridges and in parks. I wanted to get an apartment, with you. I was ready for a real job." I said. "When I talked to Marta I told her I didn't know about any sister-in-law and she looked worried. I kept pushing." I looked down at the floor. *Fuck. Could I have pushed harder?*

"That cop said you helped set up my rescue, Tay. I'm still fucked up, I know. But I'd really like to live with you," she said. And that was it. I was determined to make it happen — because wishes, and little sisters, and way too much shit…she just deserved better.

"I'm going to do whatever it takes to make sure that happens," I promised. "I'm gonna get a job, with Cook, and pay for my car insurance so I can come see you all the time. Kenny says I can live with him. And

I think there's a plan for you at Veronica's where I can visit." I was so excited about the future that I almost missed that Jenny was looking… skeptical. I pushed her about why.

"Yeah. I guess it sounds great. I just don't really see myself in school, hanging out with the kids I met before," she said, scratching at her arms. The scabs weren't healing. I took her hands in mine.

"I get it'll be hard, Jelly Bean. I know you still get…well, wanting smack. But if you want to live together, we're both gonna have to be strong, okay? Rosie wants to build a circle of people to support us. I think they're gonna meet this week with us, and we'll build a plan, okay? Some of my friends, some of the people who are helping me get over that shit with Mom." Jenny looked up at me, and I knew she didn't believe me. That it was possible.

"Will you try for me?" I asked. "Just try?"

"I don't know if you should trust me." She put her hands under her blankets, pulling them up in front of her face. "I'm not that strong. And I've done things…," she said, and a lost look filled her eyes. "I don't know if I can…." She sounded so sad, so tired.

"Let's talk about it in the morning, okay?" I was struggling to hold it together. "Things might look better then. You rest now," I said, grateful that she was checking out of the conversation anyways. She nodded her head and lay down facing the wall. Minutes later Connie came in, told me I had a ride, and kicked me out for the night.

"He'll be back tomorrow," I heard her reassure Jenny as I left. Getting to good was a lot harder than I thought it'd be.

Outside the room, I found Kenny there to drive me home.

"Hey, buddy, you need a break, to sleep. Maybe bake me some scones, okay?" he said. "Cook and Sally and I decided for you, when the hospital called Kate. Seems they don't run a rooming house." He smiled over at me, and I piled in. The tunes were good, and he handed me over a coffee. I smiled. Yes, I could use a break. Talk to people who had my back.

Later that night, while I was baking for my roommate, my phone rang.

"Taylor? It's me, Jean," she said. Like I'd ever forget the voice that gives me nightmares. "I don't have anything on tomorrow afternoon, if you want to drop by," she said.

"Oh, man, Jean, that's great!" I answered. I was surprised how excited I sounded. The next right thing.

"Great. See you about three?" she said. I agreed, and hung up, thinking about everything I needed to do to set this up.

Truck. Check.

Wine shopping. Check.

Oh yeah. Police backup. Check.

I was as ready as I ever would be.

CHAPTER 60
INTO THE SPIDER'S WEB

Dressed up in nice new clothes and holding a bottle of wine, I knocked on Jean's door. I tried to calm my rapid breathing while I fidgeted with my keys and waited. Into the web I'd stumbled, and I was determined to do it well. In spite of the sweat trickling down my spine. I knew Yousef and Andrea were waiting outside, monitoring my "button."

She answered the door in her clothes, and I breathed a sigh of relief. At least we weren't going to replay the last time and get naked immediately. Or at all, I hoped.

"Hi," I said, trying hard to sound apprehensive. "This is for you. For later." I handed her the wine and took a breath. "Just because." I smiled tentatively. She took it and moved into the kitchen to make coffee and small talk.

"So, where are you living now?" she asked.

"I'm back at Kenny's on the rare night I'm not at the hospital," I answered. "Still thinking about doing more cooking school after the summer. How've you been?" I asked, and as soon as the words were out of my mouth, it went dry. *Umm…she claims she was raped? How do you think she is?*

"I'm good. Seen anyone from the group?" she asked. "I don't think I'll be going back. I don't know about that half-way house," she said. "They sure seem different than the ones downtown." I laughed. Yeah, they were different. We talked while she handed me my stuff – some shirts, and Jenny's photo.

"I saw Padma, a while back, when she moved. I didn't make it to the group after we saw each other. I was pretty upset. I...you know."

"I remember that. Terry and I were late. I had some stuff to deal with." She didn't say anything about her trip to emergency. "It was a crazy day, for sure." We chatted a bit more about how she'd rearranged her furniture. About 15 minutes in, I couldn't put off asking her any longer.

"So, hey, Jean. I was confused by a call from the Vancouver Police a while back. They said they wanted to talk to me about an incident between us. Something about avoiding charges. Do you know anything about that?" I asked, again looking right at her. She sighed, looked out the window.

"Yeah. About that. I was mad, and I may have said some stuff to get back at you. I haven't pushed anything with them, so they'll just drop it. I was really mad." Like that just explained away her behaviour. I could feel the tension in the room increase, so just waited because I didn't know what else to do. My heart started pounding, and I picked at my new jeans.

"It was hard, Jean. I didn't know what to say. I didn't say much. But I really want this cleaned up. You know I want custody of Jenny...I can't have stories about me." And that flipped a switch.

"What the fuck? *You* came here. Pushed yourself on me. You were rough. You deserve it, whatever comes to you." I gulped air, trying to breathe my way out of it.

"But...really, I'm confused." I reached out as if I was going to touch her. "I just wanted to get my stuff. You started...you asked for the sex. Asked me to be rough. I feel like an idiot...I only did what I thought you wanted me to do...I...wanted to end it," I said, trying hard to sound like a submissive. "I get that you were angry...but...I don't understand." I let silence grow between us. The clock in her living room sounded like a cannon, ticking off the seconds.

"You only got what you deserved. You took me for everything you could get from me. Phone. Car repairs. Food. Hotels. Everything. And you tried to make me into a fool. Who's looking foolish now?" The woman was yelling, her hair flying around her head, spit flying, too. I pushed my chair back. My brain was running a mile a minute. Was that enough of a confession for the cops? I had to try to get more, I thought.

"So you just told people I raped you? Because we know I didn't...." I slid off the chair, and started to back up, head towards the front door. Which seemed to trigger her. She grabbed her coffee mug and threw it at me. Hard. I ducked, which didn't make her happy. I think she really wanted to hit me! It exploded against the wall behind my head. Jean – possessed — launched at me, yelling.

"You think you're so smart, you little fucker. I had to teach you every step. You don't even know how to fuck a girl good. You got everything you deserved. In fact, maybe we'll do it again...." She lunged at me, but I dodged her. She kept yelling. "You fuckin' played me, so I played you back. You think you're so street smart. Well, I showed you, eh? Be careful what a customer asks for, you little idiot. I hope you get labelled a sex offender...and never even get to see Jenny."

My mouth dropped open. *She hated me so much she wanted to ruin my chance to help Jenny?* I scrambled for the door, reaching it just as there was a knock.

"Everybody okay in there?" A voice I recognized. It was Andrea, but she sounded so... friendly? Like a neighbour borrowing sugar. I pulled open the door, and dodged around her, kept going.

Yousef and Andrea went in, and I ran down the stairs, into Kenny's truck. Drove a few blocks away, and pulled over, hyperventilating. Fuck, that woman was scary. I hoped I never had to see her again.

Twenty minutes later, I'd calmed down and just wanted to go back to the hospital. To the visitors lounge. To see Jenny. I texted the cops and told them where I was headed, that they could call me. I expected they'd want their clothes, or at least their button. "Hope you got what you needed," I finished. Because I knew I wasn't going to try again.

In spite of it all, I realized I didn't need revenge on Jean.

I just hoped she wouldn't do it again to me. Or anyone else.

CHAPTER 61
BROTHERLY LOVE

Jenny wanted Kate and Nora to drive her from the hospital to *Tide's End* for the circle. And I was so glad, because if I was driving and she'd even said one word about wanting to back out, I'd have burned a U-turn. Whatever she wanted, she had me wrapped around her little finger. Of course, I would have had to borrow wheels, too.

Cook and Sally welcomed me back into their midst, and Beth had given me my first-since-I-was-back pay that morning, which was amazing. But I didn't have enough for more than a few days insurance on the clunker, and I wasn't going to commit until…well, just say I was learning about commitment.

I got up early to make fresh dough for giant oatmeal-raisin-chocolate cookies, which I planned to pop in the oven just before break so they'd be chewy and warm and just about as amazing as they could be. I'd pulled all the furniture out of the way and set the cushioned chairs out in a circle. Put Rosie's bigger one by the fireplace and laid a fire just in case. Rosie's little round table was in the middle, waiting for her colourful scarf and sage bowl. We'd each bring something to add to the centre piece. I had Jenny's old picture in my wallet to add. I was so glad I'd gotten it back from Jean…it meant even more to me now. And I hoped Jenny brought Russet and her blanket.

I was setting up the mugs in a circle on the side table, making sure all the handles were facing the right way, that they were clean and polished, and that there were napkins and butter out, with just the right number of knives to spread yumminess onto warm muffins I'd also baked. And then I caught Ben looking at me from the door to the kitchen.

"Hey," he said, his voice barely clear. "That almost looks like a prayer."

"Or a wish," I bantered back and smiled at him. "Cook accused me of being OCD this morning. I told him that you'd say it was love in action." Ben smiled at me.

"How you doing?" he asked me. "Really?" I grinned back at him, putting the yellow napkins in a pattern to look like a sun.

"I'm good. Really good. Jenny and I are getting along. She's out on a pass today for this. She's getting better, her doctors say. I think she's doing good. She'll be moving to Veronica's soon, so I'll be able to spend even more time with her. I think we'll spend a few weeks there before she starts school.

"And Cook and I are working on that cooking school project. Maybe start it up next year. Beth says we didn't get funding this year. But that's good. We'll have it all planned out and ready for next time. And I'm gonna go to school and get my Cook 1 certificate. Or something." I heard my voice drop off. Felt stupid. God, I just keep going on and on. Ben does that to me. He came over and gave me a side hug, still smiling.

"You're doing great, Taylor. Really. I hear things are getting sorted with the cops. Well done, son." It still freaked me out when he called me that, but I'd realized that he called every male who was between about 8 and 25 "son." Must be an ex-monk thing. I shrugged and kept on preparing the space.

"I've been thinking about forgiveness since that night at the cabin," Ben said. "And how hard I'm struggling to forgive myself for leaving those boys at the school. I couldn't go back to them. I can't go back now – it's been years. And I'm not welcome. It wouldn't be kind or good. I do know they're safe now – I have a friend, a Brother, who keeps me in touch with the Order. My Order. And I do what I can to make things better for other victims." He shook his head. "It's hard, Taylor. I just wanted you to know I understand. Forgiveness isn't a grand act. For me, it's something I have to do again and again." I smiled and told him I'd keep thinking about it.

Before long, others were arriving. Rosie thanked me for getting "her circle" ready. I almost blushed.

And then the door opened, and in came Kate, and Nora, and Jenny. I tried not to tear up, looking at her. Her hair was washed, but still that weird colour. Maybe I'd get someone to help with that. Her clothes were ragged and hung on her. She was wearing Kate's big jacket over it all. It looked a little like when she used to play dress-up with Mom's things. Kate gave her a hug, wrapping her arm around my little sister.

Jenny looked around the room – maybe the biggest one she'd ever been in, and I could see it was shaking her up. She started to pick at her sleeves, tried to back out the door. My heart squeezed.

"Jenny! It's a bit much, isn't it? You should have seen me the first time I came in this place. I couldn't believe it. Dropped all my stuff all over the floor." I remembered that first night, when I hadn't been sure I'd even be allowed to stay in the circle…overwhelmed by the huge fireplace, the comfy couches. And now, I was so comfortable here, working all the meetings, owning the kitchen space.

She burrowed into my shoulder, and my heart nearly exploded.

"Tay? Is it okay?" she asked as I gently rocked her back and forth.

"It is so much better than okay," I whispered to her. "It is the sunshine on the other side of a terrible storm. And the best part is that you found your way back to safety." My little sister was my miracle. I brought her over to the kitchen area, where the snacks were.

"What do you want, Jelly?" I asked. "I did it all for you." She snickered a bit, nervous.

"I don't need anything just yet, Tay Bay. Kate and Nora took me to Tim Hortons on the way. I'd been dreaming of a chocolate donut and hot chocolate." I made a mental note to repay them. "And my stomach hurts all the time." Shit. Right. She pulled Russet and the blanket out of

419

Kate's coat. "Where do I put her? Rosie told me to bring something," she asked, and I reassured her the time would come.

A couple of hours later, Jenny was trying hard not to yawn into her hand, only succeeding about half the time. She'd held my hand through much of the circle, a bit overwhelmed by it all (and at first, not really understanding how it worked, who everyone was, or even that they were all there to help her).

I was overwhelmed for a totally different reason. Claire and Veronica were there and had this whole plan for fostering her – Claire's house on school days, Veronica's on the weekends. And I was welcome to join her at Veronica's when I could. The principal of the "alternative school" Jenny'd be attending – three mornings a week to begin, then four – was also there along with Dianne, Padma and Ophelia, Cook and Sally, Nora and Kate, Beth and Ben. Of course, Rosie and Hugh helped us as circle keepers. So, I almost cried when everyone showed up for us. And again when Ben, and Hugh, and Cook and Sally made it really clear they were there for *me*, that I mattered.

"Well, son, you're on quite a journey yourself, and you deserve support, too, so you can continue to be the good brother you are," Ben said. When Hugh and Cook nodded it felt warm like the best bowl of homemade chicken noodle soup after sleeping in your car in winter.

On break, Padma and Dianne came up to us, and Padma took Jenny to the bathroom. Jenny bounced off with her, and I realized maybe she needs more than just me. Like someone to join her in the women's bathroom. I smiled. Padma was the best friend ever.

"Hey, Taylor, how are you doing?" Dianne asked. When I was too quick to respond "Fine," Dianne called me on it.

"No, really. How are you?" I thought about it and teared up a bit.

"I really am good. It's all a bit much…it's been just me for so long, and before that it was just me and Jenny. This is…it feels like a lot." Dianne snickered at me.

"Well, just so you know, we're happy to do it. You don't have to worry about keeping score. Or paying us back. Or whatever. You already do that without even realizing it."

"How?" I knew I barely carried my own weight, let alone Jenny's.

"Do you think we didn't see the snacks? The presentation? Cook looks ten years younger than he did the night you came home. Sally smiles at you all the time. Don't think I don't see it."

Then we were back in circle, and Jenny was trying to stop yawning. As it started to wind down, Rosie stopped us.

"So, I'd like to interrupt this round, and move towards finishing this in a good way." People around the circle nodded. "Is there anybody who feels they really have something else they have to say? Because if not, I'm going to ask Jenny and Taylor to close us off with a few words. Ben put his hand up, and Rosie gave him the piece of pink quartz we'd been using for a talking piece.

"I just wanted to say how honoured I feel to be here today, to be a part of this, and to be in your lives. I feel so much gratitude for my life because of you. Thank you for caring so thoroughly." As he was handing the polished rock back to Rosie, he smiled. "It's really warm here today. I know because the first time I held this, it felt cold. It's really warm now." Rosie smiled.

I don't know what I said. Something eloquent like, "What Ben said." But Jenny caught me off guard by being brutally honest.

"So, I've never had this kind of thing before. And I don't think it's gonna make me all better. Or even that you'll all be here in a week. A month. I don't know." She took a breath.

"Sometimes I don't even know who I am, what I am. And inside my brain, my body even, it feels really…hard. Not like this circle feels. So even though sometimes I think my life can get better…." She looked down at her hands. "I can't promise." She looked at me, teary. "But today I feel like I could try," she admitted. I almost started crying. Cook's hand on my shoulder felt solid, and good. Rosie closed the circle.

"Thank you Cook," I said. "I'm gonna go drive Jenny back to the hospital."

"Nope. You're coming to Nora's for dinner. Kate's gonna drive her back. Jenny asked. Kenny's joining us. You can see her tomorrow. Just go say goodbye for now," he said, and I ran to the door, and gave her a hug.

"Hey, Jenny Benny. Thanks for reminding me that you need to look after you, and I need to help you but only if you want me to," I said. "Can I come by tomorrow?" She looked so tired, I let her off the hook. She headed out.

"Let me know. Really. No pressure, I'm here. We'll talk before you move. If you want." And she was gone. And tiredness crashed in on me. Good thing I didn't have to cook tonight.

A few days later, I met with Inspector Derksen, and some cops from Vancouver. I returned their clothes, button and all. I didn't really want a reminder of how I'd ratted out Jean. Some of the men at *Just Living* hadn't actually come right out and said they were pissed with me, but I could tell by their frigid shoulders that they wouldn't have made the choices I did. I'd be years gaining back their trust, if I ever could.

Which was a small price to pay for getting out of shit with Jean. They were considering what to charge her with…they talked about perjury and misleading the police or obstructing justice or something on my stuff, but now they're really doubling down on a bunch of other shit they knew about. Seems she could get anywhere from nothing to a lot of years. They think she'll plea bargain most of it away. Best part though? She's got to stay away from me. They don't think I'll owe her anything (yes, she threatened to sue me) and there won't be any charges against me. I smiled hard when I heard that. My step is lighter.

I haven't told Jenny anything about it. I don't want her to worry about me, but if I'm being really honest, mostly it's because I still feel so fucking stupid. Kenny and I celebrated, if that counts for anything. And I spent some time cooking for Padma, Ophelia and Dianne one night, thanking them for sticking by me. Delivered some cinnamon buns to

Rosie, which Hugh seemed to appreciate. I worked hard to thank Cook. And one night, I'd tried to talk to Cook about it. Being a rat. Working with the cops.

He settled me down.

"Now, Taylor, I don't know you give these boys enough credit. Yeah, it's true they don't like informants and such. Rats. But really? You think you're the first one accused of something you didn't do? Some of them think what you did was okay. They're just waiting to make sure you don't keep on doing it. And they may be a bit…shy to talk about it. They wouldn't want to be approached if they'd done it."

And that got me thinking. Maybe I'm okay here.

About a week later I got a call from Beth. She and Ben were going to pick up Jenny, drive her to Veronica's.

"We'll pick you up on the way," they said, and my stomach got butterflies.

I promised to get ready and hung up the phone. Then I tried to figure out what that meant. What do I do to help Jenny start her new life when I knew she didn't really believe it was even a thing?

I'd visited every couple of days because when I went daily, she accused me of smothering her. Sometimes we just chatted about what colour she wanted her room (Veronica let me and Kenny paint it turquoise), and sometimes she cried with me about some of the stuff that had happened to her. I tried so hard to be strong for her, never letting on that I'd had stuff happen to me too. Her stories made me cry.

I thought about something Ben had said to me a long time ago… about how sad he felt because I'd never really seen love between adults lived out in a healthy way…or even between parents and their children… and I tried to tell Jenny about it. About how we can't be expected to know how to do something we've never seen except on TV. Because really…we know stuff on TV isn't real, right? She gave me the stink eye and I knew I hadn't explained it well.

One day I went hiking with Ben, and we talked. I started to realize how fucked up I was from Mom. I'd been messed up by wanting to please her when I was little, and then she'd wired my brain for fuckup by abusing me. No wonder I felt attracted to Jean!

And I couldn't help but wonder how she'd been with Jenny. Did she set her up with Barry? Did she train her to be more vulnerable with that douchebag who kidnapped her? It's hard to explain how kids want to please even the shittiest of parents. Any adults, really. I knew I'd be unpacking this shit for years.

Beth and Ben stopped on the way to Veronica's to buy Jenny some new clothes, so when we arrived with bags filled with stuff, she looked overwhelmed. I took her to her room and together we took the tags off everything and folded her stuff and put it into a few drawers. Russet was perched on her pillows. It didn't feel anything like I'd imagined Christmas would, though, so I patted the bed, inviting her to sit down beside me.

"Hey, you. How is it all?" I asked.

"I don't know, Tay. Sometimes it feels like all the other times I packed our stuff in garbage bags and moved to new foster homes and opened up brand new packages of underwear. And we both know what that was like...." I grinned at her.

"Yeah...not exactly moving into a palace when your luggage is a garbage bag," I said. *When the fuck would they fix that for kids?* I wondered.

"Then, Kate or Beth'll say something to me...and like...I feel something different. Like this time it might work. But then I remember that even if they want it to...well...it's hard. It doesn't really feel like it could." There it was again, that feeling that nothing could ever get better. I knew it well.

"I know, Jelly Belly. It's hard to believe this is real...or even that we found it. These people, though...I don't know how to say it...they get it. Don't let their 'I-got-it-together' image fool you. They've been there. They've seen some shit, Jenny Penny...and some of them are still...

trying? I don't know how to even say it. But they do pull together, and they're helping me."

"Yeah, I get it," she said, turning away from me. She was shivering a little bit, trying hard to stay in control.

"Maybe I just need a nap," she said, and I let her off the hook. Again.

Looking back, I could have done better.

CHAPTER 62
HURTING AND HELPING

Six weeks later…

"I'm not sure what you want me to do, but you know I'm happy to do it," Kate said, smiling into the phone. Nora was wrestling Brock into his shoes, trying to get them ready for a walk in the woods. Brock was dashing around the kitchen island.

"Brock! Slow down! We want to go outside, but you need shoes, so you don't cut your feet!" Nora tried reasoning with a toddler, never a winning plan. She could hear Kate talking on the phone and hoped the walk wouldn't have to be postponed.

"As a matter of fact, we're in the process of trying to shoe the poor sod so we can come up there for a short hike in the woods, maybe pet the horses a bit. Would you like us to stop by? We will have your favourite little person with us," she said, "if we can get him shod." Moments later, she was tickling Brock, trying to clear the tension between her wife and their son.

"Cook suggested we drop by for lunch. He's got some extra sandwiches, and Rosie and Hugh are there. I think I heard Veronica, too. Are you okay with this?" Nora knew it'd be okay to say no, to guard their time together. But really, Cook only asked when something important was going on…and besides, she missed seeing Rosie and Hugh every day now that she worked so much from home.

"Let's go, Brocky Boy!" she declared. "We can run around the pond ten times or play hide and seek in the woods for *five minutes* if we get in the car seat quickly! Then Sally will have some treats for us, I bet!" Nora knew Brock loved Sally to bits, the closest thing he had to regular spoiling from a grandmother, and in no time, they were "buckled and ready for liftoff," as Kate put it.

After eating lunch, and helping with cleanup, Kate and her family headed to the barn to pet the horses, Buttercup, Tex and Thud. Tex was Ben's horse; Thud was a big old draft horse who *loved* Brock. Buttercup was a rescue who was mostly trustworthy, but they kept an eye on her around their son.

"Promised Hugh I'd ask. He wants me to get together with Beth and Rosie this afternoon. Are you okay with me staying? I think they want to talk about how Claire's doing living with an almost-teenager." In the six weeks since Jenny had moved in with the former nun, she'd tried to meet the girl's needs, but it wasn't getting easier. Nora smiled at her partner and answered.

"Of course, I don't mind. I bet Jenny is driving Claire nuts. Maybe we can steal an afternoon this week to make up for it?" Kate chuckled. She was used to Nora's reminders to prioritize health, balance, family.

"Yeah...my Thursday is completely free right now, so we could...." Kate said. Brock wouldn't care whether they hung out today or on Thursday. Soon, their little boy was getting tired, so Nora picked him up and they headed back into *Just Living* to say their goodbyes.

A few minutes later, Kate joined her colleagues as they walked out to the building between the kitchen and the barn. The Sanctuary was a small round space, big enough to host circles and the occasional craft session. It had beautiful stained-glass windows, and soaring ceilings, wooden floors and comfy chairs or cushions to sit on. As they gathered, Hugh started burning some sage to smudge the space, and Rosie welcomed them.

"Where's Taylor?" Ben asked as they settled in.

"He couldn't make it. Something about schoolwork," Cook offered.

"We decided to go ahead. We didn't know he wasn't going to be here but thought maybe the Ancestors wanted him to stay away. Rosie promised to tell him about it, as long as everyone is okay with that?" Hugh helped set the tone — consent. He opened with a pulsing drumbeat and a glorious honour song.

"So," Rosie began, "Claire seems to be having a harder and harder time coping with Jenny. Jenny…well…I worry about that little girl. I thought maybe we could get together and think about things we could do different," Rosie said. Looking around the circle, Ben felt grateful to see so many who cared about these people. Veronica nodded in agreement across from him. Taylor's friends, Dianne and Padma, were holding hands on one side, and Cook and Sally were there, too.

When the talking piece came around to him, Ben noticed his palms sweating and his breath getting shallow. Beth reached over and put her hand on his leg. His heart squeezed. *How did I get so lucky?* he thought. She knew when something was wrong before he did.

"I'm a bit worried about Taylor. Not because he's not doing excellent stuff. I think he is. But I'm worried about how little the guys around here talk to him now. Other than you, Kenny, he's kinda isolated. I'm going to talk to him about how hard that must be." Ben knew what it was like to be cut off from people who were like family.

"If I hadn't met you guys after I left the Order, I'm not sure what I would have done. It just feels…maybe risky for Taylor right now. And I'm not okay with anything bad happening to him," Ben said. "I just want to support him and Jenny. And I think he needs friends." He noticed Beth biting her lip to keep the tears at bay and smiled at her. Her face was radiant in the afternoon sun, and he couldn't help sharing a moment, a kiss, with his wife. His blessed, pregnant wife. "I am so glad for all of you," he finished and passed the talking piece along.

Beth took the talking piece when it was offered, and started to cry, quiet tears dripping from her chin. She breathed. And breathed some more.

"Everyone knows I went to see Martin last month. And last week. Whenever." She took a big breath. "It was hard. Really hard, seeing him behind those walls, in that cage, and remembering the conversations by the fires we built, the nights we sat in the field with that damned cat, Timex, and tried to understand each other." She took Ben's hankie when he offered it, dried her cheeks.

"It was also hard remembering when he was told he had to go back to that village to get full parole, and he didn't want to. But none of us were able to stop it." Beth looked up at Hugh, breathed. The Elder looked over at her with soft eyes.

"We tried to stay in touch. I tried, but…he told me no one could have," she said, as she looked at the Elder who still carried some shame for what had happened. "Even you, Hugh." She chuckled. "Yes, he even said that." Hugh smiled at her, but it didn't reach his eyes.

"When we met, Martin told me about the few days he had in the village when he was…sane. When he first got there. And how the memories came in so strong and he got wired again. He told me it was… fast…he fell into old…well, you know. Hallucinations, I guess, about all the shit that happened to him in Residential Schools, and…well, priests and the devil and stuff." She took another breath, regaining her composure when she talked about the conversation she'd had with the man who'd killed her friend.

"He's really, really sorry for what happened. And he takes responsibility. He knows we can't trust him…that he can't ever be out. He says he can't even trust himself." Beth smiled, looking around the room. "I see him here. And he told me he tries to fill his days with better thoughts, good things. He's singing again, making hobby-craft and donating it. Helping crime victims.

"But the demons are still there. The addictions. Flashbacks. Lashing out. Depression." Beth held the talking piece for a long time, just looking into the smudge bowl in the middle of the circle. Time became heavier, and when she broke the silence, the truth seemed more profound.

"I've been sitting here trying to figure out exactly what this has to do with Jenny. And Taylor. And I think I've got it.

"What happened to them? It can't be allowed to happen again." Beth looked around the circle, into each of their eyes. "Jenny has to want our love, our help. *But we have to show up even when she doesn't.* Because that's…well that's what love looks like. And for the sake of all that is real, more than anyone else in my sphere right now, she needs it." She took a breath. "They need it." Her eyes looked up to the colours splashing onto the walls from the stained-glass windows Martin had helped to make, and she blinked away more tears. "That's what stopping the tides looks like." She took another deep breath, and the circle breathed with her.

"It's not easy. God knows and so do I…that safety, like love, is never assured. And that little girl deserved to be safe. And loved. So we have to make sure she gets it now." Beth's voice was pleading but determined.

"I don't care what it takes," she said, putting her hand on her belly and handing the talking piece to Rosie, who held it in silence for what seemed like a good ten minutes, letting those words resonate in each of their souls.

And then, they made another plan.

CHAPTER 63
ONE STEP FORWARD

"Hey, Tay Bay, what'ch you up to?" I still smiled when I heard my sister's voice through my phone. She was waiting for a ride up to Veronica's. She'd been staying at Claire's, going to school four mornings a week.

"I'm doing some baking and cleaning for Cook. We've got that gathering this weekend. Why?" I asked. I loved it when she called me.

"Just wondered if you'd drive me downtown before we go to Veronica's. Not Vancouver…just downtown here." *Hmmm…*I wondered. Whatever she was up to, it'd be better if I was there, right? I made plans to pick her up in an hour, and let Sally know I'd be leaving her in charge of getting the cookies out of the oven.

Jenny'd been back at school for about three months, trying to do what she was supposed to, and taking breaks when that wasn't…well… possible. Let's just say she wasn't faking PTSD crashes. And even though "the women" – Kate, Nora, Beth, Padma, Sally and Dianne – had surrounded her, life continued to be hard for my little sister. It's hard to be in Grade 6.

I'd like to say I thought she was getting better, but truth? Sometimes when I hung out with her, I swear she was…not full-blown wired, but using. I hated that I was suspicious of my sister, and I didn't confront her, but I had gotten into the habit of monitoring her. It happened mostly on days she was at school and I picked her up…I think she'd found a "distributor" there. I wasn't sure how she was getting money to buy, but really…she wasn't an idiot. And neither was I.

Three months was a long time. Time enough to let her hair grow out and get a really cute short haircut. Enough to get my insurance on my car and start at a culinary school a couple of days a week. It gave us time to hang out, go to the movies, have friends for dinner at Veronica's. Watch Netflix. Pretend we were ordinary.

But it was also enough time to have a few peaks and valleys – times when Jenny was doing amazingly – academically, socially, whatever – and then crashes. She had been caught drinking a couple of times by Claire. I knew she was smoking cigarettes again…to cover the weed I thought. I hoped she wasn't using anything stronger than coffee to get herself going. Because, truth be told, my little sister was a firecracker – she knew how to manage the tough bits. When to pick herself up. When to calm herself down.

Living with Claire was becoming harder and harder. Driving towards her house, I started thinking about what Beth had told me…that Claire's life had been hard, too. I knew she used to be a nun…and man, did she ever still project that hard. Like, no kidding. It meant that she and Jenny didn't just butt heads but smashed them. Regularly.

And my little sister didn't bother to tell me about it. But I heard. From Padma. From Kate. And from Veronica…who Claire complained to *all* the time. I just hoped today would not be a hard day.

I knew my friends – the women, as I'd come to call them – were trying to help Jenny. And I knew sometimes she bristled against it. How do you help someone keep safe, thrive even, if they don't care about themselves?

"So…I want to drop by this guy Freddy's place for a minute if that's okay." I looked over at her. She was having a good day, her face was clear, and she was smiling. I smiled.

"Freddy?" I asked, wondering if this was a boyfriend. She swatted my arm.

"Ewww. Taylor! He's just a guy who's helping me with some stuff at school," she said. And immediately I worried. But I didn't want to wreck the mood, so I drove to Freddy's.

Pulling up I had to tell myself to suspend any judgement. Bed sheets over windows. Garbage and empty beer cans piled up on the front step. Cars that hadn't moved in months. But Freddy could be a fine boy, right? Jenny jumped out of my car and headed up the stairs. She called back to me that she'd just be a minute, so I put the window down and turned up some tunes. She disappeared into the front door. And I waited.

And waited. And waited. On the third song, my palms were getting a bit sweaty. How much do I trust her? Freddy? What are they doing? What if my sister gets hurt while I'm sitting out in the car waiting for her? Once that kind of thought gets into your head, let me tell you, it doesn't leave. I had to do something.

I paused with my hand on the door latch, counted to ten just in case she was heading out, and then…opened the car door, ran up the steps.

I knocked twice on the front door and stepped back. I could hear music pounding inside and wondered if they'd heard me. Do I try the door handle? Call the cops? I decided to knock again, this time louder, and the music was turned down. Then I heard Jenny. She was laughing, which made me feel better. I turned and sat on the porch, but a moment later the door opened.

"Thanks Freddy! See you on Monday! I'll return the favour," she said, and we walked down the path to the car.

"What the hell, Taylor? I said I'd be a minute." Little sister wasn't pleased.

"But you'd been more than 15. I have to get back to help Cook with dinner. It's his day off, but he agreed to help me so I could come get you." I didn't want to let on that I'd been worried.

"I thought we were going to Veronica's! It's our evening together!" I knew that look.

435

"I'll be home before seven. I've just got to get dinner on the table and wash up the pots. The men can clean their own dishes tonight," I said. "Besides, I thought you had work to do to make up for those classes you missed. Weren't you gonna work on that with Kate?" I asked. It was math or something. Jenny crossed her arms and pouted all the way home. Looking back, she may have been avoiding any more conversation with me.

I dropped her on the driveway, and she grabbed her big backpack and headed into the garage at Veronica's. Before I could even say goodbye, or "You're welcome," she was in the door.

I slowly opened the door at Veronica's around nine o'clock. I'd called to warn them that I'd be later than I'd expected because I was the only one on-site who could run the big sterilizer. I'd thought Sally would be there, but she and Cook had gone out to a movie, so cleanup was up to me. I was ready for Jenny's wrath, so I had a sack with some croissants for breakfast. Jenny'd loved them every time I'd baked them for her.

I was surprised when I found Veronica alone in the den watching a British TV show about midwives. I knew Jenny wouldn't have watched that.

"Hey, Veronica. How are you? How's my sister?" I asked. "Did you eat? I have some muffins for breakfast I left on the counter."

"She's good. She's been in her room all night, talking on the phone. Doing her homework, she says, but I think she may actually have friends she's talking to." Veronica looked as pleased as I felt.

Except. Really? She was suddenly acting like I thought a normal almost-teenager might? I gave Veronica a hug and told her I was tired.

"I'll check on Jenny before I have my shower," I said. Stopping at her door, about to knock, I did hear voices. But neither of them was my sister. I knocked. No answer. Shit. My gut was firing all its alarm bells now.

"Jenny? I'm coming in," I said. But the door was locked. I headed back to the living room.

"Veronica – do you have a key? I can't get into Jenny's room," I asked.

"No, that's what locks are for, Taylor. We have to trust her." I could tell by her voice that Veronica wasn't budging. But I was worried. I headed to my room to figure out what to do and sat on my bed. In the dark I saw headlights slow down out front of the house, and soon I heard car doors slamming and Jenny calling goodnight. The little shit had gone out without letting anyone know. I raced back into the front room.

"Did you give her permission? She went out?" I asked Veronica.

"Nope. She didn't ask, but I figure after what your sister's been through, we have to expect a little of this. I was staying up waiting for her." I went to the front door, but she wasn't on the porch. What the hell?

"I think she went in and out her window, at least I expect that's what she did. My middle son used to do it. I saw her getting into a car." She had a paper in her hands. "This is the license number. I'm not stupid, Taylor. But your sister's gotta have a chance for some fun, too." I was shaking my head as I walked back to her room.

"Why didn't you tell me when I got here?" I asked.

"I knew you'd worry. And she clearly didn't want us to know." I headed down the hallway, confused.

"Hey, sis…you alright?" I asked and heard the TV show turn off.

"Yeah. I'm good Tay. You finally got home!" she said.

"I've been here a while," I said. She wasn't opening the door, so I wished her goodnight, and headed to bed.

The next morning, I wish I'd insisted on a hug goodnight.

Veronica knocked at my door about 7:30, and I rolled out of bed and opened my door. She was in her bathrobe and pyjamas, looking more dishevelled than I'd ever seen her.

"Can you hear that?" she asked, and I became aware of a soft keening that was coming down the hall. She handed me a key, and I rushed down to find out what was happening in Jenny's room. *Fuck,* I thought.

"I'm coming in, Jenny," I said, opening the door with the key. And there she was, rocking back and forth on the bed, her eyes wild. She'd not gotten into her pyjamas, was still dressed in the clothes I'd seen her in the night before.

"Darlin' are you okay?" I asked, joining her on the bed. I wrapped her in my arms, and we rocked together.

"Veronica, I think you should call an ambulance," I said to the amazing woman who was saving us from ourselves.

"NO!" Jenny cried out. "No police!" I hadn't been planning to call the police, but convincing Jenny of that was impossible. She was completely distressed, but I suspected this time she was also wired. After a little negotiating she agreed to let me drive her to town, to the doctor's office at the hospital. It only took Jenny wailing in the waiting room for a few minutes for an appointment, and by early afternoon it was clear Jenny was going to have to be admitted. I wish I could say it was easy.

That's what it's been like. On and off, Jenny does okay, and then she doesn't. Sometimes she's drinking. Sometimes she's using. Sometimes I'm convinced she's turning tricks to pay for it. Miraculously, she's smart enough that when she's sober, she's doing okay in school and when she's high, she doesn't disrupt things too much, so they haven't kicked her out.

When I can, I go to school. I always do my work so that I have a paycheque. I always set some aside for my sister, for our future. I'm so glad for our life, when we hold it together.

And when we don't, I'm glad for my friends.

EPILOGUE

Six months later…

"Hey, Taylor! Give me a second and I'll come help you with that!" I heard Kenny's voice calling out as he came in the front door of the large dining room attached to the commercial kitchen.

"Hey buddy! Thanks for coming! I've got this, no worries," I said while tipping a huge pot of stew over a five-gallon pail. Another kitchen worker came up behind me and grabbed the second handle of the huge pot. Kenny stayed in the doorway, eyes on the operation.

"Man, you really do," he said, shaking his head back and forth. "That is one helluva lot of stew."

"Well, it'll be made into some piping hot soup with the addition of some more broth, carrots and potatoes. It'll help keep folks here well fed. Even in summer, living on the streets takes energy." I kept going, packing up my stuff, and wiping up the surfaces of the kitchen. I was starting to feel like I was helping at this new job I'd taken.

"Seen Jenny this week?" he asked, his voice quiet.

"She called a few times. It's hard for her…I can tell she likes to see me, but she also feels…weird, I guess." I ducked in a back cupboard and grabbed my backpack. "Haven't seen her for a while though." He smiled at me.

It had been more than a month since I'd started working at the soup kitchen in the Downtown East Side. It was the easiest way to get my time in a kitchen and still be there for my little sister. She'd bounced back and forth between Veronica's and the street, but lately had been spending more time downtown. I understood and wanted to be there for her. I remembered the conversation I had with Cook and Beth about it.

"I have to turn in my apron here," I'd started. "I got a job downtown." They knew I'd been looking but were trying to postpone my start date in the hopes that Jenny would decide to move back to the Valley. I tried to keep my voice from cracking and turned away from my friends when my tears started to pool in my eyes. "You know I wish I could stay here," I'd finished, hanging my apron on the back of the door to the pantry.

"We do understand, Taylor. And I know you can't do anything else. But don't leave us. Really. Come back and forth, stay here on your days off. Look at this as home-away-from-home," Beth suggested.

"Really, m'boy, you are welcome to eat here any time. As is that firebrand sister of yours. Come often," he said, and got up to leave the room. I knew Cook struggled with goodbyes.

And so I'd done that. Four nights downtown, in a flop house with a bathroom down the hall was all I could afford. I came and went, and they didn't charge me for too much because the soup kitchen subsidized my rent. And then, on my days off, someone from the Valley often picked me up and drove me home. Unless I thought Jenny was in a crisis and might need me overnight to look out for her. Sometimes she stayed with me, but I didn't let her actively use in my space. Beth and I had negotiated boundaries with her at Veronica's. Not actively using in-house was an important one, so I thought it would be best if I maintained that message.

Turning out the lights, I headed towards the front door.

"Do you mind if we wait a bit? Jenny said she might drop by to say goodbye this evening," I asked.

"She's outside, waiting on you," Kenny told me, his eyes sparkling. I called a quick goodbye to my boss.

"See you next week!" he called back, and I jumped for the door.

Cook was double-parked outside the doors and talking to Jenny. I stopped and took in the picture. She looked pretty good, and I didn't think I was just peering through rose-coloured glasses.

"Hey, you," I said, quietly. "How are you?" She smiled when she turned to me, looked a little frightened.

"Tay? I'm good. I need a favour." She opened her arms to me, and I moved in and hugged her, wrapping my arms around her thin shoulders.

"And?" I asked. This day had just gotten a whole bunch better. She reached into her bag, pulled out Russet who was looking remarkably clean and whole.

"Can I come back to Veronica's for a while? I've just gotten out of the hospital, and I want to try the Valley again," she confessed. I hugged her harder, and the tears started to fall.

"Did you talk to Veronica, like we planned?" I asked, knowing that wouldn't likely be a barrier.

"She said she was good with it if you were," she said.

"Awww Jelly Belly, I will always be good with it. Always." We all clambered into the crew cab, and Jenny and I sat beside each other in the back seat. "I am so proud of you," I reminded her. "And I will keep on showing up as long as you do."

We headed out, driving towards the forest I'd begun to think of as home, past where the tides end, where the pounding of the concrete jungle and the crashing waves settle down, and the river's flow is strong, and steady and reliable. And I thought about this very adult life I'd created, working to feed people comfort food, and showing up around the edges of my sister's life. Keeping up with my studies when I could and being okay with it when it didn't work out.

I'd decided early on that if I was going to spend time on the street looking for Jenny, I would be cheerful. And I'd also decided that whenever I could, I'd try to leave things a little better behind me. Cooking for others reminded me of what's waiting for us up the Valley, once Jenny's ready to join us again. Cook. Sally. Beth. Ben. Kenny. Padma. Dianne. They'd called, texted. Sometimes joined me for an evening. Dianne, Phee and Padma regularly showing up to volunteer in the kitchen. Once I'd even slept over at friends of Ben and Beth's. Showered. Eaten a great meal. Then I'd found this job and my room.

I'd continue to cook, feed people, learn about myself, and how I fit into this weird world. How I could give back.

And then I'd pray someone was making things easier for Jenny, somehow.

We'd try to make another go at Veronica's for as long as that lasted.

I'd stopped hoping for happily-ever-afters and started finding happy in what was right in front of me today. I smiled and looked at the gardens as we drove by, imagining flowers and vegetables bursting out of the dirt.

Today, I had my little sister back, cuddled up beside me, and she was sober.

It was a good day.

And that was better than enough for now.

ACKNOWLEDGEMENTS

Like many, I'm aware writing is a solitary practice that is only productive when a whole host of people help. It is certainly no different for me.

First, to my friends and family, and my neighbours at Groundswell Cohousing, who put up with my, "Sorry, I can't come out and play today," even when I wasn't writing or editing or formatting…but just dreaming in my big chair. Or napping. Or taking Mollie for another walk. Ponder walks, I call them.

Thank you for holding a place for me at your table. Our table. The Table.

Brigid, Grace, Jonah and Nat…you are my everything. And thank you for inviting Maggie and Bridget to our clan. I am truly blessed.

To the men inside at the Mission Medium Creative Writing group, who meet faithfully every two weeks, and give me such rich critique, aren't afraid to challenge me, and reinforce the places I still have to learn, grow, strengthen. Without you and your support this novel would not be. You share your stories, your impressions, and your insights into lives as diverse and rich as I can imagine. Thank you. If I could name you by name, I would, especially the regulars who let it fly right at me.

To Diana Gabaldon and Bob Dugoni, who show me every year how great writers share, help, and care for those who are inside, and writing. Thank you.

To Amity Publishing for continuing to bring my work to press. Wilma and Cliff Derksen share themselves so freely, feed me tea and chocolate and fruit on those Sunday nights when I drop in. You offer ideas, and questions, and deadlines, and connections, and wisdom. Thank you so much. Your team are amazing – thank you to Sue Simpson for her editing genius and Odia Reimer for her cover design and formatting. You made me a book! Thank you.

To Jennifer Glossop, Content Editor extra-ordinaire, who reminds me of why I'm writing, and what I (still) have to learn, who points me towards a better course. I am so glad I found you. Thank you.

To my early readers and reviewers: Avery Hulbert, Pam Pederson, Cathy Mendler, Heidi Epp, Renata Karrys, Linda Noble, Leslie Braithwaite, Anita Pybus, Darlene Wahlstrom, Gai Brown-Evans, Jane Miller-Ashton and Janice Robinson, thank you. Your insights, and willingness to share from your experiences humble me. Your feedback fueled me through the final laps to publishing. And your reviews brought a tear to my eye.

Thank you to Sammie Farrell, an extraordinary photographer who captured the essence of Russet and Tide's End so beautifully. Find her @ iriephotographs where she rocks.

And finally, to the community of West Coast authors who hold one another up, who encourage, and teach, and understand, who laugh and drink and workshop with me. Those at Surrey International Writers Conference, Golden Ears Writers, Creative Ink, Chilliwack Writers Group, and many others. Thank you, all.

All of the best of this book is because of your support. The errors, of course, are mine alone.

ABOUT THE AUTHOR

Meredith Egan is a novelist and executive coach who has worked with crime victims and prisoners for thirty years. The stories she has been privileged to hear, and the courageous people she has accompanied inspire her work. She has been honoured to learn from many Indigenous peoples and has been trained in mediation and peacemaking circles. She coaches writers and other creative folks and offers workshops and training through her *Daring Imagination* work.

Meredith has facilitated and spoken in schools, universities, prisons and communities on restorative justice, creative writing, victim empathy, and personal transformation throughout Canada and internationally, and continues to be available for this work.

In 2016, Meredith released *Just Living: a novel*. It characterizes the complicated relationships that exist in the aftermath of crime. It was extensively worked inside prison, with creative writing critique groups in medium security prisons.

Dr. Egan's first training was in Pharmacy and Pharmaceutical Sciences. She holds a Doctorate in Pharmacy from University of Alberta, and she is the principal at Wild Goat Executive Coaching, where her clients include leaders in the automotive, technology and small business fields.

She lives at Groundswell Cohousing in the Yarrow Ecovillage in British Columbia with her dog Mollie and furry feline companions.

For fun she dabbles in cooking soup for her neighbours, and sampling expensive scotch.

Meredith's four adult children still visit – maybe not only because of the hot tub, board games and amazing view.

To connect with Meredith, and access Resources for Readers, find her at

JustLivingNovel.ca
DaringImagination.ca
WildGoatCoaching.ca
facebook.com/meredith.egan.writer

Taylor Smythe dreams of having a loving family. But first, he has to rescue his little sister Jenny from the gritty underbelly of the child cyberporn industry. Taylor journeys from homelessness in the inner city to a community in the dripping forests of the Pacific Northwest to confront the relentless pounding of his fiercest pain.

Can he become the big brother Jenny needs right now, and for the rest of their lives?

Tide's End explores the many faces of sexual assault and human trafficking, and how life can shatter for those most affected – the victims.
Because #MeToo is more common than we can imagine.
As is #ChildrenToo
And even #BoysToo
It tears apart our families and neighbourhoods.

And wherever there is suffering, there are guardians and helpers who still the relentless pounding to encourage Tide's End.

Meredith Egan is an author and executive coach who has worked with crime victims and prisoners for more than thirty years. She has been trained in mediation and peacemaking circles

and has been honoured to learn from many First Nations peoples. She coaches writers and other creative folks and offers workshops and training through her Daring Imagination work.

Meredith is the principal at Wild Goat Executive Coaching where her clients include leaders in the automotive, technology and small business fields. She lives at the Groundswell Ecovillage in Yarrow, BC. with her dog Mollie, and rambunctious feline sisters Firefly and Filigree. For fun she dabbles in cooking soup for her neighbours, and sampling expensive scotch.

Meredith's four adult children still visit - maybe not only because of the hot tub, board games and amazing view.

You can find Meredith at www.wildgoatcoaching.ca for information about coaching, www.justlivingnovel.ca for information about her novels, and www.daringimagination.ca for information about her work with writers. Meredith welcomes opportunities to speak with groups about her work, and writing.